Martin Middlet[...] [...] 1954. When his f[...] emigrated to Australia in 1960, they lived in Inala, Brisbane. After attending Corinda High School, Martin joined the army and spent most of his time at Lavarack Barracks in Townsville. Martin, his wife and children now live in Beaudesert, Queensland.

Martin has always been an avid reader of science fiction/fantasy novels, though since the success of his novels he wishes he had much more time to write.

HAWK†HORN
T · O · W · E · R

MARTIN MIDDLETON

PAN
Pan Macmillan Australia

*For the Honans, Jim, Denise, Amy, Haylee and Jessica
and as always, Kate*

First published 1996 in Pan by Pan Macmillan Australia Pty Limited
St Martins Tower, 31 Market Street, Sydney

Copyright © Martin Middleton 1996

National Library of Australia
cataloguing-in-publication data:

Middleton, Martin.
Hawkthorn tower.

ISBN 0 330 35793 X (pbk.).

I. Title. (Series: Middleton, Martin, Living towers; bk. 1).

A823.3

Typeset in 10/12pt Palatino by Post Typesetters
Printed in Australia by McPherson's Printing Group

TERMINOLOGY

ACCEPTED	First level of Deisol
ADEPT	Fourth level of Deisol
APPRENTICE	Second level of Deisol
BELIEVER	Fifth level of Deisol
BIREME	Vessel with two banks of oars
CANTRIP	Simple spell
CATHAR	Protector of pilgrims and merchants
CHOSEN	Religious zealot
CRAFTER	User of the Lore
CRATAEGUS	Alliance of towers
DEIS	Religious leader
DEISOL	Death Cult
DEY	Commander of Iledrith forces
DISCIPLE	Third level of Deisol
EMULYS	Race living north of Belial
FENI	Those of the Fens
FINAL WARS	Third Lychgate Wars
FIRST LYCHGATE WARS	First war between Iledrith and Kyrthos
HIERARCHY	Leaders of the Chosen
JAEGER	Hunters of the northern plains

KOEL	Leader of the Kolecki
KOLECKI	Race living north of The Belial
LIFLODE	Grey living stone
LOREMASTER	Iledrith Crafter
LYCHGATE	Gate joining Lychworld to Kyrthos
LYCHGEM	Gems of the Living Towers
LYCHLORD	Iledrith title
LYCHSTREAM	Lights of the Lychgems in the Lychworld
LYCHWORLD	Home of the Iledrith
PANTHEON	Home of the Chosen
PICKET WEED	Noxious plant used to imprison Aves
RIGHTEOUS	Protectors of the Chosen
SAPHY	Wanderers of the northern plains
SECOND LYCHGATE WARS	Second war with the Iledrith
SEVEN-WATER	Alcoholic drink
STCHI	Cabbage soup
TRIREME	Vessel with three banks of oars
WRAITH	Nocturnal mist-like killers of the Lychworld
YCLAD	Armoured wraith

GLOSSARY

ARMOURY

BRIGANDINE	An armoured sleeveless jacket
BUCKLER	A small round shield
FALCHION	A sword with a heavy single-edged blade
LAMELLA	Small, thin, oblong steel plate attached in overlapping rows
RAPIER	A thin-bladed sword
SHORTSWORD	A short-bladed sword
SMALLSWORD	A narrow-bladed sword

CREATURES

AZUREUS	Toad-like creature of the northern Belial
AVES	Wingless, flightless birds
BAUTILAZ	Enormous beetle
DEATH CROW	Large predatory bird
DENDRO	Toad-like creature of the eastern Belial
HIRUDO	Small humanoid of the Gallowgate
HYLA	Toad-like creature of the eastern Belial
RANIDAE	Small green humanoids of the northern Belial
SKULKE	Small humanoid of the Belial

TOWERS	ILEDRITH
Dogrose	Jaax
Foxglove	Tragg
Hawkthorn	Tuatara
Hellebore	Xend
Horehound	Brescia
Knightshade	Vachell
Monkshood	Eupatrid
Snakeweed	Zaffre
Wolfsbaine	Klaze
Wormwood	Xylitol

CONTENTS

× **Lychgate**
■ **Tower**

1
CHARYBDIS

Geber staggered forward, his breathing ragged. As he pushed himself onward, his body was bathed in sweat and his face was red. It had been a big mistake to leave the others on the ridge and enter the city alone, but he had only sought to find a way to its centre. It wasn't until he had entered the city itself that he had decided that perhaps he should have a larger share of the treasure for himself.

A faint sound behind him forced him to increase his pace even further.

He had no idea whether he was heading into or out of the city—every deserted street he took looked the same as the one before. If not for his persistent pursuer he might have paused and marked the path he was taking.

A sudden sound behind him made Geber spin around in terror. Even after all his efforts, he had not managed to lose the creature which was chasing him. Earlier, Geber had rounded a corner and almost run directly into it. The sight of the tall shadow had been enough to cure Geber's passion for the treasure. He had fled down street after street until he was sure he had lost his pursuer, but the moment he stopped his headlong rush he heard once more the faint sounds of pursuit.

Rounding a corner, he came across a tall shape stretching up before him. As the creature attacked, he dropped and rolled, feeling the rush of air above his head. Climbing to his feet he turned to face the threat. In the darkness it was hard for him to see the exact shape of his attacker, but he saw enough to know that it was the same creature which had managed somehow to get ahead of him or, worse still, another of its kind.

His fears were soon confirmed as another shadow rounded the corner. Geber turned and ran as the sounds of a struggle broke out in the darkness behind him. As he ran, the sounds became louder until they suddenly ceased, leaving a strange echo filling the street.

Geber crashed into a wall and leaned against it, trying to fill his bursting lungs. The street behind him was alive with dancing points of light and his head pounded. Closing his eyes, he wiped the perspiration from his face. When he opened them again he found his sight had cleared but his head still ached from the effort of his escape.

Drawing one final breath, Geber pushed himself away from the wall and headed off down the street. Without warning, a long shadow erupted from an unseen side street. Sharp pangs of pain ripped through Geber's body as something grabbed him by his hair and neck. Geber had little time to realise what had happened before his neck was snapped with one savage flick of his attacker's wrists.

As Geber's lifeless body began to slide to the cobbled street, the attacker lifted the corpse and twisted its grip once more. Hot blood flowed as Geber's head was torn from his body. The headless corpse fell to the cobblestones, its limbs still twitching. Sightless eyes stared forward, as though suspended in the shadows, before the new owner drew the head close and vanished into the darkness with its prize.

Charybdis staggered forward, his dirt-encrusted boots scuffing the lichen-covered ground as his bare right arm brushed the damp stone wall. He could not believe his run of bad luck. They had been so close to their goal when the others had refused to wait for him and he had been left cursing them as he nursed his twisted ankle.

He had limped after his companions, gritting his teeth and swearing to himself that he would not let them get the jump on him when it came to finding the treasure. He had worked just as hard as the others to find the treasure and he intended to ensure he received his fair share.

Stumbling down one street after another, Charybdis soon found himself hopelessly lost in the long forgotten city. The walls surrounding him rose well above his one and a half metre frame and there was no noise other than the sound of his uncertain progress. A faint breeze sprang up and Charybdis cast a nervous glance towards the sky.

The narrow strip of blue was rapidly darkening

and the cold wind was much stronger beyond the protection of the walls. Huge dark clouds were rolling in from the horizon, signalling the storm which would soon unleash its fury on the ruined city and the jungle which surrounded it.

As he quickened his steps Charybdis missed his footing and his weakened ankle gave way beneath him. A loud curse escaped his clenched teeth as he fell. His elbow struck a rock projection and he felt the sharp edge cut his weakened flesh. Warm blood began to flow freely from the open wound.

He ripped the tail from his filthy blue shirt and wrapped it tightly about the wound, trying to stem the flow of blood. As he worked he again cursed those who had left him behind.

Charybdis flinched involuntarily as a terrifying scream ripped through the city. He held his breath as it reached its peak and then began to taper off. Whatever had caused the scream was still at work and the high pitched noise rose once more.

Shaking with fear, Charybdis climbed unsteadily to his feet. The scream faded, disappearing into a gurgling cry which filled him with even more dread. His injured elbow was forgotten as he leaned against the stone wall, trying to control his shaking body.

It seemed the stories were true and the city was not as dead as many believed it to be. He had heard tales of watchers, guardians of the treasure, whose sole purpose was to protect it from any outsider, but he had thought them simply stories.

His nerves under control, Charybdis pushed himself from the wall and continued down the street. He was forced to favour his injured ankle but

4

the terrible scream had added a new energy to his tired body. It had seemed to come from everywhere and for all he knew he was heading straight towards it. Each corner held a new imagined menace as he slowly eased himself along the rumble-strewn street. Rounding a corner Charybdis discovered the source of the scream.

Ryan, or what was left of him, was splattered across the cobbled street and halfway up one of the walls. His limbs had been ripped free of his body and his torso had been slashed open. His bloodied organs had been thrown indiscriminately around the street. As Charybdis worked his way slowly through the grisly mess it dawned on him that Ryan's head was missing.

He felt his stomach rise as he found himself looking down at Ryan's ruptured heart, but there was nothing in his stomach to answer the call. With one hand holding his convulsing stomach and the other supporting him against the wall he hurried on.

The cobbles were splashed with blood and he realised that whatever had slain Ryan so horribly had passed this way only a short time ago. Charybdis paused to look over his shoulder and, for a brief moment, thought of retracing his footsteps and leaving the city.

But he was reminded of the fortune waiting to be found and his greed for the riches overpowered his fears. With ears cocked for any sound from ahead of him, he drew a small knife from his belt and continued on. Rounding a corner Charybdis was stopped in his tracks.

Mercer and Kelson were fighting a creature straight from the tenth level of hell. It looked like an

Ave, but it was like no Ave Charybdis had ever seen before. It was grey skinned and at least two and a half metres tall. Its legs were long and spindly and it seemed unbelievable that they could support the creature, let alone allow it to move at such a great speed. Its arms were also long and thin, ending in wicked curved talons.

As always, Mercer and Kelson fought side by side. Charybdis had not known them before their journey began, but he had learnt much about his companions over the last five months. Mercer and Kelson had journeyed together for many years and had developed a good partnership. Both wore light mail shirts, their legs bare. Kelson's long dark hair was tied back behind his neck while Mercer's bald head was covered in a sheen of sweat.

The creature's head was elongated and ended in a bird-like beak which snapped at Kelson as he stumbled backward. He managed to duck under the blow and the creature struck the stone wall. A howl of pain rose above the sounds of the struggle. Mercer leapt for the creature's back but it must have heard his approach and spun round to intercept his attack. Blocking the intended blow, the creature grabbed Mercer by one foot and lifted him from the ground. With one movement it flicked him across the street. The sound of his leg snapping was over-shadowed by the noise made as his head struck the stone wall. If the creature realised that Mercer was dead it didn't care. It continued to attack Mercer's body as blood and brains splattered the stone walls and the creature's grey body.

Lifting Mercer's still form by its head, the creature wrenched the head from the body with one twist.

Then it stooped to pick up an object from the ground and began to move down the street after Kelson. Just as the creature disappeared from sight Charybdis realised that it had taken Ryan's head with it. It seemed the creature wanted the heads. Charybdis did not know or care whether it was for food or simply as a souvenir. What he did know was that no treasure was worth what he had just witnessed.

The Aves were creatures of the northern steppes. They were fast and savage but Charybdis had never seen or heard of one like the creature he had just seen. It was half as tall again as a normal Ave and its strength and speed were almost unbelievable. But what terrified him the most was the total disregard for life it had shown as it had butchered Mercer. The expression on the creature's face would haunt Charybdis for the rest of his life.

He turned quickly and began to retrace his steps—past the dismembered body of Ryan and down the littered street. A large drop of moisture struck the dust-filled street directly in front of him. It was followed by another and still another, until the skies opened.

The rain beat down deafeningly all about him. He raised his right hand to shield his eyes but he could hardly make out what lay ahead of him. As he fled blindly, he imagined the creature finished with Kelson and on his trail. On and on he stumbled until he collapsed with exhaustion.

It occurred to him that he must have taken a wrong turn since he did not remember it taking this long for him to work his way into the city. With the rain increasing in strength it would be stupid to keep stumbling from one street to another.

He decided to wait till first light and then climb to the top of one of the walls and escape from this place of death. Slipping behind a large block which had fallen from one of the walls, he wedged himself in between it and the wall and closed his eyes. As the cold began to work its way inward he started to shiver. Soon a small puddle of water formed about him. Exhausted, he dropped off into a dream-haunted sleep.

A scream tore Charybdis from his dreams. At first he thought he was reliving the death of Ryan and Mercer, but he quickly realised that another one of his companions was dying. Pressing his hands to his ears, he tried to keep out the terrible screaming but the sound persisted, cutting deep into his head. *Another of his companions was dead.* This latest loss seemed to weaken him more than the months of hardship he had faced. Climbing to his feet he quickly stretched the aches from his small frame and looked up just as the sun seemed to creep over the eastern stone wall.

The scream had continued for so long that Charybdis was able to get a rough idea of its source. With his idea about climbing the wall temporarily forgotten, he headed off in the opposite direction to the scream.

Now he was totally lost. He had no idea whether he was moving deeper into the city or heading for its outer edge. For all he knew he could be trapped in a small section of the city going round and round in circles. This was confirmed when he suddenly came face to face with Mercer.

His companion's head was sitting on a low stone wall just beyond his shattered body. Beside Mercer's head rested two other bloody and battered heads, those of Ryan and Emal. Emal had been their guide. She was a Cathar, the sect sworn to the protection of pilgrims. Cathars, organised by Charter Houses, entered into contracts with merchants and adventurers to protect them as they travelled the many dangerous roads of Kyrthos. With the money the Charter Houses made from these charters they were able to aid those less fortunate than themselves.

Cathars were trained in all manner of weaponry and for Emal's head to be mounted next to Ryan's meant she must have been taken by surprise some time during the night. There was a look of shock and horror frozen on her face, but compared to the other two heads there was considerably less damage.

Charybdis realised that the creature would soon be back for its trophies and half climbed and half fell over the wall. Looking at the section of wall where Mercer had been killed, Charybdis saw something protruding from the crumbling mortar between the stones.

He paused long enough to wrench it free and was soon on his way again. He risked a glance to see what he was carrying. In his hand was a long curved talon. It was flat and looked more like the blade of a small sabre, razor sharp along one edge and slightly rounded on the other. There was dried yellow blood on the bulbous end, obviously where it had been ripped from the creature's hand when it had struck the wall in the fight with Kelson.

Charybdis shuddered as he looked down at the talon, remembering the damage he had seen inflicted on Ryan's body. As he slipped the talon into

9

a pouch on his belt, another scream echoed the death of the last of his companions. He was now the last invader and, if the creature knew this, then he was also the next victim.

Looking about him, Charybdis realised that there was no place to hide. The streets were all identical, with no other openings offering concealment. It was obvious that the creature was able to track him as it had his companions, so to continue running blindly was useless. Stopping beneath a crumbled section of wall, Charybdis sheathed his knife and began to climb.

Sections of the wall threatened to give way and throw him back onto the street, but finally he reached the top and sat surveying the area about him. His views to the north and south were blocked by taller structures, buildings of some sort that he had not yet encountered. A green line of trees marked the edge of the city in the east. And to the west were more walls and buildings. But towering above them was a tall tower of green stone. It was funny, but when they had first seen the city he was sure that all the buildings had been about the same height, separated by streets and bordered by the stone walls. He had definitely not noticed the tower before and, if his companions had, none of them had mentioned the fact.

For the briefest of moments his greed tried to override his fear and convince him that it would not take him long to reach the tower and that, once there, he could easily find the treasure and evade the creature. His right hand fell to the pouch at his belt and, as he felt the curved talon, an involuntary shudder passed through him.

One side of the wall looked much the same as the other so, throwing his legs over the wall, Charybdis dropped to the other side and set off for the jungle's edge. His mouth was dry, whether from fear or thirst he did not know, but he paused at a large puddle and drank his fill from the muddied water. Raising his head from the puddle, he examined the sky. It looked as if another storm was building and he could see that it would hit before he could work his way free of the city. Rubbing his right hand over his stubbled face, he thought of the options open to him.

Continue on? Hide? Or simply sit and wait for the creature to find him? A sudden noise echoed from the street behind him. It sounded like stone on stone but Charybdis did not care what it was. He leapt to his feet and fled down the street in the direction of the city's boundary.

He could not hear anything over the noise of his own progress, so he simply ran as hard as he could. His ankle was still weak so he was forced to favour it as he ran while ensuring that, when he jumped to clear any obstacles, he did not land on his injured ankle.

His crazed run had now faded to a terrified stagger as he tried to force his legs to keep pumping. Stumbling against the wall, his injured elbow brushed the rough stone and a lance of pain shot through his arm. As he threw himself away from the wall his ankle gave out and he fell forward on his hands and face.

When he raised his hands to his injured face they came away covered in blood. His palms were lacerated and the blood from his hands mingled with that of his bleeding mouth. Placing his bloodied hands on a block of cut stone, Charybdis gritted his teeth as he tried to force himself to his feet.

A soft whistling sound echoed up the street and Charybdis turned his head just in time to see the strange grey creature round the corner. The creature was carrying four heads which it set down carefully before rushing forward.

Charybdis drew his knife with his bloodied right hand while his left hand slipped the talon from his pouch. Pushing himself to his feet and brandishing the knife and talon before him, he waited to meet the attack of the creature.

There was yellow blood on the creature's chest and arms and Charybdis knew that it would have been Emal who had inflicted all the damage. As a Cathar she had been trained in weapons to help protect those who had chartered her. Perhaps this wariness on the creature's part could help Charybdis, but he seriously doubted it.

'Stop!' Charybdis called. It seemed stupid but he did not know what else to do.

To his utmost surprise the creature did stop and regarded him with large black eyes. From this distance Charybdis could see that the creature resembled an Ave, something like a large featherless, wingless bird. Its head was continually moving, its large black eyes locked on Charybdis. He could see the blood-red hatred in those eyes and Charybdis realised that his next few moments could be his last.

'Get back!' Charybdis ordered, gesturing with his knife and the talon.

This time the creature took a step back and its eyes dropped to Charybdis' left hand. Blood was

12

dripping slowly between his clenched fingers and some of it ran down the length of the talon before forming a large drop which fell slowly to the ground.

The creature took another step backward, throwing a glance over its shoulder at the four bloodied heads. There was no escaping the creature, yet its backward steps had filled Charybdis' battered mind with a wild idea. Taking a deep breath, Charybdis stepped forward, holding the knife before him. The creature did not move but stood there looking from Charybdis to the heads and then back again.

Charybdis could not believe that the creature feared him or his small knife. He could see the creature's muscles rippling beneath its grey skin as it stood there, torn between Charybdis and its grisly souvenirs. Souvenirs? Perhaps that was it.

Charybdis lowered his knife and raised the blood-smeared talon, holding it at arm's length before him.

'It seems we both have souvenirs,' Charybdis laughed. 'Or perhaps they are more than that?'

An idea suddenly struck him.

'Come forward!' he commanded.

The creature returned Charybdis' stare and stepped forward, its head slightly lowered, its arms by its side.

'Can you lead me from this city?'

The creature tilted its head and a soft whistling sound emerged. But it did not move from where it stood.

Charybdis lifted his arm, the talon still clasped in his bloodied hand, and pointed in the direction of the jungle. 'Go!' he ordered.

The creature stooped and retrieved its trophies before moving swiftly past Charybdis and heading off towards the jungle. Charybdis sheathed his knife and followed, the talon held tightly in his left hand.

Charybdis remembered some of the tales Emal had told during the long nights on their journey south, tales of her life before she had taken to the road as a Cathar. Her people believed that all things were alive, even lost hair and nail clippings were still part of the body. Should they fall into the hands of an enemy they could be used to upset the well-being of the owner.

To that end, all lost teeth were ground to dust and released on the wind, while hair and nail clippings were buried or burned. Emal had explained that even after death a powerful enemy could use portions of a corpse's body to influence its progress in the afterlife.

Each time Emal had spoken of this she had touched a small bag beneath her tunic. The bag was made of soft leather and contained a single tooth. It had been lost by an old enemy in a struggle many years before and Emal knew that while she held that tooth she had power over her enemy. When taking to the road a Cathar was supposed to relinquish all save for loyalty to the Charter House. But Emal had explained that of late many Cathars had reverted to the ancient ways, with sword religions and old hatreds coming to the fore.

Charybdis looked down at the talon held tightly in his left hand. Perhaps the beliefs of Emal's people were true? Could it be possible? Charybdis followed the creature's progress as best he could but soon found himself falling further and further behind. Finally he was forced to stop and rest.

Sliding to the ground, he leaned back against a wall and closed his eyes. The air was cool and unnaturally still and it felt to Charybdis as if everything was blanketed in silence. Even his breathing seemed somehow soft, perhaps even slow.

2

AZUREUS

Charybdis' eyes snapped open and he realised that he must have dropped off to sleep where he sat surrounded by the silence. His hand sought the talon which had slipped from his fingers. At first he could not find it and he began to panic, but finally he located the curved talon lying only a few centimetres from his right boot.

Snatching it up, he breathed a sigh of relief. A faint noise had woken him and he imagined the creature returning to slay him now that he had lost the talon. As he held it tightly to his chest Charybdis decided that there had to be a better way.

Drawing his knife he cut several thin strips of material away from what remained of the hem of his tunic. Weaving these together, he tied a knot in the centre and slipped the talon through the knot. Then he lifted it and tied it about his neck. The convex side of the talon rested in the hollow of his throat, the wicked edge and tip pointing forward. Charybdis gently fingered his handiwork. Feeling

16

much calmer, he leaned back against the wall and closed his eyes.

When he woke again it was dark and, as his eyes adjusted to the lack of light, he was startled to find the creature perched on a rock an arm's length from him, its large eyes watching him as it sat silently like some grotesque bird of prey.

Charybdis felt a shiver down his spine as he slowly dragged himself to his feet and worked the aches from his protesting limbs.

'Food!'

The creature cocked its head to one side, its eyes never leaving Charybdis.

'Find food!' he ordered once more. This time his left hand touched the talon while his right hand touched his lips and then rubbed his empty stomach.

With a soft whistle the creature lowered itself from the rock and disappeared into the night. Charybdis gathered several armfuls of deadfall which lay against the bases of the walls and large blocks of stone and quickly set about making a fire. The thought of the creature returning unseen made him glance nervously over his shoulder. He did not know how he held control over the creature so he wondered how long the compunction might last or whether there was a limit to the distance.

Another thought crept in. What if the creature slipped from his control and he was unable to regain a hold over it? The mere thought sent another shudder through his tired, aching body.

With shaking hands, he used the flint and stone from his pouch to strike the spark. The tiny glowing ember nestled in the soft tinder and, as Charybdis blew carefully, it slowly grew. Smoke rose from the tinder as Charybdis slipped it into a ball of dry leaves and bark. Blowing gently, he watched the spark grow larger until the handful of leaves and bark burst into flames. Dropping the blazing ball into the centre of half his gathered fuel, he set about feeding small pieces of timber and bark to the hungry flames.

He got to his feet, satisfied with his work, and collected a number of the large stones, setting them about the fire to protect it. Immersed in his task, he had not noticed the return of the creature. Its beak and claws were bloodied and it held out a furred object towards him.

Charybdis was glad to see that it was not part of one of his companions. The furred offering turned out to be a large rodent minus its head. Quickly skinning and gutting the rodent, Charybdis impaled it on a stick. He then positioned it over the fire and moved himself closer to the fire's warmth. The air was still chilly but at least the rain of the night before looked to be gone. As Charybdis slowly rotated the catch above the fire he spared the odd glance for the creature which had slain his companions but now appeared to be his saviour.

The creature seemed tireless as it sat there watching the dancing flames of the small fire. Every so often it would tilt its head to one side and regard Charybdis with its large saucer-sized eyes before emitting a soft whistle. Charybdis could still see in the creature's eyes the need to kill, but at the moment it seemed to offer his only chance to escape this cursed city.

When the smell of the roasting rodent became overpowering Charybdis prodded it with his knife, testing the flesh. Happy with the results, he lifted the skewer holding the meal from where it rested over the coals and began to tear at the hot flesh. He pulled a small leg from the body and threw it to the watching creature.

Startled, the creature leapt back and then slowly regained its perch on the rock. It bent its grey featherless neck towards the offered morsel, its beak slightly parted. A sharp whistle escaped that beak before it straightened, the offered titbit ignored, its dark eyes returning to Charybdis.

'You see something tastier?' Charybdis shrugged, wiping the grease from his fingers through his long dark hair. Running a hand over his face, he realised how tired he was but knew too that he would have to push his fatigue aside and reach the edge of the city before he could sleep. He would need food. Perhaps his meal was the answer to his problems. The rat-like creature had to feed on something? Perhaps it lived in the city but hunted in the jungle which surrounded it? Climbing to his feet, he fashioned several simple torches from the deadfall in the street and, lighting one from the fire, spoke to the creature once more.

'Move,' he commanded.

The creature leapt lightly from the block, turned and hurried down the street with Charybdis in close pursuit. It moved more slowly now, as if aware that Charybdis could not keep up the pace. Every so often it would stop and look back. Once, it stopped suddenly and lifted its head high, tilting it back to release a long drawn-out whistle. The sound sent a chill down Charybdis' back as it seemed to echo about him.

Then the creature took off and he was forced to jog to keep up. The night's rest had done wonders for Charybdis' ankle and, though still tender, it carried his weight well enough. Gradually the speed of the creature increased until Charybdis found himself running once again and short of breath.

'Stop!' he gasped.

The creature came to a skidding halt and Charybdis ran into it, knocking himself from his feet. Picking himself up from the cold ground and leaning against the wall, he quickly regained his breath.

'What's the hurry?'

The creature lifted its head and opened its beak. A small thick tongue slid into view and moved from side to side as it tested the air. The beak closed and then opened again as it released the same long drawn-out whistle. This time the whistle was answered.

Charybdis drew his knife and stepped closer to the creature. 'Friends of yours?' he asked nervously. 'I certainly hope they've eaten.'

The creature stood on one leg and then another, as if impatient to be gone. Charybdis looked up and down the street but could see nothing in the feeble light thrown out by the rapidly dying torch.

He finally came to a decision. 'Go!' he ordered. The creature shot forward without a second thought and Charybdis was forced to sprint several metres before he could catch up to it.

Charybdis lit his second torch from the first and dropped the sputtering torch to the ground without pausing. Rounding a corner he found himself facing two of the bird-like creatures. One lowered its head and tried to push past its companion to reach Charybdis, but the first of the creatures stepped swiftly into its path.

Heads lowered and necks extended, the two creatures circled each other as they snapped and whistled their challenges. Charybdis moved well back from the display.

Abruptly, one of the creatures turned and fled and Charybdis found himself looking into the eyes of the second. Lowering his gaze, he readied himself for the blow which would end his life.

Dropping his gaze further he allowed it to travel the length of the creature's thin right arm until it rested on the taloned hand. With a whispered prayer Charybdis lowered the torch and saw that one of the curved talons was missing. With a sigh of relief he lifted his torch.

'Thank you,' he offered. He did not know if the creature really understood what he was saying, but he had to try. 'Shall we continue?'

Several hours later the moon sat full in the sky as Charybdis dropped his last spent torch at his feet. Leaning against a wall, he drew in deep breaths of the cool night air and tried to stop the pounding of his heart. His legs were shaking and he knew that he couldn't keep this up for much longer.

Without warning, his creature appeared. Head down, long legs pumping, it sped towards him. Charybdis had not seen it move so fast except when attacking. A croaking noise exploded from the street behind it and a dark shape appeared round the corner hot on the heels of the creature.

The shadow was squat and moved in leaps, its bursts of speed equalling that of the bird-like creature. As the pair neared, Charybdis had only a moment to draw his dagger and stoop for the burned-out torch before they were upon him.

The bird-like creature turned to face the pursuing shadow. The shadow turned out to be a small but powerfully built creature, its moist skin a brilliant blue covered in a series of dark irregular-sized patches. A narrow ridge of short spines ran down the length of its back as it squatted regarding the pair. Its front legs were long and ended in stubby-fingered hands while its rear legs were large and powerful and folded beneath it like two coiled springs. Its glowing yellow eyes locked on Charybdis.

Charybdis could hear the low rumbling growl of the toad-like creature as it tried to pass his protector to reach him. Its back arched and the spines grew in size. Suddenly it spat at Charybdis' protector, but the bird-like creature simply danced to one side. The spittle landed at Charybdis' feet, hissing as it turned the cobblestones black.

Charybdis moved back a pace and threw a nervous glance over his shoulder. At first he had not recognised the creature before him for what it truly was—an Azureus, a poison-dart frog. They were found only in the deepest jungles and had not been seen for so many years that it was thought by some that they had died out.

They were very fast and spat a corrosive poison which had only to touch the skin to kill. Charybdis danced to one side as the Azureus spat again, narrowly missing its mark. The spittle struck the wall

22

behind him and he could hear it as it ate into the stonework of the wall.

Instead of attacking, the bird-like creature seemed content to keep itself between the Azureus and Charybdis. Then he saw why.

Three more of the brilliantly coloured Azureus leapt into view. Charybdis doubted the creature could fight off four of the attackers and he knew that, should he turn and run, one of the Azureus at least would be able to get past his creature's defences and run him down before long.

Grasping his knife in his teeth, Charybdis stopped and picked up a sizeable rock and, taking aim, threw it at the closest attacker. The rock struck the Azureus directly between its glowing eyes and it leapt back with a rumble of pain. With the Azureus momentarily distracted the birdlike creature attacked, opening up the injured Azureus' side with its talons.

A second Azureus attacked but the creature swatted it from the air ripping its belly open as it did so. The long curved razor sharp talons were made for such work and the thick hide of the Azureus parted easily. The street was filled with the foul scent of intestines and urine as the gutted Azureus struck the ground and sprawled in a rapidly growing pool of blood. The dying Azureus threw itself about in the narrow street until its efforts grew visibly weaker. The first Azureus then attacked, its assault slowed by its injured side. Charybdis' protector struck swiftly, throwing the Azureus across the street. As it struck a far wall, its motions ceased.

The two remaining Azureus attacked simultaneously, one taking the creature low while the other darted to the side and then back, catching it high on one side. The first of the attackers quickly backed away leaving the creature thrashing around on the ground as it tried to rid itself of the Azureus which had by now worked its way round and locked onto the creature's back.

It looked to be the end of the birdlike creature, which had no hope of ridding itself of the attacker while it was forced to watch the one remaining Azureus. Before he realised what he was doing, Charybdis leapt forward, knife extended, and struck at the Azureus just behind its right foreleg, hoping to find its heart.

The Azureus screamed and arched its back, extending its spines, but it lost its grip on the creature's back. One of the spines caught Charybdis low on his side but, as he was already falling from the Azureus, it merely pushed him to one side, failing to break his skin. Scrambling to his feet, Charybdis leapt for the Azureus before it had a chance to rise and buried his knife deep in its neck, twisting it. The dying Azureus flexed, extending its spines once more. This time Charybdis was thrown back against the wall and a warm wetness soaked his side.

The last Azureus turned, gave one final defiant snarl and disappeared into the darkness. Charybdis raised his hand from his side and saw it was covered in bright red blood. Sighing, he closed his eyes and passed out.

He dreamed of the time when he was apprenticed to his uncle and he stood beside the glowing forge, watching as his uncle slid the blade of a longsword from the red hot coals and regarded his work. With a slight nod, he grunted and turned from the forge, then dropped the glowing blade onto his largest anvil. Lifting a hammer in his massive fist, he set about his work.

The hammer rose and fell as if it had a life of its own, never once missing its mark as it pounded the hot metal, shaping the blade even further. Laying down the hammer his uncle slid the sword blade into a nearby tub of water. Charybdis marvelled at the water as it danced and cavorted about the blade. Steam rose above the tub, temporarily obstructing his view while the hissing of the water filled his young ears.

Charybdis' uncle was a skilled craftsman, much sought after by the Cathars of the local Charter House. Even in the short times of peace his uncle had crafted fine swords and axeheads, while his apprentices produced long tapering blades for spears and hundreds of arrowheads. Charybdis marvelled at how easy his uncle made the work look, and laughed as the apprentices cursed when they made a mistake.

Charybdis had been happy in his youth. When his mother, a Cathar and a swordswoman of some fame, died in a border clash while under charter to a small party of pilgrims, Charybdis and his father had moved in with this uncle. His father had wept openly at the death of his wife, a thing unheard of amongst the Cathars, who accepted the possibility of death as part of their charter.

But Charybdis' father had followed a religion which had flourished long before the Final Wars, in a time when men had walked the roads in roles similar to Cathars. That religion had many Gods, each of which expected to have dues paid. As his uncle plunged a sword into the fiery coals of his forge Charybdis' father would offer a prayer of thanks to one God for the fire and then another prayer to a different God as the sword blade slid into the cold water. Every aspect of his life was filled with prayers.

Charybdis' parents had loved each other deeply and openly, but his father had never ceased in his efforts to coerce his wife's feet from what he referred to as the godless path of the Cathar. With her death, Charybdis soon realised that his father had replaced her with increased devotion to his many Deities.

Charybdis had hardly known his mother as she had travelled the roads under one charter then another, drifting from one Charter House to the next over the years but he had always marvelled at her tales on her all too infrequent visits.

She would tell of her most recent charters and the strange lands she had visited. But what interested Charybdis most were her stories of the Final Wars, which had taken Kyrthos to the brink of destruction.

The Final Wars had in fact been a series of smaller wars, lasting for almost two decades, between the combined might of Kyrthos and a race of outsiders.

Charybdis' mother could tell wonderful tales about her travels, but the ones which excited her son the most concerned the fighting involved in the centuries-past Final Wars. Yet when questioned further about the race of outsiders she would shake her head and refuse to name it.

'It is better not to name an enemy, my Charybdis,' she would whisper. 'For to mention a name will call attention down upon you.' And that was all she was prepared to say on the matter. She would then lift him to her lap, ruffle his hair and continue with her tale.

One story she told, and perhaps Charybdis' favourite, was about a long-dead ancestor who had fought in the Final Wars and had been taken prisoner by the unnamed enemy. He had laboured long and hard in the realm of the enemy until one day he had managed to escape. There had been nearly thirty of them when they had embarked on their bid for freedom, but only two of them survived.

Somehow they returned home, bringing great riches with them. It was then that his ancestor changed his name to Charybdis and had insisted that the first-born son of every third generation be named likewise. As there seemed no reason for not agreeing to this request a long tradition was started.

The other escapee had stayed with Charybdis' ancestor for some time, but one day he simply vanished. He had also changed his name—to Scylla— but he was never heard of again. Charybdis often wondered if a similar tradition had been started in Scylla's family.

Charybdis had lived for his mother's stories and at her death he had determined to travel and see the many places of which she had spoken, but that would need a considerable amount of money.

After the death of his father his uncle had begun to teach Charybdis the craft of blacksmithing at an early age, explaining that the feel of the forge was

27

all-important and that one was never too young to learn. Charybdis had made his first dagger when he was ten and he had cherished it for many years after.

When he had been allowed to make his first sword, the other apprentices had lifted him high and dropped him into the tub of cold water to mark his coming of age.

Charybdis wiped the water from his face and slowly opened his eyes. A heavy rain was falling, and through it he could just see the birdlike creature sitting opposite him, its shoulders hunched. The downpour had washed all trace of blood from its grey skin, but the bloodlust which filled its eyes was still there.

'Well, you won't have long to wait,' Charybdis whispered through shivering lips. 'If I don't bleed to death then this cursed rain will be the end of me.' A shiver ran the length of his body.

The creature slipped off the block and moved to his side. Its curved talons reached for Charybdis, who shrank back in fear sending another wave of pain through his body. He reached for the talon secured about his neck but was too weak to hold it.

Lifting Charybdis in its arms, the creature set off down the street. Charybdis passed out several times but each time he came to he found himself being carried down a stone-walled street in the arms of the creature as the rain beat unmercifully down upon them.

When Charybdis awoke fully he found himself nestled in a small opening. The creature was nowhere in sight and, as Charybdis moved, his body was racked by a fit of coughing. Raising himself to one elbow, he gritted his teeth against the expected pain, but there was none.

His body was covered by a thick pile of foul-smelling straw and when he pushed the odorous covers to one side he realised that he was virtually naked. More importantly, he discovered that the wound to his side was healed. Four red depressions were all that remained of the injury caused by the spines of the Azureus. As he probed and prodded his side in amazement, he saw that the injuries to his hands and elbow were also healed. Even the ankle which had plagued him for so long was completely healed.

Pushing more of the straw from him, he was shocked to see Geber. When they had first sighted the city from the ridge to the east, Geber had ordered the others to wait while he slipped quietly into the city and investigated it. Charybdis and his companions had sat silently, their greed slowly getting the better of them all day until they had talked themselves into following Geber, who they all agreed was not to be trusted. It was on the descent from the ridge that Charybdis had injured his ankle and fallen behind.

As Charybdis leaned forward to wake his companion, Geber's head rolled free of the straw. Charybdis jumped to one side to avoid touching it. The head had been torn from Geber's body, as had those of his companions. Poor Geber. It seemed that he was not the thief they had pegged him to be.

Taking Geber's head by the hair, Charybdis carefully lifted it and moved it as far as possible from where he lay. As he moved the bloodied trophy he saw more of the heads sitting in the filthy straw. It seemed the creature had brought him to its nest.

Leaning back against the side of the nest, Charybdis examined his surroundings more closely. There was something about the place which disturbed him, something beyond the presence of the heads. There was something else that he could not quite put his finger on. Then it came to him. It was the state of the heads themselves.

Charybdis brushed aside more of the straw and examined the heads closely. All had been torn from their bodies and most showed the damage caused by the struggle before their death, but there was more. Geber must have been killed shortly after entering the city, and that had been a day before the arrival of Charybdis and the others.

Charybdis had been in the city for at least three days, perhaps more, his memory was by now fragmented. But Geber's head showed no sign of turning. It was as if it had only just been removed—even the blood looked fresh. Reaching for the head, Charybdis brushed something else hidden in the straw.

It was a small tube the length of his hand and, as he took it up, he saw that one end was threaded. Slowly turning the threaded cap, Charybdis peered into the tube. It contained a white salve which filled Charybdis' nostrils with a faintly familiar honey-sweet odour. Somewhere, or sometime, he had come across that salve before.

The outside of the tube was decorated with hundreds of small delicately carved shells, long and spiralled in shape, each one the same as its neighbour, yet at the same time different in a way that Charybdis could not explain. These shells were the sign of the Cathars. One of the few things about his mother that he remembered clearly was the small shell medallion about her neck.

A soft whistling marked the return of the creature. Charybdis twisted the cap into place and dropped the tube back into the straw, then leaned back against the wall. The creature was carrying another of the rodents it had caught for him the previous day and Charybdis quickly set to work preparing it.

Once his meal was over he was careful to extinguish his small fire. He had not felt as energetic as this for many months. Standing, he stretched and marvelled at the feeling. He had always prided himself on his fitness. His short body was well proportioned and his torso was muscular, thanks to the weight of his blacksmithing hammers. His profession might have been hard, but it had kept his body sound. The journey through the surrounding jungle had taken much out of him and with his stomach full and his mind at rest, he realised where he had smelled the salve before.

It had been in a small Solanesse fishing village about three months ago. He and Emal had arrived there ahead of Mercer and the others and had taken lodgings in a reasonably clean tavern. While they were there an accident happened on one of the small fishing boats. A wire stay parted and whipped back across a fisherman's unprotected leg, opening it to the bone. The locals had just decided that the leg needed to be removed when a Cathar arrived, who was also a Crafter. She wasted little time in pushing her way through the crowd and offering her services.

The injured seaman was carried to a bench where his trouser leg was cut open. After examining the injury the Crafter eased a shell-like medallion from beneath her clothing and grasped it tightly in both hands. The Crafter's medallion differed from that of a normal Cathar in that it had a small gem embedded in the shell's opening.

The Crafter stood still for several moments, then opened a small box containing many narrow tubes, one of them containing a white salve which she rubbed into and about the injury. Once done, she ordered the wound sewn and the leg bandaged. Then she took another tube and added a small amount of a fine green powder to a cup of water which she then bade the injured man drink. By the following morning the leg had healed sufficiently for the seaman to be up and about.

Charybdis slipped his hand into the straw and rummaged round until his fingers touched the tube. Drawing it from its hiding place, he held it up before the creature.

'Where did you find this?' he asked slowly.

The Crafter in Solan had not charged much for her efforts, but Charybdis realised he could make money from the situation if the salve had been found locally.

The creature made several chirping noises and inclined its head before lifting one of its long arms and pointing. Charybdis had no idea whether it was pointing into or out of the city but he didn't care. His greed had once more overcome his fears. As he lowered the tube he surreptitiously slipped it into an empty pouch of the belt which was lying by his side.

Charybdis climbed from the nest and stretched. It felt good to be alive, though the only weapons he had were his knife and the talon. His clothing was fast turning into tattered rags and one of his boots was missing. Taking off the other boot he threw it from him and turned to face the creature.

'Where?' he repeated.

The creature took off and Charybdis followed. With his injuries healed and his stomach full, his mind was once again filled with the thought of profit. He whistled a soft tune as he jogged carefully along the deserted streets.

As the sun was about to set the strange twosome reached a large pair of timber gates. They were closed and obviously barred from the inside as they refused to budge under Charybdis' efforts. The creature seemed agitated as Charybdis tried once more to open them.

Both gates were inlaid with a strange device. Charybdis touched the metal and realised it was silver, pure and untarnished. The shape was almost manlike, only slightly out of focus. Charybdis had no idea what it meant and quickly his mind returned to the thought of the riches he would find.

'It looks as if we'll have to climb them,' Charybdis murmured.

The creature made a sharp whistling noise and began to run round in circles, its long legs and arms lifting high into the air. As Charybdis climbed the gate the creature's antics increased. When Charybdis reached the top he saw more streets like the one he had just left. But high in the distance he saw the green tower he had spied days earlier. Perhaps it was the tower which held the salve? Perhaps there would be more treasure there for the taking?

Dropping over the wall Charybdis set about opening the gates. With the bar drawn and the gates pushed open Charybdis waited for the creature to join him. 'Come!' he called. But the strange Ave continued its odd performance. Charybdis grasped the talon tightly and called again. This time the creature stopped its frenzied running and approached the gates.

The sun was just setting as Charybdis and his reluctant companion set off down the litter-filled street. The moon was full and cast a silvery light into the streets, allowing them to proceed without stopping to light a torch.

They had been walking for some time before Charybdis was brought to a halt by an incredibly obstructive heat. Sweating uncontrollably, he took a half step backwards. As he did so the heat lifted and he felt the cool of the night.

The creature was hopping up and down on one leg, its whistling soft yet urgent. Charybdis stepped forward once more and again the heat struck him like a solid blow. It was as if a barrier had been set before all who would approach the tower, but perhaps it stretched only a short distance. Charybdis took a deep breath and moved further into the torrid region.

His breath was short and gasping, his body covered in a film of sweat when suddenly he was free of the heat. As his body cooled he saw that the creature had not followed and was standing silently on the far side of the fiery barrier. Charybdis gestured for it to follow but watched in dismay as the creature leapt into the air, then turned and fled.

When slaying his companions, the creature had been powerful and quick. When protecting Charybdis from the Azureus it had been strong and fearless. But now it turned and ran just as Charybdis had done when he had first sighted the creature itself.

His control over the creature had failed. Would he regain it? What could lie beyond the torrid barrier which would send the otherwise obedient creature into such a panic?

Charybdis felt a chill on the back of his neck and a shiver passed through his body. He had the distinct feeling that something or someone was watching him. Dropping to a crouch he whipped round, knife drawn ready to face an attack. But there was nothing there. He straightened up and moved cautiously forward, knife still extended.

Ahead of him in the street was a faint haze which seemed to shift and flow from one wall to another. The moonlight reflected from small sections of the haze and, as it moved, its dancing lights mesmerised Charybdis. The lights became brighter and, as they did, the temperature dropped dramatically.

Charybdis was aware of the cold and his mind slowly registered that the haze was drawing closer. He shook his head to free his thoughts and found that the haze was almost upon him. As close as he was, Charybdis could still not see what was hidden in the haze. Not wanting to wait and find out he turned and fled.

As if his movement was a signal, Charybdis

sensed a presence behind him and he ran for the heated barrier. The hairs on the nape of his neck were standing on end and he expected to feel a biting pain in his back any second as whatever it was that pursued him caught up with him. When he felt the first touch of heat he dived and landed on his shoulder, rolling and coming to his feet just beyond the torrid barrier.

As he looked back through the barrier the haze swirled and vanished. The being it revealed sent a scream of fear through Charybdis' body. Wraith!

Wraiths were creatures of the night who stalked the darkness in search of victims. They were the creatures controlled by powerful Crafters who had called them forth from other worlds to protect their homes from the threats of their enemies. Once summoned, they remained until released. They could not be slain, save by others of their kind, and they fed on the power of the Crafter, indicating to Charybdis that a powerful being must have once lived here if the wraith was still imprisoned.

No wonder Charybdis' creature had baulked at the gate and refused to pass the barrier. No living creature was a match for a wraith. Charybdis thought of the safety of the jungle and then its unknown dangers, but again his greed overcame him. If the wraith was still here then a portion of the Crafter's power must still remain in the tower, and if so, then the treasure of the Crafter would be there also. But how to get past the wraith?

Much knowledge of the ancient Crafters' Lore was lost. How the wraiths were summoned or controlled had been a point of contention between Crafters for decades.

If the journey did not take too long it was possible for Charybdis to make the trip in daylight, but he would have to reach the tower, find the treasure and return before the sun set. He knew that what he planned was foolish, but he doubted he could make the three-month journey back through the jungle alone and, even if he did, what did he have to show for his troubles? Nothing. Absolutely nothing.

The creature quickly returned once Charybdis had passed through the wooden gates and settled himself down for the night. A small fire burned brightly and another of the rodents sat above the flames, its flesh cooking slowly in the heat thrown out by the crackling timber. The creature was its normal self, still and watchful, its eyes filled with death. But still Charybdis found himself talking to it.

'You must have been here some time?' he surmised. 'Are there more of you? A family perhaps? No? Well, it doesn't matter. I've been alone for some time and you'll find that all you really need is a place to sleep and a full purse, though I doubt you have much need for money here.'

The creature tilted its head and regarded Charybdis with its large eyes, but it remained silent as Charybdis rambled on until he finally fell into an exhausted sleep.

3
ASAL

Charybdis woke as the first rays of dawn entered the street. As before, the creature sat perched on a block of stone beside the fire, its eyes regarding Charybdis as he climbed quickly to his feet. The Azureus of the outer city had obviously not been able to pass the locked gate so after his encounter with the wraith Charybdis had returned and closed it, dropping the large timber bar into place. For the first time since entering the city he felt safe, the barred gate to one side, the barrier of heat to the other.

The wraith he had encountered the night before would be hiding, protecting its frail body from the light of the new day's sun. Nibbling on a few bones left over from the night before, Charybdis made his way towards the heated barrier. He intended to pass through the barrier, enter the tower and return before the setting of the sun released the wraith.

As before the strange Ave refused to follow him through the barrier of heat and simply stood silently by as Charybdis readied himself. He could feel the eyes of the killer locked deep within his back and, if not for the continual need for food, Charybdis would have used his power over the creature to banish it from his sight.

It was unsettling to have to depend so much on the killer of one's companions. Charybdis had known them for only a few months, but in that short time he had learnt a great deal about them and regretted their loss. After all how much treasure could one man carry? Brushing those thoughts away he checked that the talon was still secured about his neck and that his knife was wedged firmly in its sheath. With a deep breath, he braced himself and leapt through the barrier.

Again the heat bit deep, but this time he was ready for it. As soon as he was free of the barrier's influence he turned his steps towards the tall green tower. At first it was a pleasant sensation to jog through the deserted streets, his mind alive with the thoughts of treasure. But as the day wore on and the twisting streets apparently brought him no closer to the tower, he began to worry that he might have to turn back before he reached his goal.

In one street Charybdis came upon a section where the plaster from one of the houses had come down and as he ran through it he cut the soles of his feet. Gently applying the salve, he tore the last of his tunic into strips and quickly bandaged his feet before continuing.

A faint panic began to well up inside Charybdis as he noted just how low the sun was on the horizon. If he did not find the tower soon he would have to retrace his steps. But could he still find his way back to the barrier and the protection it offered? His mind made up, he turned, and began to head back towards the barrier.

His fear lent him speed as he raced down the streets, the setting sun casting long shadows about him as he pushed himself to the limit, his fear having given way to panic.

He turned a corner and saw the haze of a wraith blocking the street before him. Making a quick detour, Charybdis threw a nervous glance over his shoulder but he tripped in doing so and sprawled headlong into the centre of the street. As he quickly regained his feet he watched the haze as it entered the street and moved steadily towards him.

He could feel the cold radiating from the wraith as it approached. Not game to risk a look behind him Charybdis bolted headlong down one street after another until he was totally lost. His feet were bleeding again and his lungs were straining when, at last, he found himself in familiar surroundings.

The cold was increasing behind him as he sighted the birdlike Ave hopping about in the centre of the street just a short distance ahead of him. Using every last grain of strength, Charybdis increased his pace. When he passed a junction he felt a flesh-tearing cold as he ran within a hair's width of another wraith. His right arm was numb from the cold which was slowly working its way up to his shoulder as he entered the heated barrier.

On the far side of the barrier he skidded to a halt and collapsed in a heap, gulping in much-needed cool air. His arms and legs were shaking and he was forced to draw his knees up to his chest to try to stop shivering. The heat of the barrier had not banished the intense cold of the wraith. Beside him was a pile of deadfall and one of the rodents. The rodent's skin had been ripped from its body and it had been roughly gutted.

Charybdis looked at the creature and watched in amazement as it cocked its head to one side and then prodded the pile of timber with one of its clawed feet. As Charybdis quickly regained his composure he slipped his flint and stone from a pouch on his belt and proceeded to light a fire. The creature had provided what he needed, and without being told. It was as if it was learning from being with Charybdis.

If he had not seen this creature kill Mercer, Charybdis could have forgiven the beast, allowing himself to believe another had slain and mutilated his travelling companions. But he had been there.

His hand rose and carefully stroked the curved talon at his throat. The powerful Ave watched Charybdis as he moved, its large round eyes following his every movement. The power Charybdis seemingly had over the creature was growing. He could sense it in the Ave's movements and its attitude when it raised its eyes towards the barrier.

The two wraiths were still beyond the barrier. Charybdis set the small carcass over the flames and ignored them. His lips were cracking and his throat was dry but there had been no rain that day and the small puddles he drank from earlier were long gone. Tomorrow he would have to find a way to mark the streets he travelled so as not to pass the same way twice. Closing his eyes, he allowed himself a brief smile. There was death in all directions, but with the aid of his new companion he might yet reach the treasure and then safety.

*

Charybdis used a piece of plaster to scribe an arrow into the stone wall of the street. Over the last five days he had slowly worked his way deeper into the centre of the city by marking his path and retreating as the sun reached its zenith. He had found that the inner city was a maze of small streets and buildings set in a repeating pattern clearly intended to fool the unwary. Many of the buildings bore the same facade which had confused Charybdis on his first visit.

He looked up and found himself at the base of the tower. To his surprise he saw that the tower was not green painted stone but was in fact cloaked in a strange plant which grew from the soil close to the base of the tower. The leaves were mainly green with a brown hue, their serrated edges touched with a hint of blue. The leaves were growing in pairs between each of which was a short, wicked-looking curved thorn, much like the beak of a bird of prey.

Charybdis offered a small laugh as he stepped back and shaded his eyes against the light. The plant covered the tower totally and no matter how hard he looked he could see nothing beneath it.

Thrusting both hands into the twisted vines, he forced an opening and in the gap he found a smooth grey stone. From the outside, the plant seemed to be supported by the stonework of the tower but Charybdis could not see anywhere it actually touched it.

Charybdis shrugged and stepped back further; his imagination was running away with him. For the plant to cover the entire tower from base to top it had to touch the stonework for support.

He had seen the plant before or at least he

thought he had, perhaps he had only dreamed it, but a name came to his mind. Hawkthorn . . . The plant was Hawkthorn, its name coming from the similarity of the leaves and the thorn beak to the wings and beak of the hawk.

Charybdis carefully searched the tower for a means of entry and eventually found a tall narrow door. The Hawkthorn stopped its growth at the edge of the grey stonework and not one twisted tendril touched the timber of the door. It was as if some gardener had trimmed the plant, leaving the door free for the use of any who wished to enter the formidable tower.

The sun was still high in the sky but it was well past midday and Charybdis knew that to linger was to flirt with danger. It took a great deal of effort on his part to draw himself away from the promising door. Beyond that door lay incomparable riches, he was sure of it. His dreams had been a mixture of wealth and death, and while the deserted city held death, Charybdis was sure the tower held the wealth. Without hurrying, he retraced his steps back to the barrier and began to prepare the meal his companion had caught for him during his absence.

'Well, Asal, how was your day?'

Charybdis slowly turned the body over the coals of his fire. After the last excursion beyond the torrid barrier he had given the creature a name. Asal was reputed to have been a ruler of a far off land who had been known as the King of the Golden Pillars. It was said that he had owned seven swine which he and his guests had slain each day and dined upon each night only to rise in the morning and find the swine whole and hearty once more.

It was the same with this creature. Each time Charybdis returned he found a small pile of fuel for his fire and a skinned and gutted rodent ready for roasting.

'Well, Asal, my silent companion, tomorrow is the day. I have found the tower and a door leading into it. With luck by this time tomorrow we should be dining off silver plates and drinking from golden goblets. How would you like that?'

Asal merely twisted its long head and stared down at Charybdis. There was never any change to the creature's expression and Charybdis sometimes felt he could see his own death reflected in its eyes. Even when it had been afraid of the wraiths and had refused to pass the barrier, it had simply danced and cavorted about, whistling its strange sounds. Apparently the need to kill was the only emotion it showed. But he did not care, so long as the Ave kept him well fed.

Tomorrow. After so long, he was finally going to have the wealth he had always sought. He had been happy as a blacksmith, and he had often found himself with more work than he could handle, even though he had many skilled apprentices and offsiders to help.

For years he had laboured over the swords and armour he had made for the rich until he had amassed a small fortune ready for his retirement, after which he had intended to travel the many lands of Kyrthos. But then his Lord's luck had changed for the worse. On a raid deep into Scapol, his Lord had lost a major engagement with his enemy and been captured.

Charybdis had given almost all his savings as part of the ransom for his Lord only to find that, once free, his Lord sold him into service to help pay the war debts he had amassed. His forge cold and his profits gone, Charybdis had been forced to labour in the forge of his Lord's enemy until one night he'd had enough and, packing only a few items, he escaped.

To head east for Calcanth and home would have led to a quick recapture, so Charybdis travelled west. He was chased clear across Scapol, all the way to the border with Skarn, and then beyond. He had not even been safe when the search was called off, as the people of Skarn did not like strangers and regarded them all as thieves and escaped criminals.

It was in Skarn that he first met Emal, the small Cathar who had told him so many things about the world and life itself. Like Charybdis, Emal had no family left alive. Together, they had drifted in and out of trouble until they had met Geber. His wife had just died and he had left his home behind to seek out the wealth he had always craved. It had been Geber who had introduced them to Kelson and Mercer. Each of them had felt the itch of wanderlust and each sought a quick route to the riches they desired. Geber had heard a tale of a deserted city far to the north and, with only a few scraps of information to go on, the small party had set out on the road to adventure.

Charybdis felt sorry that he had not made the time to bury the head of Emal and the other companions he had lost, but he made a promise to himself that he would erect a monument to them in the garden of the massive home he would build with the treasures he would find tomorrow in the Hawkthorn Tower.

Charybdis quickly crossed the plaza and stood before the narrow door of the tower. He shivered involuntarily as a cold breeze whipped round the plaza's open expanse. The nights had been growing progressively colder and, with only a pair of ragged breeches for warmth, Charybdis had not rested well. The fire had been comforting but he did not know what he would do for protection and food once he was free of the city. He would have Asal, but could the Ave hunt, protect him and carry the treasure at the same time? Charybdis doubted it.

The door swung open at his touch and Charybdis, surprised to find it wasn't locked, pushed it open further. He found himself in a semi-circular room at the base of a set of winding stairs. Beneath the stairs was another narrow door, but it was locked and refused to move under his efforts.

This door was constructed of the same dark heavy timber as the main door, and it fitted snugly into the stone wall with only the faintest of cracks showing. Now that he was inside the tower he could see more clearly the grey stones from which it was constructed. The blocks were irregular in shape yet fitted perfectly and Charybdis doubted he could slide a piece of parchment between the joins.

Charybdis climbed the stairs cautiously, passing many other doors as he did so, but each one held fast. Resigned to climbing the stairs to their end he tested each door he passed until at last he found himself at the top of the winding staircase. The room beyond the door had to be the uppermost one in the tower.

To his relief, this door was unlocked and swung inward on silent hinges. Charybdis entered a circular room filled with light. The doorway and a small section to either side of it were the only solid walls the room seemed to have, the rest being constructed of a strange crystal. Smooth to the touch and transparent, it allowed the light in but kept the cold out.

The room was furnished with a long table and eleven chairs, each of which looked to be carved from a single piece of timber. The workmanship was finely detailed and Charybdis could not help but marvel at the tiny figures and glyphs which decorated the legs of the table and the backs of the chairs.

Several low stands surrounded the table and he quickly realised that he stood in a small banquet room. The previous owner had obviously entertained in this room and the thought of this reminded Charybdis of his hunger. Returning to the stairwell, he descended and tried to force one of the locked doors.

The door was made of the same dark-hued timber as the furniture in the room above, but unlike any door Charybdis had ever seen, it had neither a keyhole nor a handle. He searched the walls around the door, looking for any sign of a trip mechanism, but there was none.

Working his way to the base of the tower Charybdis was again unable to open any of the doors. Cursing his luck, he ran across the plaza and lifted a large rock which had become dislodged from a wall. Intending to return to the tower and batter down the door, Charybdis gasped as he realised that the sun was already low on the horizon.

With no time for him to reach the safety of the barrier, Charybdis realised that his only hope lay in securing the tower against the wraiths and waiting out the night. Dropping the rock, he quickly began to gather armfuls of fallen timber so that he might have a fire for the night. He threw the timber in through the door, all the while keeping a watchful eye on the plaza around him.

Struggling under the weight of the largest rock he could move, he closed the lower door of the tower and wedged the rock against it. Then he ferried all the timber to the uppermost room and set about building a small fire in its centre. Once the fire was burning he wondered what Asal would do when he did not return.

Smoke rose from the fire, but this did not disturb Charybdis. Every building he had known had vents which allowed the smoke from the burning torches to escape. He searched the chamber more thoroughly than before but he found nothing new.

Through the transparent walls of the tower room, Charybdis watched as the sun set behind the jungle to the west. A red glow filled the sky even after the sun had vanished and, for a brief moment, it reminded him of the blood of his dead companions. Glancing down, Charybdis swore as a haze entered the plaza and moved quickly to the base of the tower.

He darted across the room and pushed the table and chairs hard up against the door. If the wraith found a way through the lower door then he doubted that his makeshift barricade would hold it for long, but he had to try. His fear and greed were replaced by a sudden and unwelcome realisation that his feet were already set on the path of death and that he would soon join Emal and the others.

Charybdis did not hear the lower door open, but he could feel the coldness intensify as the wraith climbed the stairs towards him. Throwing more of his fuel upon the fire in an attempt to drive off the cold, he stood wide-eyed as the door began to shake. The smoke from the fire seemed to have nowhere to go and as it began to gather on the ceiling Charybdis found himself coughing.

The smoke reminded him of the inn where they had rested on their final night before entering the Belial. It had sat in the westernmost district of Solan, nestled against a low ridge of grassy hills. A loose-surfaced road ran before the inn, little disturbed by the insignificant number of travellers who used it.

The large guest room had been void of life but the smoke from the smouldering fire had a life of its own as it swirled away from the wide-mouthed chimney and crept across the filthy ceiling. It was only the heavily spiced drinks which had kept them there, the warm liquid filling their tired bodies with a new energy.

The five of them had continued to brave the smoke, sitting by the open door in the hope of catching a slight breeze. The breeze did not arrive but after several more drinks their meal did. It was cold and greasy and tasted of smoke, a taste that would always remind Charybdis of that almost carefree night before the darkness of the Belial fell upon them.

The Life Bringer was surely not with him the day he agreed to join this little expedition . . .

The door was shaking more violently now and one of the chairs had fallen from the table. Charybdis quickly scooped it up and held it raised above his head. As he looked up at the chair he almost laughed at the thought of attacking a wraith with a piece of furniture. When he glanced nervously around the room he saw a faint spiral of smoke being drawn into a thin crack beside the door. Lowering the chair and standing on it, he saw that the smoke was vanishing into a long crack which ran from beside the door almost to the transparent wall of the tower room.

Climbing from the chair Charybdis found that there were other cracks, four in all, which formed a rectangular outline on the wall. Continuing to search, his prying fingers found a small stone which moved slightly under his touch. He pressed harder and stepped back as a section of wall slid back and then up, revealing a small narrow passageway.

As he stepped through, Charybdis saw the door to the tower room fly open and caught a glimpse of the wraith as it entered the room. The man-like shape of the wraith was all Charybdis had in common with it. Locked under some long dead Crafter's spell, the wraith needed only to slay Charybdis for its role to be accomplished. Then the stone panel slid closed and Charybdis began to climb a short stairway. As he reached the fourth step his head passed through an opening into a round domed chamber.

The walls were the same grey stone but decorated with engravings, and the chamber was lit by a faint pulsating green light radiating from its centre. The light was coming from an enormous multifaceted gem, larger than any Charybdis had ever seen.

Easily the size of a man's head, it rested in a large shell on a low stone dais surrounded by ten smaller yet similar gems, each of them mounted in an identical shell. All but one of the gems were glowing and it was their luminescence, reflected by the shells into the larger gem, which lit the chamber. As Charybdis approached the central gem he could see his reflection a hundred times over in the cut and polished surfaces of the many facets.

Leaning against the wall was a long thick staff, its entire length worked with intricate designs. The staff was made of a light metal which Charybdis had never seen in all his years of blacksmithing. Its head was fashioned like that of an animal which Charybdis saw could almost have been Asal, or an Ave very much like him. But when he examined the head he discovered a look of cold intelligence in the unseeing eyes, not the bloodlust of Asal's.

Charybdis carefully studied the staff and realised that the repeated design was in fact a series of shells, narrow at the top, then bulbous, and finally long and tapered. The sign of the Cathar? The symbol brought back a fleeting image of his mother as she had been the last time he had seen her, the Cathar shell medallion as always about her slim throat.

When a grinding sound signalled the opening of the panel in the room below, Charybdis lifted the staff and stepped behind the gem, where he waited for the wraith. The haze seemed to drift up the stairs and hovered just out of reach beyond the gems.

The wraith standing patiently within the haze was man-like in shape and size but its limbs moved in a chilling way. As it stood at the head of the stairs, it seemed to flow back and forth, but, at the same time, Charybdis had the impression that it was motionless.

Suddenly the wraith darted forward and Charybdis steadied himself on the gem as he struck out with the staff. There was a flash of green light which blinded him and he staggered backward, swinging the staff about madly as he tried to shield his eyes from the blinding light and fight off the wraith. As the dancing lights cleared from before his eyes Charybdis saw that the chamber was deserted. The wraith had gone.

Looking down at the staff he saw that the head of the staff was moving, changing shape even as he watched. It was like watching molten metal flow from a crucible as the head took on many forms before finally slowing and then stopping. Charybdis raised the staff and saw that the head now resembled a man, rather than a creature. And there was something uncannily familiar about the man. It was he, himself. The head of the staff was now a miniature bust of Charybdis, with the same look of panic on his face as when the wraith had attacked.

If one wraith could enter the tower, then others might still follow. Charybdis quickly descended the stairs to the banquet chamber and then to the lower door.

Pushing the door closed, Charybdis was about to wedge it shut with the staff when he heard a loud click, like the turning of a key in a lock. He pulled on the door but it refused to open. When Charybdis looked down at the staff the light of knowledge was in his eyes.

The staff was the key to the tower.

*

Charybdis sat on a chair in the banquet room, his bare feet resting on the table before him. He had put out the fire and rested the staff against the side of his chair. There was a strange warmth coming from the staff and he found that it was all he needed to keep warm.

The staff must have been left behind by whomever had commanded the tower last. That much was obvious. And as the head of the staff now resembled Charybdis, did that mean that a creature like Asal had been the tower's last master? It would seem so. But Asal seemed to have little intelligence save what it needed to hunt and kill.

Charybdis lifted the staff and rested it across his thighs. In the morning he would see if he could draw Asal into the inner city and then he would set about opening all the doors of the tower and learning its secrets.

4
TRAGG

T ragg cursed. He could not see his Lychgate
from his Stronghold but he knew its exact
location and he could feel its pent-up power.
Since the closing of the Lychgate at the end of the
Final Wars, Tragg and his fellow Iledrith had been
trapped within the blood-red tinted world, surrounded by the destruction they had caused.

Nothing could repair the damage done to their
world. All the Iledrith could do was wait for an
opportunity to escape their world and re-enter
Kyrthos, a world which had been denied to them
centuries ago by the Crafters, Crafters allied with
the cursed Living Towers.

The Living Towers had been constructed as
mighty keys with which to hold the Lychgates
closed, barring the Iledrith from the world of
Kyrthos. The first of the Living Towers,
Knightshade had been constructed by two powerful
Loremasters, Crafters of the Lychworld. It was generally believed by the Iledrith that they had to have

originated on the Lychworld, as those living in Kyrthos were too barbaric at the time of the construction.

But Tragg believed that it was travellers from other worlds who had constructed the towers. The Lychworld and Kyrthos were not the only worlds to use the Lychgates for transportation. There had once been many, but now only two worlds were accessible via the Lychgates. Gone was the knowledge to open the gateways to any other world.

Several moons ago Tragg had felt the calling of a tower. He did not know which of the towers it was and he did not care. For him to feel the urge so strongly it had to be the tower which held his Lychgate secure. If a new master could reach the tower then his Lychgate would be released and Tragg would be able to set foot upon Kyrthos, and this time there would be no alliance of towers to hold him at bay.

Tragg stood up and strode the smooth stone floor to one of the narrow windows of his throne room. To either side of his throne sat his few Loremasters, skilled manipulators of the Lore of his world. With their combined powers Tragg was able to maintain a huge army, kept locked in sleep deep within the lower reaches of Deyja. His Loremasters also provided much of the food and water for those who served him, as his world was a barren wasted land, able to feed only a few who knew the secrets of the Lychworld.

Along the walls stood his Dey, the commanders of his army. They were trained and ready to die for him should an enemy of his cross the boundary and enter the region under his Lore. More to the point, they would greatly aid his army when he once more gained access to the world of Kyrthos and the riches it held.

Tragg stared out over the forbidding landscape. Veins of white lightning filled the sky as a mighty storm unleashed its fury against the long dead mountains. In the brilliant light of the storm Tragg could see the extent of his realm.

The land was tinted a blood red as the huge ball of angry fire settled behind a range of torn and jagged peaks. The range, the Dragon's Backbone, ran almost the length of the Lychworld like a living spine of stone joining all the lands of the race known as the Iledrith. As the raging sun set the land darkened until it was bathed in a soft grey light. At the base of a spur leading from one of the rugged peaks sat a squat circular fortress. Cut from the same dark stone which made up the mountain range, it sat alone in the eerie landscape.

The storms of the Lychworld were deadly and sudden, and no sooner had a storm appeared than it vanished. With the passing of the storm Tragg could see the tall thin columns of the Lychstreams which stretched upward towards the dark sky. These columns sprang from the summits of rock spires, marking the positions of the towers in Kyrthos. It was believed that these spires were the shadows of the Living Towers and the streams of lights which sprang from them simply the reflected power of the Lychgems which stored the power of the Living Towers deep within their body of living stone.

Tragg recrossed the room and sat silently on his throne of cold stone. Surrounded by his followers, he allowed his mind to fill with the whispered promises of the tower. Piercing even the great distances between Kyrthos and the Lychworld, the tower's pleadings and pledges amused Tragg. Riches, power, unending life, the promises went on and on, filling Tragg with hope that one moon soon a worthy candidate would reach the tower and master its power.

Many of the towers were once more conscious and sought the masters they needed from amongst the puny inhabitants of their world. As they drew the hopefuls towards them, great obstacles were thrown in their paths ensuring that only the most worthy reached the final goal: as yet none had succeeded.

Tragg had journeyed to the Lychstream when he had first sensed the tower's awakening. At the summit of the rock spire he had stood bathed in the reflected Lychstream. For a brief instant he not only understood the need of the tower, but heard the frail pitiful creature it sought to master it. Many had tried before and failed, but Tragg had felt the commitment in this man and the greed building up within his frail body as he drew nearer and nearer to the tower and the promised treasures.

When this one reached the tower the Lychgate would be released from its age-old barring and when the runes of the altar were traced and the blood of a female spilled upon the well-worn stone then the Lychgate would open and Tragg would be free to wreak vengeance on the world for his banishment.

His huge scaled hands gripped the arms of his throne tightly and his talons carved deep scratches into the hard stone as his red eyes lifted towards the ceiling. An age-old silent prayer escaped his lips as he mouthed the blood-filled promises to the Four Pillars of Death.

Tragg remembered an old tale he had heard about a time when those of the Lychworld still travelled the oceans and seas. Somewhere off the coast was a giant whirlpool whose waters destroyed any who were fool enough to approach. Only avoidance could save a vessel from the swift deadly waters. However, nestled against the coast was The Rock, and any who managed to avoid this Whirlpool of Destruction met their fate in the crashing waters surrounding it.

But those who steered clear of The Rock were captured and drowned by the never ceasing waters of the Whirlpool of Destruction. Tragg laughed to himself. Those who chose to travel that coast died, the only option granted them was the means they chose to do so. Such a choice was fast approaching the pathetic creatures of Kyrthos. Would it be the Rock or the Whirlpool for their destruction?

Soon the clear waters of Kyrthos would be muddied and bloodied. Events were already in motion, instigated by the Whirlpool of Destruction which would soon be unleashed upon their unsuspecting world. Only the stilling of these once gentle waters could again bring peace to the world of Kyrthos.

As Tragg rose from his throne and crossed the stone floor towards his quarters, the released power of the newly mastered tower flowed suddenly through Deyja. Tragg stopped in mid stride as the walls of his fortress throbbed with the power of the Lychgem.

Raising his head to the blood-red sky he shouted

his name for all to hear. Then, spinning on his heels, he marched back into his throne room and called for his Loremasters.

'The tower has been mastered,' he shouted, his words filling the entire fortress as they echoed from the stone walls. All who served him stopped and listened. 'Bring me armour and ready my warriors— the time of the Iledrith will once more touch the world of Kyrthos.'

Servants rushed about their duties while Loremasters gathered what information would be needed.

Several hours later Tragg strode the open plain of the Lychworld towards the distant Lychgate, his blood-red armour fastened about his huge frame. A massive helm rested upon his head and a mighty war hammer hung from his belt.

'Is all in readiness?' he demanded.

A Loremaster rushed to his side. 'All is prepared, Lychlord. We have woken the remainder of the Dey and they stand in readiness for your orders.'

'Has the Lychgate been unlocked?'

'It has, Lychlord.'

Tragg reached the stone-bordered Lychgate and turned his attention to the centre of the closed gate, where he saw a faint image. A ring of tall standing stones marked a circle about a flat rectangular altarstone supported by four short ornately carved pillars. Two of the standing stones were capped by a large flat one forming a gateway. This was the Lychgate which would take Tragg from his world to Kyrthos.

The image was only the shadow of the real Lychgate and altar and would remain so until the deep-carved runes on the altar were traced by the hand of a female. Once this was done, Tragg would be able to send his own shadow image through the Lychgate.

Eons ago it had been the females of the Lychworld who had control of the power and released the Lychgates for travel. Even now the cursed Lychgates only responded to the touch of a woman, regardless of race.

Tragg had many females, human females, but these were in the Lychworld and could not reach the circle of standing stones on Kyrthos. As soon as a woman touched the cold stone of the altar she would be overcome by an urge to touch the deep-cut runes carved into the altar's surface. Having touched the runes she would be compelled to trace the all important design, releasing the Lychgate.

To hold the gate open and allow his real body to pass, he needed fresh blood to feed the stone of the altar and it would fall to the poor unfortunate female who opened the gate to supply the blood.

When Tragg last strode the world of Kyrthos his Lychgate stood at the end of a long peninsula, a pointing finger of land stretching out into the turbulent ocean of Kyrthos.

'Summon my Dey,' Tragg commanded. 'I wish to speak with them before their warriors are awakened.'

The Loremaster, his hairless scalp covered in scales, bowed deeply and left the chamber. As he passed down the tall wide corridor he walked erect. Sentries saluted and other Loremasters bowed deeply. He had risen to a position of great power under Tragg and now was the time for him to prove his worth. He knew that there would be

Loremasters on Kyrthos known as Crafters to face, but of their power and skill he had no knowledge. But deep within his altered form he could sense his own power and knew that Tragg and his Loremasters would be victorious.

With a flick of his heavy robe he entered the training room where the Dey were waiting. 'The Lychlord commands you to his presence,' he stated.

The Dey marched from the room, their red-dyed leather armour and helmets giving the impression of miniature Traggs, but they were the offspring of humans taken in long-past wars and they knew none of the power their master possessed. The Loremasters alone were of the Lychworld, the only survivors of a breeding between Tragg and his human captives, and they knew the Lore of their world like no other.

Charybdis used the staff to open the many locked doors within the tower. He found a kitchen, a library and many small storerooms, each one filled to overflowing. He also found a small treasure room. Weeks, or even days ago, the room was all Charybdis would have been interested in, but now, after feeling the power of the staff and witnessing what it could do, he merely glanced about the room and resumed his explorations.

Once he was sure he had located and opened every door he returned to the library. Its walls were filled from floor to ceiling with all manner of books and scrolls, and several small tables were spaced about the room also holding many books of varied sizes and themes.

In the centre of the room was a low marble pedestal with a sloped top. Resting on it was a large book, by far the largest the library had to offer. It was closed but there was a wide length of red ribbon passing through its pages, marking something which had been of interest to the previous owner.

Charybdis wiped the dust from the cover and felt his fingers tingle as they brushed across the leather surface. Then he slowly opened the book and carefully turned the thick dry pages until he found the marked page. The printing was large and artistic and it took some time before his eyes adjusted to the flowing script. What he was reading was a brief history of Kyrthos, beginning at a time just before the Final Wars, a time known as the Denial. Charybdis was amazed as page after page revealed the history of his world and of those who had once ruled and then destroyed it.

It seemed there were more of these towers spread across the varied lands and that they had once been controlled by powerful Crafters who ruled the entire world. But they fell to quarrelling; wars soon broke out across the lands and nations fell. The towers and their occupants survived the wars, but there was little they could do to help the surrounding countryside as the power of the Lychgems had been depleted in the fighting.

Eventually only the towers were left and, as the centuries rolled by, man once more began to flourish and prosper, though not in the lands bordering the towers, which were thought of as evil.

Only the Hawkthorn Tower and its occupant had survived the centuries. But as Charybdis read on he learned that as this history was being written its author was dying. The end of the book would mark the end of the Crafter's life and Charybdis wondered what it would have been like to have lived for so many centuries, only to die alone in this tower.

He read on.

Once the tower's master was dead the tower would renew its power over centuries of inactivity. It would then be free to seek out a new master and start the cycle of destruction once more.

Charybdis and his companions had been lured here by the promise of treasure. What if at this exact moment other adventurers were working their way towards other towers in the hope of similar riches and glory? Should the power of the other towers be woken, Charybdis realised that a war of truly epic proportions could erupt across the peaceful land, finally encompassing all of Kyrthos.

As he closed the book after reading the final entry Charybdis realised that whoever had commanded the tower before had left him a sign. The tables were filled with books containing ancient maps and directions for finding the remaining towers. They also told how these towers could be conquered and united with the Hawkthorn Tower.

The closest of the towers was the Monkshood, located not far away, but distance mattered very little. It could be in the same city and would be of little use to Charybdis. To learn the secrets of the tower he had to stay, he had to unlock all the knowledge there was about the other towers and his own.

Having destroyed one wraith with the combined power of the staff and gem, Charybdis was sure he could defeat any other assailant who risked the centre of the deserted city. The tower was now secure, and control of the staff gave him a security he had never known.

The treasure sitting in one of the small chambers would allow him to live out the remainder of his life in unparalleled luxury, but now he had felt the power of the tower he desired more, much more.

To achieve this, Charybdis had to find others who were willing to take on the hardships. Somehow he had to find these people and persuade them to aid him in his plan. But where?

The first pangs of hunger reminded him that it was late in the day and that he had not yet eaten. Retracing his steps to one of the many storerooms he found sealed containers of dried herbs and vegetables, and a substance which looked and smelled like meat but turned out to be rather tasteless. The sooner he could lure Asal into the inner city, the sooner he'd be eating real food again.

The banquet room still smelled of smoke as Charybdis crossed to the transparent wall and watched as the sun set. He could make out the jungle to the west and for the briefest of moments he wondered what lay beyond its tangled protection. Then his attention was captured by movement in the plaza below. A wraith had left one of the many side streets and was making for the base of the tower. Charybdis felt a momentary panic before remembering that he had secured the lower door with the power of the staff.

He watched as a second wraith appeared and joined its companion at the base of the tower, their haze-shrouded bodies moving rapidly as they disappeared momentarily from sight, only to reappear when they had finished their circuit of the tower.

Charybdis held the staff closer to his chest. He knew that these wraiths were after him and that they would not stop until they had slain him, or he them. He had killed one wraith in the room above. Was it the staff alone which had accomplished that? Or was the gem the weapon he had unconsciously used?

He had to read more of the books and find out what he could about the staff and the gems in the highest tower room.

But the longer he delayed reaching the other towers, the more chance there was that another would find them first and unlock the power they contained.

The roots of the plant reached deep into the earth, well past the bedrock which supported this city and those that came before it. Its protective shroud over the tower was complete and, when the master had passed on, the Hawkthorn had turned inward on itself, resting, conserving its strength.

There had been a slight tingling travelling the length of its vines for some time before the sluggish mind of the plant realised that a living being had entered the tower. It struggled to fight off the effects of its long sleep and gradually became more aware of its surroundings.

The city was older but its familiarity soon returned as the Hawkthorn took in all about it. A jungle had grown up beyond the outer walls of the city and in its slow way the Hawkthorn wondered what other changes would have affected the creatures who had occupied the lands before the death of its master.

The Hawkthorn sent out new roots, drawing fresh nutrients to its leaves as it welcomed the warmth of the sun. In the tower wrapped in its tight embrace, the Hawkthorn could sense a strange creature. The creature was asleep as the plant had been, but it slept for a much shorter time. As the Hawkthorn studied the creature it found the familiar pulsations of the gem and staff.

However, the staff had changed slightly, adapting itself to the one it now recognised as its new master. The gem also identified the strange creature as the new master of the tower and allowed a little of the increase in power the new master had brought to trickle out into the stems and leaves of the Hawkthorn.

With the moulding of the staff into the characteristics of the new master, the deed was done. Whether suitable or not, the creature now commanded the power of the gem and the strength of the staff. There was little the Hawkthorn could do but follow.

Sending its consciousness through the many stems and leaves, it gradually strengthened its hold on the tower and sought out fresh pockets of water deep beneath the plaza.

5

HAWKTHORN

Charybdis wiped the sweat from his eyes and stared at the pulsating gem once more. Its surface was slick, as if it too felt the effort of the work he was asking of it. He allowed himself a slight smile. The sweat was his, but sometimes it was hard not to think of the Lychgem as being alive.

Since finding the gem he had worked relentlessly trying to master the forces needed to control its secrets. From his first contact with it he had felt the pent-up power. But the power the Lychgem promised would not be enough. If he was to consolidate his position and gather more of the towers to his cause, he would need others.

Concentrating on the many facets of the central gem, Charybdis projected a mind picture of what he wanted to see. Slowly at first, and then gradually faster, the gem clouded over as it filled with a seething grey fog. He bent closer to the gem and watched as a small patch of light appeared, growing steadily brighter until one of the facets was filled with life.

Charybdis found himself staring down at a deserted wet street and for the briefest of moments he felt light-headed, as if he truly floated above the muddy thoroughfare. A cloaked figure stepped into view and cautiously made its way towards a dimly lit doorway.

As the figure pushed the door open the light of the room flooded into the street and for the first time Charybdis realised that it was night. The figure removed the cloak, revealing a tall lithe woman wearing a brigandine, an armoured sleeveless jacket. The brigandine was made of small rectangular lames arranged in vertical strips, overlapping like roof tiles, then mounted on a supporting cloth or hide in parallel rows, the attachment being made by rivets whose heads were visible from the outside. This defensive construction was sewn to a quilted jacket which gave the surprisingly light garment its final shape. Such protective clothing was commonly found within the borders of Skarn, a land on the western coast of Kyrthos.

A long thin sword rested on one of the woman's hips while the leather scabbard of a wide-bladed knife occupied the other. Her thighs were bare and she wore leather boots with soft leggings laced to the knee.

Hanging about her neck on a thong of woven leather was a silver and black spiralled shell. It was the sign of a Cathar. His mother had worn an almost identical one and it had been the first thing his stubby childish fingers had reached for. He had always regretted losing it. The same type of shell had decorated the tube of healing salve, and the staff he now commanded.

The woman crossed the sawdust-strewn floor as if she owned the building and sat down opposite a huge fat man who was wedged between a table and wall. Two well-armed females stood to either side of the man and studied the woman briefly before turning their eyes back to the crowded Charter House.

'I find you well, Malek?' the woman greeted formally.

The fat man nodded as he scraped the last few battered silver coins from the tabletop into a worn, but rather large, leather purse.

'And you, Tandra? Do I find you well?'

'Only if the Strawman has anything which will rid me of this mud-cursed berg.'

Malek smiled deeply and leaned back in his chair, the straining timber protesting as he shifted his weight. A small bent servant moved from the shadows and lit the tiny red-shielded lamp which sat in the centre of the table. Bathed in the flickering glow of the lamp, the table was now set apart from the rest of the room. None in the Hall of Business would approach while the red flame burned. It was a signal to all that a charter was being negotiated.

'The Strawman hasn't much to offer these days,' Malek intoned. 'What with the southern wars and the border skirmishes to the east.'

Tandra made to rise but Malek stopped her with a word.

'However ... '

'Yes?'

'The Strawman has one charter on offer that seems to fit your particular talents.'

'And that is?' Tandra asked, trying to mask her interest.

'There is a party of five Jeremiadian priests who are anxious to reach Tamerra in time for the Festival of Shadows.'

'They've left that somewhat late.'

'Yes. Their ship was damaged in a storm and they only managed to limp into port this morning. But they are willing to pay handsomely.'

'They can pay what they like,' Tandra snapped. 'There's no chance of their making it. Why, it would take five weeks just to bypass the Omena Fens, and the Festival starts in four.'

'That is why they are willing to pay so handsomely,' Malek smiled.

Tandra brought her fist down hard on the table, momentarily distracting a conversation at an adjoining table.

'By the tenth level of hell! You can't be serious?'

'It seems that they are willing to risk the Omena Fens if it will get them to the Festival of Shadows.'

'They may be stupid enough to try it, but I certainly am not.'

'They'll pay eight Imperial silvers if you guide them through the fens, two coppers a day for food and other expenses and a double-weight silver if they reach the Festival in time.'

Tandra had been on the road long enough to know an opportunity when she heard one. 'Sixteen Imperials and three dulls per day, and the double-weight regardless of when they arrive.'

'Ten and two and they must arrive no later than the second day.'

'Twelve and two and two double-weights if they arrive before the initiation ceremony.'

'Done.' Malek smiled and extended his right fist across the table.

When Tandra clenched her right fist and placed it against Malek's it sealed the bargain and began Tandra's charter for the Strawman. It had been rumoured for several years that he did not exist and that there was only Malek. But the Strawman had grown rich and powerful since the troubled times had reached north and no-one was willing to anger him by looking too closely.

Tandra lifted the small well-stitched purse from the table and weighed it in her hand. She was tempted to open it and count the fee, insulting Malek in front of his brethren, but she quickly shook the idea from her mind and pocketed the purse as she rose.

'When do we leave?'

'I have one more charter to fill and you will be on your way,' Malek replied.

Tandra made to leave, then stopped and turned back to the table. 'Bram is in town. He is staying at the Crazy Sailor. My things are there and I'll send him your way if he's free.'

Malek nodded, then leaned forward and blew the small flame out.

Charybdis was pleased. He had sought an ally and the Lychgem had revealed this woman to him. Her conversation proclaimed her to be shrewd at business and her movements displayed both a deep-seated purpose and controlled power. She would prove a strong ally, and Charybdis would gather others around her who would aid him.

Tandra felt happy with herself as she threw her cloak around her shoulders and entered the street. Light rain was falling but the Inn of the Crazy Sailor was not far from the Charter House and she was soon there, her eyes trying to pierce the smoke-filled taproom.

Bram was alone, his back to the far wall, seated at a small table beneath one of the many smoking lamps which lit the room. Stepping over and around several crumpled forms, Tandra made her way towards the table and sat down opposite him. Bram was heavyset and wide across the shoulders and chest, promising immense strength. His hair was cut short and he had been drinking and was the worse for it, his grey eyes unfocused and squinting.

The first thing he saw when he looked up was Tandra's long dark hair, loose to the shoulders, and her red full lips. Then his eyes met her cold green ones and he cursed silently and lifted his drink to his lips.

'The Strawman has a charter,' Tandra offered. 'A rough one but the pay is good.'

Bram eyed her over the edge of his drink. She was a cold bitch, but by the Slayer's tail she could fight, and she had a good eye for a charter.

'Whas charter?' Bram slurred.

'Protecting a few priests. Malek is handling it for the Strawman. If you're interested, he's at the Charter House waiting in the Hall of Business.'

'Malek!' Bram spat.

'Well I've told you.'

Bram leaned forward and slipped a finger into

the collar of Tandra's lamella jacket. Tandra did not resist as he pulled her forward, knowing that the only danger she faced was from his breath.

'I could tell you somin' 'bout your friend Malek and the Strawman for nothin'.'

Realising that Bram was far too drunk to reason with, Tandra angled her head to one side and spat in his drink. With a curse, Bram pushed Tandra from him and snatched up his drink.

'What'd'ou wanna do that for?' he cried and stared down in dismay at his drink. Then with a shrug he threw the mug from him, hitting a young man at a nearby table in the back of the head.

The youth leapt to his feet and turned. Bram leaned back against the wall, his drunken features filled with an idiotic grin.

'You'll pay for that, old man!'

The youth started forward but was brought up short as Bram lifted his left forearm from beneath the table and rested it on the scarred table top. His left hand was missing from just above the wrist, and had been replaced by a short-bladed trident. The centre tine was smooth and thin and protruded beyond the outer two, which were slightly curved, their outer edges honed to a razor sharpness. The weapon took up no more room than an opened hand, but in the lamplight of the taproom it looked almost evil.

Tandra had seen Bram use his 'left hand' on many occasions and knew that it was indeed deadly. But more often than not the sight of the weapon was enough to save him from having to prove just how adept he was at using it.

The young man's companions grabbed him by

the arms and dragged him from the inn. Tandra heard one of them whisper the name Bram Onehand. The youth mumbled and cursed but made no attempt to break free of his friends. Tandra laughed and headed for the stairs that led to the second floor and her small room. It did not take her long to gather her few possessions and soon she was tramping through the mud towards the Charter House. As she was under charter to one of its members she was entitled to a free cell for the night.

As she approached, a one-eyed bald man in his early sixties nodded and produced a key from one of many hooks that covered the wall behind him. Tandra had plied her trade for many years and was well known in most of the Charter Houses of Skarn.

The cells were small, with barely room for a bed and a low stool. She hung her soaked cloak behind the door and dropped her light pack onto the stool. It held a change of clothes, a spare knife, a pair of old but comfortable boots, an empty waterskin, two rather worn blankets and a piece of soft leather, wrapped within which were a few of her most treasured possessions. Strapped to the outside of the pack was a light crossbow and a quiver of twenty bolts.

When Tandra had been younger, she had dreamed about the new clothing and weapons she would buy with her wages at the onset of each charter. But as the years rolled by she had come to realise that if she was to survive she could spend her money on only the most needed items.

Whenever she found a lull between charters she would travel home to Galena, a small coastal village at the base of the Kaolin Ranges where her father owned two fishing boats. Neither he nor her three brothers had allowed Tandra to enter the family business, saying that it was no place for a woman. When her anger finally got the better of her, she had gathered her possessions and left, not returning for five years.

Every coin that she could spare was secreted under a loose board in her father's storage shed. It was not the fortune she had claimed she would make, but it was growing into a tidy sum. Each time she visited, her father and brothers would bring their friends round in an attempt to marry her off.

Tandra drew a wrapped package from her pack and took out a small comb which she slowly drew through her wet hair. She had arrived home one time to learn of the death of her mother. Searching through her mother's belongings Tandra had come across the comb. Placing the comb on her chest she lay back and closed her eyes.

Charybdis straightened from the gem and rubbed his eyes. He was tired beyond belief. Once he had opened contact with the subject he had sought he had not noticed the toll it was taking upon his strength.

Using his staff as support, he descended the spiral stairs to the banquet chamber he had converted into living quarters which lacked for very little. Asal stood beside the large table. It had taken Charybdis some time to persuade the strange Ave to follow him to the centre of the city and enter the tower. It was nervous at first, continually raising its head while its tongue tested the faint breeze for any sign of danger.

Charybdis had seen Asal kill, but it was no match for a wraith and it seemed to realise this. Asal's large dark eyes were never still and they seemed agitated whenever it was beyond the safe stone walls of the tower.

But that had been months ago. Now Asal left the tower each morning and hunted for the meat Charybdis needed. There were many wild herbs and vegetables growing in what must have been gardens adjoining the plaza and, between these and the storeroom, Charybdis had little trouble in finding sufficient to eat.

The wraiths still troubled Charybdis. Their numbers had increased to nearly twenty and each night they gathered at the base of the tower. Charybdis had studied many of the books in the library, but little of what he had learned about the wraiths was of help. There was one cryptic passage about being able to entrap the wraiths and harness their powers. However, the majority of the text was in ancient Bezoarian and Charybdis had never been much of a scholar.

On his first encounter with one of the wraiths in the tower, it had vanished when Charybdis had touched it with his staff. He had subsequently learned from one of the old books that the power which had been the wraith had been drawn through the staff into one of the small outer gems.

Perhaps he could seek out each of the wraiths in turn and capture them, using his staff. But when he saw how many wraiths he had attracted to the tower he changed his mind. To try to lure so many to the tower room and trap them in the small gems was a plan doomed to failure.

Charybdis descended the stairs and entered the vast library. He had glanced through a number of books the previous master of the tower had left lying about, but he needed to know more. He slowly traversed the room, reading the titles of various books, and lifting the occasional scroll. One large scroll seemed much older than the others and, placing it upon a pedestal, he carefully untied and unrolled it.

His hungry eyes searched the text, which spoke of the Lychworld—a world bathed in a blood-red sun and filled with death. It was, he learned, the original home of the wraiths. The tower's master had used a gate, a Lychgate, which joined the two worlds and allowed the master to enter the Lychworld and enslave the wraiths. But the scroll also spoke of others of the Lychworld—the Iledrith. There was nothing but the name and Charybdis wondered what manner of race could share its world with creatures like the wraith? Still, it appeared that the Lychworld held the answer to his problems about gaining control of the wraiths. If the previous master had been able to do it, then why not Charybdis?

The swollen sun hung above the western horizon as if it had no intention of setting and then, without warning, it dropped from sight behind the grey range of forbidding mountains beyond the edge of the verdant jungle. With the vanishing of the sun darkness filled the streets of the once mighty city and from pockets of the deepest shadows the wraiths appeared once again.

Slowly they moved towards the tower and the

prey they sought. Their speed increased as their numbers swelled and they entered the plaza and surrounded the tower, their silent screams of rage and anger drifting about the heart of the deserted city.

Only Asal, high in the tower, seemed to register the forlorn screams of the wraiths. The anger of the wraiths beat at his consciousness.

A large, strangely bound book in the library contained a detailed history of the Aves. Charybdis had seen the wild Aves of the steppes, but had not known that they were the original race of this world from a time long before man arrived, or that they had once served the Hawkthorn Tower. Now, however, their memories of that time were only faint shadows.

The Aves had lived in three distinct classes: the workers, those who roamed the steppes wild and untamed waiting to be trapped and trained; the leaders of the race long since vanished; and the warriors—Aves like Asal who would defend their homes and protect the leaders. That certainly explained Asal's killer instincts.

With a movement not quite a shuffle or a hop, Asal moved to Charybdis' side.

Charybdis woke with a start. He had dreamed that he had walked in his sleep, that he had left the tower and been pursued through the many streets of the city by a horde of silent hunters. One minute these hunters were wraiths, the next instant they were all like Asal, with bloodied beaks and slashing talons. Then they were his dead companions. Headless, they sought him, blaming him for their deaths.

These dead companions then vanished and were replaced by a large red-armoured figure. Through the visor of the helm, Charybdis could see the angry red eyes. The figure rose and lifted an arm, pointing at Charybdis.

Charybdis climbed shakily from his bed and crossed to a low table which held a beautifully crafted crystal bowl and jug. He poured the cool, clear water into the bowl and splashed his face with it, removing the last of the sleep. No matter how much water he used the jug always remained full. It was one of the small cantrips of the tower he had learned to control in the short time he had spent there. And there were more cantrips and knowledge to be collected every day, but so long as the wraiths prowled the inner city Charybdis knew that his dreams and fears would always be present.

One day as Charybdis examined the Hawkthorn plant which blanketed the tower he heard a short high-pitched whistle from Asal. Each of Asal's calls had a distinct tone and Charybdis had not heard this one before. He turned and found himself face to face with a short green-skinned creature wearing a brown leather loin cloth and laced sandals. As the being approached, Charybdis realised just how short it truly was.

The top of its hairless head barely reached Charybdis' chest, but despite its short stature it moved with a confidence Charybdis found surprising. It stopped before Charybdis in the plaza and lowered itself slowly to its knees, its forehead touching the dusty ground. It had remained so until Charybdis reached down and touched it on the shoulder.

The chest of the creature was large, suggesting a great strength, and its limbs were well muscled. For all purposes it resembled a small powerfully built man. Charybdis had called the creature Bohe, after a short tree with bright green leaves which had grown about his home. Though stunted, it had provided good strong timber.

Bohe never made a sound in the months after his arrival and Charybdis grew tired of talking to him and receiving no answer. Even Asal made a sound once in a while. Still, Bohe proved to be a good servant and Charybdis determined to learn more about Bohe from his library when time allowed.

Descending the stairs to the library, Charybdis once more set about the task of discovering a way of slaying the wraiths. He pored over several tomes before his hunger made it impossible to continue. Calling Bohe to his side, he closed the heavy book and rested his eyes.

Bohe appeared before him, holding a silver platter filled with freshly picked and prepared vegetables and a silver goblet encrusted with gems. The workmanship was magnificent. Charybdis could not help but marvel at the construction of the goblet and wondered if the hands which had crafted it were at all human.

As he sipped at the wine he reflected how poor a match the wine and goblet were. The previous owner of the tower had obviously had poor taste in wines and, no matter what variations on the cantrip Charybdis used, the wines were always of an inferior quality. Even drinking them from the delicately crafted goblet had not helped him enjoy them.

Holding the wine-filled goblet before him,

Charybdis had a brief flash of inspiration. Perhaps he was approaching the situation with the wraiths from the wrong angle. As with the poor wine, he could not yet dispose of the problem, but perhaps he could alter it somehow, and then turn it to his advantage.

In a lower section of the tower was a room holding everything he would need, and across the plaza was a smith's shop. With Bohe's aid it would not be too difficult for Charybdis to rekindle the forge and put his plans to the test.

It took only two days to prepare the forge and carry all the items he needed from the tower to the smithy. Charybdis then lifted the staff, rested one end on the cold forge, and concentrated. He allowed the intense heat generated by a blacksmith's forge to flow from his mind to the staff and into the cold forge in front of him. At first the forge showed little change. Then heat slowly began to build until it glowed red, then white hot.

Satisfied with his work, Charybdis rested the staff beside the forge and took up the first of the many silver ingots Bohe had carried over from the tower.

All through the day Bohe stood by silently as Charybdis worked. Asal stood well back from the intense heat, whistling occasionally as his master worked, his attention divided between Charybdis, Bohe and the heat of the forge. He eyed them all with a cold unyielding stare.

Over the next week Charybdis spent every minute of daylight at the smithy. He had been a good blacksmith in his younger days and now, with

Bohe's strength and the power of the staff, his work was made considerably easier.

Bohe would fetch and carry, while the staff provided not only the heat for the forge, but also allowed Charybdis to use its power instead of a hammer as he worked the hot metal. Under the steady pulses of energy he generated from the staff, he shaped a suit of silver plate mail.

When he was happy with his work, Charybdis set about preparing for the first of the night's visitors. The armour Charybdis had made was not constructed for use by man. The joints were tight and offered little movement, but Charybdis was certain it would be the answer to his problem.

Atop the armour sat a drum-shaped helmet, its narrow one-piece visor raised revealing the dark interior. It was the only opening the armour contained.

With the setting of the sun, the wraiths began their short pilgrimage towards the tower. When they saw the armour Charybdis had placed at the foot of the tower they attacked it, venting their power against the unfeeling metal. As they circled the tower, the wraiths were confused by this creature which neither ran nor died under their attacks. They could sense life within the strange being and its silent, unmoving resistance drove them into a frenzy.

Charybdis waited patiently in his chamber, watching the scene unfold beneath him. Through the staff he could sense the power of the wraiths weakening, and as he studied them through one of the facets of the larger gem, for the first time he thought he could hear a faint noise.

It was like the rumbling of the sea as a strong wind drove it in over a rolling sandy beach. It was filled with many different sounds but he was unable to make out any one in particular. As the wraiths weakened and their anger increased, the cries of rage and frustration grew louder and Charybdis was able to make out the individual ones by their cries.

He was not actually hearing the wraiths, he realised, but their cries of rage were somehow registering in his mind, and as he concentrated further the sounds became more clear. Charybdis' eyes widened in surprise as softly spoken words passed his straining ears and entered his thoughts.

It had to be Bohe, he thought, and was about to direct a question to him when the commotion in the plaza increased dramatically.

The first wraith to enter the plaza was by far the angriest. But as the armour resisted its attacks the wraith grew more incensed and redoubled its attempts. Charybdis ignored all save this one.

He placed the staff across the Lychgem, projected an image of the wraith below, and waited. The wraith swirled around the armour, writhing and dancing, then suddenly drew back. The other wraiths fell silent and Charybdis increased his power. The staff was channelling his will into the gem, and then into the armour.

The wraith emitted one terrifying howl before it was drawn into the armour through the open visor. The visor snapped closed and the wraith was imprisoned. The armour moved jerkily backward, then forward, then side to side, swaying in a macabre dance as if a monumental battle was taking place within its confines. The metal swelled in places as the wraith tried to escape from the armoured silver trap.

Charybdis smiled. The armour was under a cantrip and there was little the imprisoned wraith could do. For all intents and purposes, it was now Charybdis' servant. It would lose some of its power, encased within the enchanted armour, but Charybdis now had control of a tireless fighting machine of great strength. Totally loyal and virtually indestructible, this wraith was but the first.

Happy with his work, Charybdis stared deeply into the gem, calling Tandra's form to mind.

Tandra stood on a narrow strip of land overlooking a grey expanse of water and kicked a rock into it before walking slowly to her companions. She had felt eyes on her as they began to set up their night camp but there was little she could do that would not alert whoever, or whatever, watched them.

As she worked to clear a small area for the fire she noticed Bram glance in her direction several times. The old veteran was also aware of their danger, but equally unwilling to give his knowledge away.

Tandra remembered the saying her mother had impressed upon her. 'Knowledge is power, and power is knowledge.' It had taken years before Tandra had fully understood what her mother had meant, but simply knowing that they were being watched gave her the advantage over her enemy. And by not revealing the information, she also had an edge.

Bram sat on a rock on the fringes of the camp,

seemingly ignoring the activity about him, but Tandra knew him from previous charters and knew too that his looks were deceptive. With his broadsword resting across his knees, he was industriously working at some imaginary notch with a whetstone he had dug from deep within his pack.

Tandra made a quick sweep of the camp, her practised eyes picking up the smallest detail. It was strange to see two men on the one charter. Men usually held the reins of power in Skarn. Town and city elders, tradesmen and traders, men had better things to do with their lives than protect those not able to protect themselves. For many generations it had been a woman's role to ensure the safety of travellers and pilgrims.

Her mother had once told her that it had not always been so—that at some time in the long distant past men held nearly all the high roles in life, and coveted those they did not hold. This had led to a great war which lasted many lifetimes and almost destroyed Kyrthos.

Kathryn sat beside the fire. A small round buckler was strapped to her right forearm and the hilt of a falchion lay within easy reach of her left hand. She was already skilled with each, and carried a large round shield strapped to her pack. Kathryn was only twenty years old, but she was intelligent and fast, and always watching. It was as if she had been born to follow the road of the pilgrim. If she could survive the next few years she would rise swiftly and be assigned many charters.

Tarynn was only seventeen years old and Tandra could not believe that the Strawman had offered the boy a charter. But then she thought back to the first time she had touched fists over a red burning flame. And the youth had come from the same village as Bram after all. He had grown up with the tales of Bram Onehand and had only awaited his coming of age before he sold everything and bought himself a cheap sword.

The sword was a broadsword, like Bram's, only it had been used hard over the years and was not in very good condition. Bram had shaken his head when he first saw the weapon and had strongly advised that the first coins the boy earned should go towards buying something better. Many times the older and more experienced Cathars would share their knowledge and experience with a youngster, but this was the first time Tandra had seen Bram take a newcomer beneath his wing.

Tandra squatted down beside Tarynn and rummaged through several of the bundles of supplies. 'It is possible that we will have visitors quite soon,' she told him.

Tarynn started to turn round but Tandra grabbed his arm.

'Damn you!' she whispered angrily. 'If you want to live till the end of your charter just sit still and do as you're told.'

Tarynn nodded and ran his fingers through his sandy hair. Tandra could see that the boy did not know whether to be happy or scared at the prospect of his first fight. 'If anything happens, stand by Bram. And do not leave the confines of the camp, no matter what happens.' Tandra rose and moved towards the clustered priests.

Sitting off to one side was the fifth member of the charter. Sian-vesna did not mix with the rest of the party. She refused to be drawn into conversation by anyone and at night she preferred to stay close to the priests as they slept in the hastily built camp.

Sian-vesna was a Crafter. She wore a shell medallion around her neck, as did all Cathars, but the open swollen section of her shell held a small green fragment of gem.

Tandra had met only a few Crafters in her years of travel but had often marvelled at their many skills, including talents to heal, guide and predict the weather. There were many varied Crafters, not all of whom chose the path of the Cathars for their life.

Crafters' use to a party depended on their particular physical and mental strengths, but as Tandra had not encountered Sian-vesna before their introduction in the Charter House, she was not quite sure what to expect. The Crafter wore no visible weapon and Tandra hoped that Malek had chosen wisely.

'Why must we stop so early?' Raanah whined.

The priests of Jeremiad were known throughout Skarn for their fondness for complaining. They were often referred to as the Priests of Woe.

'Surely we could make better time if we pushed on until the sun set?' Hedya added sourly.

'We must have time to prepare the camp before the sun sets,' Tandra explained.

'But could we not send the servants on ahead to ready a suitable site?' Sadira added.

'The Omena Fens are filled with dangers and we do not have the swords to protect two parties,' Tandra answered.

'We offered to pay for more but that fat man told us there were none to be had,' Sadira retorted. 'At twenty double-weights for each of us and a further one for each of the servants, I believe we should have a say in the matter.'

Tandra nodded. It seemed that the Strawman was making a handsome profit from this venture. Still, the Charter House would get its share, and use it to open new Charter Houses and oversee protection for pilgrims unable to pay their way. All who travelled the roads of Kyrthos were eligible for the protection of the Cathars, whether they could afford it or not.

'Then I'm sure that once we reach Tamerra we can approach the Charter House there about a refund on the moneys paid,' Tandra replied. She had listened to the whining and whingeing of the priests for days and was fast reaching her limit. 'I'm sure it wouldn't take more than three days.'

The priests became agitated at the thought of reaching Tamerra in time, only to be denied the pleasures of the Festival of Shadows while they haggled over money.

'I doubt there will be any need for that.' Raanah smiled. 'I, that is we, are all very happy with the way you have upheld your charter so far and we are sure that you are doing your best to get us to Tamerra as soon as possible.'

Tandra hurried away from the priests before they thought of something else to whinge about.

'I see the Priests of Woe are once more on the trail of some grievance.' Bram laughed as Tandra passed.

'I would be happy if that were our only problem,' Tandra replied with a sigh. 'There is something wrong with this place.'

Bram nodded. 'I felt it the moment we stopped. I thought it strange that you decided to remain.'

'I have little choice,' Tandra motioned, her hand taking in the expanse of dark water. 'The next high ground suitable for a camp of this size is a good day's march ahead, or several hours' back. And I don't fancy retracing our steps with our five pilgrims.'

Bram nodded. 'I doubt they'd let you. They're just as likely to sit themselves down and tell you to pick them up on the way through in the morning. I've chartered for Jeremiadians before.'

'We'll keep everyone in close tonight and build extra fires,' Tandra added. 'Perhaps we are just growing old.'

As Charybdis watched from his tower he knew that the danger they faced was real enough. An arrow's flight from where the party sat, Charybdis could sense the hunger of beasts as they waited for night to fall.

6

CONTACT

Tandra shivered. The temperature had dropped drastically during the night as a thick mist rolled in over the stagnant waters of the Omena Fens. Sometime in the distant past this series of depressions had been part of an inland sea. Shells and the remains of strange creatures could be found in many of the higher reaches.

Winding their way between the brackish waters were narrow strips of land covered in a low brush of coarse bushes. They were the only passageways through the fens and the secrets of the corridors were known only to a handful who had been willing to brave the dangers the Omena Fens had to offer.

Many fleeing the law of Skarn and its neighbouring lands had taken refuge in the desolate backwaters, hoping that they would be safe from pursuit by the law. These regions were well known to local guides and were avoided, but sometimes the Feni, as they were known, would venture out in the hope of gathering much-needed equipment to help in their struggle against the creatures of the fens.

Tandra threw more wood onto the fire and made another circuit of the camp. As well as her cloak she had both blankets drawn tightly about her shoulders. There was little wind but the biting cold reached every exposed portion of her body. Stamping her feet, she drew her arms tightly about her chest.

The skeleton-like branches of long-dead trees reached above the mist-blanketed water like the arms of drowning women. A long grey vegetation covered almost everything above the surface and Tandra imagined all kinds of creatures lurking in the shallow water at the edge of the campfire's light. Where the water caressed the land it was covered in a bright green scum which stretched out several paces. Tall razor weeds grew in clumps along the edge offering meagre protection to some of the small defenceless creatures which lived there.

Tandra turned her back on the water and allowed her senses other than sight to take over. The stench of the water and the rotting vegetation masked all other smells, even that of the campfire. And there was no sound to be heard other than the muffled movements of her party.

Gradually, she worked out where the watchers had to be. A crossbow-shot away was a thick tangle of dead branches. She had studied them carefully and had been unable to make out anything, but it was the closest cover to the camp. As she stood silently, her back to the water, she was eventually able to make out the soft sounds of movement through the water.

Tandra moved several paces to one side and, loosening her rapier in its scabbard, she stared down at Bram. He was lying on his back, his sword drawn and resting across his chest. His eyes were open and there was a faint smile on his lips.

Sensing an attack, Tandra drew her rapier and spun round, extending her arm. The thin blade took her attacker in the throat. Her attacker dropped its weapon and threw up both hands to stop the flow of blood, exposing its chest to Tandra's next thrust. The rapier entered the chest and scraped along a rib before piercing the heart.

As she withdrew her blade, more of the creatures leapt from the water. Bram rushed past her, and met the advancing creatures at the water's edge, his broadsword making short work of those closest.

A short cry rose from the darkness as the surviving attackers disappeared back into the fens. Four of their number lay dead. Tandra cautiously approached one of the figures and rolled it over with the toe of her boot. Then crouching, she tore the veil from its face to reveal the features of a man in his mid-thirties. His skin was leathery through exposure to the elements and his eyes were surrounded by deep-set wrinkles. His nose looked to have been broken several times.

The body was wrapped in a thin grey material, very light but coarse, and even though he had been out of the water only for a few moments, his clothing was totally dry. There was a thin-bladed curved dagger tucked in his belt and another lying on the ground beside his open right hand.

Bram knelt beside the corpse and spat over his shoulder. 'Feral!'

'One of the Feni?'

'Worse,' Bram cursed. 'Much worse. Our friend here might have started off as one, but he has long since gone over the edge.'

To prove his point, Bram slipped a glove from his belt and held it in his teeth while he slid it on his right hand. Then drawing back the dead man's lips, he revealed the filed yellow teeth.

'By the prophet! Cannibals and scavengers,' Bram added as he straightened, giving the corpse a kick for luck. 'They hide in the fens, pursued by only the Slayer knows what, then they seem to lose all their humanity . . . running and hunting in packs, feeding off whatever they can trap.'

Tarynn stood by the water's edge watching for any sign of another attack. Every so often he would throw a nervous glance over his shoulder at Bram, and then down at the body. Kathryn and Sian-vesna had gathered the priests and their cowering servants about the fire.

As Tarynn looked nervously over his shoulder at his fellow-travellers clustered in the centre of the makeshift camp, Bram made the sign of the fist over the corpse. This sign was used by many men to ward off evil, though very few admitted it. In the past it had been linked with the Slayer and it was widely rumoured that to make the sign was to call upon the Slayer itself for help and guidance. Many poor unfortunates who had been spied using the sign of the fist had been accused of belonging to the long-hidden Slayer Cult and then dispatched. For some time the cult's following had been growing, but it seemed times were not yet safe enough for it to be acknowledged in public.

Tarynn had never known his father. He had been raised by an uncle but had found little in his way of life to take to heart. All his life he had listened to stories of the Cathars, and now he was one himself.

Stepping to one side Tarynn watched Bram closely. Tandra could tell how strongly the young man was drawn to the older veteran. If he lived long enough he would learn much from one such as Bram. But once this charter was over it was not likely that they would remain together, as Cathars went wherever their charter sent them.

Tandra had also seen Bram use the sign of the fist and wondered if he had been part of the cult before taking to the road. It was strange for those who chose the Cathar way of life to carry any of their old ways with them on the road, but it was not completely unheard of.

When Tarynn saw the sign made by Bram he remembered his uncle talking long into the night with a cloaked stranger. They had spoken about the way things had changed since the Final Wars and how it was only a matter of time before the old cults would again rise to the surface. Had his uncle been speaking of the Slayer Cult? The pair had talked well into the night and by the morning Tarynn had forgotten many of the things he had heard before falling asleep.

Tandra rose and dusted off her knees. 'We'll run a double watch tonight. There'll be two of us, plus at least one priest and servant, awake at all times.'

'We are not here to stand watch!' Hedya complained.

'Then perhaps you'd like to take your chances with our friend's companions when they return?'

Bram suggested. 'They attacked us for food, and received nothing. If we float these bodies out into the fen perhaps they'll be satisfied, and perhaps they won't.'

Kathryn dragged the bodies to the water's edge while Tarynn and Bram stood watch.

'That's about the best we can do,' Bram said as he backed slowly into the camp.

'Shouldn't we leave?' Tarynn asked, licking his lips nervously as he stood beside Bram, his broadsword still held tightly in his hands.

'Listen to me, lad. It would be suicide to move in the dark,' Bram explained. 'One false step and you'd disappear into a bog or be sucked down into a mire. The fens are filled with dangers other than the living breathing variety.'

'But if we just sit here?'

Bram sheathed his sword and moved towards the fire. 'But we won't be sitting here, will we, lad? We'll run a watch all night and at first light we'll up stakes and move. Then we'll make a quick stop to break our nightly fast and be on our way.'

Bram pushed his way through the servants, nearly trampling two of the priests who had not moved fast enough to clear his path. He straightened his pack, drew out a dark bottle, jerked out the stopper and took a long pull. Then he slapped the stopper back into place and slid the bottle back into his pack. Shouldering the gear, he moved to the edge of the camp and leaned his battered pack against a small fallen log.

'I'll take the first watch,' he said, and yawned. 'Lad, you'd best sit with me and help keep my mind on the job.'

Tarynn grabbed his pack and was soon seated beside Bram, his broadsword resting across his knees. No one knew of Bram's past, or spoke of it if they did. Bram Onehand had suddenly appeared on the many roads of Skarn and Ceruss, his shell medallion marking him as a Cathar. When Tarynn was old enough to listen to the wandering story-tellers' tales he had often heard of the exploits of Bram Onehand. Many a night he had listened at the blanketed-door of his uncle's hall, revelling in the tales being spun.

It was on one such night that Tarynn had made up his mind that he would take to the road as a Cathar and follow in the steps of this Bram Onehand. How could he have known then that he would actually sit beside the hero of his dreams, sharing a watch and the hidden dangers beyond the dying campfire's light? With Bram seated beside him, Tarynn felt as if he could take on all comers.

Over the years Tarynn had learned that his father had worked at one of the local temples in the hope of gaining himself and his family a better position in the poor region. But something had happened and his father had been punished. Soon after that a fire had destroyed the temple and all its small outer buildings. Tarynn's father had not been seen since and it was rumoured that he had been responsible for the fire.

Tarynn had been very young when all this had happened and he often wondered what his father had been like, but his uncle had refused to speak of him, saying only that it was better not to mention his name for fear of retribution. Many of the older boys in the village had mischievously hinted that they knew his father's name, but none would speak it for fear of what Tarynn's uncle would do to them.

While Tarynn contemplated his past, the priests and their servants had spread themselves out about the fire and nervously waited for sleep to overtake them. Kathryn had dragged her pack to the far side of the camp and was sitting beside Sian-vesna, who had unwrapped several small bundles and was mixing finely chopped herbs and a white powder in the bottom of an old leather mug. Taking another smaller mug from her pack, she divided the mixture in half and handed a mug to Tandra and to Kathryn.

'When it is your turn for watch, add a small amount of hot water and sip at this,' she explained. 'It will help keep you awake and will also keep the insects at bay.'

Kathryn said nothing as she took the offered mug and placed it beside her pack.

Tandra tentatively smelt the mixture. 'What is it?'

'Simply a product of the Crafter's Lore,' Sian-vesna explained. 'Other than that I am forbidden to tell.'

Charybdis broke his concentration. He had seen enough. He had asked the Lychgem to show him somebody who could help him unite the towers and it had shown him several. There was no doubt that he would need Tandra's and her companions' talents soon enough. But first, he had to rid himself of the wraiths.

A second week's work produced another suit of armour, and when the sun set he drew the wraiths to it before trapping a second one. At this rate it would take him several months of continual work to construct the armour and entrap them all, but there was nothing else he could do.

As the months progressed he took time out from this work to seek out Tandra and the others and watch their progress. Tandra had reached Tamerra in time for the Festival of Shadows and had received her payment at the local Charter House. From there she had picked up another charter north. Only Bram Onehand and Sian-vesna were chartered with her.

By the time Charybdis' armoured servants had grown in number he found it increasingly difficult to draw the remaining wraiths into his trap. Unwilling to allow the armoured wraiths into the tower, he was forced to keep them in a building bordering the plaza. This proved no difficulty, and he thought it might have been the presence of these followers which finally had the effect of driving off the other wraiths.

Asal grew more and more agitated as the number of enslaved wraiths grew. Charybdis was in two minds about releasing or killing Asal, but he could not bring himself to kill the one living being who had helped him survive. Even though he had slain his companions, Charybdis had grown accustomed to the Ave.

Bohe paid little attention to the Ave, or the wraiths for that matter. When Charybdis needed him he simply turned and Bohe would be there.

Searching through a dust-shrouded set of shelves in the library Charybdis had finally found the information he sought. The power of the Lychgem was transferred to the tower's master by thought. This was how the towers called those who would try to master them. A tower would broadcast thoughts of wealth and power, which only those suitable could hear.

As he read further Charybdis had discovered that this was how the Aves had communicated with those who had previously ruled them. The wraiths operated the same way as did Bohe. Charybdis realised that Bohe came to his side when summoned by thought.

He sat before a huge volume and wondered if he should test his new knowledge further. All he had to do was remove the talon from his throat and call Asal to his side. He thought on the matter for a while and then decided to delay this test until he had more time.

Charybdis moved slowly down the darkened street. Ahead of him were two of his armoured wraiths, each carrying a large lantern. He had named his new servants Yclad, which simply meant clothed. To the rear were two more, also bearing lanterns, and behind them walked another two who carried an inanimate suit of armour between them.

It had been three weeks since the last wraith had been trapped and Charybdis was now forced to hunt down the remaining creatures. He could scarcely believe he was actually out looking for wraiths. How he had changed in the many months since his arrival at the Hawkthorn Tower!

When Charybdis suddenly felt an overpowering cold, he knew that a wraith was close. A swirling silver shadow appeared in the street ahead of the party and hovered there for several seconds before swooping down on them. Charybdis barely had time to raise the staff before the wraith struck.

The cold intensified and silver sparks filled the air as the wraith pawed at the shield Charybdis had erected about himself. As it turned to flee, the wraith found itself trapped and once more attacked the silvery shield. Charybdis ordered the two Yclad bearing the armour to place it beside the shield and withdraw, then he wiped the sweat from his eyes and readied himself.

He would have to drop the shield and then activate the cantrip drawing the wraith into the armour. For that briefest of seconds the wraith would be free to flee or attack. If it fled then the cantrip was strong enough to still work but, should it decide to attack, Charybdis was not sure if the cantrip would work fast enough to save him.

Initially, Charybdis had hoped to use one of the Yclad, but it had been impossible to work the cantrip through them. However, he had managed to teach one of them some of his skills at blacksmithing and now his forge operated day and night under the untiring strength of the armoured wraith.

Charybdis took a deep breath, then raised the staff and dropped the shield. For a moment the wraith hovered uncertainly in the centre of the street, then it darted for Charybdis. But the pause had been long enough for the cantrip to work. Trapped, the wraith was drawn into the armour and the visor snapped closed. As its companions led the imprisoned wraith back towards the tower, Charybdis relaxed. So when the feeling of cold suddenly struck and a wraith appeared as if from nowhere, he was taken completely by surprise. The escorting Yclad stopped. Linked to their master by the Lychgem through the staff, they were unsure of what to do. Charybdis raised the staff and waited.

Much of the power of his wraiths was now deeply embedded in the armour which entrapped them. Far stronger still than any human, the enslaved wraiths would be no match for the wraith waiting only metres from Charybdis.

The two Yclad leading the party dropped their lanterns and turned to attack the wraith. The swirling haze thinned and expanded as the wraith struck out at them. One was thrown across the street. The other staggered back a few paces before righting itself and attacking again.

Charybdis ordered the other four to join in, and then backed slowly from the fighting. The fight was between him and the tower and there were still more wraiths at large in the inner city. His only hope lay in overcoming the wraith with the aid of his servants.

The wraith made no attempt to flee or attack but stood its ground, defending itself against all comers. Charybdis' followers would continue to attack with little effect if he did not go to their aid.

The hairs on the back of Charybdis' neck stood on end and he spun around to find another wraith moving swiftly up the street towards him.

This was it. Grasping his staff firmly in both hands, he moved towards the second wraith and touched it with the staff's tip. The wraith vanished and Charybdis felt the staff grow uncomfortably cold.

His hands were numb when he turned to face the

battling armoured wraiths. The staff was still cold and he wondered if another wraith could be imprisoned within it, but he had no other choice. Stepping closer to the struggle, he raised the staff once more and readied himself for the contact.

Without warning, the wraith erupted from the fighting and launched itself at Charybdis. Stumbling backwards, he drew the staff back just as the wraith impaled itself on its tip. Again Charybdis felt the staff grow intensely cold, but this time the cold travelled down the length of the staff and he found himself bathed in the frigid life of the wraith.

Charybdis tore his cloak from his shoulders and threw it to the ground. Its silver threads glowed brightly, pulsating with the life energy of the wraith. Charybdis bent down and cautiously touched the cloak. The material was cool and felt alive under his fingers.

He lifted the cloak and lowered it carefully about his shoulders. It drew itself in and hugged Charybdis, easing his tired muscles and relaxing him. The lanterns were then retrieved and the party returned to the tower.

Charybdis was pleased with this night's work. Not only had he enslaved another of the wraiths, but he had trapped two more. How the wraiths trapped in his staff and cloak could be used to his benefit he did not know, but a little research might give him a clue.

Charybdis stared down into the large gem. Tandra had finished yet another charter and was relaxing in the southern port of Sytry. It had been a long and arduous journey, what with the surrounding lands preparing for yet another all out war. Tandra was again joined by Bram, Sian-vesna, Tarynn and Kathryn. There were eight other Cathars also resting at the same inn. Three had arrived that morning while five had arrived the day before. Both groups had been chartered to protect merchants bringing their wares to Sytry.

The party Tandra's group had protected mainly consisted of merchants dealing in weapons. They had made their dangerous journey to take full advantage of the rapidly worsening situation. Fighting had broken out along the border and only the Cathars had made it possible for them to cross the many lines. Nevertheless, at several checkpoints the merchants had been forced to part with small purses filled with coins.

Tandra had wanted the party to travel overland to Erlan and then take passage on a vessel bound for Sytry in Ceruss. But the merchants had been afraid of privateers, who had been hired by the Bezoarians to disrupt the trade off their enemy's coast. It would be much easier, they said, to hide themselves among the many travellers of the southern roads.

At Sytry, the Cathars had taken lodgings in a small clean inn on the waterfront. Thirteen Cathars in the one inn had drawn a large crowd that evening, but it had stayed quiet throughout the night.

As Charybdis watched the party straggle one by one down to break the night's fast he felt a tingling in the tips of his fingers. The sensation grew until he realised that something was happening within the gem. Releasing his contact with Tandra, he searched the gem's many facets until he felt the sensation increase.

When his sight cleared Charybdis saw a long, worn face staring at him. It was like looking into a mirror and having someone else stare back and both faces registered shock, then surprise. Then the face vanished.

Someone, somewhere, had entered a tower and used its Lychgem. Charybdis felt a moment of panic at the thought that he might have left his plans too late. If another had reached a tower and was learning how to use the gem's power, then he would need to act soon.

There was a library in Sytry that Charybdis could use to find out more about the towers other than the Monkshood. His problem lay in contacting someone who would follow his orders completely. When he returned to his chamber, Charybdis was weary. He ignored the food set out on the long table and, resting the staff against the headboard, he lowered himself onto his bed and almost instantly fell asleep.

When Charybdis awoke he felt totally relaxed. He had dreamed many times during the night, and in one of those dreams he had seen the answer to his problem. He entered the small treasure room at a lower level of the tower and lifted four fist-sized sacks of coins. Three were filled with double-weights while the third held Imperials. Charybdis studied the faces stamped on the coins but had never seen their like, which meant that these coins could date back many centuries. As he climbed the stairs to the highest room, Charybdis made ready to put his plan into action.

Placing the sacks on the centre of the large gem, Charybdis concentrated on Tandra. When she came into focus he allowed his mind to drift back and forth amongst her companions until he found the one he sought.

Sian-vesna sat silently at the end of the table, watching her brethren laugh and eat. It had been a long and dangerous charter but they had come through without loss, and that was good. She leant forward and speared a cold potato with her dagger which she was in the process of raising to her mouth when she felt a tingling sensation in her medallion. Raising her left hand, she caressed the surface of the tapered shell, fingering the gem embedded in its swollen heart.

Through her fingertips she could feel the sensation increase and, rising quickly, she left the table. Only Bram seemed to notice her departure, but he said nothing and returned to his meal. Although Sian-vesna had been on several charters she had kept to herself and had never truly joined her fellow Cathars.

Sian-vesna entered the tiny garden at the building's rear, closed the door behind her and leaned against it. Touching the gem once more, she allowed her mind to open as she did when she needed an answer to a perplexing medical problem.

Many thought that the Crafter's medallion was the centre of their power, but it was in fact a link to information.

The knowledge of any cure was available to any Crafter who sought it through the gem. Once that knowledge was acquired it was only a matter of combining the many herbs and other medicinal chemicals the Crafters carried. Or, in the case of more exotic maladies, hunting down the right ingredients.

As her mind opened Sian-vesna saw a tall green tower at the centre of a sprawling city. The city looked deserted as her sight flashed above it, but in the tower she saw an Ave and a strange green creature at the foot of a set of stairs. Up the stairs she found herself in a large circular room with transparent walls. Stationed about the walls were tall armoured men, unmoving like statues, but Sian-vesna, through her medallion, could feel the life energy pulsating within the armour. At the far end of the room sat an enormous man in flowing robes of spun gold.

The man seemed filled with power and Sian-vesna was unable to take her eyes from him as she drew nearer. The robed figure was seated on a large chair cut from a single piece of crystal and had a staff resting across his knees. On his head was a small crown of woven silver, studded with gems.

When the man spoke his voice filled her mind, almost overpowering her. 'You have been summoned here to be of great service to Kyrthos.'

Sian-vesna lifted her head and stared into the deep blue eyes of the figure.

'When you are released you will take the money I have provided and seek out a charter at the local Charter House. You will take a charter on all those who travelled with you to Sytry, and the two other parties staying at the same inn. You will seek out knowledge from the Library of Sytry on anything referred to as the Living Towers. You will be able to speak to me through your medallion.'

The speaker extended his staff and touched the medallion. Sian-vesna felt as if her mind was afire and tears filled her eyes. Through the tears she saw the image of the man fading. Softer than before, she heard his voice echoing in her mind.

'If you seek any aid I will always be ready to help in any way I can.'

Sian-vesna's knees gave out and she slid to the ground. Blinded by her tears, she took a firm hold on the door handle and dragged herself to her feet. Unsteady, but standing, she drew in several deep breaths before wiping the tears from her eyes.

She did not have to touch the medallion to know that it pulsed with power. Whoever the Crafter had been, he had linked her medallion with a power far greater than she had ever thought possible.

Sian-vesna had heard many stories of great Crafters who had left the path of healing and other talents to take up the search for true power. There were said to be but a handful of these Crafters in the many lands, and they preferred to live alone, with only knowledge and power as their companions.

The thought of the power the Crafter controlled filled Sian-vesna with envy. She imagined all the things she could do if she controlled but a small portion of these powers, but there had also been something wrong with the Crafter. She had watched his face carefully and had the impression of two beings rather than one. She shook the thought off as she imagined what feats she could accomplish with the power.

Sian-vesna looked down at the four sacks at her

feet, then gathered them to her chest and fled to her room. Slipping her robes over her head, she opened her pack and removed the travel armour she had recently packed away. It was light and well oiled and felt comfortable as she shrugged it into place. Donning her robe, she belted it at the waist, replaced her shoes with her heavy boots and hurriedly braided her hair into one long plait. Then, slipping her war fans into her belt, she lifted the sacks and left her room.

The charter she was about to purchase would draw a few curious thoughts from the local Charter House, but she cared little. It was the Lore of the Charter that none but those involved could speak of it.

There was more to the charter than she had been told, Sian-vesna knew, but it was not her place to question anyone who wished to charter a Cathar.

The inn lay only a short distance from the Charter House, and Sian-vesna was soon seated at a darkened table.

'I find you well, Joelen?'

'I find you well, Sian-vesna?'

The small red-shielded lamp was lit and the business commenced.

As soon as the image of Sian-vesna had vanished, Charybdis released the illusion. His robe and crown vanished, his size diminished, and he sat once more on a wooden chair. He had needed the illusion to convince Sian-vesna that he was indeed powerful but he had taken no chances, leaving behind a faint suggestion in Sian-vesna's mind that she should do as he ordered without question.

In fact Charybdis had felt her desire for the power the instant he had contacted her. He also knew that her loyalty to her calling as a Crafter and Cathar would compel her to place the charter as he desired. This ability to enter the minds of living creatures would prove useful. With it, he could proceed with his plans and guarantee the loyalty of all who aided him.

7

REBIRTH

Sian-vesna, Tandra and Bram approached a three-storey building of white stone. The blocks were large and well-cut with the only windows being on the third floor. A steep set of semi-circular stairs marked the entrance and, as the three climbed the stairs, they were greeted by many scholars and Crafters. Many believed it was good luck to pass greetings with a Cathar of a Charter House other than the local one.

The interior of the building was cool and heavy hangings muffled the sound of their steps as they approached a massive desk of black oak. The walls were covered in heavily laden polished timber bookshelves and short yellow candles burned at the small desks, illuminating the hunched silent readers.

'We are under charter,' Tandra explained.

The librarian nodded.

'We have been sent by the local Charter House to search out old maps or scrolls referring to the time before the Final Wars.'

Again the librarian nodded and rose from his seat behind the desk. Without a word he led them to the far side of the library where he opened a small cobweb-shrouded door. A set of narrow stairs disappeared into the darkness below. Taking a shielded lantern from a small hidden shelf, the librarian handed it to the party and departed.

'A man of few words,' Sian-vesna commented. 'There should be more of them.'

'Most librarians in Ceruss have had their tongues removed as a kind of penance against any noise they might make,' Bram noted casually.

Sian-vesna glanced over her shoulder at the retreating librarian. 'There should be more of that.'

The air was dry as they descended the stairs. In the light thrown out by the lantern they saw shelf after shelf of scrolls. There were frayed cobwebs at every corner and the books and scrolls they passed were covered in dust.

'It seems this charter is no small feat,' Bram laughed. Then he turned to Tandra. 'Was there no hint whom the charter was for?'

'Only that he lived some distance from here and could not search for the information himself,' Tandra replied. All she had been told at the Charter House was that the charter could lead to more work if it was carried out successfully. And the main thing was that it paid well, incredibly well.

'If we each take a wall we will finish sooner,' Bram said.

'But we have only one lantern,' Sian-vesna observed. When she had taken out the charter she knew that her name would not be mentioned. It was against the Cathars' most ancient laws to reveal any information about the origin of a charter.

'Then it seems we must work together,' Tandra noted as she took a scroll from the shelf and shook off the dust.

Removing the tie, she opened the scroll and quickly scanned the contents. With a shrug she rolled and retied the scroll, setting it back on the shelf.

Several hours passed before Tandra finally located anything of value. They had been sent to search for a certain time before the Final Wars, a time when there would be mention of Living Towers and those who lived in them. What Tandra had found was an old map showing Ceruss and Skarn and the surrounding lands. But as she examined the map further she discovered that there were many points of difference between it and the lands she knew today.

On the shelf where the map had been they also uncovered a small scroll which had two references to the Living Towers. One recorded the destruction of the Foxglove Tower, near the coast to the south of Sytry. It had been destroyed by the priesthood of Sytry, but there was no reason given for the act. The second was mostly unreadable and Tandra could make out only one phrase: '. . . and the *Whirlpool of Destruction* will revisit Kyrthos, bringing about its destruction.'

Sian-vesna took the scroll carefully from Tandra and touched it to her shell medallion, then she took the old map and allowed the light of the shell's Lychgem to move over the surface of the parchment.

Although she was a Crafter who specialised in healing, there were other Crafters like Orren-ker who dealt in folklore and antiquities. He would now be able to gain access to the information stored on the scroll and map through his medallion.

The road south out of Sytry was narrow and rutted, and ankle-deep in mud. But its condition did not stop the merchants as the narrow wheels of their carts churned it into a quagmire. Servants strained in their harnesses as the suction held the wheels tight and the shouts of the merchants could be heard over the cries of the servants.

When Tandra returned to the Charter House with what they had learned she was offered another charter, this time to travel south and find the ruins of the Foxglove Tower. She had expected this, but was surprised by the number of other charters that were to be offered for the same purpose.

There were thirteen of them in all. Tandra was to lead with Bram Onehand, a considerable honour for a man. Kathryn, Sian-vesna and Tarynn were also chartered. Others offered the role were Mahira of Calcanth, a veteran of even more years than Bram, Fallon, who was on her first charter, Cerise, Ferne, Phaidra and Kallem. There would be two other Crafters, Orren-ker and Lealia-shey.

Kallem knew none of these Cathars well. He had journeyed with only a few of them previously and he had kept mostly to himself. The road walked by the Cathars was still very much female orientated, and as one of the few males accepted into the profession he had always found the trail lonely.

But even though he was unfamiliar with many of the party, he had heard of Bram Onehand. For many long years now he had walked the road of the Cathars, his skill at arms growing as had his legend in all regions of Kyrthos.

Tarynn was very young and Kallem watched the youth as he tried to follow Bram's lead. What was truly refreshing was Orren-ker. Kallem had never met a male Crafter before and for some time had believed they existed only in stories.

Many of the servants ankle-deep in the mire paused in their work as the thirteen Cathars strode by. It was strange to see so many in one place other than a Charter House. And to see them alone, with no pilgrims or merchants to protect, drew mutterings from many of the servants.

One of the merchants straightened from his shouting and eyed the thirteen suspiciously. Then he quickly clenched a fist and raised it before his chest in an ancient warding to protect him from evil. Thirteen was a bad omen and the merchant told himself that he would stop early that night and offer a silent prayer to the Life Bringer.

Orren-ker wrinkled his nose at the smells drifting up from the road. 'Why is it that these idiots keep to this bog of a road when the land to either side is clear? Why don't they use it?'

Tandra laughed and patted the Crafter on his shoulder. 'The road tax in Ceruss is one dull per day's travel. The shoulder of the road costs much more and it is only used by the town's Elders, their messengers, and the military.'

'But who would know?'

'No merchant is going to allow any rival to use the shoulder for free when it means that their merchandise would reach the markets earlier,' Tandra

114

explained. 'Using the shoulder without paying the due taxes means the confiscation of the entire cargo. No merchant is going to risk that, no matter the promise of profit.'

Orren-ker nodded. Tandra was surprised by his lack of knowledge. 'How many charters have you completed?'

'This will be my first,' he answered. 'I have spent much of my life in study.'

'In my land,' Mahira interrupted, 'we have beasts of burden to draw the merchants' wagons and carts.'

'What type of beasts?' Fallon asked. This was her first charter and she had attached herself to the older Mahira in the hope of learning more than she had been taught at the Charter House.

The youngest of a large family, Fallon missed the almost continuous attention she had received at home and had thought of trying to get close to Tandra. But she could see that Tandra was busy enough trying to lead such a large number of Cathars. In fact, Fallon had never seen so many Cathars, not even in the Charter Houses she had visited.

Nevertheless Fallon was happy with her progress. She was learning a great deal from Mahira and was sure that the veteran liked her and was not just helping her because she thought it was her duty.

'Large featherless, flightless birds,' Mahira answered.

'How can a bird be featherless and flightless?' Tarynn scoffed. 'Surely it must be a different creature altogether and have nothing to do with birds?'

'The Aves have migrated across the open steppes of Calcanth since the beginning of time,' Mahira expanded. 'They move in large flocks, as they cross and recross the treeless steppes stopping only when it is time for them to mate and nest. They are as tall as a woman and are totally free of feathers.

'Their arms are long and thin and end in hands bearing wicked talons as long as your middle finger. They are razor sharp on the inside edge and can gut an unsuspecting traveller in seconds.'

'How is it that they are captured?' Cerise asked. She was also young like Tarynn and Fallon, but this was her third charter and she carried herself with the confidence exhibited only by those who have come to grips with the life they now led.

'That is known only to the Jaeger,' Mahira replied. 'They roam the steppes trapping the Aves, training them and then selling them south, across the Tante Ranges into Bezoar.'

Cerise spat and cursed under her breath.

'You have a problem?' Orren-ker snapped.

'Bezoar!' Cerise cursed and spat again.

Lealia-shey moved to Orren-ker's side, forcing Ferne and Phaidra to join their countrywoman. Hands hovered over the hilts of their weapons as the others stepped back in surprise. Tandra could not believe what she was seeing. When you accepted the path of a Cathar you forsook all ties to family and country and became one with those who shared the road with you. It was unheard of for Cathars to fight amongst themselves.

Stepping forward she raised her hands. 'Stop!' she ordered. 'There is no need for this.'

Sian-vesna had worked her way towards Orren-ker and Lealia-shey. If the need arose she would stop her fellow Bezoarians from fighting, but the

Cerussians were another matter. No-one was listening to Tandra as the party separated further, fragmenting into three distinct groups.

'By the crooked tail of the Slayer!' Bram cursed as he stepped forward.

Tarynn was taken aback by Bram's hasty movement, but then quickly stepped forward.

'This is no concern of yours, Bram,' Cerise snarled.

Bram's right fist flashed out, taking the woman on the point of her jaw and snapping her mouth closed with a distinct sound. Cerise's eyes rolled back as she crumpled to the ground. Bram stepped over the body and confronted Ferne and Phaidra.

Both women lowered their heads in shame under his steady stare. A slight turn of Bram's head brought Orren-ker and Lealia-shey into sight. They too lowered their heads and Bram could see their lips moving as they sought deep within themselves for forgiveness.

'I had not thought I would see the day,' Bram soothed, 'when we who share the same road would face one another in anger. Never have I heard of what I have just witnessed. When we reach the next Charter House I suggest that we all take time to examine what has just happened.'

Cerise moaned slightly and tried to rise, but Bram lifted his foot and kicked her neatly under her chin. 'Cerise is no longer of Ceruss. It was wrong for her to say anything about Bezoar. But, on the other hand,' Bram added quickly, turning his attention once more to Orren-ker and Lealia-shey, 'you have given up Bezoar when you took to the road with your first charter. It was wrong of you to allow yourselves to be baited like some fingerling in a shallow pond.'

Bram's voice had taken on the depth of authority and none dared face him. On one of their many shared charters Bram had once told Tandra of his life before he took to the road.

He had been drunk, as usual, and had explained that as a child he had wanted nothing more than to serve the priesthood. He had not indicated which sect, only speaking of taking his vows. Then something had happened. He had not revealed what to Tandra, and she had not asked. Whatever it was had turned Bram from the priesthood and had set his feet firmly on the road.

Tandra could not imagine what order would suit Bram, but his priestly ambitions were long past and the road had a habit of changing all those who trod it.

The traffic on the road had ground to a halt during the confrontation. As Sian-vesna moved forward to help Cerise, who was still unconscious, many of the merchants made the sign of warding. Perhaps tonight would be a good one on which to call an early stop and offer thanks to and ask protection from the Life Bringer.

Never before had they witnessed such a thing. The world was truly turning upside down when those of the road fought amongst themselves.

Tandra led the party a short distance from the road and ordered a camp set. One more day's travel and they would reach the Foxglove Tower.

The squat remains of the Foxglove Tower sat high on a cliff overlooking the ocean. Barely two storeys high, the stonework at its base was burned black, and edged in a white salt that had leeched from the stones. The higher stones showed no sign of ageing or damage.

'I thought the scroll said that the tower had been razed to the ground,' Sian-vesna commented.

'That was a long time ago,' Bram pointed out. 'Many things change with time. Perhaps the writer only believed the tower was destroyed.'

'Or somebody once tried to rebuild it,' Tandra offered. 'The upper stones appear to be newer, less worn.'

'Who can say?' Bram shrugged.

The air had become very warm and still as the wind dropped away and Tandra felt the storm coming before she saw it claw its way over the horizon.

'It looks to be brewing up a fair blow,' Bram noted.

'Let's see if the tower offers any shelter,' Tandra suggested.

The stone walls of the tower and a spiral staircase were all that remained, offering only scant protection from the wind. Kallem, Lealia-shey and Ferne were set to work rigging a shelter out of the canvases the party carried while Cerise and Phaidra hunted for enough firewood for the night.

Tandra felt ill-at-ease as she watched the storm approach and ordered that a watch be mounted. Tarynn, Kathryn, Mahira, Fallon, and Orren-ker took up positions well back from the tower but from which they had good views of all approaches.

'What are we watching for?' Fallon asked. 'There is no living thing in sight, save us.'

'And what is out of sight?' Mahira offered.

Fallon looked confused.

'Can't you feel it?' Mahira persisted.

'The storm?'

'No. More than that. There's something not quite right.' Mahira glanced quickly over her shoulder and for a moment Fallon thought she was going to make the sign of warding even though the clenched fist was a sign used by males, when they were frightened of the unknown, and never used by a woman.

'All I can feel is the storm approaching,' Fallon said. 'What is it you feel?'

Mahira shrugged. 'It is hard to put into words. When you have trod the roads for as long as I have you will understand these things. I see nothing, but there is danger close by, I know it. And so too does Tandra.'

'Do the others feel this as well?'

Mahira looked at the young girl and then at the armoured figures to their right. 'Tarynn has eyes only for Kathryn, and Kathryn is still young, but Orren-ker senses something—you can tell by the way the Crafter is holding his medallion as he studies the terrain.'

Fallon risked a look behind her. As she studied the tower from its blackened base to its ragged top she felt a chill that caused her to shudder.

'It's not in front of us,' Fallon said softly. 'It's the tower. I can feel it now. It's the tower that is not right.'

Sian-vesna knelt by the tower's base and pushed aside the thick growth of weeds. Nestled against the wall was a knee-high bright green plant. Its leaves were thick and shone as if oiled. Atop the stem was a long spike of flower of the softest purple.

It was the most beautiful flower Sian-vesna had ever seen. She leaned forward and pulled a weed from beside the plant, then drew her dagger and loosened the soil around the flower. She poured a small amount of water from her pouch at the plant's base. The flower's fragrance was almost overpowering as she worked over the plant. It must have been the plant which had given the tower its name.

As the sun set the party settled into the protection of the tower's walls. The rain grew heavier as the night drew on and Tandra ordered the watches to take up their positions. One pair stood by the opening, staring out into the rain, while another pair remained beside the fire, feeding the fuel they had collected into the hungry flames.

Tarynn sat beside the fire, watching the guards at the door in the flickering firelight. Bram rested against the cold stone wall, his breathing heavy. Tarynn could smell the drink on his companion's breath, but said nothing. Bram was a hero to the youth, one of the first males to have been accepted by a Charter House.

When it came time to make decisions, Tarynn often found himself watching the veteran. He had seen how Bram silently agreed with most things Tandra ordered.

A sharp noise from the crumbled stairs drew Tarynn's attention. It could have just been a loose stone unsettled by the wind and rain, but as he turned back to the fire he heard the noise again. Bram had not moved, nor had Fallon or Cerise. Tarynn stepped carefully over the sleeping bodies until he stood at the base of the stairs. Their canvas did not reach very far and, looking upward into the rain, he could see nothing.

When Tarynn heard the noise once more he drew his sword and cautiously began to climb the stairs. He could feel his heart beating loudly as he climbed and swore that it was loud enough to wake his companions, but they still didn't move. As he climbed he realised that something was wrong. From the outside the tower was only two storeys, yet already he had climbed higher than that and had not come to the stairs' end.

And there was no rain within the tower, although he could still hear it falling beyond the wall. Tarynn stopped to wipe the moisture from his brow and lick his lips. As he took a step backward he heard the sound again. He could not risk a look over his shoulder, yet he somehow knew that his companions had not stirred.

When Tarynn heard the sound again, it was much closer. He steadied himself against the wall and took a deep breath before resuming his climb. At once he found himself engulfed in a frigid, mind-numbing cold. Ahead of him on the stairs was a dark shape.

The young Cathar lashed out with his broadsword and cleaved the shadow in two. As the sword cut through the shadow Tarynn's mind filled with a silent scream as the intense cold rushed down his arm and into his chest. Then he felt a reassuring glow of warmth from deep within.

'All is well,' came a strange voice echoing round Tarynn's pain-clouded mind.

Sian-vesna rolled in her sleep disturbed by a dream. One of their number was being slowly killed while the others stood about doing nothing. She tried to help but found she was restrained by an unpleasant cold sensation in her chest. Again, she tried to aid her fellow Cathar but her attempt was foiled once more. This time the cold was considerably more intense.

Calming herself, she concentrated on helping her companion and slowly she reached for her medallion. But as her fingers touched the shell-wrapped gem they were scorched. The sudden pain woke her with a start, her soft cry enough to snap Bram from his stupor.

Sian-vesna reached for her medallion again, but the searing heat was still there. Bram searched the camp for any sign of danger and noticed that Fallon and Cerise had not responded to the noise. When he realised that Tarynn was missing he rushed towards the tower's opening and the storm beyond.

'No!' Sian-vesna shouted. 'Not out there. Up.' She gestured to the stairs as she got to her feet, ignoring the mumbled questions and curses of her companions.

Bram rushed for the stairs, Sian-vesna close behind. A few steps up and out of sight of the camp they found Tarynn. His sword was drawn and extended, his left hand resting against the wall as if to steady himself. Bram reached out for Tarynn but a restraining hand from Sian-vesna stopped him and she moved past her companion, lifting her medallion before her as she did so.

The heat in the gem increased and its light filled the narrow stairwell. Bram and Sian-vesna made out a darker shadow on the stairs above the motionless Tarynn.

Through the gem in Sian-vesna's medallion, Charybdis saw the shadow for what it truly was. A wraith. But a wraith so weakened by a long and enforced solitude that it lacked the strength to descend the stairs. It sat before them like a mist-shrouded spider, luring its prey into its web.

In the Hawkthorn Tower Charybdis raised the staff and, placing his left hand on the Lychgem, he forced his will into one of its facets. As he stared down he felt himself enter the gem. As if in two places at once, Charybdis watched his barely visible self pass through the many facets of the gem until it confronted the wraith.

Charybdis reached out and touched the reflected form of Sian-vesna. He raised his staff and struck the wraith a blow. The wraith vanished and Charybdis felt Sian-vesna pull away from him. Allowing himself to drift back to his tower, Charybdis felt the slight life-force of the Foxglove Tower as it cried with hunger as its last defender vanished.

The instant Charybdis had entrapped the wraith its hold over Tarynn and those still sleeping below vanished. Tarynn's broadsword fell from his lifeless fingers as he slid down the wall and was caught by Bram. Slowly the veteran lowered the still form of Tarynn to the rain soaked stairs.

Sian-vesna leaned against the wall of the tower, unable to help Bram. When the shadowy attacker had vanished she had felt the medallion on her chest erupt with life. Its strength flowed into her chest, filling her with a deep warmth. Where she touched the tower's wall she could feel some of the power seeping out and surging through the hungry stonework.

She quickly regathered her thoughts and knelt beside Tarynn. There were shouts and confused questions coming from the camp below, but Bram and Sian-vesna's only thoughts were for Tarynn. Sian-vesna lifted his hand and, shocked by the chill of his skin, she felt his chest for any sign of his life-force. There was nothing but the intense cold.

As she touched the body of her dead companion Sian-vesna sensed something was wrong, but in the back of her mind she heard a gentle voice reassuring her that all was as it should be.

Slowly she straightened. 'He's gone,' she whispered, as she placed a hand on Bram's shoulder. 'The Slayer has had his way and Tarynn has started his greatest charter as he searches for the Life Bringer and eternal peace.'

Bram wiped the tears from his eyes and lifted his face to the steady rain. He howled at the night, venting his grief into the darkness, then lifted Tarynn into his arms and carried him down into the camp. Sian-vesna paused. She had noticed a shadow vanish up the stairs. Closing her eyes, she shook her head and then examined the stairs once again, but this time she saw nothing. Again the voice whispered that all was as it should be.

The camp was in turmoil. Wakened from their forced stupor, no-one knew what had happened. Three of their number were missing yet the sentries had neither seen nor heard anything before Bram's howl indicated that one of their number was dead. Then Bram appeared carrying Tarynn's body. Sian-vesna followed closely.

'There was something on the stairs,' he

explained. 'Tarynn must have heard or seen something and gone to investigate.'

'But there was nothing?' Cerise argued.

'We sat by the opening and there was no sound or movement from within or without,' Fallon protested.

'It was the tower,' Sian-vesna stated. 'Remember we sought a Living Tower, and the Foxglove Tower is one of them. I thought it was simply a name, or that if the tower was ever alive it was long since dead. But I was wrong. There is a new life-force within the tower and Tarynn encountered one of its defenders.'

'What was it?' Bram asked.

'It was a wraith,' Sian-vesna replied. The answers were in her mind but she did not know where they had come from. The small plant growing against the wall of the tower was the new life-force, she could sense that, and the wraith had been weakened by the need for the strength it generated.

'Are there likely to be more of them about?' Mahira wondered.

Again Sian-vesna knew the answer. 'There would have been once, but now they are all gone, returned to the Slayer.'

'How?'

'Perhaps it was time. Or the tower was so hungry it fed on its defenders until only one weakened wraith remained.'

Bram look up. 'Weakened?'

'A wraith at full strength would have destroyed the entire party. There would have been nothing we could have done about it. As it was we were lucky. The effort of slaying Tarynn overtaxed it and it died before it could feed.' How could she explain to them what had happened when she was not sure herself?

'We are safe here then?' Tandra queried.

'Now, yes.'

'Place Tarynn's body beside the door,' Tandra ordered. 'We will send him on his final charter at first light.'

Bram lowered the body to the ground and slid down the wall beside it. He lifted his right hand and wiped the rain away from his face, knowing that it hid his tears. Sian-vesna seemed sure that there was nothing which could have been done to prevent Tarynn's death. But Bram was angry with himself for allowing it to happen. He had drunk deep from the small flat flask resting at his hip and for this weakness Tarynn had died.

Tandra watched as the wet earth covered Tarynn's form. Across the canvas coffin, his broadsword and scabbard were laid in a cross above his chest. Beside him rested everything he would need before he reached the Great Charter House. Food, water, spare clothing and items given him by his companions. Only Bram had failed to add anything to the small pile of stores.

As the last of the canvas was hidden from sight, Bram stepped forward and tossed a small silver flask into the grave. Then he turned and strode away. Looking up at the clear blue sky, Bram cursed himself once again. 'Listen to me, lad,' he whispered. 'That flask caused your death as sure as any wraith. I can not bring you back but I swear that I will see you have not died in vain.'

Bram raised his hand and slowly drew an outer edge of his trident across his right cheek. Blood flowed down his chin and dripped onto his mail shirt. It was an ancient ritual Bram had used as he vowed to avenge his companion's death, dating back to the time just after the Final Wars when only women walked the road on charters. None would stand in the path of a Cathar, yet many were the hardships faced by man. It was a sign to all that the wearer of the scar sought someone's death and that none should stand in the way.

Charybdis strengthened his contact with the Foxglove Tower, feeding it small amounts of stored power from his Lychgem. Slowly, he was able to confirm that the tower was still alive, after a long dormant period. As the plant grew back it began to feed it with the limited power it could gather from the earth beneath its roots.

Before the new master of the Foxglove Tower could do anything, Charybdis had linked both towers to the one power source. Slightly faster now, he fed power into the Lychgem of the Foxglove Tower. The strength of the plant increased as the power passed through it and into the liflode, the building stone of the tower. Like the plant, the tower would also grow—expanding stone by stone until the gem appeared in its upper chamber like the seed of some strange petrified plant. The Lychgem controlled the power which the plant gathered and stored within the liflode.

Charybdis released the wraith trapped within his staff and imprisoned it in the Foxglove Tower as a deterrent against future intruders, and as a reminder to the new master of where the power truly belonged.

Joining the Foxglove and Hawkthorn Towers had cost Charybdis dearly from the power stored within his tower. But as the Foxglove Tower grew, Charybdis' power would gradually increase too, and he now had an ally. The new master of the Foxglove Tower was in Charybdis' debt and between them they would seek out more towers.

8
REPAYMENT

The return journey to Sytry was uneventful and as the tired, silent party of Cathars entered the town, they made straight for the Charter House. Like all other Charter Houses, it was located in the centre of the town, bordered by brick buildings on three sides while its front opened onto a narrow side street.

As Tandra's party entered the building it was met by retired Cathars and the building's servants. Word of what had happened on the road to the Foxglove Tower had reached Sytry and there were many questions which needed to be answered. Tandra soon found herself in a small room with one of the oldest Cathars she had ever seen.

The woman's face was so wrinkled that her mouth seemed to remain in a continual pucker and her eyes resembled small craters. Around her neck hung a shell medallion which was different from any other Tandra had seen. Its outer edge was worn smooth by the handling it had received over the long years.

'I am Faina-lai,' the woman explained. 'I have questions which need answers. Perhaps you will be able to help me in my search.'

'It all started . . . ' Tandra began.

The woman raised a hand, silencing Tandra.

'The incident on the road to Sytry is indeed a grave matter,' Faina-lai agreed. 'But it is not that which concerns me. Others of the Charter House will seek out what transpired on the road south.'

Tandra was confused. If not over that incident, then why had she been summoned here?

'The charter granted to you and your companions was brought to us under unusual circumstances. In fact it was brought to the Hall of Business by one of our own. To be exact, by one of those who accompanied you on the charter to the Foxglove Tower.'

Never before had Tandra heard a charter discussed by any Cathar save those under the charter as they sat by their lonely fire in some far and possibly hostile land. It was obvious that Faina-lai was held in high esteem in the Charter House and this confused Tandra even further.

'The Charter Houses of Kyrthos have kept a vigil over the centuries since the end of the Final Wars for any sign of the Living Towers regaining power. It was these towers and their masters who caused the wars leading to the Final Wars which saw the people of these lands pushed almost to the point of extinction.

'The towers were constructed some time in our distant past. The architects and their reasons for building them are unknown but, whatever the purpose of the towers, they controlled an immense power.

131

'It is written that as each of the towers grew in strength they began to fear their neighbours, wondering if the other towers sought to increase their hold over the lands by gaining control of the rest of the towers. The inhabitants of the towers built cities and towns from which they drew huge armies to defend their borders. Eventually the many lands fell to warring amongst themselves.

'Councils, Governments and kings fell beneath the strength of the Living Towers and it was not long before each tower ruled one of the many lands of Kyrthos. Warfare escalated and there were only a few survivors.

'But the Living Towers had fared little better. Many of them were defeated by the combined strengths of the other towers and all but a few of the remaining towers lost their masters and withdrew from the war not wishing to follow the fate of the other towers. Of the few remaining towers with masters there was nothing left for them to do but try to draw the last remnants of the population to them.

'But the damage had been done and those few pitiful survivors wanted nothing to do with the Living Towers and fled from them, settling in the lands no longer under their control. Over the centuries the Living Towers were virtually forgotten, spoken of only in myths, but it seems they are still intent on playing a part in our lives.'

'Who set the charter?' Tandra asked. To answer her question would break the greatest vow any Cathar could take.

Faina-lai fell silent and her head tilted forward. She allowed her eyes to rest upon the clean stone floor of the room.

'Regardless of the dangers which threaten us,' she said, 'there is no way that I can break my vows. I will tell you that she is still part of the party, and will be continuing the charter with you.'

'Continuing?'

'Yes. There was a second part to the charter, which paid for a small force to seek out the Living Tower known as Monkshood. It is located far to the north beyond the jungles of northern Skarn and Scapol.'

There were five jungle regions north of Skarn and Scapol, but over the years they had been joined under the one name, Belial. It simply meant ruin or destruction, and was another name for the Slayer himself. None but the most foolhardy ventured anywhere near the Belial.

'Of late,' Faina-lai explained, 'many travellers and adventure seekers have wandered north attempting to find the treasures spoken of in myths. It appears that at least one of their number has passed the Belial and entered the realm of a Living Tower.'

'How do you know this?'

'When the charter was granted the name used by the go-between was Crataegus. It was said that he lived to the north and was a bedridden scholar, unable to make the journey south. But our Crafters have discovered another meaning for the name. It was the title used by many of the Living Towers during the Final Wars, when they pooled their power for protection.

'The Monkshood was one such tower and we can find no mention of its destruction. Others of the Crataegus included Snakeweed, which was defeated by enemies, and another which sits on an island to the north-east surrounded by a sea filled with deadly creations of its own design. Foxglove was destroyed by the Charter Houses of Skarn, Ceruss, and Scapol. And finally there is Hawkthorn. Nothing is known about Hawkthorn, but it is believed that after the war it went to great lengths to slay any who knew about it, and then used the ignorance of its presence as a protective shield.'

'But somehow the knowledge of it survived,' Tandra added.

'Yes.'

'But the records of the Sytry library state that the Foxglove Tower was destroyed by one of the priesthoods.'

'That is how it was written,' Faina-lai agreed. 'It was thought wise not to let those who oppose us know we had the power to destroy one of the Living Towers.'

'But you did not destroy it,' Tandra interrupted. 'The tower still stands, at least its lower section does.'

'It is written that the plant was torn from the ground and used to fill the lower level before the tower was set alight. Only a few of the stones remained standing.'

'The tower is now two storeys high,' Tandra said, 'and the higher stonework looks to be new. Sianvesna also found a small strange plant growing at its base.' Tandra then went on to explain what had passed that night, including the death of Tarynn.

'This is most upsetting,' Faina-lai mumbled. The information had clearly upset the old woman. 'The plant draws its power from the depths of this world, and it is stored within the liflode which makes up the tower. The power is wielded through a gem, the Lychgem, which links the tower's master with the stored power. All three live and, combined, they are a formidable force. If what you say is true then we must act immediately. I will organise a party to revisit the Foxglove Tower while you and I and your eleven companions continue north on your charter.'

'But . . .?' Tandra interrupted.

'When we reach the tower, if it still stands, we must destroy it,' Faina-lai declared. 'There is no other way to stop this Crataegus from gaining control of it.'

The thirteen Cathars strode the road north as if they owned it. Each of them, save Faina-lai, carried a large pack with sufficient rations to allow them to reach Erlan without having to stop and purchase more. Faina-lai had insisted that they start as soon as possible and that word of the progress of the party she had organised to revisit the Foxglove Tower would be waiting for them in Erlan.

Tandra knew that the Charter Houses had many methods for sending news from one House to another, but she had no idea how this was accomplished. Those who worked in the Charter Houses were as dedicated and loyal as those who walked the roads and their secrets stayed with them.

The Bezoarians had crossed their northern border many times in the past, but since their neighbours had garrisoned the three passes through the Tante Ranges, Bezoar had been contained. Over the years a new state, Obira, had arisen between Bezoar and Ceruss. It was settled by Bezoarians unhappy with the way their homeland was deteriorating. Many of the War Hawks of Ceruss had welcomed the split, as it had given them access to regions long controlled by Bezoar. And with the continual border disputes there was always work for a strong arm and a quick sword, and this meant profits.

Those who chose to break away from their traditional lives in Bezoar and take up life in Obira were sick of the continual warring of the Bezoarian leaders and wished for a life of safety for their children.

The rulers in Bezoar were always looking to expand their control of the surrounding lands with either a soft word or a swift blow. But with the separation, aided by Ceruss, there arrived a time of greater bloodshed as the Bezoarian forces tried to take back what they claimed was rightfully theirs.

To the east lay Tulda, Deccan and Hrubsice, small lands ruled by a succession of Kings and Princes until any true regal lineage was lost. For the most part these lands were isolated from the rest of Kyrthos and many strange and deadly creatures could be found lurking there. Slowly, and then much faster after the King of Tulda had been assassinated, the three lands threw their military might behind that of Bezoar.

Obira had called on Ceruss for more assistance, and had received it. But now the two forces faced each other across their common border, jockeying for position. Calcanth had called up many of its reservists and marched them south to reinforce their mountain garrisons.

Scapol had taken the opportunity to break the

shaky truce which had existed for six years and cross the Berdun River into Calcanth and sack several of the small border towns.

The Charter Houses of these lands were quickly transferring their funds out of the troubled regions as they tried to speak of peace with all those involved. For the present any party under the protection of the Cathars was still able to cross the inflamed borders, but none knew for how long this would continue.

Faina-lai stared out over the Shaylee River and watched as the ferry drew closer. The far bank was packed with soldiers of fortune who were making their way south from Skarn and Scapol to help fight the Bezoarians.

'I fear we will soon encounter trouble,' Faina-lai predicted.

'Perhaps they will let us pass,' Tandra said wistfully.

Bram shook his head. 'I have spoken to several of the ferrymen and they have told me that they have been ferrying spirits and ales across the river all morning. Merchants have set up tents on the banks, turning them into taverns. These muddy islands of greed and drunkenness have been doing a roaring trade.'

'Perhaps we could wait till dark?' Faina-lai suggested.

'It will take more than the setting of the sun to get us safely past that lot,' Bram grumbled.

Tandra nodded her agreement. The old veteran had at first said nothing, but as they moved further north it became obvious that he did not appreciate the presence of Faina-lai. Tandra had no idea why.

Perhaps Bram felt that she was too old for the hardships of the road.

'Could we not swing west and pick up a vessel off the coast?' Bram asked.

'The Cut is filled with shipping,' Tandra answered, 'but none of them is interested in running a few Cathars when they can make several fortunes running supplies and weapons into Brisk.'

'Then we will have to take our chances with the rabble.' Bram sighed. The ferry struck the riverbank with a crash of timbers and its ramp dropped as the Captain shouted orders and curses at his crew.

'Get a move on, you lazy louts. If we're not across the river with these supplies before the sun sets, Vizard will have my guts.'

Two new members of the crew paused and laughed.

The Captain was a short round man with dark matted hair covering every portion of exposed skin. His thick beard and long untidy hair seemed lost within themselves, like the mane of some wild cat of the plains. Three parallel scars ran across his face where his right eye should have been.

'You may find that funny now, you fresh-skinned bastards, but I'll be sure to take your balls with me when I visit Vizard's tent.'

The men hurried about their work.

'We need passage across the river,' Faina-lai called.

'Find some other way,' the Captain called back. 'I haven't the time for passengers.'

'None of the other vessels is willing to take us,' Faina-lai explained.

'Then find another way,' the Captain growled.

'What other way?' Tandra called out.

'Walk for all I care,' the Captain spat. 'You're wasting my time. I have no room for you on board.'

'Is there room in your purse for our coins?' Bram shouted above the chaos.

The Captain looked at the caller and his one good eye opened in surprise. 'Bram, you old sow's bastard. Aren't you dead yet?'

'Hardly,' Bram scoffed.

'But I still don't have time for you, old friend. Vizard owns this vessel and my soul.' The Captain glanced down at the deck. 'A sorry sight as she may be, she's been my home for many years and I'd hate to lose her.'

'There are thirteen of us,' Bram called back. 'We wouldn't take up much room and we'd be glad to help with the loading. Free of charge, of course.'

'The fare is one Imperial and you get your backs into it and you've a deal,' the Captain shouted.

'One . . . !' Tandra sputtered.

Bram raised a hand to silence her. 'Done and done,' he answered.

'Then don't just stand there,' the Captain shouted. 'Get that one good hand of yours dirty and help this useless trash with their work.'

The Cathars threw their gear on board and quickly set to work. One of their number was left watching over the equipment, as they trusted neither the Captain nor his crew. And although it was Bram who had negotiated the deal, it was he who ended up standing beside the Captain grinning down at his fellow Cathars as they loaded the ferry.

'They work like old women,' the Captain commented dryly.

'They're working better than your sorry excuse for a crew,' Bram laughed. 'Tell me, do you actually pay them to loiter on the bank like that?'

'By the prophet it's good to see you again, old friend,' the Captain whispered. 'We had thought you lost.'

'Simply misplaced,' Bram answered. He'd not heard that form of greeting for many years and it brought back a flood of memories.

'Have you news of your boy? Did you ever find him?'

Bram nodded, his memories soured by the question.

'How is he?'

'Dead,' Bram sighed. 'Almost a month ago now. We were on a charter and he was killed during the night.'

'Did he die well?'

'He did,' Bram answered. 'But there was no time to tell him who I was. He died believing his father had deserted him all those years ago.'

'The Land of the Dead is a dangerous place for one such as he,' the Captain said, making the sign of the fist before his chest. 'May his sword edge never dull and his eyes remain keen.'

Many males of the western lands believed that death was simply a passing to another world, no better or worse than the one in which they now lived. But the passage to this new world was through the Land of the Dead, which was reputed to be more dangerous by far than any Kyrthos had to offer. Still, it was a journey that had to be made.

The Captain and Bram were of an old breed of fighter who deeply believed that life was a continuous war. It took place on many lands and in many worlds, until either they or the Slayer were defeated.

'Thank you, Lyronn.' Bram smiled. 'You always were a good friend, one of only a handful who believed in me all those years ago. It was a trust that could have cost you and your family their lives if I'd been found.'

When the loading was almost finished, Lyronn cupped his hands around his mouth and began to shout orders. Pulleys squealed as the ramp was raised. The Cathars collapsed atop the cargo but the crew were not so lucky and soon, under the lashing tongue of the Captain, they were at work in the rigging guiding the heavily laden vessel across the river.

The Shaylee River was quite wide, but only near her mouth was she deep. Slow of current and filled with silt, the Shaylee rambled from the Tante Ranges to The Cut. It had once been proposed that a bridge span her calm waters, but there had been many accidents as it was being surveyed.

Lumber and tents had mysteriously caught fire and no member of the party who strayed from the camp was ever seen again. Finally it was decided that a bridge was not needed and the way of life of the Shaylee and those who worked her muddied waters returned to normal.

'Cut any good throats lately, Lyronn?' Bram asked as he watched the riverbank fall away behind them, their previous conversation forgotten.

'Probably not as many as you,' the Captain

replied. 'Since when have you walked the road? The last time I heard you were . . .'

Bram silenced his old friend. 'It is not the time to speak of the past,' he said. 'What is needed is some way to pass the rabble on the far bank.'

'Not much chance of that.'

Bram winked at Lyronn. 'There's always a way.'

The riverbank was filled with the angry shouts of too many men in the one place. Fights were breaking out all along the water's edge as large men with clubs rushed forward to lay low the struggling figures.

'Lyronn, you miserable river rat. What in the Slayer's name is taking you so long?' called Blackleg, a short greasy man who was wearing a tattered jacket over patched and dirty leggings. His left leg was a battered wooden stump slightly shorter than his right giving him a rolling gait. Brushing his dark hair from his eyes he stared up at the bridge.

Lyronn looked towards the bank and saw Blackleg limping down the sloping timber path towards the river. The black mud on the bank had been churned into a foul smelling quagmire by the men seeking water at the river's edge.

Bram looked down at the disgusting water and spat. Mercenaries were short-lived. If they weren't killed in battle or betrayed by their employer, they died of one of the all too many diseases which followed the campaigns like an unseen sword of pestilence killing all it touched.

'Vizard has sent me to hurry you up,' Blackleg shouted.

'One day, Blackleg, I will take that wooden leg of yours and shove it up your arse and set fire to it just to watch you hop around.'

'Words, Lyronn!' Blackleg called back. 'You still owe Vizard the money you borrowed to help that wife of yours.'

Bram felt rather than saw Lyronn stiffen.

'Why you'd throw good money after bad I don't know,' Blackleg laughed. 'It cost you enough to pay off her indenture to Vizard. I would have thought that was more than she was worth. But obviously she was better than I remember.'

Bram placed a hand on his friend's back. 'You borrowed money from that filth?'

'She was ill,' Lyronn whispered. 'I would have sold everything I owned, including my soul, if I could have made her well again.'

'Dead?'

Lyronn stared down at Blackleg. 'She owed Vizard money and he claimed her as payment. Then he gave her to Blackleg who treated her badly. One day my debt will be paid and then I'll entertain Blackleg handsomely and introduce him to some of the ways that seem to have been forgotten in these civilised times.'

The Cathars, robed and hooded, laboured down the ramp under the weight of the cargo. Blackleg had his thugs on hand to keep the watchers at bay as the precious cargo of spirits was unloaded. When the last keg had reached the stockpile the robed figures melted into the crowd and vanished from sight. Lyronn watched them disappear before turning his red-rimmed eye back to Blackleg.

On the edge of the bedlam there was a large camp of merchants waiting for their opportunity to cross the river. Not willing to pay the exorbitant prices charged by the Captains, they waited patiently for the mercenaries to move on. Tandra and Faina-lai approached the party and were met by cries of recognition.

A further thirteen Cathars would strengthen the merchants' camp considerably and they readily offered their hospitality to the party. With the increased numbers of Cathars the few mercenaries who had been lurking about the edge of the camp vanished.

Eight caravans with their merchants and servants with fifteen Cathars was one thing, but add another thirteen Cathars and the campsite was well above the reach of even the most foolhardy of mercenary companies.

Bram excused himself and wandered off in the direction of the noisy throng. He could not decide whether it was the noise or the smell which upset him most as he approached the temporary town.

Three drunken leather-clad mercenaries barred his path as he entered the camp.

'I'll be buggered,' the tallest one said, and then laughed. 'That's the ugliest woman I've ever seen.'

'That's no woman, Meran,' the largest grinned. He was wide shouldered and his upper arms were almost the size of his companions' legs. 'That's a man what likes to travel with women.'

'Well, well, well,' the smallest of them smirked. 'What's it like to be serviced by a different bitch every night?'

Bram lashed out with his right fist and smashed the man in the mouth, throwing him from his feet and into the side of a tent which collapsed under his weight. Curses and squeals erupted from within as the occupants tried to disentangle themselves.

'What's it like to have no teeth?' Bram snapped.

A second of the mercenaries made to step forward, but the beast of a man laid an arm across his chest. 'Now's not the time, Meran,' he whispered. 'See to Frapps.'

The words were not lost on Bram as he strode on.

In the centre of the seething mass there was a slightly raised area on which three red silk tents had been erected. Bram strode for the centre tent and was met by five Cathars. Their chain mail and leather chestplates were polished and well-kept and their visored eyes showed that they were ready to uphold their charter.

'I find you well?' Bram greeted.

The suspicion was replaced by surprise and then welcome smiles.

'I find you well?' one replied.

'Well met, Bram Onehand. What brings you to this corrupted place?' another of them asked. 'This place is not fit for beasts.'

'I am on charter,' Bram answered, 'and just passing through.'

'I wish our charters were reversed,' a third Cathar added. 'This place is tainted.'

'I wish to see Vizard,' Bram said.

'He's seeing no one.'

'He'll see me,' Bram explained.

One of the Cathars vanished into the largest of the tents.

'Have you had trouble?' Bram asked.

'Nothing a few broken bones didn't remedy.'

'Vizard will see you, but you must leave your weapons with us.'

Bram nodded. He slid his broadsword and knife

from his belt and ducked into the tent. The interior was decorated in light hangings and the air was sweet with incense. Vizard rested on a pile of cushions at the tent's rear. His golden hair was long, drawn back by a leather thong, and he wore a light long-sleeved mail under a sleeveless silken tunic. A beautifully crafted longsword rested naked across his knees. He was the same age as Bram but the years had been kinder to him.

'By the prophet, I'd thought you long dead,' he commented as Bram straightened.

'Hardly,' Bram answered. As he crossed the tent he kicked the silken cushions from his path.

'No ritual greeting for me?' Vizard faked a hurt tone. 'Has it been that long?'

'There was never any love lost between us, Vizard. You proved that years ago.' Bram raised his left hand slightly and the polished metal caught the light of the lamps.

'But it has helped in your reputation from what I've heard,' Vizard commented. 'Besides, it did not stop you from saving my life when those Jaeger were going to skin and gut me.'

Bram snorted.

'Perhaps you should have let them?'

'No,' Bram explained. 'Then I would have no reason to be here now.'

'Ah! Payment time.' Vizard grinned.

'What is your life worth, Vizard?'

'What is it you want?'

'Lyronn's debt marked paid in full.'

'You always were a loyal friend, Bram.' Vizard sighed. 'All right, his debt is cleared and we are now even.'

146

Bram turned and left the tent without a backward glance. As he passed the five Cathars one whispered: 'Watch your back.'

In the tent Vizard raised a finger and Blackleg appeared from the shadows.

'Do you want him slain, Master?' he asked.

Vizard nodded. 'But make it quick. We were once the best of friends, and one does not want one's friends to suffer.'

'Yes, Master.' Blackleg hesitated, as if lost in thought.

'And I would advise that you take a dozen of those large brainless idiots with you.'

'A dozen, Master?'

'Bram was something special in his youth. And I doubt that time has tempered his anger.'

Blackleg bowed deeply. As he left the tent, Vizard's steward handed him a small purse to pay the men who would be needed. Blackleg had amassed a small fortune in his dealings with Vizard and was always alert for any chance of increasing it. Tying the purse to his belt, he signalled for two men to join him. Pay for two to do the job and keep the rest. Three of them should be more than a match for a one-handed drunk.

Bram chose a different route through the tents as he strode quickly towards the welcome fires of the merchants' camp. A shadow appeared from his left and Bram slashed out with his 'left hand', taking the attacker across the throat. Warm blood spattered Bram's face as a gurgling sound echoed from the shadows.

Another figure rose almost directly in Bram's path and revealed itself as the beast of a mercenary he had encountered earlier.

'Frapps is dead,' the huge man said. 'That blow of yours snapped his neck. And by the sound of it, Meran has not fared any better.'

'Then it seems you are the only one left,' Bram whispered.

'Not quite.' The voice was soft and Bram had heard it before.

The club wielded by Blackleg struck Bram on the shoulder instead of the head and he was simply thrown off balance rather than knocked unconscious. His left shoulder was numb but he dropped to one side and snapped a kick out at the legs of the big mercenary. The crunch of bone and a gasp of pain brought a smile to Bram's lips.

Straightening himself quickly, Bram reached out and took the mercenary's head in his right arm and twisted it. The neck snapped with a dry sound, like the breaking of a twig. The speed and savagery of Bram's attack had stunned Blackleg, who still stood to one side.

Bram stepped forward and Blackleg held up his hands. 'Vizard will pay you well if I am returned unhurt,' he pleaded.

'What is it now?' Lyronn asked as he saw Bram approaching. 'That bastard Blackleg learned of your passage and has demanded a cut of the fee or he'll inform Vizard.'

Bram grunted under the weight of the sack he carried as he climbed the ramp and dropped his load unceremoniously to the deck. Then he stood up and began massaging his left shoulder where the club had struck.

'Your debt to Vizard is paid,' he offered.

Lyronn made to protest but Bram stopped him. 'Call it a wedding present to you from an old friend.'

Lyronn was taken aback by the statement.

'And here is a present for your late wife. I only wish I had been able to meet the woman who captured you.'

He left the vessel without another word.

Lyronn stepped forward and nudged the sack with the toe of his boot. A muffled cry escaped the sack and a smile crossed the Captain's face. Then the smile turned to tears. As he saw his friend disappear into the darkness he lowered his eyes once more to the sack at his feet.

'Cast off!' he cried gleefully.

'But the sun has set,' his first mate offered.

'I can see that, you idiot,' Lyronn shouted. 'You think me blind? Now cast off and be quick about it. I have an appointment mid-river that has been a long time coming.'

Vizard sat alone in his tent as the first echo of the scream reached the tent town. It rose and fell and almost vanished before it increased once more to its full pitch. Vizard nodded in satisfaction. Whoever was manipulating the victim was a true master at his work, Vizard thought, and it brought a smile of professional pride to his lips.

9

IMPOSTERS

Fallon and Kallem were scouting well ahead of the party when they saw the column of smoke swirling upward from the ridge in front of them. They took cover behind a clump of fallen ash trees as Fallon strung her bow and slipped the cover from the quiver.

Taking his cue from Fallon, Kallem removed his shield from his left shoulder and slipped his left arm through the straps, pulling them tight with his teeth. He licked his lips nervously as he slid the longsword from his belt and tested its edge on his thumb.

Fallon stretched up over the trunk of the fallen tree and searched the ridge line for any sign of movement. Kallem slipped several paces from his companion and, looking up, saw the first of the crows as they spiralled down.

Kallem spat and, turning his back on Fallon, made the sign of the fist across his chest. As a lad he had seen the sign made many times by the older boys and men of his village. Not wanting to show his ignorance, he had never asked its true meaning. But on the night he was to leave home he approached his father, judging it the right moment to ask him about the Slayer. Kallem learnt that the Slayer was a being which haunted the Land of the Dead, waylaying travellers on the long journey to the many other worlds.

It was once believed that making the Sign of the Slayer in the face of evil or bad luck was a brief prayer to the Slayer, preparing your way for the perilous journey across the Land of the Dead.

The Death Crow was the worst omen a person could see. In a dream it meant approaching death, and when seen in the distance it meant certain death. The Death Crows were a large black form of Aves, like the ones found on the Steppes of Calcanth. Unlike their earth-bound cousins, they were covered in wide black feathers and their powerful wings could lift them to a height well beyond the sight of man.

But even soaring so high, the Death Crows missed nothing below them. They came to ground only to feed and nest and on the open plains they were feared above all else. Even the great cats which roamed many of the northern plains fled at the first shadow which rolled across them.

'Kallem!'

Fallon gestured towards the ridge with her bow. Kallem nodded and made for a low clump of bushes, then veered right. He dropped to his belly just short of the crest of the ridge and worked his way forward. At the crest he peered down the ridge at a scene of carnage.

Wagons burned fiercely and sections of smoking canvas rose on the warmed air, dancing above the fires like miniature Death Crows. About the wagons were strewn the bodies of at least fifty people of various ages. They were twisted in death, and many had been pierced by more than a dozen long-shafted arrows.

Chests and crates lay open between the wagons and Kallem could make out the slashed food sacks. Whoever had raided the undefended party had not been interested in plunder. Murder had been the only thing on their minds as they butchered the innocents.

Kallem waved to Fallon, who quickly joined him, and they moved cautiously down the gentle slope of the ridge. Fallon nocked an arrow and drew it back partway, ready to complete her drawing and release in one motion. Kallem raised his shield and peered nervously over its steel rim as he reached the scene of carnage.

Young children were sprawled in death beside their parents, most of them grouped between two of the wagons. Around them were scattered the mutilated bodies of their menfolk.

Fallon circled the bodies several times before she straightened and released the tension on her bowstring. Glancing up at the circling Death Crows, she watched as first one than another slowly turned on one wing and glided off towards the horizon. They must have fed recently, for the sight of two intruders would not have stopped them landing and feeding on the corpses.

Fallon moved about the fallen, kneeling occasionally to examine a print or disturbance to some rock or branch. She made several circuits before she stopped and pointed with her longbow.

'There were about twelve of them,' she commented before turning her attention back to the bodies. 'All professionals by the looks of it, and well practised at this sort of thing. They came in from the south-east, paused, and then struck the wagons. They were allowed to get in quite close before the first blood was spilt, so it seems these poor people had no idea they were in danger. It even looks as if several of the men went out to greet their murderers.'

'How long ago?' Kallem asked.

'About two hours, maybe less.' Fallon pointed to the north-west. 'They headed off that way and they weren't in any particular hurry.'

'Why should they be?' Kallem snapped. 'The bastards made sure that there were none left here to follow them.'

Fallon moved further out from the corpses and started a swing around the wagons in the hope of learning more about the attackers. Kallem returned to the ridge and signalled the remainder of the party to approach.

It took the rest of the afternoon to bury the dead and the sun had set before the party lifted their packs and left the burned-out wagons. They would set up their night camp far beyond the destruction of the small party. Even with the corpses buried there would still be the normal nocturnal predators, attracted by the scent of death.

The Death Crows had remained on the wing all afternoon, circling an unseen spot on the horizon. The Cathars placed extra sentries that night and kept an eye on the large birds as they circled, and the terrain about the camp.

There were stories of raiders massacring one caravan only to lure a second and larger one into its grasp. But foremost in the sentries' thoughts was the fact that one of the Death Crows could be down on them in an instant. They also knew that the Death Crows would come to ground once they had left the site and uncover the bodies with only a few strokes of their powerful talons. By then they hoped to be some distance from the graves, and only Fallon offered the scene behind them a glance as they strode off.

The bodies had belonged to the Saphy, a nomadic tribe of religious extremists who believed the land held all they needed to know about their Gods. Continual travel would one day take them to a special place where the secrets of extended life would be found. They were skilled tradespeople and the metalwork they peddled was greatly valued.

They generally roamed the plains but were sometimes found as far east as the Steppes, where they were used by the larger landowners as labourers during the harvest months. They were very rarely armed, and the few weapons they might have carried would have been of little use against their killers.

The Saphy wore small gems, Sardius, about their throats as a sign of their devotion to the land. Before the dead had been buried, Fallon searched the bodies but had found none of the gems. Their absence affected Fallon even more than the bodies they had just buried. The gems were small and she had never seen one worth more than an Imperial in all her travels. Perhaps they were worth stealing, but they were never worth the cost in lives that Fallon had just witnessed.

Fallon had been raised in a small village along the Eutha River. As a child she had watched the multi-coloured Saphy wagons as they approached across the open plains bordering her village. She had watched too as the Saphy children ran madly between the wagons while the adults set up for the bartering to follow.

Fallon had never been allowed to mix with the Saphy children but she had sat for hours at a time and watched them play. She had taken to the road when she had come of age, aching to be rid of her way of life and to see some of the sights the Saphy must have encountered on their travels.

The coastal town of Brisk was alive with merchants and its small secure harbour was filled with every type of vessel imaginable. Coastal schooners sat close inshore, their crews toiling to load supplies brought from the brimming warehouses. The food was bound for Sytry and then Hardwick, where it would be used to feed the massed forces of Obira and Ceruss.

Triremes and biremes filled the outer harbour as scores of longboats scurried to and fro like water beetles, slowly filling their huge holds. Some of the triremes carried fightingmen on their upper decks and were clearly ready to sail once their supplies had been taken on board.

Well out beyond the protected waters of the

harbour the warships of Ceruss were prowling, eager eyes turned to seaward watching for the first glimpse of sail or flash of reflected light. The Cerussian fleet was huge, but it was spread along the coast of Kyrthos in an attempt to protect its merchant shipping.

The raiders of Bezoar edged their way north along the coast, preying on any shipping they encountered. If the Captain of a captured vessel was not willing to take a southerly heading and unload his cargo in one of Bezoar's ports, then he and his vessel were considered an enemy and the vessel was put under a skeleton crew.

Tandra found an inn willing to take them and they were soon taken to their rooms. Brisk was one of the new towns which were sprouting up across Kyrthos, which boasted little law and large profits. As yet none of them had petitioned to the Charter Houses for one to be built and the Cathars, not liking what they had seen of them, had not offered to build any.

After their evening meal, Fallon, Phaidra and Cerise wandered the town. At the docks they watched in wonder as the activity of the day continued into the night. Huge braziers filled the air with an acrid stench and threw a half-light across the docks. Phaidra found a noisy tavern in one of the side streets off the dock and the three entered its smoky interior.

Approaching the bar they ordered their drinks and sipped at them as they surveyed the room. Most of the occupants were seamen, but there were also a few rough-dressed officers of the local militia and three leather-clad Cathars.

Fallon made her way through the crowd towards

the Cathars, who were drinking and laughing loudly. As she reached the table one of them looked up, her mouth hanging open as she saw the shell medallion about Fallon's neck.

One of the Cathars seated at the table was a drunken male, his long matted hair held back by a leather band which seemed to cut deep into his forehead. The other two were women in their early twenties, one of whom wore her hair short, and had a face streaked with grime. The other sat wide eyed as she watched Fallon approach.

'I find you well?' Fallon called above the din of the room.

The three looked at each other before one of them nodded and they returned to their drinking. Retracing her path to the bar, Fallon ordered another drink for herself, although this time she did not touch it when it arrived.

'They are not Cathars,' she whispered. 'They are dressed like us, and each wears a shell medallion, but they are not of our kind.'

'Why would they pretend to be Cathars?' Phaidra wondered.

'You're not joining your friends?' A tall greasy-haired man had approached the trio on the far side of the bar. 'They have been here for some time,' he added. 'There were more of them but the others lost interest in the place once they'd sold their gems.'

'Gems?' Fallon snapped.

'Yes,' the tall fellow answered as he wiped his filthy hands on his apron. 'They came in earlier with a good number of Sardius gems. I gave them a good price for them and then all but those three left.'

Fallon turned her back on the barkeep and he

wandered off down the bar still trying in vain to scrub the dirt from his hands on his apron.

'So that was how they were able to get so close to those poor Saphy,' Cerise offered.

'They were dressed like Cathars,' Phaidra added angrily. 'And in this lawless region a Cathar would be treated like a messenger of the Life Bringer. It would mean at least one night of safety.'

'Shall we tell the others?' Cerise asked.

'There is no time,' Fallon answered. 'They could leave at any time.'

Fallon glanced across at the table just as one of the three looked up. Their eyes met and for a brief instant there was understanding. Leaping to her feet, the short-haired imposter made for the door. Cerise pushed herself off from the bar and blocked her way while Phaidra and Fallon moved towards the other two.

The drinkers realised that something was wrong and a deep silence settled over them as they watched. The short-haired female made a grab for her sword but Cerise kicked it from her hand the moment it was free of her scabbard and whipped hers up. The man leapt to his feet, not as drunk as Fallon had thought, and hurled his mug at Phaidra before drawing his sword.

Fallon blocked a blow aimed at her head by the third imposter and sent a backhand slash across her attacker's chest. The tip of her sword skated across her opponent's mail shirt before she could bring her arm round and aim another blow at Fallon's head.

Phaidra met the attack of the male with her shortsword raised and her knife held low in her left hand. He lunged at her but she turned his blade aside and stepped in close, stabbing upward as she did so. The knife slipped into his groin just below his mail shirt and his sword dropped from his fingers. He slipped to the ground, trying desperately to staunch the flow of blood.

Cerise ducked under a wild swing and stabbed upward, catching her attacker off guard. Following up her advantage she put pressure on the woman until she backed into a table. Momentarily distracted, she failed to see Cerise's strike until it punched its way through her leathers and entered her chest.

Fallon's opponent dropped her sword and stood still, her arms by her side and her eyes wide with fright. A startled cry from Phaidra drew Fallon's attention back to Cerise. Five more women dressed as Cathars entered the bar. At the sight of two of their number down four of them turned and fled at once, while the fifth drew her sword and struck out at Cerise.

Cerise was turning just as the narrow point of the smallsword entered her throat and her movement caused the sword to bite deeper, then tear itself from her throat in a spray of blood. The short-haired imposter made for the door but staggered and fell as one of Fallon's knives took her low in the back.

Cerise's killer stood her ground by the door, a long shadow falling across her upper face as she surveyed the room. She was also dressed as a Cathar, in light leathers over chain mail, a shell medallion about her neck. Her eyes were large and dark, accented by swirling tattoos, but her features were hidden by the shadow.

She raised her right hand and clenched it across her chest, index and little finger extended in a northern variant of the Sign of the Slayer. With a silent laugh she turned and vanished into the street. A throwing knife struck the door frame just as the imposter turned, missing her by a hair's width.

Fallon was fuming as she turned and faced the injured imposter. Phaidra rushed across the room and knelt by Cerise's side.

'She's dead,' she called.

With a growl of rage more animal than human, Fallon flicked out her blade and opened the throat of the terrified woman. Before the body struck the floor she crossed to where the injured male lay, his bloodied hands pressed firmly to his groin. Without pausing, she grasped the man by his filthy hair and cut his throat too. Phaidra tore the shell medallions from the throats of the three imposters and dropped them to the floor, crushing them beneath her boot.

Phaidra and Fallon lifted Cerise and carried her from the tavern. There was no sign of the imposters in the street and they were not interrupted as they made their way back to their inn.

A scream burst the silence and Tandra threw herself from her bed just as the door to her room crashed open. Two figures rushed into the room, the blades of their knives glinting in the half light. Tandra whipped her blanket from the bed and threw it at one, tangling her as she rushed forward.

Dropping quickly to the ground, Tandra lashed out with her foot and grunted in satisfaction as she felt it make contact with her attacker's knee. A sharp cry answered her attack but Tandra was already moving as the second assailant neared.

There was no time to draw her sword and, in the confines of the room, it would have put her at a disadvantage. Grabbing a chair, she crashed it across her attacker's head and then leapt for her throat. The feel of a coarse beard told Tandra that this attacker was male. Throwing her assailant onto his back, she dropped a knee into his stomach and, grasping his head by his greasy hair, drove it down hard against the floorboards.

A shadowy figure rolled on the floor by the door, one leg folded up against its chest. Snatching up her attacker's knife, Tandra crossed to where the figure lay and quickly dispatched her.

Taking up a second knife, Tandra leapt for the hall. She could hear fighting coming from the rooms along the hall and suddenly a door splintered and two struggling shapes crashed headlong into the hall.

Kathryn blocked a hand holding a wicked blade and drove her forehead against her attacker's nose, smashing it. Blinded by blood, her attacker lost some of her eagerness and Kathryn maintained the initiative with a knee to the stomach. Wrenching the knife from her hand Kathryn drove it deep into the woman's chest and then turned.

Tandra saw the look of triumph turn to pain as a shadow darted from another room and buried a knife deep into Kathryn's back. The shadow took off down the hall, pausing only at its end.

Tandra was by Kathryn's side in a heartbeat but the young Cathar was already dead, her blood staining the old timber floor of the hall.

In the half light of dawn streaming in through the open window, Tandra saw a tall powerfully built woman. Her hair was pale and short and she wore only a light leather breastplate and kirtle. Her legs and arms were free and Tandra noted the dark tattoos which decorated her upper face and surrounded her eyes. The woman at the window paused and raised a hand in salute before disappearing from sight.

Bram appeared, his sword and trident bloodied. He and Tandra searched the rooms and found more of the imposters. Most of them were dead, but a few still clung to life. Bram questioned them, none too gently, but it was obvious that they were not going to speak. Whoever had hired them had filled them with a fear far beyond the threats offered by Bram. As a sign to all others who might think of portraying themselves as Cathars, Tandra ordered the injured assailants dispatched.

Amongst the bodies they also found Lealia-shey. The Crafter had been stabbed in her sleep, a fate which might have befallen all of them if not for the scream which had alerted them. Lealia-shey's shell medallion was missing, taken by her killer.

In the last room searched they found a Saphy youth. The young girl explained that she had been the sole survivor of the attack on her family and had followed the killers to Brisk.

Her hands were bloodied and at her feet was a short-bladed curved dagger. Beside the dagger lay one of the imposters, her throat cut. Tandra could not help but notice the other injuries the girl sported.

Tandra tore a sheet from the bed and covered the young girl's hands. 'It was you who warned us!'

162

The young woman nodded as she tried to wipe the blood from her hands without looking down at them.

'I am Yahudah,' she announced. 'I followed this one here and, when she was not looking, I cut her. She screamed and I was scared. Then she turned on me and I was forced to cut her again. When she fell to the floor I knelt beside her and cut her throat. All my life I was brought up to believe that violence was wrong. Yet now my family is dead and I have killed.'

'We are all forced to do things we do not like,' Tandra said by way of consolation. 'It might be best if you were to come with us.'

Yahudah nodded.

The bodies of Cerise, Kathryn, and Lealia-shey and all their possessions were taken from the town in the early morning and buried in unmarked graves in a small hollow protected by a ring of young pines. Theirs had been senseless deaths and many of the party insisted that they stay and find those responsible.

'Cerise knew the dangers she faced when she took to the road,' Faina-lai explained. 'And Lealia-shey and Kathryn were killed in a cowardly attack that will not go unavenged. But for now we have a charter to fill and they would be sad if they knew their deaths led us astray.'

'But their killers must be punished,' Ferne pleaded.

'They will be,' Tandra insisted. 'Not only for the death of Cerise and the others, but for the massacre of the Saphy. In these times we Cathars are the only true balance people still have. While we function normally, going about our tasks and charters, there will remain a slight balance in the lands. But if this atrocity is allowed to go unpunished, then more will try.'

'Then what are we to do?' Mahira asked.

'We will journey to Erlan as we had planned,' Bram promised. 'And there we will tell the Elders of the Charter House and allow them to make the decisions. Our new companion, Yahudah, will accompany us.'

All agreed, though most would rather have sought the slayers of their companions.

Tandra separated herself from her companions and tried to suppress her anger and her sorrow. She thought about what she had said about Cathars providing the only true balance people still had and she knew she was right.

For centuries the Cathars strode the many roads of Kyrthos, protecting the innocent and poor while aiding the rich and merchant classes. They had always been looked upon to uphold the law and in many towns their Charter House was also the seat of justice. But should it be known that imposters were abroad, then the Cathars' rule would be severely weakened.

Two weeks later the party reached the outskirts of Erlan. Footsore and tired, they made for the centre of town and the waiting Charter House. As they entered the street holding the entrance they found a large crowd of angry townsfolk shouting insults and waving their fists in the air.

Faina-lai slowed the party but ordered them to keep moving towards the entrance of the Charter House. As they reached the edge of the crowd they were seen for the first time and a cry rose above the shouting.

'Murderers, thieves!' The cry was taken up by more and more of the crowd until the entire street rang with the accusations.

Angry faces confronted the party as they continued to move slowly towards the entrance of the Charter House. At first it looked as if the crowd would refuse to let them pass, but as Tandra and Bram reached the first of the shouting townsfolk they parted and the party moved on.

Surrounded by the noise, the party looked about nervously for the first sign of trouble that could herald the death of many. The crowd was largely unarmed, but some weapons appeared above the shouting mob. Those in the rear tried to push forward while those at the front pushed back, not wishing to be any closer to the Cathars than necessary. As the crowd swayed back and forth one of the noisiest of the protesters fought his way up to the Cathars and raised a staff above his head as if to strike Sian-vesna.

Bram grabbed the youth by his tunic and pulled him off balance. Ferne chopped him across the wrist, loosening his grip on the staff, and Tandra grabbed him by the scruff of the neck and drew him close. Holding the youth like a shield Tandra increased her pace through the crowd, the rest of the party following close on her heels.

As they reached the Charter House the huge double doors opened. Several of the retired veterans appeared, wearing armour which had not seen the light of day for years. Tandra stepped to one side and allowed the party to pass her before stopping in front of the open door, her protester still gripped tightly by his crumpled tunic.

'What is the meaning of this?' Tandra shouted above the din. 'Why are you here?'

'Murderers, thieves!' shouted those at the rear of the crowd.

'Who accuses us?' Tandra called back. 'Put away your weapons and step forward to be heard.'

Most of the crowd fell silent and turned to face a small group on their edge.

'Don't deny it,' one of them cried angrily. 'I saw Cathars attack my caravan on the plains of Scapol two months ago. I hid in the long grasses and watched as they butchered the entire caravan.

'It took me weeks to get out of Scapol and longer still to make my way here. Then what am I told? That it could not have been Cathars and that I am either mistaken or lying.'

An angry murmur rose from the crowd as they turned their attention back to Tandra and the struggling youth.

'On the southern plains of Scapol,' Tandra began, 'we found a clan of Saphy who had been killed, apparently massacred by a band of Cathars.'

The crowd surged forward and Tandra was forced to hold the youth before her as stones flew from the rear of the crowd.

'But they were not Cathars,' Tandra shouted above the angry rumbling.

'When we entered Brisk three of our number stumbled on a group of the imposters. Three of them were slain, but one of our number was also killed. Later we were attacked by the remaining imposters. They hoped to silence us so that word of their deeds would not reach any Charter House. They knew that we would not rest until all had been made to pay for their actions.

'Six more of their number were killed, but again the cost was high. Two more of us perished under the blades of the imposters.'

'Words,' came a cry from the shadows. 'Mere words. Where is your proof?'

'I am their proof,' Yahudah said as she stepped forward to stand beside Tandra. While Tandra was tall and muscular Yahudah barely reached her chest. The young Saphy was thin and her hair was long and straggly and covered half her face. Her skin was tanned a healthy gold from her years of travel.

'I survived the massacre of my family,' she explained. 'I was on a distant ridge when I heard the fighting. As I reached the scene I saw the last of my family cut down and the attackers destroy all their possessions. They took nothing save the Sardius gems my people wear and the few coins some of us were carrying, and then they were gone.

'I followed them to Brisk, where I lost them in the crowds, but I continued to search for them. I located them just as they sprang their ambush on Tandra and the other Cathars. Believe me. I am here to tell you that the killers were dressed like Cathars, but they were not Cathars.'

The crowd had settled down and some of them were even turning to leave when the same voice rose from the shadows. 'All well and good to have a trained Saphy, but we are talking of real people. Can you prove that it was the same party that was responsible for both attacks?'

'If you would like to enter the Charter House,' Bram called from the open doors. 'I'm sure we can satisfy even you.'

The crowd turned to wait for an answer, but no further sound came from the shadows and the crowd slowly dispersed.

'That's twice you have helped us,' Tandra said to Yahudah.

'You buried my family,' she answered. 'I had no time to do it if I was to follow their killers, and I am still indebted to you.'

10
RAISSA

Charybdis paced the floor of the Lychgem's chamber, wondering if what he had done was right. When he sent the Cathars he had chartered through Sian-vesna south to the Foxglove Tower he had known that it would be protected if it still possessed any of its ancient power. The wraith there had been weak, but it had carried out its role well, leading to the apparent slaying of Tarynn. But Charybdis had woven an illusion before the Cathars and the real Tarynn rested safely in the tower. Because of his youth it was easy to convince him of Charybdis' role as a benefactor.

Now, with the Foxglove and Hawkthorn Towers linked, Charybdis felt a little safer. It was one less tower he had to concern himself with. Tarynn now controlled Foxglove's growth as it drew strength from the Hawkthorn Tower, but the ancient tomes in Charybdis' library revealed the names of other towers that could pose a potential threat. The face he had seen in the Lychgem still hung before

Charybdis and he waited for the inevitable to happen. Both he and his unknown opponent sought the remaining towers.

But perhaps what concerned Charybdis even more was a second reference he had found to Lychgates. It was a bit more detailed, but it still only said that Lychgates represented a great threat.

Charybdis had contacted Sian-vesna whenever he needed information on her party's progress and had been distressed to learn of the deaths of Lealiashey, Cerise and Kathryn. He had not known these Cathars, but their deaths worried him. What is more, he had no idea if their deaths were linked to the towers.

What Charybdis needed was insurance. He knew that one of his Yclad could journey to the Monkshood Tower and meet up with the party when it arrived. But would the imprisoned wraith be an aid or a hindrance? The power emanating from the Yclad would be enough to draw any opposition towards the party. No, he needed something different.

Charybdis descended the spiral stairs to his private chamber, where one of the Yclad awaited him. He had perfected his mind control over the wraiths as he had over Asal, and now allowed them to serve him in the tower. Asal was at first disturbed by their presence but had grown used to the company.

A raid on the tower's armoury had allowed Charybdis to supply his Yclad with either huge double-bladed axes, two handed broadswords or massive war hammers. No ordinary fightingman could have wielded the combined weights of the weapons and armour but his wraiths managed it easily. Charybdis had wondered briefly about who might have wielded the weapons for the previous masters but then his thoughts returned to his problem.

Tireless and obedient, the Yclad protected the inner city from all intruders. Charybdis had no idea of how many treasure hunters might have reached the city over the years, but it was obvious that none before him had succeeded as he had and discovered the power it had to offer.

At about the same time that Tarynn faced the wraith on the stairs of the Foxglove Tower, Charybdis sent his armoured wraiths into the outer city with orders to destroy or evict any living thing they came across. It was Charybdis' hope that he would soon be able to draw people to the northern city and open its gates once more to a living population willing to work for the city and, of course, for Charybdis, its master.

Charybdis leaned his staff against the polished table and began his midday meal. Bohe stood silently in the background, always ready to fulfil Charybdis' wishes. By using the power of the Lychgem, Charybdis had managed to learn a smattering of Bohe's language, but still could not learn where he came from or if there were any more like him.

As always, Asal hovered in the background throwing nervous glances from one Yclad to another. Its soft whistling filled the circular chamber and Charybdis smiled as he ate his fill. After all the hardships he had faced to reach this city and the tower at its heart, he could never have imagined the power he would command. He stroked the staff and allowed his smile to broaden into a laugh which filled the tower and continued until tears began to run down his cheeks.

Gasping for air, he steadied himself against the table. More and more often, his emotions released themselves in uncontrollable bursts. One day he had found himself kicking out at a stationary Yclad when the creature had not moved from his path fast enough. Now here he sat, laughing for no good reason.

Charybdis rose unsteadily from the table and, taking up his staff, he climbed to the uppermost room. Resting both hands upon the gem, he closed his eyes and allowed his breath to slow. As he eased his mind into the heart of the Lychgem, all that concerned him was his future as Master of the Hawkthorn Tower.

He found himself in a small eight-sided chamber, each of whose crystal walls was suffused with a different pulsating colour. The light was not bright but it was sufficient to illuminate the chamber. As he slowly turned and studied each of the walls he knew that he was still standing in the upper room of his tower, his eyes closed, his hands resting upon the Lychgem, but the vision before him was so real that he could almost imagine he had been drawn into the gem, standing in the master facet.

Each wall, as well as the floor and ceiling, represented another of the many abilities of the Lychgem. Through one of its facets, he had used the power of the gem to contact those he needed to aid him. And through another of the facets he had felt the first awareness from another of the towers, while through yet another he had met and enslaved the wraith of the Foxglove Tower.

Looking down at the reflection at his feet, Charybdis saw himself as he had been when he had entered the gem. He wore a cloak of the finest silk decorated with strands of woven silver and gold. Upon his right breast was a strange design in silver. It was in the shape of a man, yet blurred and almost unrecognisable. It was in fact the wraith he had imprisoned in his robe during his brief venture into the city.

Trapped by the cantrips locked within the silver threads of the cloak, the wraith awaited its release. Charybdis would never know cold or excessive heat again as the power of the wraith protected him. This was the Charybdis of today.

When he looked up Charybdis saw himself in the ceiling. This time he saw the Charybdis of old, a sweat-lathered blacksmith plying his trade over the open coals of his forge. He was not as finely attired as the Charybdis at his feet but there was a healthy glow about the image as he toiled over the glowing metal he dragged from the fire.

Stepping towards one wall Charybdis found himself facing another image of himself. The figure was also robed, but the robe bore many more silver inlaid decorations revealing other imprisoned servants who awaited his call. The wall radiated a faint golden hue which gave Charybdis the impression that he was surrounded by wealth.

Moving slightly to his right Charybdis found himself staring deeply into a grey shrouded landscape. There were shadows in every corner and the horizon was lost in a blood-red glow. As his eyes became adjusted to the dim light Charybdis saw a figure standing in the distance. Again, the figure was robed, but the aura of wealth the other robed figure had commanded was gone.

Instead of riches and golden light there were only long deep shadows. The figure was totally alone, isolated. Not caring for the scene before him, Charybdis drew in a breath and looked deeper. The lonely figure was indeed he. Gone were the protective wards which had decorated his cloak, instead it was as grey as the landscape which surrounded him.

Then Charybdis noticed the eyes, and with a stifled cry fled the facet. He shook as he opened his eyes and found himself standing before the Lychgem once more. The memories of the strange faceted chamber haunted him. He had been reminded of the difference between what he had been and what he now was. And the golden facet had shown him a future of wealth. But the shadow facet had shown him a bleak and lonely time ahead.

Worst of all, he could still see the eyes of the poor wretch in the shadows. Deep-set and dark-ringed, they were filled with a suffering beyond belief. Was this also to be his future? Did all of the facets hold a similar scene? And if so, would each of the futures come to pass or only one prevail?

The party of Cathars rested at Erlan for five days, gathering their strengths and steadying their convictions. They would continue with the charter to find the Monkshood Tower, but they would do it without further aid. The Elders of the Charter House of Erlan and of those of the surrounding lands had decided that the imposters posed a greater immediate threat to their existence than the towers. Tandra was to take the remaining members of the original party to seek out the Monkshood Tower.

'And you believe that the towers are truly more important than finding the imposters?' Tandra asked. 'Even though the Elders believe otherwise?'

Faina-lai nodded. 'The imposters will cause us a great deal of trouble in the coming months unless we can put an end to them. But the towers are just as deadly a threat. The Foxglove Tower was thought to be destroyed and we found it otherwise when we sought it out. Only, some of the Elders can't see that!'

'But a large party was to be sent to the Foxglove Tower from Sytry,' Tandra added. 'Surely they have destroyed it by now?'

'Yes,' Faina-lai confirmed. 'They reached the tower some time ago. However, their efforts to enter it were thwarted by another of the shrouded killers.'

'But the wraith was destroyed,' Tandra argued. 'Sian-vesna destroyed it after it slew Tarynn.'

'That might be so,' Faina-lai continued. 'But when the party reached the tower they were confronted by another, and stronger, wraith. None of the Crafters was able to destroy it.'

'But . . .?'

'There is more,' Faina-lai interrupted. 'The tower is now twice the height it was when you visited it, and the small plant at its base now totally covers its outer stonework. Even during the hours of daylight, when the wraith could not leave the tower, it was impossible to gain entry. The stairway was filled with a barrier of tearing cold which stopped all attempts.'

'How is that possible?'

'We believe that another tower has been entered by one or more beings who have gained control of the power pent up within its heart. Whoever it is has managed to feed power into the Foxglove Tower and help it recover from its centuries of deprivation.'

'Then why do we help by seeking out the remaining towers?' Tandra questioned.

'When we find the Monkshood Tower we are to ensure that it does not become a threat.'

'How is this to be done?' Tandra asked.

'One of our number took the charter into the Hall of Business. As we near the tower we will ensure that she does not accompany us into the tower. Once there we will seek out any sign of a small green-grey plant growing at its base, and when we discover it we will destroy it.'

'The plant?'

'The plant is the Monkshood. That is how the tower received its name.'

The ten Cathars left Erlan well before the sun's rays had appeared above the eastern horizon. Still cloaked by night, they moved silently through the darkened streets. As they reached the edge of town the large gates were opened just enough to allow them to slip quietly through.

Without a pause or a backward glance, the party was soon well beyond the sight of the guards in the watchtowers to either side of the main gates. They had been paid well by the Cathars to allow the party to leave town early and none was willing to question why. Striding beside the Cathars was the small cloaked figure of Yahudah. The young Saphy had refused to be left behind, explaining that she still owed a debt to those who had buried her clan.

Tandra and Bram tried to talk the young girl out of accompanying them, but her mind was set.

A week later, at the southern tip of the Omena Fens, Faina-lai called the other Cathars about her and drew out a map which she spread on the ground and weighted down with several stones. Then she stood up, dusted off her knees, and examined the expectant faces staring at her.

'We search for the Monkshood Tower,' she explained, and pointed down to the map's top left hand corner. 'It is believed to lie somewhere north-west of the Belial, cut off from the rest of Kyrthos by the jungle and the off-shore reefs. Orren-ker has studied our problem and believes he has come up with a way of reaching the tower in the shortest time and with the least difficulties.'

Orren-ker stepped closer to the map and nodded at Faina-lai. 'I have consulted the information available to me through the gem of my medallion and have found mention of another tower called Snakeweed. It lies far from here in northern Scapol, and once our business is finished at that tower it would be an easy matter to reach the Custodians, a large cluster of mountains on the border between Scapol and Skarn and then travel downriver to the general region of the Monkshood Tower.'

'Is a detour wise?' Bram asked.

'I wonder that too,' Fallon added. 'Haven't we enough on our plate without adding more to it?'

177

'The Snakeweed Tower seems of little conse-
quence,' Mahira told them. 'It is the journey through
the Belial that we must deal with, and if we can
travel that dark jungle faster by river from the east
then I say so be it.'

'Couldn't we just make for the Custodians from
here, without seeking out another of these cursed
towers?' Kallem asked.

'The detour would be minimal,' Faina-lai offered.

'And the river passage through the Belial?'
Kallem pressed.

'It would make the journey through that shadowed jungle all the quicker and safer.'

'I'm for that,' Kallem stated firmly. 'I know of
several who dared the Belial, and none of them has
returned. If we must enter that infernal place, let us
pass through it as speedily as possible.'

'Couldn't we try the ocean route?' Phaidra
ventured. Ferne, standing beside her, nodded in
agreement.

'The reefs off the coast are fatal,' Bram explained.
'There is no known way through them, and the few
vessels with Captains mad enough to try to sail
round them have been lost in the savage storms
which lash the northern tip of Kyrthos most of the
year round.'

Sian-vesna sat silently beside Tandra. She knew
that the one who had chartered her would want
them to make all haste to the Monkshood Tower, but
if a detour meant the discovery of another tower,
perhaps he would be content.

'What are your thoughts, Tandra?' Sian-vesna
asked.

'I will abide by the decision of the party,' she

answered. Then she turned slightly towards Sian-vesna and whispered: 'We must speak.'

The two women moved away from the other Cathars. Once out of earshot, Tandra took Sian-vesna by the arm. 'Faina-lai believes there is one amongst us who has sided with whomever sent us on this charter.'

'But how?'

'I don't know,' Tandra whispered. 'I believe that the only way to reach the tower lies in travelling downriver, the coastal route is no option.'

'Then what?'

'If you, Faina-lai, Bram, Yahudah, Kallem and I seek out the Snakeweed Tower and journey west to the Monkshood while the others try the ocean approach, we will have rid ourselves of the possible traitor. Should the traitor raise her hand against the progress of the other party, we will still have a chance of reaching the Monkshood Tower.'

Sian-vesna only nodded, unable to say anything.

Finally it was decided that the party would divide. One group would take the detour and seek out the Snakeweed Tower before continuing their search, while the other would chance the frequent storms and risk a coastal route beyond the Belial.

Tandra climbed to the crest of a small ridge and watched as Orren-ker, Phaidra, Ferne, Mahira and Fallon disappeared from sight. She had appeared to oppose the idea of dividing the party but, seemingly without notice, she had proposed many good arguments to separate.

Turning her attention from the departing party, Tandra looked down from her vantage point and studied the small company which remained. Bram and Kallem stood deep in conversation while Sian-vesna, as always, sat well apart from the small band of Cathars. Faina-lai rested by the small campfire with Yahudah seated beside her.

Sian-vesna noticed Tandra watching them and wondered if she truly believed the traitor was in the other party. Traitor? Sian-vesna turned her attention back to Faina-lai as she sat before the fire. Tandra had mentioned that the old Crafter believed there was a traitor in the party. If only she could confide in her companions, then she could dispel this myth of treachery, but Charybdis had insisted that she say nothing about the charter.

Bram only half listened to Kallem. His throat was dry and he needed a drink more than life itself, but he had gone this far without one and he was not going to go back on his pledge now. He raised the water-skin and took a long drink of the cool water. Swilling some about his mouth, he spat it on the ground at his feet. It was a mistake to have brought the Saphy, she was too young. And that old Crafter Faina-lai was only going to slow them down. The sooner they reached the tower they sought, the sooner Bram would find out more about Tarynn's slayer.

The roads throughout eastern Skarn were for the most part deserted as Tandra and her party made good time towards the border. Farmers and share-croppers were busy with their harvest and many called out as the Cathars strode by, asking if they wished to earn two dulls a day working in the fields. Tandra thanked them for their offer and continued on.

Most of the workers had been lured away by tales of riches to be found in the fighting to the south. Tandra and the others knew that the tales of waiting treasures were false and that all that awaited the eager were hardships, hunger and possibly death.

They crossed the Eutha River by barge and spent their first night in Scapol, with the river to their backs. The small cluster of huts on either side of the river had been deserted, with only the bargemen and their families remaining.

Sian-vesna had travelled in silence, deeply disturbed by Tandra's words and Faina-lai's accusations. She had taken the charter to the Charter House and had helped in its undertaking. No matter how long she thought on the matter she did not consider herself a traitor. She was bound by law not to tell anyone of where the charter originated, but her fears grew daily nonetheless.

At the first opportunity she contacted Charybdis in the hope of learning more about Faina-lai's misconception, but he sat on his golden throne surrounded by his armoured guardians and simply laughed at her worries. He then explained that the traitor Faina-lai spoke about was not her and that she was to aid in the discovery of the person. Again, he assured her that she was not the one sought.

As the sun set the rough-dressed men moved closer to the outer huts, the sound of their movements covered by the sweeping wind which had sprung up during the afternoon. They had watched as the Cathars entered the deserted village and would have attacked at once if Raissa had not held them back.

Olsenn stopped and watched as his men moved closer to those they sought. Raissa and her companions had stayed behind in the shadowed depression of a small wash, but he could feel her eyes on his back. She was a strange one, Raissa. She wore the identifying tattoos of the Solanesse Deisol Cult, the Cult of Death whose worshippers believed that the sun died each day as it set, and that another was born to rise the following morning. Cult members believed that each time they died in the service of their Deis, their religious leader, they were reborn further up the Ladder of Life.

Solan was a cold barren northern land and very few visited it. Olsenn had passed through it many years ago and had learned a little of the cult when he sat out several months in one of the filthy cells of the local Lord. The cell next to his had held a Deisol member awaiting execution for the murder of a local merchant who, it seemed, had been cheating one of the isolated Shrines of Deisol.

This cult member was unimpressed by the threats of the Lord's men as they tried to learn whether he had acted alone or under orders of the Deis. In the weeks prior to the execution, Olsenn had been under the impression that his fellow prisoner was trying to convert him to the cult.

Olsenn paused and listened for any sound from the group of huts that indicated that he or his men had been heard by the travellers but he could hear nothing above the keening of the wind.

Raissa had offered enough Imperials for him to retire, should they succeed in their mission. He had not liked the thought of killing Cathars, who had a reputation for being fierce fighters. On the rare occasion when a Cathar fell, those of her Charter House always sought revenge. This did not promise the type of future Olsenn was planning for himself, but his group outnumbered the small company of Cathars three to one, and that was the type of odds he preferred.

Olsenn straightened slightly and a piercing bird call escaped his dry lips. Bunched tightly together, his men started forward. As one passed close to Olsenn he seemed to trip and, when he did not rise, Olsenn moved to his side and rolled him over. Protruding from his chest was a short-shafted quarrel. Olsenn bit back a curse as he spun round to face the huts.

The door of one of them burst open and figures rushed out. At once, the sound of clashing steel filled the area between the huts. Olsenn threw one nervous glance over his shoulder and then launched himself into the fighting.

Raissa and her three companions watched the proceedings from the safety of the gully. Tavira rose to go to the aid of those they had hired but Raissa placed a restraining hand upon her shoulder and drew her back into the shadows.

'They have been paid well for this night's work,' she explained. 'There are more than enough of them to gain victory.'

'And if they fall?' Tavira asked.

'Then we will need all our strength and wits to defeat the Cathars without aid.'

Taya and Yolane threw worried glances at one another. Raissa and Tavira were all who remained of the first mission sent south by the Deis. Yolane, Taya, and Elin had been sent to seek out Raissa and learn of her success. However, there had been little success and Raissa had sent Elin home with messages for the Deis. She had kept the other two with her, and they had found Olsenn and his bunch of cutthroats on the road as they followed the Cathars.

At first Olsenn had eyed Raissa and her companions as a worthwhile target, but some quick talking on Raissa's part convinced him that there was more to be made by helping them rather than killing them.

Tavira peered up over the edge of the gully and realised that Olsenn may well have been right in his decision to cut their throats and take what he had rather than risk his life and those of his men for more. Olsenn's band was faring badly and if Raissa did not leave the gully and throw the weight of her numbers behind him, he would surely lose.

'We must help them,' Tavira pleaded. Taya nodded her agreement while Yolane merely watched.

Raissa rose and Tavira released a pent-up sigh. Then, to her amazement, Raissa turned her back on the fighting and disappeared into the night, calling softly for the others to follow.

Tandra slipped a knife into the belly of her attacker, feeling the blade scrape against a rib. With a twist of the knife she pulled it free, stepping to one side as the figure before her collapsed. Bram knelt beside another figure and, sliding his trident beneath the struggling body, cut its throat.

A flick of his wrist sent droplets of blood spattering across the dusty ground. The sounds of fighting had eased and the deep silence of the night returned, locked beneath the sorrowful crying of the wind. Back at the small hut they shared, Tandra retrieved a lamp and brought it back with her. Kallem appeared round a corner, limping, a slight cut on his right thigh. The rest of the party made their way towards the light.

Tandra rolled the corpse of the closest attacker over with her foot and squatted beside the bloodied body. She took in the aged mismatched armour and the patches of rust decorating the shortsword.

'Nothing more than common bandits or cut-throats,' she stated matter-of-factly.

'But why did they pick such a miserable little village to attack?' Kallem asked. 'What could they possibly hope to find here?'

'Apart from us?' Bram added quickly.

'You think they were after us specifically?' Sian-vesna interrupted. 'You don't think it was an accident?'

'I don't know,' Bram replied. 'But if they were locals they would have known this village was long deserted.'

'And if they were not from around here?' Faina-lai pressed.

'Then what brought them here?'

Bram spat on the corpse at his feet and turned towards the hut. 'Whether accident or fate, there may be more of them about.'

Kallem moved to join Bram and Sian-vesna followed quickly, calling for him to show her his wound. Yahudah moved to Faina-lai's side. The old Crafter glanced down and smiled at the young girl.

'Get some rest,' she advised. 'We have a long way to go and will need our strength.'

Faina-lai and Tandra stood in the lamp's light and examined the body-strewn ground. The wind had increased during the fight, bringing a cold bite to the air, and Tandra shivered.

Finally Faina-lai broke the silence. 'It was no accident,' she whispered. 'I have no evidence to support that statement, but I feel deep down that they were looking for us.'

'Well, they found us,' Tandra pointed out. 'And they paid dearly for it.'

'But did they pay enough?' Faina-lai added.

11
DEISOL

Raissa sat before the small sheltered fire. Taya, Tavira, and Yolane were already rolled in the blankets, sleeping the sleep of the Believer. The cutthroats were no match for the Cathars, Raissa had known that, but she had hoped that the attack might have killed enough of them to make their charter seem impossible. Raissa had been fascinated by the fellowship of the road and had studied the Cathars for many years.

They were a strange breed of people dedicated to their cause as strongly as any Deisol was to the Deis. The Cathars protected those who were weaker, but accepted payment only from those who could afford to pay. They followed the path of the Cathars yet they worshipped many different religions and, though at most times their many lands were at war, they still worked side by side for the advancement of their beliefs.

Raissa drew the blanket tighter about her shoulder. The movement startled Tavira and in the dancing firelight the small swirling tattoos of her apprenticeship filled her pale face with colour. Swirling colours covered her eyelids and cheek bones like the extended wings of some exotic butterfly. And like the butterfly, the lives of a Deisol passed through many phases.

Upon Tavira's right temple were the twin wheels of life. Identical and interlocked, they represented the ever present life cycle of the wearer and of their god: birth, duty, death—the continual cycle of the Deisol.

Raissa lifted her right hand and touched her own tattooed eyes and twin wheels, allowing her fingers to trace the long narrow sword tattoos which rested in the centre of her forehead. The tip of the sword stopped just above the bridge of her nose. The sword was a badge of honour worn only by a few, but Raissa remembered the blood which had been spilt to gain the tattoo . . . and it had not been her blood which stained the grass floor of the forest. Her left temple held the all-seeing eye of a Disciple who had learnt the true nature of death through injury and lost companions.

In the years to come Tavira would also receive many more tattoos which she would continue to wear proudly. For now the only tattoos she wore were those of the Accepted and Apprentice. To follow would be those of a Disciple, an Adept, and finally a Believer. There were many other badges of courage and authority a skilled Deisol could gather. Of these, the greatest were those given in the presence of the Deis, the religious leader of the Deisol. None questioned her decisions and all bowed to her knowledge gained over a long lifetime of service to their God.

Raissa had been a follower of the Deis since she was old enough to walk the long path from her dormitory to the Hall of Investiture. There she had said nothing as she passed the large portals of the Hall and made her way to the raised dais beneath the magnificent golden sun. Its far-reaching rays radiated across the room ... gold leaf on the ceiling, silken banners inlaid with gold on the walls, and small hand-crafted golden tiles on the floor.

Raissa had walked the path of the setting sun and reached the dais, where she raised her tiny hands towards the golden sun. The Deis herself had been upon the dais that morning and she had smiled and offered her hand to the tiny child who climbed the tall steps to the dais.

It had been at the hands of the Deis that Raissa had received her tattoo of Acceptance. How proud she had been as she walked back to the dormitory to collect her pitifully few belongings. As one of the Accepted, she had slept with the children for the last time. Now she would sleep with her older sisters and brothers in the sparsely furnished rooms of the sect houses.

Raissa closed her eyes and allowed the small warmth of the fire to relax her. It had been another ten years before she had been summoned into the presence of the Deis once more, but that scene was etched deep in her memories.

'She is here, Holy Deis.'

'Allow her to enter and ensure we are not disturbed,' the Deis had ordered.

'By your will, Holy Deis.'

The Disciple backed from the room and motioned for Raissa to enter. As Raissa crossed the

189

threshold of the Hall of Investiture, the massive gold inlaid doors swung closed behind her and met with a gentle sound which echoed throughout the chamber. The Deis lifted her head from the parchment she had been studying and smiled.

'Come closer, Raissa,' she sang. The Deis had kept a close watch on the young Raissa for many years. There was something special about her that the Deis had recognised the first time they had met.

Raissa's excitement grew at the sound of the Deis' voice. It was not the tone the Deis adopted in speaking to one of the Accepted, Apprentices, Disciples, Adepts, or even Believers. Rather, it was the voice of a true follower speaking with another. Raissa almost sprang forward, her legs seemingly acting under a will of their own, and crossed to the table before the Deis.

'Look closely, Raissa,' the Deis crooned, and Raissa's eyes dropped briefly to the parchment. 'You will have need of the knowledge soon enough.'

It was an ancient map of northern Kyrthos showing the northern provinces of Skarn, Scapol, and Calcanth. Solan and the Belial were represented in great detail, as was the chain of islands and reefs off the western coast.

Raissa was attracted to several strange markings and searched the map for some reference to their meaning. But she could find none.

'They are the Living Towers of Kyrthos,' the Deis explained. 'This map was made by an Adept when the towers were at the height of their power. Note the slightly different spelling of the names and the increased size of the Belial.'

There was an island chain marked to the north of

Solan that was on none of the maps Raissa had ever seen. And the Belial stretched from the northern shores of Kyrthos well beyond the current boundary of the Custodians and merged with the Fens. Some of the rivers did not look quite right, but Raissa could not put her finger on exactly what was wrong with them. Scrawled in a dried red ink across the northern expanses of the map was the word 'Crataegus'.

Raissa raised her questioning eyes to the Deis, who smiled in return. That smile filled Raissa with a sense of well-being and devotion.

'What am I to do?'

'The occupiers of the towers are the long-time enemies of the Deisol. For many centuries the towers have sat lifeless, their masters long dead and their power diminished. But of late the towers have begun to stir from the long cold death. First it was simply the yearnings of the towers for the times past, when they ruled this land under a cloud of steel.

'We could learn nothing from our libraries and the Adepts we sent west never returned. But there's worse news. One such tower has wakened and has sent its strengthened call out to the others, trying to draw any to its cause.

'By using greed as its bait and power as its net, it hopes to regain the status it has lost. You must seek out this tower and kill its master and all who aid it. Study the map once more—mark well all its ancient details. Then gather what followers and equipment you need for this journey and enter the Inner Shrine. I will hear of your life and ready you for the perilous journey which you must take.'

Raissa lowered her eyes to the map once again as the Deis left the chamber. She smiled inwardly. To tell the story of one's life in the Inner Shrine before her companions and friends meant that the mission would end in death. For the Deis to be present at the telling was the greatest of honours. Once the hearing was over, Raissa and her companions would be dead to all the Deisol.

Should they complete their mission and return, then, like the rising sun, they would be born anew. And at the moment of their rebirth they would find themselves that one step closer to their ever dying God.

Tandra called a halt and stared at the towering wall of rock. She and her five companions stood at the southernmost tip of the Custodians, a cluster of ragged peaks which gave birth to four of the seven major waterways of Kyrthos. From there the small party would turn their footsteps east, crossing the upper reaches of Scapol until they reached the Snakeweed Tower.

Night was still several hours off, but Tandra ordered a camp set. There was a small sheltered spring at the base of the rock face and the hollow in which they stood was protected from the strengthening wind by a ring of young spruce trees.

'We're in for a cold night,' Bram offered as he took note of the change in the weather which rode the evening's wind.

As Kallem cleared a small area of dry grass and deadfall and began to lay out their fire, Yahudah searched the hollow for fuel. She made several trips until she had built a large pyramid of logs and branches beside the growing fire.

Sian-vesna stood on the lip of the hollow and stared back over the trail. All day, and indeed for all the weeks since their attack at the village, she had felt that they were being followed, but she had been unable to prove it to her satisfaction.

Bram was also convinced that there were unseen pursuers on their back trail and on more than one occasion he had dropped back in the hope of catching sight of them. He had seen nothing, but this had only strengthened his suspicions.

Faina-lai rested beside the fire. She had told herself repeatedly that she could make this journey, but her old bones were proving her wrong. Each day was a new experience in pain and she tried to reveal nothing of her troubles as she struggled to keep up with the others. She knew that they would insist on taking her to where she could get help if they learnt of her difficulties, and Faina-lai could feel that time was growing short.

She had steered the party towards Snakeweed on a chance, but as they drew ever closer she realised that they were destined to journey to the lost tower. Tandra had chosen their campsite well, and should Faina-lai decide that she must remain here she would be well sheltered from the harsh elements until she had time to regather her strength.

Tandra watched her five companions closely. She could see that Bram was convinced that they were being followed and she had no doubt that he was right. He had changed immensely since Tarynn's death, and she was disturbed by the extent. He had turned inward on himself, studying his every move and whim instead of the surrounding lands. At least the presence he felt trailing them had broken a long period of silent introspection.

Bram had not taken a drink of anything stronger than water since Tarynn's death. There had been many opportunities but Tandra noticed that he had turned his back on them. Over the last few weeks he had lost a great deal of weight from his waist, and once again resembled the Bram Onehand of old.

She had spoken of this at times with Faina-lai, but the old Crafter said that Bram would soon find himself again. Whenever the two women spoke Tandra could almost touch the exhaustion she sensed in the old Crafter. On many occasions she had been on the point of pausing and seeking aid for Faina-lai, but each time she had stopped herself. What they sought was far more important than the well-being of one of their number.

Yahudah was never far from Faina-lai. It was as if she could also feel her aged companion's weariness. But like Bram, Yahudah had also begun to withdraw inward. There had been no more attacks on them and she was denied the opportunity to extract the vengeance which she deeply sought.

Faina-lai had cut Yahudah's hair short, making it more manageable, and with a few items of clothing donated by the party and a good bath the young Saphy looked just like another Cathar walking the dusty roads of Kyrthos.

Meanwhile, Kallem had taken to their new task with an eagerness which reminded Tandra of her younger self. He tended to keep apart from the two Crafters and seemed to be nervous around Tandra, which left him only Bram for company.

Sian-vesna was always alert, and whenever they stopped she would watch over their back trail like a mother watching over her nest. Each night she was the last asleep, prowling the edge of the camp like some nocturnal hunter, and as the sun rose so too did Sian-vesna. Quickly she would free her shell medallion from her clothing and, with it gripped firmly in both hands, search out the surrounding land.

Tandra had noticed a strained silence which had arisen like a wall between the two female Crafters. This was strange. Cathars usually kept themselves apart from their Crafters on a journey, so when two or more Crafters came together they spent every moment in each other's company, whispering secrets and trading knowledge. But Faina-lai and Sian-vesna were somehow different. Something known only to the two of them was holding them apart, and it was becoming more obvious as the days progressed.

Orren-ker wondered how the other party was faring as he lay on his back, trying to find sleep. More priests passed beneath his open window, their constant noise dragging him back to consciousness. Tamerra was a noisy place regardless of the time of day or year. Priests and pilgrims from all over Kyrthos arrived at the religious town at all hours of the day and night.

There was nothing really special about Tamerra. There were no miracles, no saints. The churches of the town were small and for the most part nondescript. But that had not stopped the travellers.

Orren-ker sighed as another party of priests moved noisily towards the Inn of the Sheltering Pilgrim. Realising he was not going to find sleep this night, he threw his cloak about his shoulders and wandered down the hallway towards the smoke-filled dining room.

Wagoners, Cathars and an assortment of armed men and women filled the room to capacity. They had arrived with the many religious parties but did not share their zeal.

As he passed through the dining room and out into the street Orren-ker heard the words of a hundred different conversations, all of them battering their way into his tired brain. Once the door was closed behind him, he leaned back against it and briefly closed his eyes.

The door was pushed open from within and Orren-ker staggered forward several paces. A small group of wagoners erupted from the inn, eyeing him suspiciously as they staggered past, arm in arm. Orren-ker could smell strong liquor on their breaths as they laughed and joked.

He headed off down the street, away from the drunks. Twice he was forced to take shelter in closed doorways as parties of priests marched blindly by, deep in their prayers.

Eventually he turned into a narrow street which seemed blanketed in silence. Even the incessant noise of the chanting priests vanished, replaced by a deep silence which eased the tiredness from his exhausted body. Orren-ker approached the one door which showed a light, drawn to it like a moth to a flame, and peered inside at a large room.

A varied group sat on the floor on large

overstuffed embroidered cushions. Many wore the simple robes of various priesthoods, while others wore the silken finery of well-to-do factions. Some wore dirt-stained travel leathers, while others were clad in the armour of many of the lands of Kyrthos. There was even a green-robed Chosen sitting alone in one corner.

In the centre of the group was a small clear space holding only a large cushion.

'What is this place?' Orren-ker asked.

A short man wearing the soft grey robes of the Obiran priesthood turned and inclined his head in welcome. Orren-ker acknowledged the look. 'This is a place where one comes to hear answers.'

'Answers to what?' Orren-ker pressed.

'Answers to whatever truth you seek.' The priest smiled.

Orren-ker returned the smile and silently cursed this priest and all those of the priesthood for the infuriating way in which they spoke. Never would you receive a straight answer from a priest while there was still breath in his body to spin a riddle.

A silence fell over the room as a small bent man entered by one of the side doors and made his way through the crowd toward the open space in the room's heart. He was thin to the point of emaciation and wore only a simple toga of white cotton, belted at the waist with a length of frayed cord. His battered leather sandals made a strange scuffling noise as he moved. Lowering himself onto the silken cushion, he looked up quickly at the door and smiled at Orren-ker, beckoning for him to enter and be seated.

The soft murmuring which had gradually filled

the room stopped and the thin man became the centre of everyone's attention. 'I see that others have felt the calling and have journeyed far to hear the simple words of Sy-emon.'

Many of those in the room nodded in agreement, never once taking their eyes off the thin man.

'In the long lost years of our history,' Sy-emon began, 'we were not the true rulers of this world of Kyrthos. But after a dark time of terrible bloodshed we found ourselves alone. Those who had ruled this world were all but destroyed by their greed for power and their lust for riches.

'And the time is fast approaching when history will repeat itself in all its bloody glory, and another race will vanish. This time it will be our turn to walk the path of the Lost across the desolate Lands of the Dead, and we will not be alone. You have heard me speak many times of the power of the Living Towers and the hold they place over mortal men.'

Orren-ker's interest was pricked by the mention of the Living Towers and, as he watched the old man talk, he saw his bright, almost eager eyes turn towards where he sat and lock upon his own.

'There is a time fast approaching when the power of the Living Towers will once more be set free upon the world and with it will come a time of dying. Many times you have heard me speak of the past and the future as if they were the same. Well, in a way they are. Whatever has transpired in the past still lives to haunt us in the future. All we can do is learn by past mistakes and ensure that these are not repeated.'

The listeners nodded in agreement and Sy-emon paused momentarily before continuing.

'A Living Tower is all powerful, yet alone it cannot stand the ravages of its enemies. The plant surrounding it draws its power from the very earth we tread, then it is stored deep within the grey liflode walls of the tower. Its power is regulated by the Lychgem, which sits in the uppermost room, but this power may only be wielded through the strength of the master ... by someone who has bested the tower and survived. But still the tower needs others of its kind for protection from its enemies. This protection comes in the form of us. We are the true power of the Living Tower. It is one of us who will master them, and it will be we who don our armour to answer the master's call and protect the tower. It is our blood which will be spilt upon the ground as we wrestle both to preserve and master these Living Towers.'

'But what will happen to us?'

'What happens to all men when they are given the power of the Gods? They fall to warring upon each other until they are no more.' The talesman's voice took on a different quality and he seemed to stare directly at Orren-ker as he continued. ''Ware the whisperings of the *Whirlpool of Destruction*, for it has the power to unleash bloody death upon this world for generations to come.'

The crowd badgered the talesman with questions, but Orren-ker felt as if he had been the only one to hear the talesman's last statement.

'Was that war called the Final Wars?' a youth called from beside Orren-ker.

'No! The Final Wars was simply the term given to the hundreds of wars which led to the destruction of the towers and their masters. What I have spoken of were the First Lychgate Wars and the times that followed.'

'Tell us of the Final Wars,' the youth called.

'Perhaps another time,' Sy-emon said as he slowly rose from the silken cushion. 'I have spoken of the past long enough, and now it is time to speak of the future. Who will pay for the tale they have just heard? And who will return tomorrow to hear another?'

Cries of acceptance sprang from the audience as a shower of coppers flew through the air and fell dancing and spinning at the talesman's feet. Orren-ker waited until most of the coins had landed before he drew an Imperial from his belt and flicked it to the old man.

Many in the crowd turned and studied Orren-ker, eyeing him suspiciously.

'A tale of such wealth demands wealth in payment,' Orren-ker shouted over the din.

This brought shouts of agreement and a veritable cloud of coppers landed at the old man's feet. Three small boys erupted from a side door and began to gather the coins under the watchful eye of Sy-emon. Every so often the old man raised his eyes from his busy apprentices and regarded Orren-ker with his shrewd probing eyes.

Charybdis' powers grew daily as he laboured over the Lychgem. His Yclad had cleared the outer city of all dangers, herding most of its strange and deadly creatures into the surrounding jungles, killing a few and capturing the rest. But the city was a massive one and the task had taken some time to complete.

The captives were Aves, like Asal, and Charybdis quickly made them part of his schemes. Like Asal, Charybdis simply needed something which was a part of them to control them totally.

As he stood at the transparent wall overlooking the plaza, Charybdis stroked his chin in thought. Better than fifty of the Aves were now under his control and he had set them about the outer city, repairing the damage that had been done as the tower had drawn from its surroundings, trying to prolong its life. The power contained within the tower had been used to keep the buildings of the city from falling into rubble over the decades since their abandonment. But as the power of the tower had diminished the outer section of the city had been allowed to age.

The Hawkthorn had continued drawing the energy of the world and storing it in the living liflode, but the Lychgem had been allowed only a trickle of this power to maintain the city. Its previous master had obviously ordered most of the work to be done by the inhabitants themselves. But as the populace and finally the master had passed away, the tower had been required to see to more and more of the city. The Lychgem could regulate where the energy was to be used, but only a new master could allocate more of the power it needed to its cause.

Charybdis, however, had better uses for the power stored within the tower and for the moment the efforts of the Aves would have to suffice.

Like Asal, the Aves eyed him with a deep hatred and their need for blood was palpable, but they were locked under his command. Charybdis ordered the inner gate to the city locked and guarded, which allowed Bohe the freedom of the inner city without fear. It was obvious that Bohe had not previously seen an Ave, and in the time he had served Charybdis he had never shown a moment of fear in Asal's presence. But Charybdis' followers were few and he did not wish to take chances with any of them.

With the inner city secure and repairs proceeding slowly—the Aves not being built for manual labour—he put the next phase of his plan into action.

Charybdis had used his newly acquired power to try to reach out to the south, beyond the entanglements of the Belial, and draw more followers to his cause, but he had failed. The Belial was simply too large a region.

The west and north offered only ocean and reefs which held no life that interested Charybdis, and to the west lay Solan.

In fact Solan was ripe for picking despite the fact it held the Deisol.

Charybdis knew that he could draw many of the Solanesse to his city, but his efforts would also show the Deisol just how much his power had grown. And from his library Charybdis had learned that the Deisol had been one of the strongest enemies of the Living Towers.

The Deisol believe that they must die repeatedly in the service of their God to progress through life was the opposite of everything the towers stood for. The Living Towers' ability to grant almost continuous life had brought the anger of the Deisol down upon the original masters, and Charybdis was not going to allow them to hinder him in any way.

*

Tandra's party were only a few weeks' travel from the Snakeweed Tower, and the other five Cathars under Orren-ker were making good time towards the coast, where they would attempt to hire a ship. Sian-vesna was worried. Charybdis had been able to gather that from the messages she sent. She was convinced that Faina-lai knew of her association with Charybdis and was watching her.

Charybdis agreed, but said nothing to Sian-vesna which would upset the young Crafter any further. He had merely told her how close she and the others were to the tower and left it at that.

Over the past few weeks he had come close to telling her that she was not the only one under his guidance. But each time he had convinced himself that telling her would aid his cause, for some unknown reason he had changed his mind at the last moment.

Tandra watched as the billowing cloud in the distance grew wider, stretching itself along the horizon as far as the eye could see.

'Is it a storm?' Kallem asked.

'That's no storm cloud, lad,' Bram cursed.

'Fire?'

'No, lad,' Bram explained. 'Something far worse.'

A deep noise was closing in on them—a continuous rumble which was carried through the ground as well as the dust-filled air.

'Aves,' Yahudah said, her voice almost unheard above the growing noise. 'We had better find cover. It is not wise to be trapped on an open plain.'

They were only a few hundred metres from the base of the Custodians and Tandra turned at once towards their protection. But before they had covered half the distance the rumbling grew louder still and the first of the large flightless birds emerged from the dust cloud like strange apparitions.

'The rocks,' Tandra shouted. 'Get to the rocks.'

Yahudah was the first to reach the fallen rocks at the base of the cliff and clamber over the smaller ones to safety. Tandra and Kallem reached them simultaneously, both skidding to a halt and turning to their companions.

Sian-vesna was helping Faina-lai, with one of the old Crafter's arms hooked about her neck. Bram gauged the distance and speed of the Aves and cursed as he dropped his pack and swung Faina-lai over his shoulder. With his right hand holding her legs and his left arm raised for balance, he ran for the cover of the rocks.

Sian-vesna was already carrying Faina-lai's pack and she bent to retrieve Bram's.

'Leave them both,' Bram called over his shoulder.

Sian-vesna did as he commanded and ran towards the rocks. The stampeding Aves were so close now that she imagined she could hear their soft whistling above the pounding of their feet.

As she reached the rocks a hand stretched out and dragged her to safety as the first of the maddened Aves flashed by. Tandra watched as the vast sea of creatures raced along the base of the cliff, their clawed feet kicking up a choking dust cloud which enveloped the small sheltering party.

Climbing the top of one of the larger rocks Tandra watched as the Aves reached a section of scree which curved slightly away from the cliff face. They turned in their maddened run and followed the scree until they were headed out into the open plain.

Then, just beyond the far edge of the wheeling flock, Tandra discovered the cause of the Aves' panic. Appearing and disappearing in the dust cloud were several figures. They were matching the speed of the Aves and, as they closed in on the terrified creatures, Tandra could see that they were swinging short leather thongs above their heads.

As one of the figures appeared briefly beside the party Tandra heard a high pitched whistling. She felt a tug at her ankles and looked down to see Yahudah peering up, her dusty face streaked with tears. Tandra helped the young girl climb to her side.

Yahudah wiped the dusty tears from her eyes and then smiled as she saw a small section of the herd turn in on itself. The leading Aves struck the side of their flock and a number of them started milling about at the base of the cliff while the rest of the flock ran off into the distance.

As the dust finally began to settle Tandra could eventually see who had been chasing the Aves. It was hard to tell whether they were male or female, as each was encased in soft leather clothing which covered them from the soles of their feet to the small hoods and masks which hid their faces. But the manner of dress did not capture Tandra's attention so much as the means of transport. The strangers were in pairs, standing in small three-sided two-wheeled carts drawn by a trio of harnessed Aves.

'Jaeger,' Yahudah laughed excitedly, nearly falling from the rock.

12

WINDSONG

Orren-ker stared down the gentle slope at the peaceful little town of Stable. Once in the town the small party would seek out a vessel with a Captain brave enough, or mercenary enough, to carry them north beyond the fringe of the Belial. The northern coast of Skarn was never travelled as the reefs and shoals which marred the coast were uncharted.

Many small islands dotted the dangerous waters about the reefs, but as far as Orren-ker knew none of them had been settled. The storms were sudden and fierce and only the foolhardy travelled anywhere near the region unless they had a very good reason.

Mahira signalled for the others to join them. 'It looks as if we'll have a warm drink inside us and a soft bed to sleep on this night,' she said with a laugh.

'About time,' Fallon commented. 'What I'd give for a hot roast and a chunk of freshly baked bread! I'm sick of travel rations.'

'Me too,' Ferne added quickly.

'Just how long will we be staying here?' Phaidra asked.

'As long as it takes to find a ship and Captain to take us north,' Orren-ker answered.

'Oh. That long,' Phaidra sighed. 'I had hoped we would have been gone by the time winter had arrived.'

'But that's still weeks away,' Fallon scoffed.

'And how long will it take us to find a Captain willing to brave those waters?'

'We won't know until we try,' Orren-ker called over his shoulder as he strode down the slope towards the town.

As the party approached Stable they noticed that the town was quiet and clean, its cobbled streets wide and well tended. The only signs of life were the thin tendrils of smoke rising from the chimneys of the thatch-roofed timber houses. Like all towns in Skarn, Stable used huge amounts of the large soft woods of its forests in its construction.

The timber was cut into long wide planks and the clinker-built single-storey houses were sturdy and offered a warm haven from the frequent winter storms.

'Phaidra, take Fallon and see if you can get us a room at the inn,' Orren-ker ordered. 'Ferne, Mahira and myself will see if there are any suitable vessels in the harbour.'

Phaidra nodded for Fallon to follow her while Orren-ker and the others headed towards the small harbour. Stable was a relatively new town, built to support the settlers moving into northern Skarn in their neverending search for free land and the freedom to farm it.

Others sought the rich minerals previously unmined due to the proximity of the Belial. Those who sought the undeveloped wealth of the north had no time for the tales of terror of the Belial. However, only a handful of the many parties which had struck out north had returned, and their members told tales of such horror that many took a vessel south at once, leaving behind whatever hopes they'd allowed themselves.

The harbour of Stable sheltered a small range of vessels, mostly coastal freighters waiting for a favourable tide. As the sounds of war grew ever louder to the south, their goods were in increasing demand.

Mahira stared out over the water, shielding her eyes against the reflected light. She had spent most of her youth in a small town like Stable on the upper Berdun River and Orren-ker would bow to her knowledge when it came to choosing the vessel best suited to their undertaking.

'That one,' Mahira stated, pointing to a trim-looking bireme. 'She looks to have a shallow draft, but she should be able to handle any storms and she's well-kept. Her timbers are clean and her brass work shines.'

'It looks a bit small,' Ferne offered tentatively.

'We're not looking for a warship or a heavy transport. She's small but fast,' Mahira explained. Then turning to Orren-ker, she added, 'She's the best ship this harbour has to offer for our purposes.'

'You're sure a galley will suit our needs?' Orren-ker asked.

'She's not a galley, she's a bireme,' Mahira answered. 'See the double bank of oars, she probably has a crew of a hundred or so and will be well suited to the shallow waters we will need to navigate.'

'Then it's settled,' Orren-ker said. 'Let's see if we can find its Captain.'

The three of them made their way to the waterfront where it took only a few questions to learn that the bireme was called the *Windsong* and her captain was Garrig, a local who had moved south but returned to Stable after making his fortune. It seemed he had dealt in small but dangerous cargoes, which paid well enough for him to buy the *Windsong* and return home.

Garrig was a short heavy man, his clean-shaven face worn to the consistency of leather by the years of relentless sun. His hair was white and drawn back behind his neck, held there by a ring of woven silver thread. Orren-ker felt lost as he stared into the proud Captain's deep black eyes.

'What port are you heading for,' Garrig asked smiling. 'If it's south of Sytry you may find the cost high. I've no intention of being inducted into the Bezoarian navy just yet, and that's what's happening in those parts.'

'If it's the south you're worried about, then fear not,' Orren-ker explained. 'We are bound for the north.'

'North? What manner of business have you north of here?' Garrig asked, the smile replaced by curiosity, and possibly concern.

'We are under charter to travel beyond the Belial,' Orren-ker said. 'There you will put us ashore and await our return.'

'That's all?' Garrig laughed uneasily. 'Just sail up

the coast and put you ashore. That short length of coast is the most dangerous stretch of water in all of Kyrthos. There are more reefs and shoals scattered along it than any other I have sailed.'

'But we must reach . . .' Orren-ker stopped himself before he mentioned the Monkshood Tower. 'We must pass beyond the Belial.'

'A charter, you say?'

'Yes.'

'Payment?'

'Once the price is decided upon we give you a Letter of Marque which you will hand over at any Charter House of your choice, and there you will be paid, the amount being added to the charterer's bill.'

Garrig pulled at an ear as he stared out over the waters of the harbour. 'One hundred and fifty Imperials for the journey there and back, and another two Imperials for each day that we wait for you.' Garrig had journeyed up the coast further than perhaps any other Captain. But the rewards were scarce and not worth the risks involved.

'Done and done,' Orren-ker agreed. The two touched knuckles before the Captain hurried back to his ship to ready her for the coming journey.

Orren-ker and the others caught up with Phaidra and Fallon outside a small inn. 'We have found a ship and sail on the evening's tide. So we will not need any lodgings.'

'That's good,' Phaidra said. 'This is the best inn in Stable and I'd not sleep here if they paid me.'

'Trouble?'

'It seems they don't like Cathars,' Fallon explained. 'Word of the raids has reached here, and without a Charter House to ease the trouble and put forth the true story of the imposters they believe the rumours that Cathars are raiding the caravans we are meant to be guarding.'

'Then perhaps we should just step in there and put them right on a few things,' Mahira offered. 'It won't take long.'

Orren-ker held up a hand. 'This matter is not worth the time,' he said. 'We have enough trouble as it is. What we must do is get a message to the closest Charter House and allow them to settle the situation here. We can inform them of our plans at the same time.'

'But what of the rumours?' Phaidra complained. 'Aren't we going to set them straight?'

'In a few hours we will be out of this small-minded town. In a day or two it will be forgotten. Now let's find a slightly more friendly place and see about a meal before we leave.'

Garrig sat behind his helmsman as the *Windsong* left the harbour of Stable, her sails furled. The piper played a lively tune and the rowers worked their oars in time with the music. The *Windsong* was soon free of the harbour and Garrig ordered her sails be made ready.

With a favourable breeze the *Windsong* made good time and, as the sun set, the *Windsong* was well clear of Stable, her bow thrusting north through a strengthening swell. Several young lads appeared from below deck and moved quickly about the resting rowers, handing out wedges of white cheese and large slabs of a coarse black bread.

'It is too dangerous to have an open fire on board, even for cooking,' Garrig explained. 'Should a meal need to be prepared we put ashore. Once we reach unknown waters we will do that each night and sleep on the beach. It will keep the *Windsong* safe.'

'Won't that lengthen the journey somewhat?' Ferne inquired.

'No more than running up on some reef in the early hours of the morning,' Garrig observed. He barked an order to his first mate and then, tugging at his right ear, returned his attention to his passengers. 'Exactly what business have you so far north?' He was always one to sense a good profit to be had.

'It is a charter and we are unable to speak of it to any non-Cathars,' Orren-ker quickly explained.

Garrig nodded. 'I see. And this charter has been entrusted to just you five?'

'No . . .' Phaidra said, but Orren-ker interrupted, stepping between her and the Captain.

'It has been a long day and we are in need of rest,' Orren-ker told Garrig. 'Is there anywhere special you wish us to sleep?'

'There is a sheltered area below deck for passengers,' Garrig answered. 'The crew sleep under the stars.'

Lights were hung from the rigging, which gave the *Windsong* a festive appearance, and the five Cathars moved below deck. Wrapping themselves in their blankets, they swiftly fell asleep.

The first to wake, Orren-ker lay wrapped in his blanket, listening to the wind singing in the rigging. The vessel was clearly well named, he thought. By the time he climbed on deck Garrig was already on duty, seated behind the helmsman with one eye on the sails and the other on the horizon.

Garrig raised a hand and a young lad raced forward with bread and cheese. 'Here,' the Captain offered. 'Come and break the fast with me.'

Orren-ker took the proffered bread and cheese and sat on the deck beside Garrig, slowly eating as he watched the crew go about their work. The cheese was rich and moist while the bread was dark and coarse, opposites like the region they now travelled, which was beautiful to the eye but with an underlying deadliness to it.

'We are making good time,' Garrig noted. 'If the wind holds from the same quarter then we should reach the first of the reefs some time tomorrow afternoon.'

'Are there no maps of this area?'

'No,' Garrig replied. 'We have well-made charts for most of the coast of Kyrthos, but this region has nothing to offer the honest trader so no effort has been made to make detailed charts. I have some old parchments which show reefs and shoals, but these can only give me a rough idea of what is to come.'

'I suppose that is better than nothing.'

'Aye. But not by much.'

All day and well into the afternoon the *Windsong* ran before the wind. But when the sun was halfway to the horizon the wind dropped and Garrig ordered the sails furled and all hands to the oars. The water was almost flat as the crew strained at their oars, the piper playing his tunes beside the Captain.

The first mate dropped from the rigging and

moved swiftly to Garrig's side. Orren-ker and the others were too far away to hear what was said, but the mate pointed off towards the shore and then gestured to the sun. Garrig nodded and tapped the helmsman on the shoulder.

The muscles of the helmsman's shoulders bunched as he threw his weight against the tillers and turned the vessel in towards the shore. Each tiller was attached to a long steering oar, one on each side of the stern platform.

'Easy oars!' the Captain shouted, his voice reaching above the crashing of the breakers. 'Raise oars!' The oars were lifted dripping from the water, allowing the *Windsong* to run on. 'Inboard!' The oars were quickly drawn in as the bow of the *Windsong* struck the gently sloping beach.

Several of the crew leapt into the churning water and fought their way up the beach, a long cable carried over their shoulders. More crew then dropped over the side and on each wave they manhandled the *Windsong* further from the water. With the vessel secured, Garrig ordered wood be collected and shelters erected.

A small watch was left on board while the rest of the crew set about raising canvas awnings and gathering armfuls of wood for the night's fires. The first mate and three of the crew entered the dark jungle that bordered the beach and vanished into its shadows.

Strange cries and calls rose from the jungle but the crew paid them no heed as they set about their work. Soon the first mate returned, his arms, and those of his men, filled with a strange cargo of four or five large rock-like objects.

A short length of wood was sharpened into a stake and driven into the ground, then the protruding end was also sharpened. The first mate then knelt before the stake and struck it with one of the objects. The sharpened end of the stake drove deep into the coarse husk of woven hair. The husk was soon removed by working it around the stake. Inside was a fist-sized nut.

Leaning sideways, the first mate sat the nut upon a rock and rapped it with the pommel of his dagger. At the third strike the nut cracked and a clear liquid began to escape. The first mate deftly separated the halves, trapping what liquid he could in one of them.

Giving one half to Orren-ker, he handed the other to a young lad who rushed off towards Garrig. Orren-ker raised the shell to his lips. Several of the crew had gathered about him and were laughing. The first mate looked up from where he worked on another of the nuts and nodded.

'Drink.'

Orren-ker sipped at the liquid. It was unlike anything he had tasted before and he was surprised at its coolness. He took another sip and passed it to one of the waiting crew. Soon the liquid was gone and one of the crew began to attack the nut's fleshy interior with a small ship's dirk. This white flesh was even more pleasant than the liquid.

More of the crew appeared, their arms filled with the large nuts, and the beach was soon filled with the sound of tearing husks and breaking shells. More of the crew stepped from the jungle, this time carrying armfuls of strange fruits.

The crew laughed and joked so much as they

handed the half shells from one to another that Orren-ker began to wonder if the liquid was some form of natural alcohol. The fruits were soft and filled with sticky juices which made them difficult to eat. Fires were then lit and a hasty meal of beans and more of the coarse black bread was prepared.

The sounds from the jungle did not cease at the setting of the sun and Orren-ker wondered just how they were supposed to sleep with all the noise. But sleep they did.

When Phaidra woke early the next morning, the sun's light was barely visible above the horizon. One of the crew's night watch was throwing fuel onto the fire while others patrolled the beach and the deck of the *Windsong*, the curved blades of cutlasses protruding from their thick cloaks.

Phaidra glanced about the silent camp. At this rate of progress their party would leave the *Windsong* in a week, possibly eight days, leaving them a short walk inland to the tower. Her eyes flicked over the still-sleeping forms of Orren-ker, Ferne, Mahira and Fallon. It had been weeks since the two groups had separated and Phaidra wondered just how the others were going.

Ferne and Fallon woke soon after and began to roll their blankets. Mahira simply sat and watched the breakers as they rode high up onto the beach, signalling the rising of the tide. She yawned and stretched her back, then climbed to her feet and crossed to the fire.

The large pot of beans hanging over the fire was just beginning to bubble. Mahira scooped some from the pot with a wooden spoon and slapped them on a thick slice of bread. Recrossing to her blanket, she sat down and began to work on the meal. Others joined her and soon the beach was filled with men chatting as they prepared to leave the beach.

The first mate crossed to where Garrig sat, deep in conversation with Orren-ker. He whispered into his Captain's ear before pointing down the beach and then into the jungle. Garrig and Orren-ker quickly leapt to their feet, the Captain lifting a wide belt of tooled leather and buckled it about his waist. Loosening his sabre in its scabbard, he followed the first mate down the beach.

Five men who had slept around the furthest fire, wrapped tightly in their blankets, had not realised anything was amiss until they had woken to find one of their number missing. The sand was disturbed but there was no sign of their shipmate.

Orren-ker gripped his medallion and studied the bordering jungle, but he could sense nothing dangerous. Garrig called four of the crewmen to him and started out toward the jungle. Phaidra and Mahira joined them as the first mate subdued the crew's mumbling and ordered all stores and equipment be put back on board the *Windsong*. The grumbling continued as the crew worked, their eyes not on what they were doing but on the dark wall of the jungle.

Garrig signalled a halt and studied the jungle floor for any sign. The ground was covered in a thick layer of dead leaves and branches, but there was no sign that anyone had passed this way.

'Deserted?' Phaidra whispered.

'Here?' Mahira scoffed. 'I doubt it.'

'Then what?'

'Wandered off for a leak more than likely, and lost his way,' Garrig observed. 'One direction looks much the same as another once you're far enough away from the beach.'

Mahira felt ill at ease as she followed Phaidra through the humid jungle. Insects bit at her exposed skin and sweat ran down her face and back, making her wish she had stayed on the beach. As they passed a large moss-covered log Mahira noticed a small area had been scraped away, as if by someone climbing it.

She moved around the log and came across a slight trail, narrow yet well travelled. After only five or six paces Mahira was brought to a halt. Lying on the trail just ahead of her was a torn and bloodied blanket. Off to one side were the remains of a pair of canvas trousers.

As the crew all wore the same type of trousers these had to belong to the missing crewman. There were numerous paw prints and scuff marks about the bloodied blanket, but it was impossible to tell the direction in which the attackers had fled.

Shouts of surprise and savage snarls filled the jungle about her. Mahira slipped her shield from her shoulder, drew her longsword and rejoined the trail left by the others.

She sensed rather than saw the shadow as it leapt from the jungle to her right. She raised her shield and batted something from the air, driving her sword deep into a bloated body as it tried to rise again.

The creature was squat, with huge staring eyes, long hind legs and small forelegs which ended with surprisingly human-like hands. Its markings were dark green to a dull yellow and it had a sickly looking white underbelly. The upper body was covered in short horns.

More sounds erupted from the jungle and Mahira rushed to join the others. As she rounded a bend she found a crewman down and one of the creatures sitting on his chest. Kicking it from its prey she ran it through and dragged the stunned crewman to his feet, pushing him before her as she rounded another bend. Phaidra, Garrig and the other two crewmen were battling a dozen or more of these ugly creatures.

As she joined their struggle she heard Phaidra curse. 'What manner of creature are they?'

'Hylas,' Garrig answered. 'A few have been sighted, usually in the Cloud Forest of northern Skarn, south of the Velarch River. They usually flee at the first sight of man, and never have I seen them in this number.'

One of the Hylas raised its head and its wide slash of a mouth opened. There was a flash of purple as its long tongue shot out, striking one of the crewmen in the face. He dropped his cutlass and fell to the ground, his face covered by his hands. Muffled sounds of pain escaped through his fingers as they tore at his face.

Phaidra thrust out her shortsword, its blade passing through the Hyla's eye and entering its brain. As the dead Hyla slipped from Phaidra's blade a strange pungent odour arose. Glancing about her in all the confusion, Mahira noticed that several of the dead Hylas were swelling, blowing up like full waterskins.

'Get back,' Garrig cried.

As the crewmen and Cathars retreated from the remaining Hylas one of the bloated bodies exploded, spraying the surrounding foliage with a mixture of yellow gore and intestines. The pungent smell grew even stronger.

'Back to the beach!' Garrig ordered, the arm of one injured crewman about his neck.

The three remaining crewmen began to cut their way frantically towards the beach. The sounds of something moving through the jungle could now be heard to either side of the trail. But no matter how fast the crewmen cut at the tangle of brush and vines, they seemed to make no headway.

Mahira flicked her longsword effortlessly to the right, cutting a Hyla down in mid-leap. The instant its body struck the ground it began to swell, exploding before they were several paces from it.

A small amount of its yellow blood spattered on Mahira's legs. She screamed and reached down to wipe off the thick yellow blood, but Phaidra stopped her. Then grabbing a handful of leaves, Phaidra wiped the blood from Mahira's legs as best she could.

Mahira waved off Phaidra's offer of help and limped off after Garrig, who had slowed his withdrawal as he ensured that none of the Hylas followed. Never quite in sight of Garrig and his three crewmen, the Cathars were able to follow the loud curses as one or another of them was caught up on the many thorned and stinging plants.

Suddenly they found themselves free of the jungle and only a few paces from the bow of the *Windsong*. Some of the crew were in the water easing the bireme off the sand and into the gentle swell. The oars were then readied and the *Windsong* swiftly backwatered away from the beach.

The crewmen who had journeyed inland told the others of the Hylas and their attack. The face of the man who had been struck by the Hyla was burned a deep angry red. His eyes had swollen closed and his lips were cracked and peeling.

'It's a good thing he didn't get too much of the saliva in his eyes,' Orren-ker said as he rose from examining him. 'It has burned his skin quite badly and it will be days before he is fit for duties.'

A few of the crew were crowded around Orren-ker and the injured crewman. 'Do we turn back?' one of them asked.

'Why?' Garrig asked, hands on his hips, his body leaning forward at the waist waiting for an answer.

'One dead and one injured,' another crewman tallied.

'How many did we lose when we tangled with that Bezoarian Freebooter?' Garrig countered. 'Tell me. How many?'

'But that was different. It was our lives then.'

'And now? How is this different?' Garrig again tugged at his right ear as he took a pace forward. 'If we run at the first sign of trouble, who will hire us? And what will then become of our precious lives? Perhaps we could become farmers, or herdsmen?'

The crew mumbled, some of them still not convinced they shouldn't turn and head for a safe port.

'The pay is good,' Garrig continued. 'And I've never taken undue risks with your lives, you know that. If we can open a way north and chart a course through the reefs and shoals then we will make a fortune selling our information to others who wish to test the northern lands.'

The grumbling still came but it was quieter, and there were fewer men listening to it.

'Reefs dead ahead!' came the cry from the bow look-out just after midday.

'Ease the stroke,' Garrig ordered. He left the stern platform, ran forward and climbed the main-mast. In the distance was the broken whitewater which marked a submerged reef. It seemed to stretch right up to the beach and Garrig doubted that even with the shallow draft of the *Windsong* it was passable.

Descending the mast he ordered the helmsman to change course to port and the piper to pick up the pace.

'I take it we don't go through here?' Orren-ker observed.

'No. We'll have to try further out,' answered Garrig curtly before turning his attention back to his vessel.

As the afternoon wore on, the thin strip of land vanished over the eastern horizon, leaving the *Windsong*, its crew and passengers with only the reef for company in the vast expanse of ocean. The sun was still two or more hours above the horizon when the mainmast lookout reported a large sandbar ahead.

'If we push on we might not find another suit-able place before darkness falls,' Garrig observed to Orren-ker.

Orren-ker agreed. He hoped they would not

have any problems this time, but the sandbar was empty. Not even the smallest of plants appeared to have withstood the high tides and storms and established a toehold. Garrig ordered the *Windsong* cut in towards the waiting sandbar, and as the keel of the vessel touched the sand several of the crew dropped over the side and eased her as far up onto the bar as was possible. Then a hasty camp was set and wood for the night's fire carried up from the emergency supply the *Windsong* carried.

The bare sandbar was soon covered with a number of canvas shelters and a roaring cook fire, with a large pot suspended over it giving off the now-familiar smell of boiling beans. Sacks of the black bread were dropped over the side to waiting hands who carried them up the beach and deposited them beside the sweating cook and his assistant.

'We've only enough wood for the one fire,' the first mate said as he and Mahira waded ashore. 'But we should be safe from them critters way out here.'

13

JAEGER

Charybdis stood before his Lychgem and looked deep into the many facets. It was some time since he had felt the presence of the other and he wondered if the face he had seen was only a strange reflection of his own and not a warning that another tower had been breached.

He had searched out each of the towers within his range but could find nothing to show they had awoken. Yesterday he had spoken to Sian-vesna and knew that her small party was close to reaching the Snakeweed Tower.

Charybdis had chosen another to help in his plans, but as yet had not revealed the existence of his helper to Sian-vesna. In good time he would identify his second Cathar, but for the moment he would have to content himself with waiting.

One of the Jaeger stepped down from the strange cart and walked slowly towards the dust-covered party, unhooking and drawing back the soft leather veil which covered all but the eyes. Tandra saw the face of a young woman streaked with sweat.

The young woman approached Tandra and her party, her eyes never still as they examined every detail of the six strangers. Finally she stopped before them and raised her right arm, her hand closing into a fist. Tandra matched the fist with one of her own and the pair touched knuckles in the Cathars' ritual greeting.

The young Jaeger removed her leather-wrapped helmet and shook her braided red hair free.

'I find you well?' Tandra offered.

'I am Neroli,' came the reply. 'My sister, Amalee, travelled south many years ago to become a Cathar. The good deeds and skills of the Cathars are known amongst my people. Be welcome.'

'Thank you,' Tandra answered. 'I am glad that your sister has chosen to place her feet upon that path. I am sure she does her family proud.'

'Great things were expected of her here, amongst our people, and our father did not take her going well.' Neroli was interrupted as another of the Jaeger moved towards them.

'My brother, Aleron,' Neroli whispered.

The youth tore aside his veil and Tandra could not help but notice the sneer which covered his youthful face. 'Father will not be pleased,' Aleron grunted. 'You know what he thinks of Cathars.'

'It is not for you to greet our guests on behalf of our father,' Neroli snapped. 'I'm sure father would not want his guests insulted in his name.'

'Guests? Who said they are to be our guests?'

'I did, Aleron,' Neroli said, moving to stand

beside Tandra. 'I would like to hear more about the Cathars and how they managed to draw our sister from us.'

Aleron spat as he turned.

'Pay little attention to my younger brother,' Neroli quickly added, emphasising the word younger.

Aleron spun round, his fists clenched.

'See to the Aves,' Neroli ordered. 'Fence those we have turned and prepare a campsite.'

Aleron seemed on the point of arguing, but said nothing as he stormed off towards the nervous Aves.

'He seems to think that he should be in charge of the hunt this season,' Neroli explained. 'But father said he has to work one more season before he's allowed to. One cannot lead without the respect of those they lead.'

'That's true,' Tandra agreed. 'The same principles are impressed upon our young Cathars.'

Neroli nodded. 'Come, I would meet the rest of your party and then we can discuss why you and my sister found the road so acceptable.'

Large coils of rope were lifted from the rear of the small carts and a rope fence was quickly erected about the milling Aves. On occasions a restless creature would try to make a break for the open plain beyond the working Jaeger, but a firm jab from a Jaeger's stave soon persuaded the Ave that escape was impossible. Long poles were used to build the fence and, as several of the Jaeger pulled the ropes taut, a large sack was dragged from another cart.

Lengthy strands of green-leafed vine were drawn from the sack and carried to the hastily constructed fence. Two of the Jaeger began wrapping the vines around the higher of the fence's strands. Even as the two worked the Aves drew back, pressing themselves against the rock wall.

Once the fence was finished and Neroli had set her night watches, she joined Tandra and the others. The tired party sat beside the dying fire, the evening's meal, stchi, resting well in their stomachs.

'Why do you allow the fire to go out?' Kallem asked. 'The night's air does not seem cold but surely there are wild animals about?'

Neroli laughed. 'More creatures roam the night this far north than you could possibly imagine. But the grass, though short, is tinder dry this time of year and the region is prone to sudden wind storms which could seed the dry grass with hundreds of sparks from an untended fire.'

Just as Neroli finished, a branch in the fire snapped. In the ensuing silence Tandra could hear the whistling of the Aves as they bunched together beneath the face of the cliff.

'What is the vine they used on the fence? It hardly looks strong enough to stop them?' Tandra inquired.

'It's called picket weed,' Neroli explained. 'The Aves don't seem to like it. It is found high in the Custodians, clinging to the rock faces and is very difficult to gather.'

'How does it work?'

'The smell is quite overpowering,' Neroli continued. 'Not to us but to the Aves. They only have to approach the vine and they become agitated and back away. We store the picket weed in damp sacks of woven cloth. This keeps the plant alive as long as possible and helps retain its fragrance. Originally it was used on our western borders. It was strung about our night camps to ward off the wild Aves of northern Skarn.'

'I would have thought all Aves were wild?' said Tandra.

'These you see before you are indeed wild,' Neroli agreed, 'but once captured they are easy to train and will never revert to their old ways. But the northern regions of Skarn were once home to a larger breed of Ave. Murderous and unpredictable, they roamed the lands bordering the Belial, wreaking havoc.'

'I have never heard of them before,' Tandra admitted.

'They were wiped out generations ago,' Neroli said. 'They were too great a threat and they were hunted down to the last, though it is possible that some still survive in the Belial protected from their hunters by the forest's lethal reputation.'

'How could there be two types of Ave so radically different?' Tandra asked.

'One of our camp followers, an old man who tells stories about our night camps, tells of a race much like the Aves who were once rulers of this land. He speaks of a high society which ruled, a worker society whose sole purpose was to labour for the good of the land, and a warrior society whose only thoughts were to kill all outsiders.'

'Where did he learn this?' Tandra muttered. She had heard many tall tales during her years on the road and knew when to take one with a grain of salt. This sounded remarkably like one such tale.

'He claims to have learnt it from a knowledgeable

creature in a library far to the south, where no Jaeger has ever trod. He also claims that he has seen and spoken to the Aves who are descended from those ancient rulers.'

Neroli rose and left to check on the sentries. Before long two tired Jaeger entered the camp and helped themselves to the stchi which had been left beside the dying fire. While the rest of the camp slept, Tandra lay awake for some time listening to the scuffling sounds of the Aves and their strange whistling.

As Tandra's eye closed there rose a soft music which gradually grew until it smothered the noises made by the Aves. Raising herself onto one elbow, she searched the darkness for the source of the sound.

Tandra lay awake and listened to the many tunes played by the unseen musician. They were breathtaking and eerie at the same time and she had never heard anything like them before. The more she heard the more she wanted to find the musician and see what manner of instrument was played.

Tandra woke as the sounds of activity grew and worked the aches from her back and arms before snatching up her boots and crossing to a large dead log which had been propped beside the fire. She upended her boots and shook them well, checking for unwelcome visitors. Tandra had once travelled with a woman who had failed to do so, and she still vividly remembered the cry of pain released as the woman tore the boot from her foot, allowing the armoured menace of a cavalry beetle to fall free.

Cavalry beetles could be found in all the lands of Kyrthos. They were large and black, armoured in overlapping layers of shell, and each sported a long narrow horn on the top of the head. It was from this horn, or lance, that the beetle had received its name.

Stamping her feet into her boots, Tandra crossed the camp until she neared the cook fires. It seemed they were having stchi again to break their nightly fast. Tandra didn't mind the soup, made from a head-sized round vegetable built up in layers of green leaves.

Neroli met Tandra with a smile. 'The Season of the Hunt draws to a close and so we are forced to endure stchi once more.'

'Anything is better than the travel rations we have been forced to eat of late,' Tandra answered. Her nose twitched as she glanced quickly at her companions.

Neroli laughed, louder this time. 'It is the stchi soup. You will get used to it after a while. The disagreeable effect it has on one's stomach soon vanishes.'

Tandra and the other Cathars finished their meal and the Jaeger set about breaking the camp. Everything was stored neatly into the strange two-wheeled carts, the last being the picket weed and the rope used to corral the Aves during the night.

'What was that strange music last night?' Tandra asked a Jaeger as he straightened up from packing a coil of rope away.

'It was Kaela,' he answered.

'One of the hunters?' Tandra pressed.

'No. When Kaela was young he was caught in a stampede. He only lived due to the intervention of a travelling Crafter, but his left foot was damaged, somehow twisted, and he has not been able to use it well enough to join the hunt.'

'But if he played the tune last night than he must have been here?' Tandra questioned.

'Kaela and Aleron were close friends as children and he allows him to travel with the hunt. Each night Kaela sits himself beside the flock, or above it, and plays his flute. The tunes seem to settle the nervous beasts.'

'Is that why he accompanies you?'

The Jaeger shook his head. 'He travels with us because it is Aleron's wish. Aleron is too good a hunter not to have with us and he has said on many occasions that the first time Kaela's role on the hunt is questioned then so is his.'

Bram and Kallem joined the pair as they spoke and Bram nodded as the Jaeger finished his tale. 'Comradeship is a thing valued greatly amongst the Cathars.'

'The Jaeger too.'

The Jaeger returned to his work and the rest of the party joined Bram, Kallem and Tandra.

'Do they know of the tower?' Kallem asked.

'I have not yet asked them,' Tandra stated.

Sian-vesna nodded. 'We have heard so many disquieting stories about the towers it may not be wise to advertise that we are seeking one of them.'

'I thought you wished to reach the Snakeweed Tower as soon as possible?' Bram queried.

'Safety,' Sian-vesna explained. 'We must reach the tower as quickly as possible, but we must do so safely or we may not be able to reach the Monkshood Tower which is our true destination.'

231

'My father always said that a job rushed was a job failed,' Kallem added. 'Perhaps we should simply ask directions of the Jaeger. We know that if we travel east, following the Custodians, we will reach the Berdun River. Where the river and the mountains touch we should find the tower.'

Neroli approached and the conversation died.

'I am sorry that you could not travel with us to our summer camp,' she said with regret. 'My mother would have been interested in hearing stories of your years on the road.'

'We too would have enjoyed learning more about your people, Neroli,' Tandra said, 'but we are under charter to seek out a place believed long lost.'

'And you travel east?'

'Yes, as far as the river and then north. Perhaps we will meet again when we are returning?'

'None who has approached the tower has ever returned,' Neroli warned.

'How did you know we were going to the tower?'

'There is nothing in the region you speak of save the cursed tower. Every generation or so a group of young Jaeger decide it is time to learn the truth about it. They never return. Once a great and powerful hunter's son was lost and an entire clan trekked north to seek and destroy the tower.'

'Did any return?'

'None,' Neroli replied. 'It seems that any friendship we would have made is now doomed to failure.'

'Ghosts!' Aleron scoffed. 'They have been telling stories about the ghosts of the tower since I was a child.'

'Since?' Neroli questioned.

'The tower holds a secret which should only be known to the Jaeger,' Aleron insisted loudly.

'The tower holds death,' Neroli answered.

'Children's tales,' Aleron said, laughing.

'We once sought a tower far to the south,' Tandra offered. 'It had been destroyed and stood only half its old height. A storm approached and we were forced to spend the night there, sheltering in its weak protection. During the night one of our number was lured upward and on the stairs he met a creature from the heart of any nightmare. He was dead when we found him but the wraith was still there and it was Sian-vesna who slew the creature and allowed us to retrieve the body of our fallen companion.

'None of us heard a noise, and did not realise that Tarynn was gone until it was too late. We have since learned that the towers which once dominated these lands were protected by killers such as that wraith. If you have lost people to the protectors of the tower, then it is more than a children's tale.'

'But you still intend to travel there!' Aleron snapped, his extended finger stabbing Tandra's shoulder like a spear.

'Yes,' Tandra replied. She locked eyes with Aleron, throwing out an unspoken warning, but if he recognised the warning for what it was he ignored it.

'Then the dangers are not as severe as you would like us to believe.'

'We know of the danger and are prepared for it,' Tandra pointed out. 'Could you say the same?'

*

Raissa and her companions—Taya, Tavira and Yolane—had swung wide during the night, passing the camp of the Jaeger and their six guests. They pushed themselves hard until they were sure that the Cathars would not catch them before they reached the tower.

As she sat by their small shielded fire sipping at the hot drink Yolane had prepared, Raissa smiled. 'Late tomorrow we will reach the tower,' she noted. 'We should have several hours before the Cathars arrive, so the search must be swift and sure.'

In the soft light, Raissa unrolled a grey parchment and noted both the sketched tower and the marked spiral staircase within. There were many unnamed rooms, but only one interested her. At the top of the stairs was a large chamber and set to one side and above it was a smaller domed-ceilinged one. It was in this chamber that they would learn the truth.

'In the uppermost room of the tower we will find the answer to our questions.'

'Will the tower be defended?' Taya asked.

'I have read,' Yolane added, 'that the towers were protected by demons of the night who roam the world between the death and birth of God.'

'It is true,' Raissa told them. 'There are many foul creatures who wander the world of the night while our new God awaits birth. But the creatures you speak of are from a time long ago. There may be defenders, but these we will overcome.'

'What is it that the Deis expects us to find?' Taya asked.

'Proof that the towers are once more awake,' Raissa answered. 'Proof that they are again willing to take a stand in the order of things and disrupt the lives of those chosen to follow God.'

'Is it true that those who worshipped the masters of the towers believed in life eternal?' Tavira whispered.

'Yes,' Raissa confirmed. 'And worse yet, they rewarded their followers with extended lives, breaking the ritual cycle of life and death which God demands.'

Raissa was the last to sleep. She sat beside the fire, feeding small twigs into the hungry flames as she allowed her mind to travel back to a particular time in her youth.

Her long training finally completed, she had stepped from Apprentice to Disciple. She was then sent to a small outpost on the eastern edge of the Belial where it had been reported that an unseen creature was raiding the isolated settlements. Raissa had arrived with three others and they set about gathering information from those who had witnessed the attacks.

The creature involved was a Dendro. Although they were large and squat, Dendros moved with surprising bursts of speed which left their prey unable to defend itself. The Dendros were armed with retractable spines down their back and a venomous saliva which they spat. The spines also proved to be poisonous and those who closed with the creatures died quite horribly. Artrea had examined the dead and found that there was no cure for the poison which had twisted their bodies in death.

Raissa was the youngest of the four and it was left to her to help the locals bury their dead. Meanwhile, Calli, Artrea and Jabina searched the forest closest to the settlement seeking out any trail which might prove useful. But they found nothing.

After the setting of the sun the four Disciples patrolled the edge of the settlement while the survivors waited behind locked and barred doors. As the moon rose above the small cluster of dilapidated huts a noise reached Raissa's straining ears from the forest.

When she called to the others they withdrew, allowing whatever was approaching to reach the moonlight before they attacked.

Abruptly, a shape leapt from the darkness of the forest. It was squat, and reached no higher than Raissa's thighs. In the moonlight Raissa saw that it was coloured a magnificent red, with dark blue legs.

Its eyes, which were jet black and large, sat above a gaping toothless mouth. It made no sound as it watched the four Disciples. Then, with an almost unbelievable burst of speed, its huge rear legs straightened, catapulting the creature at Calli. The beast knocked her to the ground where she dropped her torch and rolled to one side. When she regained her feet, Calli held a long-bladed dagger in each hand.

Artrea lifted her spear and rushed forward but the creature leapt again, this time towards Raissa.

Raissa lifted her sword, but she knew that she could not stop its attack. Closing her eyes she waited for the moment of death when her spirit would be released to begin its long journey. When the blow did not come she opened her eyes a crack and saw her three companions struggling with the creature.

Jabina battered at its head with her mace while Artrea and Calli clung to its back to stop it from escaping. Calli screamed as she was suddenly thrown from the creature's back. Artrea rolled to one side and rose, her spear finding its way deep into the creature's side.

With a deep rumbling growl the creature leapt forward again, knocking Jabina from her feet and tearing the spear from Artrea's hands. The sound of broken bones filled the air. Jabina cried out in pain and rushed forward, but the creature moved again.

Artrea lay where she had fallen. Her legs had taken the full weight of the creature, and were twisted at impossible angles. It was obvious that they were badly broken. Jabina rushed the creature once more but it spun about and faced her, its head rising to shoulder height, its mouth gaping.

Another of the growls reverberated as it lowered its head. Raissa could see its large black eyes as it turned slightly, taking her in as well as Jabina. Then, as if deciding she was no threat, it turned its full attention back to Jabina.

With one leap it reached her but Jabina was too quick and stepped to one side, bringing her mace down on the creature's head with all the force she could muster. A sharp crack followed the blow and for a moment Raissa thought the creature dead. But, slowly, it turned its bulk towards Jabina.

Raissa willed her legs to move. As she took a step towards the battling pair she found herself free of the fear which had held her for so long. She ran up behind the creature and leapt to its back, throwing herself to one side as the spines extended. Rolling free of the creature, she reached up and grasped the spear still embedded in its side and drove it deeper with all her strength.

The creature raised its head and spat a grey globule of saliva which struck Jabina in the chest. As it spat it leapt forward, but Raissa refused to release the spear and was dragged along with it. The creature crashed to the ground and began to thrash about. Raissa pushed the spear deeper still into its now bloated body.

Without warning, the creature lay still. Raissa climbed to her feet and looked down at the lifeless body. Its open mouth revealed a large yellow tongue from which saliva was dripping slowly to the grass, sizzling as it touched the damp grass. Raissa pushed her hair from her eyes and turned towards her three companions.

Jabina was dead, a large smoking hole in her chest where the saliva had struck. Her face was twisted in pain but her death must have been swift, as she had not uttered a sound. Raissa straightened her contorted body and turned to Artrea.

Her legs were smashed and the flesh about the bone had burst. Many blood vessels had been ruptured and she had died from the loss of blood while the others had fought.

Calli was also dead. There were two deep punctures in her chest where the spines had burst their way through her leather armour. Her face was also twisted in pain.

Raissa gathered what she would need from her companions and turned her tired legs towards the huts of the settlement. Her companions might be dead, but they were now starting the first leg of their eternal journey upward towards their God and one of the new lives offered to all those who served.

With the freeing of the spirit the body was no more than a carcass, food for the many scavengers and carrion which would soon be drawn to the region by the smell of death. But these too were God's creatures, returning all to the beginning so they might again live their new life taking them closer to God.

Raissa opened her eyes and stared into the sheltered flames of the fire. As a reward for her deed she had received the sword tattoo on her head.

She had led a party back to recover the bodies of her companions. As they had entered the small clearing the first thing Raissa saw were the accusing eyes of her dead companions. Unlike other cultures, the eyes of any dead Deisol were allowed to remain open, allowing them to find their way towards their goal.

Tandra and Bram stood at the base of the tower and followed its vine-covered shape upward. If it had been destroyed in the past then it had since been repaired as there was no sign of damage.

'Do we enter?' Bram asked.

Tandra looked at the darkening sky and shivered. 'No,' she decided. 'We'll wait till morning. If there is a wraith present we will need the light of day to confine it to the tower.'

'There is a small stand of trees which would make a good campsite,' Kallem offered. 'It's far enough from the tower that we should be safe, yet it will allow us to watch it until the sun rises.'

Tandra eyed the tower with a deep-seated fear. The memory of what had happened to Tarynn made her loath to be anywhere near this structure, but there was nothing she could do.

'Perhaps the river might offer a better defence,' Yahudah offered. 'My people believe that evil roams the world during the hours of darkness, seeking out the unprotected. Our ancient grandmothers have sought out many ways to protect us from such dangers. One of these safeguards is running water. Whenever we found a wide stream or river with a sandbar in its centre we would camp there, safe from the dangers which prowled the banks.'

'We aren't far from the river,' Sian-vesna noted.

'Why would you listen to her?' Kallem argued. 'Her people are nothing but wanderers who know nothing of the world. They believe in demons and ghosts and jump at their own shadows.'

'My people have travelled these lands from the time when your family scratched in the earth for their food,' Yahudah answered angrily. 'Our ancient grandmothers knew the many dangers this land, and others, offered. And they knew how to protect us from them.'

Kallem opened his mouth to answer but Bram stepped to his side. 'It hardly matters which of you is right,' he observed. 'Soon the sun will set and we need a place to camp. We know that the wraith which killed Tarynn was no demon, ghost or figment of somebody's imagination so I suggest we take all the precautions we can. And if that means getting our feet wet, then so be it.'

Kallem shrugged and shouldered his pack. He might still believe differently, but he was not about to argue with Bram.

'It's the river then,' Tandra agreed. 'Gather firewood as there's sure to be none where we will camp.' The party quickly moved off towards the river.

There had not been time to search the base of the tower for signs of recent passage. If they had done so they would have seen the recent tracks made by the booted feet of four people. They would have also seen the open door and the woman at the base of the stairs. Her body was frozen in death, her tattoos the only colour on her pale white skin, her open eyes staring out blankly.

14

LYCHGATE

'Why is it that this region has not been charted?' Ferne asked. She sat on the stern platform of the *Windsong* with the other Cathars, Garrig, Royden the first mate, and the helmsman Uzziel. Except for the sentries, the rest of the crew were asleep.

The roar of the waves crashing upon the reef was almost deafening and the Cathars had found it hard to sleep, but not the crew. They were used to the cacophony the ocean sometimes offered and seemed more at ease on the sandbar, surrounded by uncharted ocean, than they had been on the beach the previous night.

'When there's a profit to be made a way is always found to get the goods to and from the dealers,' Garrig said. 'But the north has not yet been opened to the traders and the merchants, so no-one has bothered to enter these waters.'

'No-one?'

'Oh, there would have been adventurers

travelling these waters for many years, but they have either found nothing of value or . . .'

'Or?'

'Or they have not returned to tell of their finds,' Garrig pointed out. 'I know of no-one who claims to have journeyed north beyond the reefs since long before the Final Wars.'

'Then why do you try?' Orren-ker asked.

Garrig laughed. 'If I didn't try you'd have a long swim ahead of you.'

'But why?' Ferne insisted. 'The money?'

'Partly,' Garrig agreed, 'but more likely because no one else has done it. The *Windsong* is a strong ship, she can handle any storm we might encounter. As long as we keep a careful watch we should be able to decrease the risk.'

'Then what are the dangers?'

'The unknown,' Garrig replied, tugging once again at his right ear. 'It is always the unknown that people fear.'

'But once we know what we face then it will no longer be the unknown,' Phaidra offered.

'That's right.' Garrig laughed. 'Each day we will sail further into the unknown until one day we reach our destination. Then, as we sail home, we will be travelling a region we have already sailed.'

'What of your crew, Garrig?' Orren-ker asked.

Garrig turned to his helmsman. 'Uzziel, what say you?'

'The crew will follow the Captain no matter where he leads them,' Uzziel replied. 'He has treated them well over the years and they have come to trust him.'

'Aye,' Royden agreed. 'If we sailed north with no

profit in sight the men would still follow Captain Garrig out of loyalty.'

'Enough of this talk,' Garrig protested. 'Let's have a look at that old chart we have and see what we might be expected to face over the coming days.'

Uzziel unrolled a small piece of faded parchment whose edges were cracked and uneven. Orren-ker saw what was supposed to be the coast of Skarn. And pushing out to the west was a series of reefs and shoals, drawn in great detail.

'I think the man who drew this was an artist rather than a sailor,' Uzziel sighed.

There was no scale to the chart and one could only guess at the extent of the reefs. There was however an indication of the direction of the prevailing winds, and their strengths at certain times of the year. Whether these were any more reliable than the chart itself was unknown.

There were several crosses marked on the chart, with dates and names scrawled in beside them, but the ink used for these entries was of low quality and had faded so much it was unreadable.

'It seems that something of importance happened at these points,' Garrig noted. 'What it was we may never learn.'

'Look here,' Ferne said. 'Doesn't that look more like an island? The way it has been drawn, it looks to have a beach surrounding it.' In the centre of the island there was a strange mark: two vertical lines, joined by a horizontal one at their top.

'Possibly,' Royden answered. 'But if it was low tide when this was drawn we might find nothing there if we arrive on the high.'

'Then again, the maker has gone to a lot of

trouble to show us that it is different from the reefs and shoals,' Uzziel noted.

Garrig nodded. 'We'll find out soon enough. Royden, see that the sentries are as alert as they should be and I suggest the rest of us get some sleep. We can speak more on this tomorrow.'

Mahira drew her blanket close about her neck and shoulders but she found it almost impossible to sleep. Each time she moved the sand packed down a little bit more and it felt as if she was lying on solid stone. She briefly wondered how the other party were faring. If they had not been delayed they should have reached the Snakeweed Tower and have done what was necessary.

Phaidra rolled on her side, her back to the wind. She could hear the faint movements of the others and knew that they were also finding it difficult to sleep. Above the sounds of the waves Phaidra heard the murmuring of the wind. Like a gentle prayer, the sound seemed to repeat itself continually. The hypnotic sound continued until Phaidra realised she was whispering a long-forgotten prayer from her childhood.

She had taken the path of a Cathar as a way of escaping her father. He had been a priest in a small village at the source of the Shaylee River, high in the Tante Ranges. But when Phaidra was quite young her family had moved to Hyghspur and her father had become one of the Chosen, a sect of religious zealots.

As she grew up her father continually pushed her towards a future in the priesthood. Her mother would remain silent while her father bullied and pressured his daughter into taking special classes at the temple which he told her would aid her in later life.

One day her mother spoke out against Phaidra's father and he flew into so great a rage it caused Phaidra to flee the house. She took refuge in a small tumbledown hut in a narrow valley behind her village. It had been a day or more before she was found by the Righteous, who were the guardians of the Chosen, and taken to the temple to await her father.

When he arrived he said nothing, but Phaidra was punished for the trouble she had caused. She spent the next week locked away in the temple listening to her father's praying. The prayer was a short one to ward off evil and he had repeated it endlessly until Phaidra covered her ears and grovelled on the floor. Finally she agreed to do as he wished and was allowed to return home to gather a few things that she would require.

Finding the house deserted, Phaidra, frantic with worry, hunted down a neighbour and was told that her mother had waited for her. But when Phaidra did not come, she had simply packed her belongings and left, believing her husband when he told her that neither he nor their daughter wanted to see her again.

Phaidra was so furious with her father she left the house at once to seek him out. But then she realised that, should she return to the temple, she would never be allowed to leave again. So she collected whatever might be of use to her and left her home, in search of her mother. She followed the trail through the mountains and down the Shaylee River to the fledgling town of Brisk, where she had lost it.

After wandering for several months Phaidra met

a caravan of merchants under the protection of four Cathars. She had been befriended by the Cathars, and when their charter was over they had taken her to a Charter House where she had received her training.

In each town or village she entered she would inquire after her mother, giving a brief description and her name but she had never found any sign of her. Phaidra had never returned to her father. He was as lost to her as was her mother and she pledged that things would remain that way until she found her mother.

Phaidra lay awake for some time, recalling the places she had visited and the faces of old friends, but one face eluded her. Since the day Phaidra had found her gone, her mother's face had been lost to her.

The next morning the *Windsong* was buffeted by strong winds out of the west which threatened to drive her onto the reefs. But the Captain handled the vessel well and all day the crew fought with oar and sail until they found another suitable place for them to spend the night.

Day after day the epic struggle against the sea was repeated until eventually, after almost two weeks, they reached the island on the north-western tip of the chain of reefs.

It was little more than a large sandbar on which vegetation had somehow taken a firm grip. Tall palms and tangled vines formed a solid wall of living greenery at the edge of the beach. As the *Windsong* was run up onto the sand Garrig ordered archers to keep watch on the jungle. Then he gathered the Cathars, Uzziel and Royden to the bow of the beached vessel.

'If we are not detained we should have enough water to reach the coast, but it would be helpful if we could locate some fresh water to augment our stores.'

'Will I take some crewmen and make a search?' Uzziel asked.

'No,' Garrig said. 'There is much to be done on board before we continue and you will be needed here.'

'Then it looks as if I will be seeing more of this island,' Royden noted.

'Take three or four of the men,' Garrig added.

'And us?' Orren-ker asked.

Garrig nodded. 'I would appreciate it if a few of you could accompany the party. They are good men, but if there are dangers hidden in this jungle then they will need help.'

Mahira, Ferne and Phaidra cut their way into the jungle, followed by Royden and four of the crew. The temperature soared and the party was soon bathed in sweat. Hidden roots tripped them and thorned vines snared them as they cut their way deeper.

This jungle was not like the last one they had entered. There was no birdsong or animal cries, and the silence was only broken by the cursing of the crewmen and the noise of their work. After an hour Royden called a halt. His clothing was plastered to his body and his long black hair was hanging limply, soaked with sweat.

'We must rest,' he gasped. 'The heat is incredible, I can hardly breathe.'

Mahira nodded and gestured for the others to stop. Phaidra carried on for several more paces before stopping, while Ferne moved to the rear of the party and kept watch over their back trail. One of the crew carried a hemp-covered jug which he passed to his crewmates, Royden, and then the Cathars. The liquid was fiery and Mahira found herself more thirsty after drinking from the jug.

'Go easy on that,' she advised. 'We are carrying only one waterskin and whatever it is it doesn't quench your thirst.'

'It's only seven-water, missus,' one of the crew laughed.

'Aye,' offered another. 'You should try it when it's not watered down.'

'That's enough,' Royden ordered. 'Stopper the jug.'

The crewman slammed the cork stopper into the neck of the jug then smiled as he licked his fingers clean. 'It mightn't quench a thirst but it certainly takes your mind off being thirsty,' he added as an afterthought.

Phaidra appeared. 'I hear running water just ahead.'

The party hurried after Phaidra and soon found themselves at the edge of a large circular pool of dark water. A tall waterfall at the eastern end fed the pool and a narrow channel running off to the west allowed the pool to maintain the same depth.

'Look here,' Phaidra called.

Mahira stepped to her side and stared down at what Phaidra had discovered.

'The pool's not natural,' Mahira observed. She ran her hand along the rough cut stone which bordered the pool, then reached down into the dark waters where the stonework continued. 'Someone has built this. The Life Bringer only knows why.'

One of the crew tasted the water. 'It's fresh, right enough.'

'Where does the water come from that feeds the falls?' Ferne wondered aloud. She scrambled up the steep side of the falls and disappeared from sight.

'What's that?' said Royden.

'What?' Mahira asked.

'In the water,' Royden said, pointing. 'There by the edge of the pool. Something is reflecting the light.'

One of the crew peered at the water, then stripped off his shirt and sandals and slipped into the pool. Taking a deep breath he dived beneath the surface. Bubbles marked the place where he had vanished and as the bubbles stopped he reappeared, something clutched triumphantly in his hand.

When the Cathars had dragged him from the pool they saw that he held a thick gold bracelet, worked like a chain. One of the crew laughed and unstoppered the jug and took a long pull at the liquid.

'Is there more of it down there?' another asked as he too stripped off.

'The water's too dark to see if there's more, but if we feel along the bottom we might be lucky.'

'I don't know,' Mahira cautioned.

'What harm can there be?' Royden asked. 'We have seen nothing since we arrived. What harm can there be if we gather a few trinkets for later?'

Mahira shrugged. It had nothing to do with her what the crew got up to. She had simply been asked to watch over them while they searched for water. Phaidra joined her as they watched the four crewmen dive again and again, each time returning with some treasure grasped firmly to their chests.

'Mahira!' Ferne stood at the top of the falls and beckoned for the others to join her.

The climb was easy beneath the vegetation. The slope was made of large blocks of stone laid upon one another like a giant staircase.

Phaidra was the first to reach the top. 'What have you found?'

'More stonework,' Ferne answered.

Behind a wall of jungle they could see a large circular area paved with cut stone and bordered by a low sloping wall. They cut their way through the vines and stepped out onto the paved area. There were six tall thin fingers of cut stone around its perimeter, and at its centre was a large stone slab supported by four short pillars. Two of the fingers of rock were capped by a long block of stone.

The three approached the central stone. The rock was dark, much of it covered in thick red moss. The end that was free of moss was much darker than the rest.

'I don't like this place,' Phaidra whispered. 'There is something very wrong here.'

Mahira had the same feeling of disquiet and lifted a hand to stop Ferne as she moved nearer the stone. But Ferne simply pushed her hand away and reached out and touched the large block.

She walked around the block, her fingers tracing faint outlines as they trailed across its cold surface.

'I fear we have stumbled on some ancient altar-stone,' Phaidra whispered. She had seen drawings of similar stones in her studies at her father's temple. They were of a time long before the Final Wars, long even before the time of the Living Towers.

'Let's leave,' Mahira advised. 'Come, Ferne.'

The young Cathar looked across the stone at her companions but it seemed as if she did not see them. Placing her other hand upon the stone she began to trace the deeper patterns.

Mahira backed away from the stone and her heel touched the sloped wall. She glanced down, then shuddered at the sight she saw. Reaching from the tangled growth was a tiny skeletal hand. Her own hands trembling, she knelt down and pulled some of the foliage away to reveal a tiny skeleton.

Phaidra heard Mahira gasp and quickly joined her. More of the skeletons were revealed as Mahira pulled back more of the vines. The entire wall was made up of the skeletons of children, hundreds perhaps thousands of them.

Still touching the stone, Ferne felt a strange warmth flowing through her hands. She had never felt so alive. Her entire body was glowing with life as she felt the warmth flow along her arms and drive deep into her. She heard her name called but she was far too happy where she was to answer.

'What are we going to do?' Phaidra pleaded.

Mahira walked steadily towards the altar and walked quickly around it until she stood beside Ferne. Grasping the girl by the shoulders, she shook her, trying to wake her from her stupor.

A piercing cry lifted above the jungle, breaking the silence. To Mahira's left the area beneath the supported stone began to fade as a white swirling fog appeared. As the fog thinned Mahira saw a strangely carved stone gateway, covered in carved runes, appear. Cut deep into the stone, this lettering was ancient beyond all dreams. Phaidra had seen similar runes before but she had no idea what they meant. All she knew was that something was going to happen that they did not wish to witness.

Mahira reached for Ferne again but the young Cathar twisted from her grasp and ran towards the opening gateway. Through the grey fog, Mahira could see a figure drawing nearer.

'Mahira!' Phaidra called. 'We must leave.'

The figure moved even closer and Mahira backed away from the open gateway. A hand gloved in red leather reached through the gate and took hold of the stonework, as if pulling itself through the gate. A second gloved hand joined it and a figure slowly appeared.

Phaidra had dragged Mahira from the stone area surrounding the altar by the time the figure emerged. It stood close to three metres tall and was encased in red-dyed leather armour. A massive helm covered its head and a huge war hammer was strapped across its chest.

The being arched its back and lifted its arms towards the sun. A cry of pleasure escaped its hidden lips. Stepping forward, it took Ferne by the arms and lifted her to the altar.

15

SNAKEWEED

Bram reached the edge of the river and found himself standing on a two-metre embankment overlooking a wide stone-filled waterway. The water level was low, a rapid ribbon of water working its way down the centre of the wide causeway. Several large sandbars protruded into the swirling current.

Sliding down the embankment, Bram walked across the rock strewn river bed until he reached the water's edge. A large sandbar ran out into the river only a few metres to his right and he began following it out into the river.

The water was clear where the bar ended and Bram could see the sandy bottom. He waded out into the cold water, forcing his way against the current until he reached another sandbar. It was quite large, with more than enough room for the six of them and a good sized fire. They would have to gather all the fuel they needed to see out the night, as the sandbar had been swept clean of any driftwood it might have possessed.

Bram rejoined the others and told them of his find. 'Nobody will be able to reach us without first crossing the river, and with the moon full tonight our watch should spot them easily.'

Sian-vesna and Faina-lai gathered firewood while Yahudah and Kallem manhandled a large log across the sandbar. Once the log was alight it would burn all night. Bram and Tandra walked back to a point from which they could see the tower in the distance.

It stood like a dark pinnacle against the setting sun whose dying rays caught the green-leafed vine making it appear to writhe and dance about the stone walls, as if alive.

As Bram and Tandra turned their backs on the tower and joined their companions, another set of eyes watched the tower.

Raissa eased herself back through the foliage. She and her three companions had reached the tower ahead of the Cathars and had found a concealed door leading to its heart. Taya had no sooner opened the door and entered than the stairwell was filled with her screams. Yolane rushed forward to aid her, but Raissa held her back.

'We must aid her,' Yolane shouted above the screaming.

Before Raissa could answer, the screaming stopped and Taya's body tumbled round the bend in the stairs and crumpled to a halt at their feet. Raissa reached down and felt for any sign of life, but there was none. Her body was as cold as ice and there was already a stiffening of her limbs.

'She has started her journey towards God,' Raissa sighed.

Yolane began to cry.

'Do not mourn our sister now that she begins the greatest journey of her life,' Tavira smiled. 'Be happy that she has been allowed to continue her progress towards God.'

'But she was so young to start her journey,' Yolane cried. 'She always spoke of the great things she would do before starting on that journey. She should have been allowed to finish what she set out to do. It is not right.'

'But that is the beauty of it,' Raissa replied. 'When the unbelievers die, their role in life is gone. But when we are set upon the road towards our God we know that our lives will take shape once again. There in that time we will be given the chance to continue our work.

'Like the setting of the sun. It throws all the lands into darkness and despair, yet we know that another sun will be born and rise, bathing us all in a new hope.'

Raissa looked up as the final rays of the sun slipped over the horizon and quoted an old saying: 'With the dying of the sun we greet the night and pray that the sun will be reborn and return the light of life to us, its most loyal followers.'

Tavira and Yolane bowed their heads and remained silent until the last of the sun's light had left the world, filling them with a darkness as dark as the night itself. As the shadows gathered about them, Raissa observed the full moon sitting high above the horizon.

'Not tonight trickster,' she laughed. 'You play at being the sun but you are only there to allow those who oppose God to do their evil work. In your faint light they live, and if they bother us tonight it will be beneath your pale presence that they will perish. But remember even your light is only a faint reflection of God's.'

A cold wind sprang up and Raissa drew her blanket tighter against her shoulders. She would have liked to have a fire. It was always good to sit about a warm and friendly fire and talk about the past, but they were too close to the Cathars' party camped in the riverbed.

Someone travelling with the Cathars knew of the old lore. Many times Raissa had taken shelter from the evil of the full moon behind the barrier of running water, but tonight she and her companions would just have to take their chances.

The night was half worn when a shadow came up from the riverbed and approached the tower. It moved directly towards the door but stopped short. Raissa waited for the scream that she knew must come, but the night's stillness remained unbroken.

The shadow circled the tower for some time, then ran off towards the river. The sun would rise, reborn, in perhaps two hours. Whoever had entered the tower had not met the same fate as Taya. Raissa was tempted to examine the tower more closely herself, but decided against it. They had already lost one to the tower, now they would need all their strength to complete their mission. To die was to take them one step closer to God, but their training did not allow them to simply throw their lives away.

At the river encampment, Bram had relieved Kallem and stood his watch at the edge of the sandbar closest to the shore. His blanket was pinned about his shoulders and his sword was held firmly in his right hand, its blade cradled gently in the crook of his armoured left arm.

It was hard to pick out any movement in the shadows so he simply stood his watch and listened to the wind and to the water flowing past the sandbar. He took time to identify every sound, so he could pick out any noise that might be made by an intruder.

As he sat beside the raging fire, Bram stirred idly at the glowing logs with a length of driftwood. The wind had risen and was howling down the river valley, adding to the eeriness of the night.

Despite the crackling sounds of the fire, the rushing of the swift flowing river, and the howling of the wind, Bram felt as if he was wrapped in a cocoon of silence.

The riverbank was nothing but a dark outline sketched by a dim moon. Bram's companions slept restlessly behind him, their occasional stirrings adding to the night's noises.

Bram drove the stick deep into the fire, sending a shower of glowing embers high into the air. Snatched by the wind, they swirled about his head before vanishing. Bram had the uncomfortable feeling of something being wrong beyond the light of their fire. He also had the distinct feeling that he could do nothing to stop whatever was brooding in the darkness of the night.

He had felt that same feeling when he was a youth, on the night that his parents had been killed in a border raid. And then again on the night he had been dragged before the Hierarchy of the Chosen.

The Chosen were a group of priests who believed they had heard the word of Iman, a long-dead prophet who it was said had spoken to all of the many and varied Gods of Kyrthos. It was written that he had met with them and talked at length before deciding on which path he was going to follow.

However, he had been slain by an assassin before he had been able to tell his followers which of the many Gods was the right one for them.

The priests of the Chosen felt that it was their purpose to follow in the footsteps of Iman and seek out the Gods and test them. But unlike Iman, they used the path of torture and pain rather than enlightenment. They raided monasteries and temples, carrying off those they wished to subject to their tests. After enduring many and varied tortures, these captives were made to admit the weaknesses of their faith.

The Chosen were under the protection of Uvelrez, a powerful Boyar of Southern Scapol. And the Chosen's Pantheon was hidden high in the Tante Ranges, well away from the prying eyes of the unbelievers or the avenging hands of those who had lost loved ones to the single-mindedness of the priests.

Bram had been drawn to the Chosen by promises of land and of protection for his family. At first he had worked about the Pantheon, but he rose quickly in the eyes of those who watched over him and soon wore the uniform of the Righteous, a religious guard whose sole role was to protect the Hierarchy.

He was only recently married when he was taken to the Tante Ranges, and while his wife Lene was giving birth to their first child, a son, Bram stood a lonely watch one cold night. A strong wind had sprung from nowhere, making it uncomfortable to be outside the protective walls of the Pantheon. Bram walked his lonely beat, his thoughts with his wife.

The instant his watch ended he had sped home to find his son well, his loud wailing filling their small two-roomed cottage. He lifted his son in his arms and drew him close, and as he held the squirming baby he named him Tarynn. But a strange uneasiness hung over him as he watched his son cry his hunger into the first rays of the morning's sun.

When he sought out his wife he found her wrapped in a sheet, laid out on their bed. She had died just as their son had reached life and Bram was struck a deep blow as he knelt beside her still form. Drawing back the sheet he took in her peaceful beauty and allowed his eyes to roam her face, searching for every detail, etching her every feature into his mind.

The next day Lene was buried and Bram had sat by the grave, his infant son sleeping peacefully in his father's protective arms.

Several weeks later Bram learnt the truth of that night. His wife had been tended to by a midwife and four of the Chosen, their role being to see that the innocent child arrived hearing words of a prayer which would protect it from evil.

The midwife drew Bram to one side and begged him to forgive her for not trying harder to stop the Chosen as they had gone about their perverted business. During the labour one of the Chosen had worked off her boredom by asking Lene questions about her earlier life. Lene had spoken freely of her home and father and of their short time together. But the questioning became more intense as it continued, until the prayers were forgotten.

As Bram listened to the tale unfold his anger grew. His wife had died under the questioning of the Chosen and they had called it just. They had sought out evil and found it in his young wife.

Bram entered his home, where he lifted his armour down from its stand and buckled it on. Then he belted his sword about his waist, lifted his shield down from the wall and strapped it to his arm. Testing the edge of his sword against his thumb, he cursed those who had slain his beloved. Then leaving his son with the midwife he had started up the long climb to the Pantheon. Recognised at the gate he was passed through, a word of greeting the only sound from the two sentries.

Bram grunted an answer and forced a smile between clenched teeth as he passed the two armoured figures and made his way to the spiral stone staircase which would take him to the level which held the chambers of the Chosen.

There were more guards stationed along the lengthy hallway. Outside the Chosen's chamber stood four of the Righteous, who were also four of Bram's closest friends. They had trained together and had walked as one their ordered sentry posts on many a cold night.

Bram raised his shaking hand in greeting and Lyronn raised his in return, a smile filling his face beneath his metal-studded helmet. But Lyronn's smile was short lived when he saw the expression on Bram's face.

'Couldn't spend the night without us,' Kalt offered. Always the joker, Kalt was the youngest of the group.

'He has come to relieve us,' Fewr suggested

light-heartedly. 'I have heard it said that he fights like four men.'

'I have heard that as well,' Vizard said, 'but I have yet to see any sign of it.'

Lyronn said nothing but watched Bram's expression as each of his friends spoke. His tense facial muscles betrayed an anger and a rage which were barely held in check. Lyronn lifted his shield higher, but Bram saw the movement and leapt forward, pushing the surprised Fewr into Lyronn.

Bram then brushed Vizard and Kalt aside and threw himself at the door. It splintered under his weight. Bram charged into the chamber, where he saw one of the Chosen who had been with his wife when she died. Rushing forward he struck the man with such a blow that he was lifted from his feet and thrown back against the stone wall of the chamber. His skull crushed, the priest was dead before he toppled to the ground.

Cries of alarm echoed about the chamber as priests tried to make good their escape. Bram could hear the sounds of armour as his friends entered the room but he paid them little heed. When he spied another of the Chosen, Bram brushed two priests aside before reaching her side.

As he grabbed her arm and dragged her around, she struck out at him with a knife which had been concealed in her robes. The blade glanced off his armour and sliced Bram's right forearm. But he seemed not to notice the wound as he reached out and grasped the terrified woman by the throat and crushed the life from her.

A shout from behind him had Bram spinning around, lifting the dead woman as he did so. His four friends were lined up before him, their visors closed and their shields raised.

'Release the Chosen!' Lyronn ordered. His eyes pleaded with Bram as he spoke.

Bram threw the dead Chosen at his friends, knocking Lyronn and Fewr from their feet. Vizard was forced to step quickly to one side, hampering Kalt's movements in the process as Bram leapt for another of the Chosen. Bram's sword flicked out and, with a two-handed grip, he struck the head from her shoulders in a spray of blood.

Searching for the fourth and final of his wife's killers, Bram found him. Velser was cowering across the chamber, a young priest gripped before him as a living shield. Velser's face was contorted with fear and his mouth worked quickly as he prayed.

But now Lyronn and the others had regained their feet and moved to block Bram. Two stood between him and Velser, their stance telling him that, should he choose to attack again, he would find them ready. The other two stood by the only door, ready to deny Bram the chance of escape.

'Put up your sword, Bram,' Lyronn commanded. 'This is madness.'

'They killed Lene,' Bram shouted. 'And he is going to pay for it just as the others have.'

'Your wife died,' Vizard offered. 'There was nothing any of the Chosen could do to prevent it.'

Bram lowered his sword and repeated the tale the midwife had told him. As he did so Velser edged closer to the door. The two Righteous before him followed his movements and kept themselves between Velser and his accuser.

When Bram had finished the chamber was filled

with silence. Lyronn looked to the Chosen and saw in his eyes that Bram was telling the truth.

'Kill him!' Velser screamed. Spittle flew from his mouth. 'Kill him! Now!'

None of the priests moved. The four Righteous stood their ground looking from one to the other, then to their friend and the terrified Velser. Finally Lyronn sheathed his sword and stepped forward, his hands raised.

'If what you have said is true, and the midwife can confirm this, then we should take it before one of the Hierarchy,' he stated. 'If he did have a hand in Lene's death then it's right that he be made to pay for his crime.'

The Chosen stood rooted to the spot, his eyes wide with fear. Bram spat at him and threw his sword to the tiled floor. Fewr and Kalt stepped forward and stood to his side, their swords still drawn but resting by their sides.

Lyronn turned to Vizard. 'Let no-one leave the chamber until I return with one of the Hierarchy.'

Vizard nodded and stepped before the open door after Lyronn had left.

Velser straightened. With Bram unarmed and watched by the two Righteous, he had regained some of his composure and whispered to one of the frightened priests. With a nod, the priest started for the door, only to be stopped by Vizard.

'Let him pass,' Velser ordered.

Vizard stood his ground, his armoured bulk blocking the door.

'Step aside,' Velser screamed, spittle again flying from his mouth. 'You risk sharing the fate of this one.' Velser pointed at Bram.

264

Vizard licked nervously at his lips. Velser stepped out from behind the priest and stepped towards the door, lifting one arm as he did so and pointing at Vizard.

'You have a family, Righteous. Would it be wise to jeopardise their lives as well as your own?'

Vizard threw a glance at his companions, then stepped to one side and allowed the priest to scurry past. The clash of armour heralded the arrival of the white-cloaked Pantheon guards, their tall white crested helmets and leather-bound shields all that could be seen beneath their white cloaks.

Velser stepped forward and commanded the guards to enter and take Bram. Vizard, Fewr and Kalt were undecided as to whether to allow the guards to take Bram but Velser was not going to be denied.

'Three of the Chosen have been slain,' he explained. 'They were killed by that one.' He pointed at Bram, a sneer riding his lips. 'Take him away. He is to await the pleasure of the Hierarchy.'

Bram was ushered from the room.

'These three failed in their role as protectors of the Chosen,' Velser continued. 'They are to be escorted to their barracks, where they will await their punishment.'

As the three Righteous were escorted from the chamber Velser gestured for the guard officer to approach. The guards were responsible for the security of the Pantheon, and there was no love lost between them and the Righteous.

'Bram is to be moved to one of the lower levels of the dungeon and kept isolated until I have time to see to him personally,' Velser whispered. 'If any ask, he was confined on one of the upper levels but managed to escape.'

'And the wardens?'

'If they fail in their duty then they are to be punished. We cannot have dangerous men allowed to wander the Pantheon at will, now can we?'

The officer nodded and left Velser alone in the chamber. Apart from Bram and the four Righteous, three priests had heard Bram's tale. During the night he would have to arrange at least three accidents if his role in the death of Bram's wife was to go unheralded.

Lyronn had already told his tale to one of the Hierarchy when news of Bram's imprisonment reached them. There was also the news that an old midwife had been found dead beside the road joining the Pantheon to the village. She had been stabbed more than a dozen times.

The Hierarchy sent for Velser and when the Chosen arrived they sat silently as he spun his tale of misunderstanding and deceit. Lyronn was on the point of interrupting several times, but one of the Hierarchy had raised a hand silencing him.

When Velser's tale was finished he excused himself from the presence of the Hierarchy and fled to his private chambers. Bram was sent for but it was found that he had escaped. One of the wardens was found dead, his neck broken, and the other had been arrested and questioned by the Pantheon guard before being executed.

The three members of the Hierarchy ordered the release of Vizard and the others and with some reluctance ordered that Bram be arrested on sight and charged with the murder of the three Chosen and the warden.

The Hierarchy had come to know Bram well in the short time he had served as a Righteous, but there was nothing they could do to alleviate the situation. Velser had many friends amongst the more fanatical sects of the Chosen and there was no accusation against him that would stand up to close scrutiny.

Lyronn rejoined his three companions just as word reached them that one of the priests who had witnessed the fight had fallen from the upper ramparts.

'So it continues,' Lyronn cursed as he grabbed a battered leather pack and began stuffing spare clothes into it.

'What continues?' Vizard asked. 'And what are you doing?'

'The midwife who told Bram of Lene's murder is dead. Bram is missing, supposedly escaped. And now one of the priests is also dead. I find it a little too convenient that all who witnessed Bram's tale are dead or perhaps soon to be.'

'But there's us?' Fewr offered. 'We were there. We heard Bram's tale and can speak before the Hierarchy if need be.'

'Fewr's right,' Kalt added.

Vizard nodded his understanding and grabbed another of the packs from the wall and began filling it. 'We can get supplies from the kitchen,' he explained as he drew his tabard over his head and threw it against the wall.

Fewr and Kalt followed suit and soon the four

were walking briskly down the darkened stairways towards the warm kitchen, and eventually the dusty road which led to the village and safety.

In the small dark cell, his head in his hands, Bram listened to the approaching footsteps. A blinding light burst into the room as the door was dragged open. The light was temporarily blocked as figures crowded into the room. Bram leapt to his feet and lashed out, striking one of the intruders on the jaw, but he was soon overpowered by the number of Pantheon guards.

A torch was lifted and Bram laughed when he saw that it was Velser's face he had bloodied in the brief struggle. Velser leapt forward, a snarl on his face and punched Bram in the mouth repeatedly in an attempt to stop the laughing. But Bram kept up his mocking laughter, spitting out the blood which tried to fill his mouth.

Velser stepped back, his shoulders shaking in rage. He snatched a sword from one of the guards and ordered Bram turned, his face to the wall. Bram straightened his shoulders, waiting for the blade to enter his back, but his arms were drawn from his side and held against the wall. As Bram awaited his fate, a strange calm came over him.

Without warning there was a searing pain at his left wrist. His strength increased by the pain, he wrenched his arm free and saw only a stump where his hand had been.

Velser backed from the room, the bloodied sword forgotten in his hands. He glanced up and down the corridor, then licked his lips. 'I will return tomorrow,' he tormented, 'and remove the other hand. But for now I must seek out your son and see that he does not have the evil in him that his mother and father had.'

Bram screamed in rage but the guards pushed him against the wall and quickly exited the cell.

Drawing his left arm in close to his chest, Bram beat on the cell door with his right fist. He had been prepared to die, but he had thought his son safe.

Eventually he collapsed on the floor by the door, not knowing what to do next. As he sat there he heard footsteps approach. The small window in the door opened and a tightly wrapped bundle dropped to the floor beside him.

The bundle was wrapped in a torn section of tabard worn by the Righteous. Inside was a small phial, a piece of white cheese and black bread, and a leather-sheathed dagger. The phial held a white salve Bram recognised as a healing ointment used by Crafters. He applied the salve to his left wrist, wrapped the stump tightly in the section of tabard and lifted himself to his narrow cot.

Bram sat silently in the darkness, chewing slowly on the coarse bread and cheese. When they came in the morning they would expect to find him weak from the loss of blood, but he would be waiting for them and if they had injured his son he would see the entire Pantheon destroyed.

A log collapsed in the fire and Bram woke from his dream. He was sitting on the riverbank, his 'left hand' resting in his lap. The dream had been so vivid, so real, he could almost feel the pain in his left wrist. He threw more fuel into the fire, struggled to his feet and walked about the camp, trying to work the stiffness from his body using the same exercises he had employed as he had waited for his warders to return.

They had come for him the next morning and as he heard the key turn in the lock he had burst from the cell, his eyes ablaze. There had been four of them and as the last one died, Bram had snatched up a sword and fled. He had walked a sentry's post for some time and knew all the narrow ways and darkened stairs.

It did not take him long to flee the Pantheon, but before he did he started a fire in the lower levels which quickly spread. In the village he discovered that his brother had fled during the night, taking Tarynn with him, and that Lyronn and the others had also fled.

Still inflamed by his anger and loss, Bram reasoned that it was Vizard who had betrayed him. It was Vizard who had allowed the priest to leave and the Pantheon guards to enter. He vowed to seek out Vizard and have a reckoning with his old friend.

Returning to the present, Bram looked in the direction of the tower and wondered how they were going to destroy something which had perhaps stood longer than the forest it bordered. The Foxglove Tower had been destroyed once, but it was alive once more, its evil already causing the death of one of their number.

Bram drew the memory of Tarynn from deep within him. He had not seen the lad since Lene's death, but when he found himself standing before a young Cathar setting out on his first charter, he knew the youth was his son even before the name was spoken. The years apart could not hide the resemblance to his mother.

When he had realised who the youth was Bram had been torn between telling the lad the truth or simply saying nothing. All through their charter he had watched the youth closely, holding himself back from stepping in and helping him when he encountered difficulties.

But then they had reached the Foxglove Tower and it was all too late. In one brief moment he had reached for the lifeless body of his son realising that all the things he should have said would now never be heard. He had pledged himself to find the one responsible for Tarynn's death, and by the Slayer he would.

The faintest of sounds snapped Bram from his thoughts. As he stood stock still, waiting for the sound to be repeated, he knew that it was not his imagination. There was something or someone out there. Something dark, its shape undefined, moved swiftly along the riverbank and disappeared into the shadow of a short twisted bush.

Then he heard the sound again. It was the faint noise of dislodged pebbles. Whatever was on the bank was not alone, and one or more of them were trying to descend the steep embankment. Without taking his eyes from the source of the noise, Bram backed up until he felt his heel touch the sleeping form of one of his companions.

Kicking sharply he heard a grunt then a whispered question.

'What is it?' Kallem asked.

'Something comes,' Bram answered and returned to his post, leaving Kallem to wake the others.

Bram saw a flash of something moving swiftly

through the darkness, this time closer, almost at the water's edge. Whatever it was, it was small and fast and the darkness did not hinder it. His eyes ached as he strained against the darkness, trying to find the shadow once more.

A soft footfall signalled the arrival of Tandra.

'Where?' was all she asked.

'Just across the river,' Bram whispered. 'At least two, probably more. One on the bank and another at the water's edge.'

'Jaeger?'

'No,' Bram answered. 'Something small and fast.'

The water in front of the pair suddenly erupted as three small figures leapt from it and attacked. Bram took a step back and cursed loudly as one of the attackers went for his throat and the other wrapped itself about his thigh.

Ignoring the sharp pain that lanced upward through his leg, Bram held the first attacker at arm's length, impaled on his trident. Then he flicked it from him and struck at the other with his sword. The sound of bone on flesh drew another curse from Bram. However, it was followed this time by a coarse laugh.

The camp behind him was in chaos as more of the creatures shot from the water and wrapped themselves about arms and legs. The pain in Bram's leg grew worse and he realised that the small thing had bitten him. For a moment he feared poison, but shook the thought from his mind as he realised that there were more than enough of the attackers to slay them all, with or without poison.

Tandra had killed the one that had attacked her

and was busy cutting the throat of another which had attached itself to Yahudah. Bloodied, the young girl jumped to her feet brandishing her knife. Sian-vesna and Faina-lai stood back to back and cut at the small creatures as they darted in for their attack.

Kallem was in the most difficulty. He was down, with at least a dozen of the small creatures squirming over him. He had two creatures by the throat and was bashing their heads together as Bram reached his side. Kicking one attacker away, Bram slashed at another with his sword. Kallem threw the two dead attackers from him and ripped another from his back, driving its head into the sand, breaking its neck. An injured creature crawled towards Bram but he quickly stomped the thing into a bloodied mess before helping Kallem to his feet.

Kallem was covered in blood, nearly all of it his own. His sword was lost and he wobbled unsteadily as he drew his knife and turned to seek out more of his attackers.

Suddenly Bram found himself shielding his eyes as the sandbar was bathed in a bright light. A soft chittering noise filled his ears as he tried to find the attackers in the unexpected light.

As his sight cleared he saw Sian-vesna standing in the centre of the sandbar, her shell medallion held before her face, her eyes closed. She was whispering something that Bram could not hear, but that did not matter as he could see the results of her words. A dozen or more of the small dark creatures were trapped in the brilliant light. Child-like, they stood enthralled by the light, their dark smooth skin shining. There was a loud chittering sound from the riverbank and, as quickly as they had appeared, the creatures vanished.

Bram crossed to the fire and kicked half the fuel they had gathered into it. The dry tinder caught almost at once and soon the sandbar was lit by the growing flames. Sian-vesna sighed and lowered her medallion to her chest. Opening her eyes, she swayed slightly and Faina-lai was forced to reach out to prevent her from falling into the fire.

'What by the crooked tail of the Slayer were they?' Bram swore. 'And where in the Ten Living Hells did they come from?'

'Hirudo,' Yahudah answered. Even though she stood beside the roaring fire, she shivered as she spoke. 'They are the Hirudo, a disgusting race of creatures which live on the blood of those they trap.'

'If you know of them why didn't you warn us?' Kallem demanded.

'I have never seen one of the Hirudo before,' Yahudah replied. 'I only know of them from descriptions given to all children of the Saphy by our Grandmothers.'

'Are they to be found often in this region?' Sian-vesna asked.

'No. My Grandmother told me that they're only to be found in the waters surrounding a small chain of islands far to the north-east.

'As a youth my father and several of his friends followed the Berdun River north to its source. They saw several small islands just off the coast, but when they tried to reach them they were attacked by the Hirudo.'

'Then what are they doing this far south?' Bram asked.

'Perhaps they were drawn towards the tower,'

Faina-lai offered. 'We are here to ensure that none reach this tower and gain its power. Perhaps the tower realises this and has drawn old allies to its cause.'

'Then the sooner the tower is destroyed the better,' Yahudah said firmly.

Sian-vesna glanced at Yahudah and saw that Kallem was also watching her. Looking up, she found Faina-lai's large eyes locked on her own.

'Then I suggest,' Sian-vesna began, 'that at first light we enter the tower and destroy it.'

Bram and Tandra agreed but Faina-lai, who did not drop her eyes from Sian-vesna's, said nothing.

Woken by the sounds of fighting, Raissa placed a restraining hand on each of her companions and whispered for them to be still. The sounds of combat increased and Raissa judged that it was coming from the Cathars' camp.

Small shadows were darting about the top of the embankment and Tavira stifled a soft curse when she saw one of them enter a patch of moonlight.

'Hirudo,' she whispered.

Raissa could feel Yolane shudder at the word and squeezed her shoulder tightly. 'Say and do nothing,' she ordered as she drew her companion closer.

Yolane and Tavira lowered themselves back to their blankets, their eyes wide with fear. The Hirudo were a parasitic race whose homeland bordered that of the Deisol. Sitting on Solan's eastern border, the Bay of Darkness was shunned by all who knew the dangers the region had to offer.

In times long past a powerful Crafter had created

the Hirudo, as well as several other equally disgusting races, and had set them free in what was then a bay used by smugglers. It was rumoured that he had lost a great deal of money to one of the smugglers and this was his means of revenge. The appearance of the Hirudo and their cousins soon put an end to any smuggling which may have taken place amongst the many islands in the chain used to protect the small smugglers' vessels and their illegal cargoes from the frequent storms of the region.

There was a larger island in the heart of the bay but it was shunned by all as a place of immense danger. None who had dared cross its shores had ever returned.

Not only was the smuggling curtailed, but so too were all forms of trade between the islands. None dared approach the water's edge as the Hirudo lurked in the shallows, waiting for the unsuspecting. They did not kill their prey, they overwhelmed the poor fool and drew the blood from its body until unconsciousness came. Then they would leave what was left to one of their larger and perhaps more dangerous cousins.

'What are we to do?' Yolane whispered.

Raissa ignored the question as she sought to calm herself. Slowly she dredged all she knew about the Hirudo from her memory. Then with a silent prayer to the Deis for a speedy rebirth of the sun she slowly opened her pack. Inside was a small shielded lamp. Opening the small door, she gently slid a finger in and felt the wick.

Satisfied that it was damp with fuel, she opened a small pouch at her belt and drew out her flint and tinder box. It would take only seconds for her to strike a spark and then a few more precious seconds to transfer it to the lamp. The Hirudo were not afraid of light, but they preferred the darkness. A bright light held them mesmerised as it did with many animals of the night.

Raissa drew her companions in even closer so she could whisper her instructions to both at the same time. 'If we are attacked, hold them at bay while I light a lamp which I have prepared. At first they will be unsure of how many of us there are and, by the time they know, we will be safe within the protection of the lamp's light. They will freeze as it reaches them. Strike out quickly then and kill all within reach.'

As she spoke a bright light appeared to Raissa's right. Hidden by the embankment, the three Deisol were able to watch as the Hirudo stopped their movement, held enthralled by the radiating light.

A sharp call snapped the Hirudo from their dreams and they silently melted into the shadows, two passing dangerously close to where Raissa and the others hid.

'One of their Crafters has called up a light,' Raissa offered.

'Deis be praised,' Yolane sighed. 'I had felt my feet upon the road to our God, but obviously it was not to be so.'

'There is time aplenty for God to call you to her side,' Raissa laughed. 'And when the time comes no Crafter is going to make any difference.'

Sian-vesna and Faina-lai set about cleaning the injuries sustained by the party. The bites of the

Hirudo were not poisonous, Yahudah assured them, though a wound caused by one did take some time to stop bleeding.

'Their saliva must hold a potion which keeps the blood flowing freely,' Faina-lai reasoned. 'The faster they can draw the blood the faster they are nourished.'

'Father said you just clean and bind the wounds and then allow them to heal by themselves,' Yahudah explained.

'Will they return?' Kallem asked. 'Or will the fire now keep them at bay?'

'No, the fire won't hold them off,' Yahudah answered. 'Even the bright light would only have held them. We would have to kill them to be free of their danger. It was the call which took them from us.'

'Call?'

'Yes,' Bram laughed. 'I heard it. Just after the light appeared there was a sharp barking sound from the darkness. Then the Hirudo vanished.'

'Whoever guided them here called them back before we could kill more of them,' Faina-lai stated firmly. 'It was not the creatures themselves which were called by the tower, but whoever controls them.'

'Then they will return?'

'It is . . .'

A terrifying scream echoed across the river. Bram had never heard such a sound before. It was as if the very soul of some poor innocent was being ripped from them while they were forced to watch. Shivers ran the length of his spine as the scream continued far longer than he thought possible.

When the scream came to an abrupt end Bram

made the sign of the fist before his chest, not giving a damn who saw him. Yahudah rushed to Faina-lai's side and buried her head in her cloak. Backing away from the water's edge, his eyes wide with fright, Kallem swung his sword arm back and forth as he sought the hidden danger.

Raissa had seen the tall cloaked shape which had crossed the open ground to the base of the tower and then disappeared into its dark heart. Only three heartbeats later the terrible scream had broken the stillness of the night.

As with Taya, three heartbeats were all the time the cloaked shape was given to see its slayer in the dark interior of the tower.

'Who was it?' Yolane asked.

'Whoever controlled the Hirudo,' Raissa answered. 'It was summoned here with implanted thoughts of greed or power, but it was unable to pass the guardian on the stairs.'

'Why would the tower summon someone and then slay them?' Tavira wondered.

'Only the most resourceful will pass the killer on the stairs and reach the heart of the tower and the power it offers,' Raissa answered. She spoke quietly, as if to herself, but the others were so close that they could not fail but hear. 'Only someone driven by the need for wealth or power will try to enter the tower, and only one willing to sacrifice all will pass the killer the tower has as its protector.'

'Are we to try for the tower?' Tavira asked.

'No,' Raissa answered, easing the worries of her companions. 'We are simply here to ensure that none enter the tower and live. That role is being performed most adequately by the tower's own guardian.'

There was little sleep on the sandbar as the five tired Cathars and their young companion waited for the sun to rise. They sat about their fire, trying not to think of what might be watching them from the shadows of the river's edge.

The party broke camp as the sun rose. No thought was made of breaking their fast. They had nearly been killed by creatures who spent their lives in the water. All they wished to do was get as far as possible from the river whose protection they had sought.

Bram and Tandra looked at the tower. It was obvious that both thought it less of a threat than what they had faced during the night. As they approached the tower a cloud of dust appeared from the east and soon they saw a handful of the carts used by the Jaeger racing towards them.

The Aves drawing the carts were reined to a halt only metres from the party, covering them in a cloud of dust.

'Greetings.' Aleron grinned as he jumped down from his cart. Turning to his companions he added: 'Stay with the chariots, it won't take me long.'

Before anyone could stop him he turned and sprinted for the tower.

'Stop him,' Tandra cried.

But it was too late. At the base of the tower Aleron turned and laughed. 'You might have fooled my sister but you are no match for me,' he shouted. 'I have heard of the treasure which rests at the top of this tower and I will have it for myself.'

Aleron glanced down at the bodies at his feet and shrugged as he stepped through the door and vanished into the tower. Raissa counted from where she lay concealed a short distance away. A scream rang out and Aleron's companions had a difficult time holding the Aves in check as their only thought was to head for the horizon.

Tandra and Bram reached the door just ahead of Sian-vesna. Tandra drew her sword but Bram touched her forearm. 'What use is steel against a wraith?'

Tandra looked down at the strange dead woman lying at the base of the stairs. She wore well-kept armour and carried a longsword. Her hair was braided and tied back, but it was her eyes which interested Tandra the most. Around her eyes were tattoos similar to those she had seen on the leader of the imposters who had taken four Cathar lives and Yahudah's entire clan.

Beside the body of the woman was another. This one was dressed in dark soft clothing, like a Feni. Was this the one who had brought the Hirudo here?

Sian-vesna shouldered her way past the pair and stared up into the darkness. The screaming had stopped and she could neither see nor hear anything.

During the night she had held her medallion close and had listened to the whispered words of Charybdis as he had told her what to do. She knew that there were at least four wraiths inside the tower. They had now fed on the life-force of three bodies— the strange woman lying at her feet, whoever had brought the Hirudo, and now Aleron.

Sian-vesna took a deep breath and entered the

tower. The moment her foot touched the bottom step she felt a presence ahead of her on the stairs. As she touched the second step she was filled with a deep tearing hunger. What she was feeling was the hunger of the wraiths. Clutching her medallion even tighter she placed her foot upon the third step and the light vanished and the world spun.

16

LYCHWORLD

All about Charybdis was a thick swirling mist which flowed back and forth like the waters on a lake. He stared into the mist through Sian-vesna's eyes, unsure of what he would find. He had expected to meet a wraith on the stairs and, after enslaving it, move upward towards the tower. But he had not expected this.

He could sense that Sian-vesna was on the verge of panic. Easing her thoughts, he commanded her to advance, her medallion raised before her. He felt a tingling down his back and Sian-vesna spun around just as a wraith appeared out of the mist.

The wraith was unlike any Charybdis had seen. It was more manlike and its form was fixed. It did not waver as had the others he had contacted. The wraith extended a hand and walked towards the terrified woman. It could sense the fear emanating from her and knew that she could do nothing to stop it from taking what it needed.

Just as the wraith's hand was about to close on

Sian-vesna's wrist, Charybdis thrust his consciousness through the medallion and took control. He
extended Sian-vesna's hand and touched the wraith.
A tearing wind appeared and with a silent scream
the wraith was torn apart.

Had Charybdis used his power through the
medallion he would have been able to tap the power
of the wraith. At the Foxglove Tower he had taken
the power and used it to feed his own creatures, but
this time he was unable to do so. Instead, he could
feel the power flow into Sian-vesna.

Easing himself back slightly, he allowed Sian-
vesna to regain control of her body. She was confused. She realised that she had been attacked and
that she had destroyed the wraith, but she was not
sure how. As she stood in the mist she could feel the
power welling up inside her.

With the medallion still raised, she turned herself
in a slow circle and took in her surroundings. The
wraith on the stairs at the Foxglove Tower had been
a shadow, unfocused; the one she had just encountered was sharp and true. Its outline had shown it as
a creature resembling a man in more ways than she
had thought possible.

By following her line of thought, Charybdis
came up with the only answer. Wraiths looked the
way they did because they were not truly in their
world. Only their life-force was present and it was
with this that they killed. It was also how they were
trapped. Somehow, on touching the third step of the
tower Sian-vesna had entered the world of the
wraith, the Lychworld.

Charybdis was taken by surprise as Sian-vesna
dropped to the ground and rolled, reaching out with

her medallion to touch the wraith which had appeared before her. He felt a brief flutter of panic but managed to push it down where he could control it.

It was more than possible that Sian-vesna could be slain in this world, but could he? She had shown herself competent in handling the wraiths and perhaps it was time for Charybdis to leave. Gathering his strength, he thought of the gem in his tower room and closed his eyes. When he opened them he found that he was still seeing through Sian-vesna's eyes, trapped in the world of the wraiths.

Bram and Tandra waited for the scream they knew had to come, but there was only silence. Sian-vesna had somehow destroyed a wraith at the Foxglove Tower. Was it possible that she could repeat it here?

'It is as I thought,' Faina-lai interrupted.

'What is?' Tandra asked.

'When I told you that you were chartered to find information about the Living Towers, it was on Sian-vesna's behalf.'

'What?' Bram cried.

'She is the agent of whoever has already conquered one tower, possibly two, and who now seeks a third.'

'Which towers?' Bram asked, totally confused.

Faina-lai drew the pair from the tower's opening. 'The Foxglove Tower is now under somebody's influence,' she explained. 'I have kept in contact with my Charter House and have learned that the party sent to destroy the tower was stopped short of it by a force they could not pass. The tower is now almost complete. Somebody is quickly rebuilding it.'

'And Sian-vesna is under this somebody's control?' Tandra asked, not wanting to believe what she had heard.

'We do not know which tower holds her master. But should she succeed in reaching the uppermost room of this tower then her master will control three towers. And as you can see, this one is not in need of any repairs before its power could be tapped for other purposes.'

'But how?'

'The towers are built of a stone called liflode which stores the very life-force from the world beneath us. The plants which cover their walls drink the power from the deep of the land and store it in the living stone, awaiting use. In the uppermost room of this tower is a Lychgem which allows the master of the tower to transfer the power from the stone for his own use. With it he is able to carry out deeds of mass destruction.

'The Cathars were originally intended to walk the roads of Kyrthos protecting any who asked from whatever dangers lurked, but we were also to seek out any knowledge of these towers and keep it for a time when it might be needed.'

'If the towers are so powerful what could possibly destroy them?' Kallem asked.

'They have a weakness. They need to attract a master, one who can pass their defences and reach the Lychgem. Once faced with the gem, the tower knows that the power and wealth offered will overcome all resistance.'

'Then the secret is to slay the defenders and

reach the upper room of the tower,' Bram suggested, 'but to reject the power and wealth the tower has to offer.'

'If the power is rejected, could it then be used for other purposes?' Tandra asked.

'No,' Faina-lai replied. 'The power can be used for many purposes, but the Lychgem regulates it and will allow it to be used for one purpose only.'

'And that is?'

'The strengthening of their grip upon the land and the people working it.'

Sian-vesna could see nothing about her but the swirling mist, but knew that and still stood on the third step of the tower. She took a deep breath and began to climb the stairs, soon finding her head clear of the mist which had obscured everything. Within only a few more steps she found herself totally above it.

To her left was a rock face of grey stone, to her right a sheer drop to the swirling mist. Looking down she could see nothing but the grey blanket. Charybdis saw more.

Sian-vesna was standing upon a narrow sloping trail. Above her stretched a finger of rock, its summit bathed in a bright glow of reflected light. Charybdis lifted Sian-vesna's left hand and placed it on the rock face. It was warm and the texture was like a dry skin rather than the cold rock he had expected.

Again Charybdis directed Sian-vesna to examine the surrounding terrain. He could see nothing below the level of the mist, but in the distance he could detect another bright glow. Off to the east he made out a thin white column of light reaching upward until it was lost from his sight. There was another fainter one to the south-east.

Urging Sian-vesna onward, he climbed toward the top of the finger of rock. Another wraith appeared before him. Again, it was more manlike, its features frozen rather than the shifting ones he knew in his own world.

The wraith wore thickly woven grey clothing which looked as if it was plaited from the fog which hid the base of the rock finger. The wraith stepped closer and Sian-vesna raised her right hand. Her left was fisted about her medallion.

At the sight of this the wraith took a half step backward. Charybdis commanded Sian-vesna on. Step after step the Cathar moved upward while the wraith slowly backed away from her. Charybdis increased their pace until the wraith was forced to turn and run.

When Charybdis felt a tug at his control over Sian-vesna he realised that his Cathar host was finally aware of her true surrounds. In his attempt to tighten his control he almost ran into the waiting wraith. He sidestepped the extended arms of the wraith but in doing so moved too close to the pathway's edge.

Loose stones rolled beneath her feet and Sian-vesna began to slip over the edge. Charybdis screamed, his screams and fear allowing Sian-vesna to break the control he had over her. As she grabbed frantically at the edge of the path, she dropped the medallion.

Sian-vesna's arms were almost wrenched from

their sockets as she hung out over the grey mist, searching frantically for some type of toehold. The wraith reached down for her, and when the grey-clad hand touched her right hand, Sian-vesna screamed in pain.

Charybdis suffered the same pain. Fire twisted through his head, searing his eyes and throat. He opened his mouth to scream again but found he could not utter a sound. The pain flared deeper until he felt it reach deep into his chest, towards his labouring heart.

Just before she had slipped over the edge Sian-vesna realised that Charybdis was inside her, controlling her. The pain searing through her eased. She had pushed him away but she knew that he was still there, fighting for his life against the wraith. She also knew that the wraith would turn its attention to her as soon as it had finished with Charybdis.

Sian-vesna released the rock edge with her right hand and snatched at the medallion. The pain of her full weight upon her left arm was excruciating but she did not have much time as she felt the struggles between the wraith and Charybdis ease within her.

She located the medallion and grabbed it, then concentrated on the wraith. A surge of power blew about her like a wind, threatening to dislodge her weakened grip. Above the wind she heard the death cry of a wraith.

Sian-vesna drew herself up slowly over the rock edge and lay on the path, her back to the rock wall. Her arms were on fire and her legs cold and numb. There was a large blister on the back of her right hand where the wraith had touched her.

Searching deep within herself she found

Charybdis cowering, as he sought to heal himself. His injuries were horrific, his skin was burnt and blistered, his eyes blinded. But he still clung to life. Sian-vesna sensed that he was as much a prisoner within her as she was a prisoner within the tower. If either of them was to survive then she had to reach the summit of the rock finger.

Sian-vesna dragged herself to her feet and resumed her climb, her left hand steadying herself against the wall while her right hand clutched the medallion. After what seemed an eternity she stood on a small flat platform atop the rock finger. The wind blew about her, dragging at her clothing as she fought for balance.

At the centre of the platform was a bright sphere, its radiance reaching up like a column of light. Beside the source of the light was the tall figure of a wraith, clothed like the others.

'Welcome.'

There was no discernible mouth, yet Sian-vesna definitely heard it speak.

'I have dreaded the moment of your arrival,' the wraith pulsed.

Sian-vesna heard the words but did not understand.

'The Lychgem has been calling a master for many generations and I have fought with it, ordering my followers to slay all who entered the tower. But its call was too strong and I knew that one day one would come.'

The wraith turned from the light and lifted a wand it held in its right hand. A flash of light sped from it and struck Sian-vesna on the medallion, throwing her backward. She teetered on the edge of the platform, screaming as she fought to regain her balance before the wraith could strike again.

Lights flashed about the centre of the platform, dancing and weaving themselves about the source of the light column. Then the wraith spoke.

'The Lychgem wishes to protect you but that is impossible. It may desire a new master, a role which I cannot take, but I can still block its power.

'I have struggled long with the Lychgem of the Snakeweed Tower. Hundreds of my kind were lost upon our world in the attempt to wrestle this icon from its rightful owner.' He held the wand aloft. It was short and thick.

'This was carved from a branch cut from the Tree of Death on the banks of the Lost River. My followers fell in their hundreds as we fought the defenders of the tree until we were forced to face the Ferryman himself. The battle took many lifetimes, but finally we were victorious and thus armed we attempted to make this tower our own.

'But, incredible though its power may be, the wand gave me only a faint glimpse of the power locked within these walls, a power that is rightfully ours.'

'Why yours?' Sian-vesna asked. She could feel her strength returning. The longer the wraith spoke the stronger she was growing.

'The cursed plant that draws the power of this world also taps ours, which has long passed the point where it is able to heal itself. So as your world prospers under the towers, ours dies.'

'But how are you here?'

'I was able to use the trickle of power at my command to open this tower to the Lychworld. It is much the same as a Lychgate and I hoped to draw the tower through and thus remove your race as a threat. But I was able to open only this stairwell and upper room. Your arrival marked the death of the last of my brethren, and your final moments among the living.'

The wand reached out again and another small sphere of light struck Sian-vesna's medallion, searing her hand. Again she screamed. Sian-vesna eased her grip on the medallion so she could lift her hand and survey the damage, but a wild cry from within her stopped her actions.

'To release the medallion means death,' Charybdis pleaded. 'The wraith can inflict pain but it cannot kill us without touching us. Should that happen we will have a chance to destroy it. And it realises this. See how it keeps its distance.'

'But how can I fight it?' Sian-vesna implored.

'You cannot,' the wraith laughed.

'No, you cannot,' Charybdis agreed. 'But hold, help comes.'

Bram and the others heard the screams echoing down the stairs and knew that Sian-vesna had finally met the wraith. As the echoes of the scream faded, Tandra drew Bram away from the door.

'There is nothing we can do for her,' she sighed.

'It was for the best,' Faina-lai offered. 'If she had reached the gem then the tower would have fallen to her master.'

'She was a companion!' Bram spat the words. 'She was of the road and I have fought beside her many times. We have only your word that she was a traitor. Where is your proof?'

Tandra was surprised at Bram's anger. She was

also surprised at herself. She had accepted Faina-lai's words as truth, without asking for a shred of evidence, and it took Bram to speak the obvious.

Tandra turned to Faina-lai, her eyes asking the questions.

'No!' Bram shouted.

Tandra spun round as Kallem darted into the tower, his sword drawn. Taking the steps two at a time, Kallem sped up the stone spiral staircase until he stood before a closed timber door. Pushing on the door, he felt it give and pushed harder. When the door was wide enough open for him to slip through he entered the room.

To the left of the door he found the telltale cracks which heralded the secret door. Without pausing, he opened the door and climbed the stairs. In the centre of the room was a pedestal beside which were the shadowy figure of a wraith and the exhausted form of Sian-vesna. She was barely able to stand and Charybdis' form was superimposed over hers.

As Kallem started forward the wraith turned to face him. Kallem knew that to confront it without adequate protection meant certain death. In the back of his mind he heard the whispered words of Charybdis: 'Forget the wraith. Touch the Lychgem and he will die. The gem—that's all that matters.'

Kallem reached the large Lychgem and its smaller companions. He reached out and placed his open right hand on the gem. The wraith screamed and vanished, its wand falling to the floor. Sian-vesna collapsed and, with a sigh, Charybdis fled from her body and passed through the gem back to his own form.

Charybdis looked down at his hands and saw

that they were once more whole. Raising them to his face, he touched his nose and mouth and realised that the damage done to him was only in his astral form—while abiding in Sian-vesna.

He was thankful that he had not placed all his eggs in the one basket. The thought of using another Cathar had come to him in a dream and he had leapt at the opportunity. He did not have the tower as he had planned, but at least it was now controlled by one who would ally himself to Charybdis and his cause.

Sian-vesna staggered down the stairs towards her friends. As she came into sight Bram leapt forward to support her. He lifted her in his arms and sat her carefully on the ground, her back against one of their packs.

Tandra handed him a waterskin and Bram gripped the stopper in his teeth and pulled it free, offering the refreshing water to Sian-vesna. She gulped the water and began to choke.

'Take it easy, lassie,' he urged. 'There's plenty of time and water.'

She sipped at the water, her smile relaying her thanks.

'What happened in the tower?' Tandra asked. 'We heard you scream and thought it was all over.'

Sian-vesna smiled weakly. 'There was a wraith on the stairs, and then two more further up. I managed to destroy them and reach the top of the tower before confronting the last one. It stood by a large gem and spoke to me. Told me that it was there to stop the tower from falling into the wrong hands.'

'How did you defeat the wraiths?' Faina-lai asked.

'I don't exactly remember. I held my medallion out and touched the first and second and then they were gone. The third I merely thought of defeating and it vanished in a tearing wind. The fourth attacked me before I had a chance to defend myself. If not for Kallem we . . . I would surely have perished.'

'What of Kallem?' Bram asked.

'Kallem is no more,' Sian-vesna lied. 'He distracted the wraith and was slain, but thanks to the distraction I was able to slay the final wraith. When I had recovered enough strength I staggered down the stairs, knowing that you'd be waiting.'

Faina-lai turned towards the tower. 'All the wraiths were destroyed, you say?'

'Yes.'

Faina-lai stepped towards the door but, as she did so, a gust of wind appeared from nowhere and the door slammed closed. She tried to reopen it but it refused to move. There was no handle on the outside, and no sign of a lock or hinge. No matter what she tried, the door refused to budge.

'It's for the best,' Bram mumbled.

'You fool,' Faina-lai cursed.

Bram sprang round and faced the woman, his hand resting on the pommel of his dagger. Tandra reached forward and placed a restraining hand on his shoulder. 'We do not fight amongst ourselves,' she whispered.

'Nor do we speak falsely of our own kind,' he snapped as he glared coldly at Faina-lai. 'You said that Sian-vesna would take the tower for her master. It looks to me as if you were wrong.'

'It is not over yet,' Faina-lai told him.

'It is as far as that tower is concerned,' Yahudah added. 'That door is shut fast and no-one's going to open it.'

'Now what?' Bram asked Tandra. He ignored Faina-lai.

'We do as we always planned. We seek out the Monkshood Tower,' Tandra answered.

'And this tower?' Faina-lai asked.

'None may enter it,' one of the Jaeger called. 'With the door closed fast there is no way to enter its stone embrace. When we return here we will tell our Fathers and a watch will be placed upon this place.'

'Good enough.' Bram looked down at Sian-vesna and saw that she had fallen asleep. 'When do we leave?'

'She will need time to regain her strength,' Tandra answered. 'We will have to rest here for a short while.'

There was no body to bury but the Cathars paused and remembered their lost companion, Kallem.

'It would be an honour if you and your party would share the comforts of our settlement,' another of the Jaeger offered. 'We have sufficient room in our chariots to carry you.'

'Done,' Bram snapped. Then he lifted Sian-vesna into his arms.

As the party climbed aboard the Jaeger chariots, Kallem watched. He saw Bram turn and regard the tower, making the sign of the fist before his chest before he too climbed aboard and the chariots raced off toward the southern horizon.

Kallem turned from the transparent wall and examined his new surroundings. There were riches and power to be had here and he knew then that he had made the right choice. He was now the Master of the Snakeweed Tower, ally to Charybdis , Master of the Hawkthorn Tower and Protector of Tarynn, Master of the Foxglove Tower. A word sprang into his thoughts. He had no idea what it meant but all he could think of was the word, Crataegus. Somehow that word eased the small fears which remained. He looked out over the land that would soon fall under his command—and Kallem smiled.

Charybdis lay on his bed, his mind filled with thoughts. When he had entered Sian-vesna's consciousness he had been one with her. He remembered the view he had seen from the rock finger.

The columns of light had been generated by the Lychgems. He had seen similar columns in the distance. Did that mean that they shone from the summits of other rock fingers? Was it possible to reach the towers from the wraith's world as well as his own?

The strange wraith had mentioned something about a wand, but Charybdis had been in too much pain to hear all it said. A wand, a battle, a Ferryman and the Lychworld were the only memories he had of those final moments in the upper room of the tower. When his strength returned he would contact Sian-vesna and learn more about what had happened.

Climbing from his bed he found Bohe at his side and, with the creature's aid, he made his way to the library. Charybdis had discovered the index system the previous owner used and he looked up the word Ferryman.

Charybdis soon found a wealth of information. As the ancient myths related, there was a land, the Land of the Dead, from which it was possible to enter other worlds. But to enter the Land of the Dead you first had to cross the Lost River by the only transport available, a small ferry.

There was a price charged by the Ferryman but it was minimal. And across the river there were many dangers still to be found, but the book did not describe them, referring instead to other volumes. But Charybdis had learnt what he needed for now.

If the towers were so powerful drawing the strength of but two worlds, then what would their power be like if he could link them to others?

The valley was steep-sided, barren and forbidding. At first glance, it looked to be deserted, void of any life or sign that anyone had ever entered it.

But locked in the shadows was a circle of standing stones. Two of them were capped and a grey mist swirled as if trapped between the long blocks of stone. As the mist solidified a gate of rough-hewn timber appeared, hanging on large hinges of beaten metal. The gate swung silently open and a tall powerful figure appeared.

Jaax, the Iledrith, turned his face towards the dying sun and rejoiced in his freedom. He smiled briefly at the crumpled form of the young Saphy girl slumped upon the cold stone altar. She was as beautiful in death as she had been in life. Her blood had flowed across the altarstone, filling the runes and giving life to the Lychgate.

Crouched beside the altar was the twisted figure

of a man dressed in rags. His few teeth were black and rotted, his hands thin and dry as he twisted them in the ragged tunic.

'I have brought the offering you desired, Master,' the pathetic creature whinged. 'I hope it pleases you.'

Jaax regarded the miserable wretch, his fingers aching to draw his longsword and remove the snivelling thing from the world. But he knew that he would have need of its help if he was to remain undetected.

A wave of his gloved hand was all that he offered the wretch, but it was enough. With a soft dry laugh the ragged man crept back from the altar and rested his filthy back against one of the cold standing stones.

Jaax drew a triple-edged dagger and crossed to the alter. Dipping the blade into the last of the runes he watched as the dull grey metal turned a brilliant red as it drew the blood from the T-shaped rune.

He turned to the Lychgate and began to trace the runes about the gate with the blade of his red dagger. As it touched the stone, faint wisps of smoke rose into the cool mountain air. The runes were well worn by time and weather but as the dagger traced their ancient lines they seemed to rejuvenate.

Jaax sighed and withdrew the dagger from the stonework. The blood which had been trapped within the blade was now gone, transferred to the runes above the Lychgate.

'I return to my realm.' As he spoke, Jaax looked over his shoulder at the cowering figure. 'When all is in readiness I will return.' Then, turning towards the pathetic figure, Jaax extended an armoured arm and stabbed at him with a finger. The ragged man jumped to his feet, his face filled with terror. 'You will have more offerings ready for me when I return. I will have need of their blood if I am to bring my forces through the Lychgate. Is that understood?'

The man attempted to speak but his mouth refused to work. He tried to nod but he shook so much from fear that his body bobbed up and down as he strove to make his answer clear.

Jaax nodded. Then he turned sharply and stepped through the Lychgate which closed swiftly behind him.

The trembling figure clung to the standing stone as if, even after the departure of the Iledrith, he could not gain control of his limbs. Silently he cursed the day he had wandered into the mountains seeking refuge. He had come upon the circle of standing stones by accident and had immediately known their significance. But he had not turned and fled. He had sat and watched the stones for some time before making his way into their centre.

In times past he had been a man of power. He had controlled many men and had been chosen to lead the path of man towards the one true God. Chosen. That had been the title he had served under. His very words had had the power of life and death. But the time came when he had been attacked in his own rooms, attacked by one who had been trained to guard him.

He had taken steps to have the person punished, but the Righteous were a close-knit company and the imprisoned guard had escaped, aided by an unknown friend. The Hierarchy had refused to take the matter further, saying that it was best if the facts of the case were left muddied on the off-chance that the real reason for the deaths would surface.

Velser pushed himself off from the standing stone and staggered a few steps towards the altar. He had lived off the miserable land surrounding the stones and their deadly secret for many years, fearful of leaving sight of them in case he lost his bearings, or some other found the stones and opened the gate before he had the opportunity.

When a young Saphy girl had wandered into the valley, Velser had seized his chance. Her blood had been warm as it flowed across the smooth stone of the altar, filling the runes. His heart had rejoiced as the Lychgate appeared and the Iledrith entered the world. But his desires and greed had been short-lived and the terrible power of the Iledrith had borne down upon him, crushing his will.

All those years ago he had cut the hand from the man who had tried to kill him and he had intended to carry on until his enemy was no more. The Iledrith appeared able to read his deepest memory. Pain had seared through every part of Velser's weakened body as the Iledrith cut him with its serrated-edge longsword. Finally the pain had been too great and he had passed out, only to awaken whole. What had transpired had been only a dream.

But the pain of his torment was still there. It was never ending and, to ease it, he was forced to carry out the will of his Master. And even though it was the Iledrith who tortured him, Velser blamed another for his suffering. One day he would be returned to his position of power and he would make his old enemy pay. He would find his true tormentor and make him suffer for his wrongs.

'Your time is short,' Velser screamed into the still mountain air. 'I have gained an ally and I will hunt you to the ends of the earth.'

Velser paused and relished the thought of vengeance.

'Your time has come, Bram!'

17

ILEDRITH

Kallem had little time to adjust to his role as master of the tower before he heard the now-familiar voice of Charybdis. Orren-ker and the others had risked the Western Ocean and reached an island holding an old altar.

'What is it they have found?' Kallem demanded as he stood before the Lychgem in the Snakeweed Tower, an image of Charybdis before him.

'It is a place most foul,' Charybdis cursed. 'It is from a time when the world was new and things of great beauty and of great evil strode the lands. It is a Lychgate to the world of the Iledrith. In times long past they would pillage this world, killing all who stood before them save women of child-bearing age.

'The captured women were taken to the altar beside the Lychgate, where dark ceremonies of evil worship were carried out. Then they were taken through the Lychgate to the Lychworld, where they were mated with the Iledrith. The Iledrith were not human and the births were few. Those children who were born were carried from their mother at birth and taken before the Iledrith.

'A grotesque cross between Iledrith and human, they were able to control the Lore of the Lychworld and were therefore of great value.

'Male human children were tested and those who survived were made warriors or slaves. Many of the females were taken back through the Lychgate to be sacrificed within the circle of standing stones. Only the best were kept to continue the breeding program.'

'Are they immortal, these Iledrith?'

'They live until they are slain. There is no writing which mentions an Iledrith lifespan. They are a race who yearn to pass through the Lychgate, and enter this world. But the towers are not just the locks warding them from Kyrthos. They are also the keys to their release.'

'Are Mahira and the others in danger?'

'They are if they remain,' Charybdis warned. 'But I cannot warn them while they stay within the boundaries of the altar. However, you could.'

'How?'

'You know them. If you open your mind to me I will be able to reach across the great distances and pierce the evil barrier of the altar.'

'But by opening my mind to you I could wake as your slave and not your ally,' Kallem argued.

'I wish only to aid those dear to you,' Charybdis replied softly. 'It matters little to me whether they live or die. The others will reach the Monkshood Tower.'

'But if they don't?' Kallem countered. 'If they also run into something . . . unknown, then what will happen to your plans?'

'It makes no difference. I can only reach them with your aid, and to do so I must be allowed to enter your mind.'

'I'm afraid not,' Kallem answered. 'Your plans are of no concern to me.'

'But your friends are.'

'You must do something!' Kallem yelled.

'I can do nothing,' Charybdis pleaded. 'Nothing without your aid.'

Kallem looked down at the scene at the altar as the Iledrith drew Ferne closer. Her armour and clothing were gone, strewn about the cut stone floor, and she lay naked on the altar. Her arms were raised and her face filled with passion.

'All right!' Kallem shouted. 'What do I have to do?'

'Nothing,' Charybdis crooned. 'Just close your eyes and relax. Think of nothing but me and my voice.'

Charybdis entered Kallem's mind and with the link was able to add the power of the Snakeweed Tower to the two he already commanded. With such additional power he was able to send a driving thought across the great distance.

Orren-ker sat upright, a pain tearing through his skull. As he clenched his eyes tightly to squeeze the pain from his head, in his mind he saw Mahira and Phaidra on the edge of a stone platform. On the platform itself was Ferne and a creature straight from the tenth level of hell.

He leapt to his feet and rushed into the jungle, ignoring the startled cries of Garrig and the others.

As he pushed his way through the thick foliage he cursed himself for allowing the three to leave the safety of the beach and travel inland. Faint words in his mind told him over and over what had to be done.

Mahira tried to pull away from Phaidra but her hold was too tight. 'We must help her,' she begged.

With one last effort Mahira freed herself from Phaidra's grasp and, leaping forward, she took her dagger from her belt, drew back her arm and let fly. End over end the dagger flew until it struck the armoured back of the stranger. The dagger spun onward, through the body of the stranger, and buried itself in the centre of Ferne's naked chest. Ferne's lifeless body fell back onto the altar, her head striking the stone edge.

The blood seeping across the altarstone was all that was needed for Tragg to return to his world and bring his true body, not the shadow form he now wore, through the Lychgate.

The armoured being lifted its head and cried out, causing the trees to shiver and the ground to shake. Turning slowly, the protected figure faced the two Cathars.

Phaidra could see the glowing red eyes of the being through the narrow visor of its helm. It lifted one gloved hand and Mahira started forward. Phaidra drew her knife and, reversing her grip, she struck Mahira a sharp blow on the back of her head. Mahira dropped to the ground, unconscious.

The visored eyes locked on Phaidra. She could feel the power of the being as it sought to take control of her will. Slowly at first, and then faster and faster, she began to recite a simple prayer her father had taught her. At first her tongue stumbled over the words, but it was not long before the familiar phrases began to flow freely.

The being lifted its visored face toward the sky and a terrifying laugh echoed from the helm. Again it turned its red glare upon Phaidra.

'Thou cannot deny me, woman,' the Iledrith thundered. 'I hath travelled across the breadth of my realm for thee. Thee or another of thy kindred. For I am Tragg, the Hammer.'

Phaidra continued to recite the prayer, but, even as she resisted, she could feel herself drawn closer to the being.

Orren-ker reached the site of the struggle just as Phaidra stepped upon the sacred stones surrounding the altar. As the armoured figure lifted both hands and held them out towards her, Orren-ker grasped the medallion about his neck and drew in the power he would need.

He did not know exactly what he was doing, but if he obeyed the whispered words which now appeared in his mind he believed his companions would survive. Pointing his left hand at the figure, he took a deep breath.

Tragg saw the puny interloper and realised that he was about to be attacked. Holding the woman with his will, he calmly awaited the onslaught. His true body was quite safe, still beyond the Lychgate, and his shadow presence could not be damaged. Suddenly the figure twisted and a small ball of fire shot from his hand, not towards the armoured figure but towards the open Lychgate.

The Iledrith screamed his rage and quickly dropped the woman as he tore the hammer from where it was secured across his chest. When he reached the open gate he sensed another attack, but he deflected it with his hammer.

Tragg examined his attacker and realised that the human was under the control of another, one far from here. To attack the human the Iledrith knew he would have to lower his defences, and this would allow the human to attack the open Lychgate once more. The human would die, but Tragg realised that the one behind the attacks would remain quite safe, protected by distance.

The Lychgate was struck by a ball of force. Another blast could damage it, perhaps trapping Tragg on the wrong side of the gate, a thing for which he was not ready. Tragg stepped back into the Lychgate, his hammer raised before him until the last moment. 'Thou has bested me, human, but our lives will cross again.'

Tragg raised a mighty fist towards the blood-red sky. He had been denied that which he needed most, a passage from his dying world to one filled with riches. But he would not be denied for long. The gate had been opened and the blood of the female had filled the deep-cut runes on the altar.

It was the curse of his race. A human female had to be sacrificed before the physical body of an Iledrith could pass through the Lychgate.

A condition of use for the Lychgates had been set long ago. Only the blood of a female could open the gates as females were the most prized and protected beings on Kyrthos. In recent centuries the price of a female's life had been reduced so low that with the waking of the towers the Lychgates were once more accessible.

Orren-ker collapsed to the ground. Behind him he heard the sounds of approaching men as Garrig and some of his crew drew nearer.

Tragg vanished and the Lychgate closed.

Kallem released a deep breath and opened his eyes. The image of Charybdis was gone, Phaidra and Mahira had been saved and the Iledrith driven off. Kallem knew from his brief touch with Charybdis' mind that the Iledrith could re-open the Lychgate from his side. It could be opened by a human female touching the altar, tracing the deep-cut lines of the ancient runes carved within the stone, followed by a blood sacrifice. Both had now happened.

He had been wrong about Charybdis. He had thought that once in control of his mind Charybdis would not return it. Perhaps his alliance with the Hawkthorn Tower was a good thing after all.

Charybdis laughed uncontrollably and rocked back and forth, supported by the gem's pillar. When he regained control of himself he wiped the sweat from his face and the tears from his eyes. He had saved his Cathars and at the same time ensured an alliance with the Snakeweed Tower. He had returned control of Kallem's mind, but not before he had added a slight doubt about Charybdis' dishonesty. He had also touched slightly on the thought of loyalty. Kallem was now a puppet of Charybdis as surely as was Asal.

*

Orren-ker knelt beside Phaidra. Her heart was racing and she was gasping for breath. Mahira was still unconscious.

He crossed to the altar, but even before he reached it he knew what he would find. Ferne's naked body lay back across the cold stone, the pommel of a knife protruding from between her breasts. The back of her head was matted with blood and a large pool had formed on the altar.

The area between the standing stones showed no sign of the gate or their visitor. The arrival of Garrig and several of the crew drew explanations from Phaidra and Orren-ker.

'Where are Royden and the others?' Garrig demanded.

'We left them by the pool,' Phaidra answered as she helped the still groggy Mahira to her feet.

Once she was upright, Mahira pushed Phaidra away and staggered towards the altar. Orren-ker stood in her path, his hands raised.

'You will do no good here,' he whispered.

'I must see,' Mahira begged.

'No,' Orren-ker ordered.

'But I killed her. I threw my knife and it struck her in the chest.'

'It was not your fault,' Orren-ker consoled. 'There was nothing you could do about it. Nothing at all.'

Orren-ker tenderly put an arm around Mahira's trembling shoulders and turned her away from the altar. His mind was still filled with the world he had seen as he had rushed to his companions' aid. There had been a face, neither old nor young, but it had offered to help him in his fight against the Iledrith.

Iledrith? That was the name or the race of the being he had driven off, yet he did not know what it meant or how he had come by the name.

Someone had contacted him through his medallion and then lent him aid in his fight. Perhaps another Crafter of the Cathars had come to his aid. But how had his saviour known?

They descended the steep slope until they reached the pool. Beside it was a pile of golden trinkets, surrounded by a large-linked chain of gold. But there was no sign of Royden and the other crewmen.

Garrig ordered a search, but it did not go well. His men remembered Phaidra's description of what had just happened and none of them wanted to stray too far from their companions. Garrig approached one of the younger men and spoke quietly with him for some time before they both moved to the edge of the pool. The nervous youth stripped off his shirt and dived into the dark waters which did not have time to settle before he was back, climbing frantically from the water. He was shaking and his face had lost all sign of colour.

'Did you find anything?' Garrig implored.

The youth nodded and pointed. 'They're down there,' he whispered. His eyes were wide with fright and his voice trembled. 'Wrapped in long lengths of golden chain.'

'All of them?'

He nodded.

'All four?'

Again he nodded.

One of the crew bent to pick up a large golden brooch.

'Leave it!' Garrig snarled. 'I'll not have one piece of that gold taken aboard my vessel.' The crewman looked as if he was about to protest, but Garrig motioned for him to be quiet. 'That gold drew four good men to their deaths and I will not see it do its evil work upon any more.'

Garrig crossed to the pile of gold and began throwing brooches and bracelets into the dark water. When he had finished one of the crewmen joined him and they lifted the large chain and dropped it into the pool. There was a brief final flash of gold as the chain struck the water and vanished.

'We must leave here at once,' Garrig ordered.

'Ferne will need burying,' Orren-ker said.

'I'll not expose my men to any of the dangers this accursed place has to offer,' Garrig replied. 'We will be on the beach once you have finished, but no matter how deep you bury her I fear it will not be deep enough.'

Orren-ker and Fallon retraced their steps to the altar. They lifted the body of their companion down, wrapped it tightly in cloaks and carried it into the jungle. There they cut two large poles to act as a litter.

'Garrig is right,' Fallon whispered. 'We cannot bury her deep enough to protect her from the evil of this place.'

'Do you suggest we just leave her here?'

'No. Of course not. But we could take her back to the *Windsong* and bury her at sea far from this evil place.'

Orren-ker wiped the sweat from his brow. 'I thought only of a burial, but she could never rest safely here. We will take her back on board if Garrig allows it, and bury her far from here.'

As they passed the pool they gathered Mahira and Phaidra and began their arduous journey to the beach. Garrig was only too happy to be free of the island and ordered his crew aboard and the vessel freed from the beach at once. Under desperate oars, the *Windsong* pulled herself away from the island.

Ferne's body was washed and wrapped in a large section of canvas, the sailmaker stitching closed the shroud which was weighted down with several large stones. Then the canvas-shrouded Ferne slid over the rail of the *Windsong* and into the sea.

'May your sword stay sharp and your eyes keen,' Orren-ker intoned, 'as you set your feet upon your final road.'

One by one, her companions threw a small gift into the waters that would be her home for all eternity.

'What will we do tonight?' Phaidra asked.

'I'll not put back to that island,' Garrig stated firmly. 'Not even if it was a choice of there or the ocean opening up and swallowing me.'

'Then what?'

'We carry an anchor in case there is no suitable beach,' he explained. 'We'll use that tonight. And tomorrow night if need be.'

The Iledrith cursed his luck as he strode the red-shrouded terrain of his home. He had lived in this red hell for longer than he cared to admit. Never hungry yet never knowing the satisfaction of a fresh kill. Never hounded by his enemies, yet never comforted by the sounds and smell of death as his hammer smashed the life from some living creature.

313

As he strode across the rough terrain he stared and cursed at the sight of the Lychstreams reaching upward from the summits of the rock fingers. It was the awakening of these fingers of rocks and their shadows, the towers, in that other world which had allowed the Lychgate to be opened. But it had been the same power, channelled through some unknown source, that had driven the Iledrith back through the gate when he was so close to feeding.

The altarstone and the circle of standing stones were made of liflode, the same material from which the Living Towers were constructed. As the Lychstreams were awakened, so too were the towers in the world beyond the Lychgates. And as more of the towers drew their power from the world, so too would more Lychgates appear, each one waiting for some poor soul to enter the circle. Any male approaching would feel the terror of the circle and the altarstone it protected. If a female entered, then she would be drawn towards the stone and the runes it bore.

Tragg had been forced back to his world. But the blood on the altar was still fresh and he ordered two cohorts of his warriors, commanded by one of his best Dey, through the Lychgate. The Dey were his commanders, the cream of his long breeding program. They knew only Tragg's thoughts, and were willing to die for him should the need arise.

Of the once-mighty race of Iledrith, only a handful remained. They had fought their almost continual wars amongst themselves until the race faced extinction.

*

With the winds now driving them away from the dangers of the reef, the *Windsong* made faster time east than it had west. In less than two weeks it was off the coast of northern Skarn, well beyond the grasp of the Belial.

'Where to from here?' Garrig asked.

Orren-ker took hold of his medallion and stepped to the rail of the *Windsong*. He concentrated on his medallion and thought of the many maps he had copied. An old parchment appeared before his eyes and he quickly studied the features on it before it vanished.

'We need to travel for several days north. Until we come to a large bay,' he said. 'You will anchor in the bay and await our return. We should be no more than a few weeks.'

Garrig gave his orders and the *Windsong* was soon cutting her way north.

Orren-ker sat with Mahira and Phaidra, easing their feelings of guilt. Fallon had helped in any way she could, but she too felt the strength of the depression which had overtaken her two companions.

As the day wore on, the sky to the west darkened and the sea turned violent under the whipping of a savage wind. As the size of the waves grew the crew became more agitated.

'We'll have to find shelter soon,' Garrig shouted above the wail of the wind, 'or it'll be too late.'

Orren-ker drew out his medallion and again consulted the old maps he had copied. Searching the dry parchment, he found a reference to a small settlement which had been deserted, long before the Final Wars. It was built above a gently sloping beach and had been the home of a clan of fishermen until disaster had struck.

'There's a suitable beach not too far from here,' Orren-ker called.

Garrig nodded and ordered the helmsmen hard over. With a new bow officer clinging for his life, the *Windsong* turned her battered bow towards land. She was not a heavy craft and the waves toyed with her as she neared the beach.

As they approached the beach, riding one wave after another, Garrig ordered the sails struck and the mast lowered and secured. At the last moment the order to raise oars was given, but some of the crewmen were injured as the three-metre oars touched the beach and were torn from their hands.

When a large wave eventually threw the *Windsong* up the beach, Orren-ker swore he heard the sound of snapping timbers. The crew scrambled over the side and the ship was secured. Exhausted, the crew then collapsed.

Garrig and Orren-ker stood on the dunes and looked out over the violence as the waves crashed against the small strip of beach. On the sand the crew were scattered, too tired to even attempt a fire. Behind the dunes stretched a flat, arid terrain. Orren-ker could not believe that it could be so dry so close to the Belial.

'I've seen stranger things,' Garrig said. 'I once sailed a river right through the heart of a desert. There we were surrounded by sand. We must have looked a sight to any of the natives.'

'How long is this storm likely to last?'

'A day or two, no more.'

By the afternoon of the second day the storm had

begun to lessen in intensity, but with the drop in the wind came the heavy rain, soaking everything in sight. Canvas shelters had been erected but these had been raised to keep the wind at bay, not the rain, and soon everything they had brought from the *Windsong* was soaked.

All through the night they sat huddled on the beach, their misery increasing as the wind rose again, freezing wet clothing to the bodies of the tired and miserable crew.

As the light of day appeared the crew climbed wearily to their feet and, after a quick breaking of the fast, all equipment was loaded aboard the *Windsong*.

The sea was still up and when they were on their way once more, Garrig was forced to detail several of the crew to man the pumps.

As predicted, the *Windsong* reached a large bay, at the far eastern edge of which they found a steep shingled beach. There was a large stand of trees and the game looked plentiful, but Garrig was not taking any chances. The *Windsong* was anchored and a small party sent ashore. Once a good campsite was located more of the crew landed the supplies the Cathars would need to reach the tower. More supplies were brought ashore and Garrig decided to keep a watch from the higher ground to the east rather than from the vessel.

That afternoon the sentry rushed into camp to report a large body of men moving towards the bay. There was only one small boat ashore and the strangers would be upon them before Garrig could ferry all his men back to the *Windsong*.

With fifty-seven of them ashore there were

enough left on board to defend the *Windsong* where she sat out in the bay. Waiting quietly in the stand of trees the crewmen and Cathars watched as the small figures in the distance grew into squat and dark-skinned men. They were carrying long spears and oval shields but they approached the bay as if they expected to find nothing there.

When they crested the last rise before the bay and saw the *Windsong* and then the small camp, they went berserk and rushed down the slope to attack the intruders. Cutlasses rose and fell as the attackers were cut down. Mahira, grabbing her first chance to release the anger which had grown inside her, leapt into the centre of the fray, her longsword cutting a bloodied swathe before her. The creatures threw themselves insanely at the crew but they were slowly beaten back, their screams of frustration echoing in the ears of the defenders.

Phaidra was leaning against a tree to catch her breath when another group of natives appeared. As the party readied themselves to meet the new threat, a cry from the bay captured their attention. The crewmen who had remained aboard the *Windsong* were also fighting for their lives against a group who had worked their way up from the south, swimming out to the vessel while the crew had watched the fighting ashore.

'That's why they didn't care about their losses,' Garrig cursed. 'They intended to keep us busy while they took the *Windsong*.'

'Fire!'

Garrig saw a thin strip of smoke rise from the deck of the *Windsong* only to be caught by the breeze and blown away. As he watched another plume of smoke appeared, and then another. The second wave of attackers were happy to stand on the crest and watch the struggle for the *Windsong*.

'Why are they waiting?' a young member of the crew asked.

'Perhaps they believe that if the vessel falls into their hands then we might surrender without any more bloodshed,' Mahira said.

'Would we surrender?' the youth asked.

Mahira reached down and drew back the top lip of one of the slain natives. The teeth were pointed and yellow. The youth shuddered as he looked from the body to the waiting natives.

The crew left on board had beaten off the attack and doused any fires. As they watched, another group, even larger than the first, entered the water and swam out towards the vessel.

Garrig could hear Uzziel's curses as the anchor was raised and the oars manned. Slowly, with barely half her oars manned, the *Windsong* crept from the bay towards the safety of the open ocean. When they saw that their prey was escaping, the natives turned and swam back towards the shore.

'At least the *Windsong* is safe,' the youth sighed.

Mahira was not so relieved. 'Unfortunately, that leaves us as the only entertainment.'

As if they had heard her words, the waiting natives attacked. Mahira reached for the youth to push him behind a tree but when she found no-one there she risked a quick glance. The youth was dead. A thrown spear had driven its way through his chest and a thin trickle of blood ran from the edge of his mouth. There was a look of surprise on his face.

The attack was short but bloody and when the

natives withdrew they left a large number of their brethren dead on the beach or in the stand of trees.

Under the watchful eyes of Garrig and the Cathars, the crew set about felling a number of trees which they lashed into a temporary palisade. A tall tree was marked as a watch tower and soon one of the crew was perched precariously high in its branches.

As the day wore on the palisade took shape. Progress was slow at first, but the small party eventually found themselves surrounded by a stout wall as high as a woman. In all that time there had been no sight of the natives or the *Windsong*.

'How long will the *Windsong* hold off shore?' Mahira asked Garrig.

'Probably until Uzziel sees that we are safe. Then he should put back into the bay.'

'He'd better hurry,' Fallon added. 'That storm looks like it's about here.'

Garrig had watched as the storm moved closer to the coast, but there was nothing he could do. Uzziel was in command now and it was up to him to see to the safety of the ship. It would be useless beating off the natives if the *Windsong* broke her back on some shoal.

'We'll just have to sit it out up here and wait,' Garrig reasoned. 'There's little else we can do.'

The natives reappeared along the long ridge, only to vanish as the storm blew in. Under the cover of the driving rain Garrig ordered more of the trees felled and the palisade strengthened. The stores which had been brought ashore were stacked in the centre of the fortified camp, with two crewmen acting as sentries. The lookout was still high in the tree, but he had seen nothing on the plains east of the camp for several hours.

'If the *Windsong* does not return for whatever the reason,' Orren-ker ventured, 'how long can we hold out?'

Garrig looked at the pile of stores. 'About a month,' he calculated. 'There was enough food and water brought ashore for your party to travel to the tower and return. And sufficient stores for a sizeable party to remain ashore.'

'Then we must wait for the *Windsong* to return.'

'For how long?' Mahira asked. 'We do not know what has befallen her—the storm, a reef. Perhaps they put into another bay and were attacked again. We can't sit here and do nothing.'

'What would you have us do?' Garrig asked.

'Find some way to communicate with these natives. See exactly what it is they want.'

'I thought that was obvious,' Garrig snapped.

'You are a long way from your vessel now, Garrig,' Mahira replied. 'On the road, we Cathars live by our wits as well as our sword arms. It seems pointless to remain here fighting for this strip of beach.'

'If we tried to leave, do you think the natives would allow us?'

'Who knows?' she answered. 'But we must try.'

'There is also more at stake here,' Phaidra added. 'If the natives are a threat to us now, then they will be more troublesome once we start towards the tower. The problem should be settled here.'

When next the natives appeared on the ridge, Orren-ker and Phaidra stepped from the palisade and began to walk slowly towards them. Mahira and Fallon waited just out of sight, their weapons drawn.

'You have a plan?' Phaidra asked.

'No.'

They walked in silence until they reached the base of the ridge. Orren-ker raised his arms to prove that he carried no weapon and continued alone. The natives looked the same as the ones who had attacked earlier, but they were dressed differently.

As Orren-ker approached, one of the natives also stepped forward. He wore a leather breech-cloth and sandals which laced to his knees. There were a multitude of tiny coloured shells woven into the long thin plaits which covered his head.

'We come meaning no harm,' Orren-ker offered.

'Why come at all?' the native asked.

'Our vessel was damaged and we put into the bay for repairs,' Orren-ker lied smoothly.

The native spoke softly with a shorter man who stood to his right. His chest was a mass of healed scars and his head had been shaved some days ago, as there was now a thin covering of stubble.

'You can stay,' the native agreed. 'But you must pay.'

'For the death of your men?'

'They are Emulys,' the native said dismissively. 'Animals! Their lives are worthless. My people hunt and kill them wherever they are found. Their village lies near ours and if we had the strength we would wipe them from the sight of God.'

'Then what must we pay for?'

'For the right of passage.'

'What is the cost?'

Again the native conversed with the scarred

man. 'Five offerings,' he answered.

'Offerings?'

'Five of your people to be offered up to the Nightones.'

'Gifts?'

'Sacrifices.'

'I must speak with my people about this,' Orren-ker said. 'If your price is not acceptable is there another offer?'

'Death for all of you.'

Back in the safety of the palisade Orren-ker told the others what he had learned.

'What in the Ten Living Hells is a Nightone?' Mahira asked.

'Perhaps only the Life Bringer knows,' Phaidra speculated.

The natives were waiting, many of them sitting on the ridge, drinking from skins and laughing amongst themselves. They looked to be in no hurry to collect the price they had set.

'It cannot be long before the *Windsong* returns,' Garrig offered. 'Speak with them again, see if there is some other way. Above all things, keep them talking.'

Orren-ker and Phaidra returned to the native and his scarred companion.

'You have the price asked?' the native inquired.

'I have been instructed to ask about the Nightones? We have never heard of them before.'

The scarred man nodded and sat cross-legged upon the ground. The taller native followed suit and soon the two Cathars were sitting on the dry grass of the ridge. A young native approached, carrying a leather bucket and four small beaten copper cups which he placed between the seated figures. He then retired.

The taller native smiled and opened his arms, tilting his head forward as he spoke. 'I am Izak Vy Bryn, Koel of the Kolecki. And this,' he gestured to the scarred man at his side, 'is Jere Vy Vachel, my Oathman.'

'I am Orren-ker, a Crafter of the Cathars. My companion is Phaidra, also of the Cathars.'

'Well met,' Izak greeted. 'I arrived too late to stop the bloodshed. I hope you will think about our offer.'

'The price is somewhat high,' Orren-ker commented, 'but we will give it the thought it deserves.'

'That is good,' Izak stated. 'The blood price must be paid by all. Even those in high standing must offer up a sacrifice when the time arrives.'

'When exactly is that?' Phaidra probed.

'The offerings are taken to the Totem and the sacrifices are made when the moon is high.'

Phaidra sipped at the drink she had been offered. It was quite strong, with a pleasant taste, but after the third sip she found that her head began to spin.

'Where is the Totem?' Orren-ker asked.

'Many weeks' travel to the sunrise,' Izak explained. 'In the search for offerings we have been forced to travel far across the many lands. The Emulys have also been set a task by their God and they too seek out offerings, preying on the clans of the Kolecki.'

'Will we meet with these Emulys again?' Phaidra asked.

'If you do it will mean more bloodshed,' Izak answered.

'What is the Totem?' Orren-ker asked.

'It is a place where God once spoke to our Oathmen.'

'Once?'

'It has been many lifetimes since our God has spoken to any of our Oathmen,' Izak explained. 'At first it was thought that somehow we had sinned. When we first set foot upon this land our people had heard the word of God, but as the years passed his words vanished and we were left wandering.

'Recently we have learned that the Emulys have been sacrificing captives and slaves at the sacred altar in an effort to reach their God. It seems they have been successful because, soon after, they started a holy war which can only lead to total destruction.'

'But, what exactly is the Totem?' Orren-ker repeated. He feared the worst.

'It is one hut placed upon another that reach upward towards God,' Izak explained. 'Only the lower hut has a door, and it is through this opening that the offerings are thrown.'

'Have any returned?'

'None.'

'And you have been forced to produce more offerings of late?'

'Yes.'

Orren-ker climbed to his feet. 'It may be possible that we are able to help you,' he said. 'I must speak with my people and I'm sure we will agree to your terms.'

Orren-ker signalled for Phaidra to be silent as he

walked back to the palisade. When they entered its protection, Phaidra sprang around, her face contorted with anger.

'How can you agree to help these savages?' she stormed.

'Think.'

'Think be damned,' she raged. 'They want five of us to sacrifice to their God, all in the hope that he will tell them how to destroy their neighbours.'

Garrig, Mahira and Fallon joined the pair. Orren-ker quickly outlined what had taken place and Garrig too became angry, realising that there was only his crew to offer as sacrifices.

'Just who do we give them?' Fallon asked.

'That's easy,' Orren-ker answered. 'You, me, Phaidra, Mahira and one other.'

'Are you mad?' Garrig asked.

'Their Totem has to be the tower we seek,' Orren-ker replied. 'What better way to find it than to be guided right to it?'

This quietened them.

'They will lead us right to the tower.'

'And then they will throw us in,' Fallon added.

'Exactly,' Orren-ker said. 'They will throw us into the tower. Isn't that where we wish to go?'

'Won't they be slightly angry when we emerge, and their God has not spoken to them?' Fallon argued.

Mahira turned to Orren-ker. 'You said that none have ever returned from the tower.'

'That's what we were told.'

'Then we will be the first. Our words could be the words of God they are waiting to hear.'

Garrig pulled at his ear as he thought about all that had been said. 'All well and good, but if they see through your charade, you're all dead.'

'No deader than we would be if we stayed here and the *Windsong* failed to return,' Mahira added.

18
AWAKENING

It had taken two weeks of hard travelling for Tandra's party to reach the source of the unnamed river high in the Custodians. They had been guided by Neroli, using the chariots of the Jaeger. Even so, the journey had been difficult and Bram doubted they would have made it if not for the tireless efforts of the Aves.

Neroli stepped from the chariot. 'You will have to travel a few kilometres downriver before you can safely launch a raft,' she observed as she eyed the fast flowing water.

The river erupted from a narrow gap in the mountains behind them, hurling itself down the steep slope of the gorge. If they launched a raft here it would be smashed to kindling against the gorge's sheer sides.

'You have helped us more than we could have hoped for,' Tandra offered.

'I did it for Aleron,' Neroli whispered. 'He sought power and it killed him. If all the towers are like the Snakeweed, then they must be stopped from drawing more people to their deaths.'

'We will succeed if it is at all possible,' Tandra assured her.

'I would ask one favour,' Neroli said. 'You have every right to deny it, but I must ask all the same.'

'Ask.'

'I wish to journey with you. I wish for a chance to avenge my brother's death.'

Tandra turned away from the Jaeger and watched the whitewater as it seemed to fight with itself for a place in the gorge.

'The journey will not be easy,' she said at last.

'It will be made easier by more hands,' Neroli countered. 'It will take many willing workers to construct and then steer a raft down this river.'

Tandra smiled. 'Perhaps you are right. A journey of this magnitude seems beyond the strength of four, no matter how dedicated.'

'Five,' Yahudah interrupted. 'I have travelled with you this far and I will not be turned back now.'

As the supplies were unloaded from the chariots, Tandra and Neroli talked quietly, well away from the others. Faina-lai sat beside Sian-vesna and Yahudah prepared a quick meal before they set off. Faina-lai was confused by what had transpired at the Snakeweed Tower. She had known in her heart that Sian-vesna was aiding someone in the attempt to reach the towers, but she had made no attempt to master the Snakeweed Tower. Instead she had staggered from it, saved from the wraith within by the sacrifice of Kallem.

Bram stood some distance from the party and watched the progress of the Jaeger. He had heard

Neroli ask to accompany them and he thought it a good idea, though he did not interrupt Tandra as she contemplated her decision. Yahudah was a child and Faina-lai old and twisted with hate. Sian-vesna and Tandra were the only ones Bram could count on, and this journey was far too dangerous for just the three of them to manage.

Finally it was agreed that three of the Jaeger would join with the party. Neroli and the brothers, Cyrille and Xever. Without delay, the eight began to wind their way down the narrow treacherous path which followed the river's edge.

In places Tandra swore the path had been cut into the rock face by human hands. But other sections were of loose stone and she shook her head, realising that the path they followed was a sloping ledge, and nothing more.

Once free of the gorge the river opened out and the waters slowed. The river was still far too fast for them to think of launching a raft, but the signs were good that they would soon find a safe place.

After a hasty meal they erected the few tents they carried and all but Bram and Xever climbed inside. A light rain started to fall and Bram cursed his luck as he strode about the camp. Finally he wedged himself into a large crack in the rock from where he could watch out over the camp. On nights like this he would once have taken refuge in his small silver flask, the burning liquid warming his body from the inside, fortifying him against the cold. But that time was long past. Each time they had stopped to catch their breath, Bram had felt the need for a drink, but each time he fought off the impulse. The cold lifeless body of his son, Tarynn, was always before his eyes.

Xever sat beside the fire, keeping it well fuelled against the chilling rain. The only sound from the mountains and trees around them was the singing of the rain as the wind blew it amongst the branches and crevasses of the overhanging rock face.

Bram sat his watch, his sword resting across his knees. The silence disturbed him. It was not right. The trees about the camp should have been filled with life. The faint light of the half moon did not penetrate the deep shadows of the jungle and only offered a fleeting glimpse of the campsite itself. Not for the first time, he would have to rely on his other senses to locate any dangers.

His watch was nearly at an end when Bram heard a shuffling noise from the trail. The noise stopped and Bram leaned forward, straining for any other sounds. Somewhere in the night a stone was dislodged. It rolled down a steep slope, collecting others as it did so. Then came the sound of someone falling, followed by a faint curse.

Bram slipped silently from his perch and worked his way towards the intruder. Whoever lay at the edge of the camp had not moved and, as he drew closer, Bram detected the dark outline of some thing or person lying beside the trail.

There were more sounds, this time emanating from his right, from the camp itself. Bram froze. Obviously Xever had heard the noise and was also investigating.

The intruder was going nowhere and Bram decided it was far too dangerous to encounter the Jaeger in the dark, lest he be mistaken for an intruder. The only thing he knew about these new companions was that Neroli's sister had become a Cathar some time in the past.

Another noise betrayed Xever's position as he tried to move silently up on the intruder. The intruder must have heard the noise as well because there was the sound of more loose stones as he moved. Bram saw the shadow as the intruder slipped something from his belt. Believing it to be a dagger, Bram lifted his sword and readied himself for the attack.

Softly at first, and then louder, a gentle piping sound reached above the stillness of the jungle. The piping came nearer until Bram heard surprised voices rising from the camp. Xever stood and moved towards the sound, his sword sheathed.

'What, by the dust of the Great Plains, are you doing here?' he cursed.

'Playing,' came the answer.

'How did you get here?'

'I walked. Though I must admit you set a fast pace. I thought I was never going to find you.'

Neroli and Tandra reached Bram's side and in the light of the torch Tandra held high, Bram saw that the intruder was the crippled Jaeger, Kaela.

'He can't come with us,' Faina-lai argued.

'Then what are we to do with him?' Bram asked. 'I agree that the journey will be too much for him. But we cannot just leave him here.'

'I did not say we should leave him here,' Faina-lai protested. 'All I said was that he could not come with us.'

'Then by the Ten Living Hells, where is he to go?' Bram erupted.

Kaela sat beside the fire, chewing on a piece of

black bread and spicy sausage. He had known that following the party was a crazy thing to do, but now that Aleron was dead he might never be allowed to join another hunt. So he had slipped away from the other Jaeger, hiding deep in the jungle as they had searched for him. He had watched from his hiding place as they eventually gave up the search and left.

As Kaela hobbled onward through the night he realised that he might never catch up and that he could die alone in the darkness of the jungle. On several occasions he had been tempted to lift his flute and play a light-hearted tune to ease his worries, but he was no woodsman and the thought of attracting any of the strange creatures of the jungle was terrifying.

'Then he comes,' Tandra decided. 'If he can not stay here then he must come with us.'

Bram grunted with satisfaction. He glared at Faina-lai as he passed her and approached the fire, where he grabbed a piece of sausage. Then he sat and chewed on his meal silently, allowing his anger to settle.

After his brush with the Chosen, Bram had been shunned as a cripple. A man with only one hand was no man at all, he had often heard. But he had shown them. In a small village at the mouth of the Shaylee River in northern Obira, Bram had found an old blacksmith who was willing to make his 'left hand'. The small trident had taken many months of trial and error before the weapon was perfected.

It had taken Bram a considerably longer time to master the unique weapon, but with the perseverance of a desperate man he had succeeded. The thought that Kaela would not be allowed to join them simply because of his twisted foot angered Bram.

'Enough excitement for the night,' Tandra called. 'We rise with the sun so get to your blankets.'

Cyrille and Sian-vesna were on the next watch, so Bram drew his blankets to one side and wrapped them about his shoulders. When he saw Kaela huddled on the far side of the fire, Bram pulled one of his blankets free, rolled it up and threw it over the fire to Kaela who caught it and gave the one-handed Cathar a nod of thanks.

Raissa cursed loudly as the chariot lurched to one side. She righted it by throwing her weight in the opposite direction just as another turn appeared.

'If you don't slow us down we'll never catch them,' Tavira shouted above the noise of their passage.

'We lost three days,' Raissa answered. 'If not for those two Jaeger we came across, we might never have caught them. At least now we have a chance.'

'But if we lose their trail in the dark, how will we ever find it again?' Yolane asked.

'We know where they are heading,' Raissa assured her. 'We have only to follow the direction they took until we reach the river. Then we will find their trail.'

The sound of chopping echoed about the camp. They had been felling trees all day and had nearly enough for their needs. Again it was left to Bram to take charge. Tandra was amazed at the number of skills he could master. It had all sounded so easy at the planning stage. Get to the river and raft down it until the region of the tower was reached. But who could build a raft strong enough to withstand the unleashed power of the river?

Bram had worked as a deckhand on a freight raft on the Eutha River. Once the journey ended they had trekked overland to their camp and then built another raft ready to repeat the trip. Bram had not stayed with the rivermen long, but he had made enough trips to know how to build a raft strong enough to survive any river's anger. This raft would be a simple affair, with a shaped raised bow, a square stern, and a low-roofed cabin small enough to leave the polemen room to operate.

The setting sun beat the party and they were forced to down tools before the job was done. The hard work of cutting and trimming the trees had left them with a healthy appetite. They had intended to hunt for whatever supplies they had needed, but they had still seen no life in the canopied jungle around them.

When the axes had fallen silent, the deeper silence of the jungle covered the camp like a shroud. As they sat and rested, each member of the party threw nervous glances over their shoulders at the darkened jungle.

It was harder to get to sleep that night and Tandra felt uneasy as she sat her watch. They had made a great deal of noise all day, and if there was something or someone out there, then the sounds would lead them straight to the camp. The sound of Kaela's flute drifted softly over the restless sleepers and Tandra relaxed as the soothing melody reached her, easing her tense body.

The flute continued to play long after Tandra had fallen asleep. Kaela sat beside the fire playing tirelessly. Not far away, Cyrille sat in the bough of a tree, his eyes alert for danger.

They were on the edge of the Belial, and many tales of danger and death had filtered south to the plains of the Jaeger. They usually told of the fool-hardy who had entered the Belial in search of treasure. Few returned and those who did were crazed by their experience, speaking of unseen death, winged horrors and other creatures of the Belial not meant for human eyes.

The mighty Belial had once stretched far to the south, covering the plains of Scapol and Calcanth in a dense living jungle. Solan and northern Skarn had also lain under this living canopy. Cyrille had found it hard as a youth to believe the tales he had heard concerning the Belial. If true, how was it that the jungle has grown so small over the generations? Surely the creatures of the jungle would have protected their homes from the invaders? And if the Belial had been alive, then where was the life now?

Raissa leant against the cold rock wall. She shuddered as she tried to steady her quivering muscles. Yolane and Tavira were also ready to drop. In all of their training and experience they had never had to push themselves to such extremes. But they had lost a great deal of time and they would have to push themselves even harder if they were to catch the Cathars.

*

The first day of the raft journey was taken with great caution as the river was still fast, and cut by rapids. The sight and sound of whitewater filled all in the party with fear. After each of the rapids Tandra would order the raft to the riverbank, where they examined the ropes and logs for damage. Should one of the logs work free or a rope fail, then it would be certain death to enter further whitewater.

Rocks jutted from the raging water at odd angles and intervals, threatening to smash the raft to pieces should they meet. Bram stood at the stern of the sturdy vessel, his feet spread and his legs braced as he locked the long steering oar under his left arm. All that stood between the party and the cold water was Bram's strength and skill.

Tandra called an early halt to the day's travel and they soon sat before a warm fire, their soaked clothes strung about the small clearing like battle flags. Muscles ached and their heads still pounded from the continual noise of the rapids. It had become a personal thing with Bram to steer the party down the river, defying everything it could throw against them. He had managed it in his youth, but the strain was taking its toll.

As their exhaustion lifted they again took note of the ominous silence of the jungle. Bram shivered, even though he sat close to the roaring fire. They had not covered all that many miles, their progress delayed by the number of the rapids they had been forced to shoot. Their speed would increase as the river slowed and widened, but the deeper they reached into the Belial, the deeper Bram's sense of dread became.

*

Perched high in the forked branch of a tree, and well out of sight of the party, sat a round woven nest of silk. The white silk had long since been dirtied, its outer skin covered in leaves and small growths, but for the first time in decades there was movement from within the dried-out nest.

Against the light of the setting sun there was the faint shadow of movement. First it was slight, as if unsure. Then it became more agitated at the sudden realisation that it was time to venture out into the world once more. One side of the woven nest began to bulge, and then came the faint sound of bursting as the old silken threads parted.

The actions within the nest became more energetic and leaves rained down on the thick carpet of deadfall covering the jungle's floor. Finally a small clawed hand burst through the silken bindings, flexing in the cool air of the night. The rent expanded and a smooth hairless head and narrow shoulders slowly appeared.

Claws locked onto the nest as the Skulke pulled itself free. Hanging by one arm, it stretched its limbs as the bloodflow returned to its small body. Then it released its hold and dropped to the floor of the jungle. Instantly, its head rose as it sought that which had woken it.

A long tapered tongue flicked out from between its small serrated teeth, testing the air. It turned its eyeless head slowly until at last it tasted the breeze-carried flavour of its prey. The Skulke's limited memory recalled the taste of man and of how he had entered the jungle and hunted its kind to the point of extinction.

The Skulke did not flinch as another of its kind dropped to the ground beside it.

As the first Skulke turned to pursue the taste, more and more of its brethren dropped from their silken nests wedged high in the old trees.

Cyrille's watch had ended and Xever sat high in the tree, his eyes closed, concentration intense as he tried to make out any sounds from the darkness and silence of the jungle. Gradually he made out a soft chirr, which seemed to come from everywhere at once yet from no particular direction. The sound was like the trill of a hundred grasshoppers and as it increased, Cyrille dropped from the tree and quickly woke the others.

As they stood beside their crumpled blankets and the dying fire the noise increased further until it was almost deafening.

'What in the Ten Living Hells is that?' Bram cursed.

'I don't want to know,' Tandra shouted. Her answer was barely audible above the noise, but as she reached down and snatched her blanket and boots from the ground beside her, the party quickly followed. Nothing was stowed. Everything they had used in the camp was simply thrown on the raft as the party clambered aboard. Poles were lifted and soon they were pushing themselves off from the riverbank.

From out of the darkness a small form appeared, its short legs propelling it at an unbelievably fast pace. When it reached the edge of the river it simply threw itself at the raft. Bram kicked it from the rough-cut timber, swearing as his naked toes struck the creature's head. With a faint splash the creature fell from the raft and disappeared into the dark water.

By then more of the creatures had appeared.

As they reached the edge of the river they simply launched themselves at the raft, their small claws locking onto timber and flesh alike. Bram grabbed one of the Skulkes and cut its throat with his trident, then threw the carcass at another of its brethren. Both disappeared beneath the water and never rose.

Another of the creatures had attached itself to Tandra's right leg. Bram cut its throat but it would not relinquish its grip, even in death. Forced to cut the creature's arms from its body, Bram threw the corpse from him with a snarl. Tandra still had two small arms locked on her thigh as she lifted her sword and went to Sian-vesna's aid.

As the party fought off the creatures they drifted closer to the riverbank, allowing more of their fearless attackers to reach the raft. Tandra looked up and saw that the riverbank was alive with the small disgusting Skulkes and that the bodies of the living and the dead had formed a causeway to the raft.

The chirr of the creatures had increased as the raft drew nearer, but without warning it became so loud Tandra thought her eardrums would burst under the pressure. As she peered at the riverbank she saw six wavering lights erupt from the jungle and leap amongst the creatures.

While the Skulkes on the raft continued their fight, those waiting on the riverbank erupted in panic. The lights drew closer and Tandra saw three women carrying a torch in each hand. They struck out at the creatures as they forced their way closer to the raft.

For a short time the small creatures pushed back from the sputtering torches. Some of the more adventurous ones threw themselves at the women as they neared the raft, but they were beaten back by the heat. When the raft bumped against the bank more of the Skulkes leapt for it. At the same time the three women reached the raft and stepped from the riverbank, their torches almost dead.

One of the women dropped a torch and tore two more from her belt and lit them before handing them to Bram and Xever. The other two strangers repeated this until half the party stood at the raft's edge, holding off the creatures while the rest lifted the poles and pushed them out into the current.

As the last of the creatures was kicked from the raft, Tandra and the others collapsed. Each of them bore wounds, slashes, bite marks and deep cuts. Tandra drew her dagger and cut at the small arms still locked on her thighs while Sian-vesna forced herself to crawl amongst the party, helping where she could.

As she reached one of the newcomers she stopped, shocked by what she saw. Sitting together were three women with brilliantly coloured tattoos etched around their eyes.

Tandra cut the last of the small arms from her thigh and turned to face the three.

'What is it you want here?' she demanded.

One of the women raised her head, then lowered her eyes to her exhausted companions before answering. 'We saved your lives,' she proclaimed.

'If not for us you would be on your way to the Skulkes' nests.'

'Skulkes?' Bram probed. 'Is that what those foul creatures are called?'

'Yes,' Raissa answered. 'When they sense prey they wake from their slumber and attack. Their only bane is fire. Like all beings of a jungle, they respect its power.'

'But what are you doing here?' Tandra asked. There was something familiar about their leader. Could she have been the one they had encountered at the inn in Brisk?

'We are on the same mission as you,' Raissa answered. 'We were sent by our Deis to stop the awakening of the towers.'

'But you attacked us?' Sian-vesna explained. 'Three times you have attacked us.'

Before Raissa could answer, Yahudah threw herself at the woman, knife drawn. Raissa blocked the clumsy attack and grabbed the young Saphy by her neck. Picking up the dropped knife she held it to the girl's throat. Then with a laugh of contempt she threw Yahudah from her and flicked the knife over the side of the raft.

'You killed my family!' Yahudah screamed. 'We had done nothing to you but you attacked and slew us without mercy. Why?'

'We had nothing to do with the attack,' Raissa insisted. 'We only crossed the path of those responsible later. Besides, the weak are prey to the strong,' Raissa recited. Yolane and Tavira nodded at Raissa's words. They had been taught from birth that only the strong survive.

'They are not gone,' Tavira offered. 'They have but taken their first footstep on the path to God.'

'And it seems that you are also about to embark on your journey to God,' Faina-lai snarled.

The old Crafter drew her dagger and everyone on the raft armed themselves ready for battle. Everyone except Bram.

'Enough!' he shouted above the sound of the river. 'There is certain death on the riverbank, and certain death should we strike whitewater unprepared. Are we to massacre ourselves out here as well? If we are, then stop the raft, I'd rather fight the creatures of the jungle. At least they know their enemies.'

'These are our enemies,' Sian-vesna shouted. 'They have killed our companions. Or have you forgotten?'

'I have not forgotten,' Bram said softly. 'If they are indeed the ones. But for the moment the Belial is our only enemy.'

'No!' Yahudah cried.

'Whitewater!' Xever shouted and pointed downriver.

The progress of the raft increased and the raft began to buck fiercely. Bram gripped the steering oar and threw his weight against it as he steered them around a large boulder directly in their path. Raissa leapt to her feet and threw added weight against the steering oar.

The others lifted their long poles and struck out at the passing rocks, pushing the raft off as they did so. The raft dropped into a sinkhole, the water poured over it, throwing Raissa from her feet and washing Yahudah over the side. Instinctively, Raissa reached out and, grabbing the young Saphy by the hair, drew her back to the raft's side where she was plucked from the water by Tandra.

As suddenly as the whitewater had appeared it vanished, and the raft was once more in calm fast-flowing water. The enlarged party collapsed with exhaustion, except for Bram and Raissa who kept the raft in the centre of the river, propelled by the steady current.

19
WRAITH

By the third day the waters had ceased their frantic rush and the thick silent jungle the party had encountered in the mountains was now filled with life. In fact a cacophony erupted which sent everyone's senses reeling.

'I had thought the silence unnerving,' Bram observed, 'but this continual noise is almost unbearable.'

'Life brings hope,' Raissa stated firmly. 'The jungle above was filled with the silence of death, a death far removed from any God. This jungle bears the life and death struggles of many creatures, watched over and warded by their many Gods.'

'What would you know of life and death struggles?' Faina-lai commented. 'You know of only death.'

'There cannot be death without life,' Raissa corrected. 'Nor can there be life without death.'

Bram interrupted before the unsteady peace could be broken. 'I suggest we put ashore and prepare a meal. A good feed and a warm fire would help us all more than this incessant chatter about Gods and death.'

Raissa nodded. But Faina-lai stared at Bram as he eased the steering oar over, aiming the blunt bow of the raft toward the vine-blanketed bank. By cutting at the vines and drawing on the overhanging branches, Bram soon had the raft snuggled secure against the riverbank.

It would be the first decent camp the party had set since well before entering the mountains. On the raft there had been little room and the uneasy truce had been necessary for the safety of all. But now, as they stood upon dry land and eased the aches and cramps from their muscles, old thoughts crept back.

Yahudah sat high in the branches of a willow which overhung the river and the camp. She watched the Deisol as they went about the camp. On the downriver journey they had convinced her that it was Olsenn's band who had attacked and killed her family. Their excuses had sounded plausible and Yahudah believed them, but as she watched she could feel her old doubts return.

Neroli and her companions sat beside the fire, drying themselves before its raging heat. They were not used to the continual soaking they had received as they had battled the river. As Neroli allowed her eyes to wander the camp, a strange uneasiness filled her.

Cyrille and Xever had followed her when she had decided to join with the Cathars on their dangerous journey, Kaela had come later but she still felt responsible for him. The pain of the death of her brother had not yet eased and, as she watched the faces of the Cathars and Deisolites, she wondered if it had been the tower alone which was responsible for her brother's death.

As soon as the camp was established, Sian-vesna called the other Cathars to her side. She was concerned that the Jaeger and Deisolites might pick this point to try to hinder the journey.

'That's ridiculous,' Faina-lai scoffed. 'This has nothing to do with them. It is the danger from within that we must guard against,' she warned, eyeing Sian-vesna.

'Are we to be bored with these implications again?' Bram said sharply. 'You have done nothing but point accusing fingers at Sian-vesna since you joined us. Have you nothing better to do with what little years you have left in life?'

'She works for our enemy,' Faina-lai accused.

Tandra positioned herself between Bram and the old Crafter. Faina-lai's tale had sounded plausible until Sian-vesna returned from inside the Snakeweed Tower. At that point Tandra had begun to have her doubts whether the old woman's tale was indeed the truth.

Raissa watched as the Crafters' dispute became more agitated. She also kept an eye on her fellow Deisolites as they drew themselves further away from the arguing Cathars.

'What is happening?' Yolane asked.

'They are questioning their faith,' Tavira answered, 'as I am questioning mine. Is it not wrong to seek death as we do? Perhaps we should be happy to bask in the light and warmth of our God rather than trying to seek her out in death?'

Yolane was taken back by Tavira's rash

statement. Then as her anger erupted she leapt on her companion, her hands seeking her throat.

Raissa rose quickly to avoid the fighting. She had felt a malevolence the moment they had landed, but she had thought it simply the after-effects of the Skulkes' attacks, which had been almost continuous since their first sighting. But as she looked about the camp she realised that there was something wrong with this place beyond the lingering presence of the Skulkes.

A weight upon Raissa's shoulder drove her to the ground and curved fingers sought her eyes. She rolled as she fell and threw the weight from her. Yahudah spun across the campsite, stopping only when she struck the base of a massive tree.

Quickly regaining her feet, Raissa kicked Yolane in the midriff and, as her fellow Deisol rolled gasping for breath, Raissa drew her dagger and rapped Tavira sharply behind an ear with its hilt before turning her attention to the rest of the camp.

All eyes had turned to Raissa as she broke up the fight, but they were filled with anger rather than surprise. Everyone was angry with someone else.

Bram felt his anger rise, but whatever fury he felt he sensed was not really his own. Somehow he was feeling the anger of his companions multiplied many times. Grasping Tandra's shoulder, he spun her round and landed a blow on her jaw which laid her out cold. Faina-lai turned, a shriek on her lips, but another blow crumpled the old Crafter to the leaf-littered ground.

Sian-vesna stood shaking. Her hands hid her face and her head was tilted as if listening to someone. Yahudah had not moved since she had struck the tree.

Neroli could not understand what was happening. She knew that, in some way, these people were responsible for the death of her brother but she was not sure how. As she made to rise and join the fight, a restraining hand rested on her shoulder.

Kaela smiled at her, his eyes wresting some of the pain from her heart. But she gathered her strength and leapt to her feet. Kaela allowed her to rise, knowing that he could do little physically to stop her and the others from fighting. He too could hear whispered words of anger echoing about inside his head but he pushed them from him, knowing that they were not real. Raising his flute, he began to play a simple song.

It was the first tune he had ever learned and, though it had been easy to master, it took all of his conscious effort to play it now as anger and violence raged about him. Slowly at first, and then slightly faster, his fingers danced the length of his flute, marshalling the tune until it rang out above the chaotic fighting.

Raissa stood before her two companions, protecting them from any attack. Bram moved about the camp as if looking for someone to vent his anger on, but could find no-one. Neroli, Xever and Cyrille had been frozen by the sound of the flute, their memories flooded with images of happier times surrounded by friends and family.

As the feelings of anger suddenly vanished, and those standing collapsed to the ground, their bodies shook uncontrollably. Kaela kept up his playing, his mind straining for the first hint of danger, but he could find nothing. Eventually he lowered the flute from his lips and looked about the camp.

There was confusion mixed with fear as those who were still conscious realised how close they had come to ending the journey there in the clearing. Sian-vesna was perhaps the first to recover, her hand seeking out her medallion as she sought an answer from Charybdis. But he knew nothing of what had befallen them.

'The Belial is huge and for the most part unexplored,' he explained. 'There are so many things which happen about the Belial it is impossible to say what manner of peril you have encountered.'

'What are we to do?' Sian-vesna asked. 'Will all of the jungle be like this?'

'We encountered nothing like that on our journey to the Hawkthorn Tower,' he replied, 'but you are far from where we travelled.'

Sian-vesna broke the contact and looked about the clearing. 'It would be best if we left here,' she said to Bram.

He nodded and hurriedly gathered the few items that had been unloaded before marshalling his companions. As soon as they were on board, he pushed off from the bank, letting the current take them where it would.

They drifted as long as they dared, but as the sun touched the uppermost reaches of the jungle Bram leaned on the steering oar and steered the raft to the bank. Their arrival quietened the jungle as they set up their small camp but, as the sun set, the strange chorus of calls and cries returned. Tandra repressed a shudder at the number of hidden creatures waiting in the jungle. Their cries were almost deafening.

Another fire was lit and the party settled down to a hasty meal before the sentries were set.

The danger of the Skulkes had been overshadowed by the strange attack of the unseen enemy. As the party travelled downriver they had tried to describe exactly what they had experienced, but found it impossible. All they could remember was that an intense feeling of anger had overwhelmed each of them.

A scream cut through the camp and was choked off before anyone had the chance to act. Bram tore a burning branch from one of the fires and sought out its source. A quick search revealed that Cyrille was gone. There were drag marks indicating something had emerged from the river and taken the Jaeger. There was nothing to be seen in the water and no sign of Cyrille along the river's edge.

The party moved further from the river and settled down to try to sleep once more. Nervous eyes were cast in the direction of the river and hands rested on weapons as an uneasy silence fell over the camp.

With the rising of the sun the party set out downriver, not breaking their fast until they were safely on their raft. Neroli had taken the time to whisper a few words at the spot where Cyrille had vanished before leaping aboard the raft. Xever was the last to leave the camp, his eyes searching the riverbank for any sign of his lost brother.

The river grew wider the further they moved into the jungle, and it slowed its mad progress as it widened. Swarms of insects attacked those on the raft, seeking every exposed piece of skin on which to feast. Without warning the raft lurched heavily to one side, as if struck by a sunken obstacle. Just as it righted itself the raft was tilted again, this time so far that Bram thought they would all end up in the water.

Straining ropes snapped and two of the logs began to drift loose. Yolane drew a length of rope from the steering oar and knelt to tie the two logs back in place. As she worked she glanced over the side into the dark water, then cursed and leapt to her feet.

'There was something there,' she shouted.

'What?' Faina-lai asked urgently.

'I don't know. All I saw was a large shadow dart beneath the raft.'

Again the raft lurched. Arms flailing, Yahudah struck the water and disappeared beneath its surface. She reappeared several metres away and struck out towards the raft. Then she vanished, a great disturbance marking her disappearance.

Raissa dived into the river and swam to where the young Saphy had vanished. Diving beneath the surface, she too vanished. The party stood, weapons drawn, trying to locate their unseen enemy or their missing companions. Raissa broke surface within an arm's length of the raft and Bram threw himself down and reached out for her. Tandra dropped to his legs as Raissa looked about to pull Bram from the raft.

'There was no sign of her,' Raissa told them when she was back on the raft. 'But there's something large down there. It brushed against me as I searched for her.' Raissa looked down and saw that her leg was bleeding, and that a large area of skin had been scraped away.

The dark water revealed nothing of what was

hidden in its depths. And as the current drew them ever onward each member of the party farewelled Yahudah in their own way.

Charybdis watched the progress of both parties. If the weather held then Tandra's party would reach the tower first—that was if any of them remained alive. When Charybdis and his companions, Emal, Geber, Mercer, Ryan and Kelson had struck out towards the Hawkthorn Tower and the treasure, they had expected to come in from the north. They had touched the unnamed river Tandra's party now travelled only once, and that had been to cross it on the last leg of their journey.

Whatever the creatures were that attacked the raft, they seemed satisfied for the moment. Charybdis was relieved, as he was loath to aid Sian-vesna any more than he had to. Faina-lai obviously knew that the younger Cathar was under someone's influence and he did not want her to convince the others. He would need Sian-vesna at the Monkshood Tower if he was to succeed in gathering it under his protective wing.

But if the attacks on the party were allowed to continue unchecked, then none of them would even reach the Monkshood Tower. His decision made, Charybdis set about organising what needed to be done.

Three days after the loss of Yahudah, the party found themselves at the junction of two mighty rivers. The river they travelled flowed north, but

Sian-vesna had learned from Charybdis that they had to follow the western flowing tributary if they were to reach the tower they sought.

The jungle closed in even more tightly and in many places the light of the sun did not reach the water. It seemed the main strength of the river flowed north for the western course they now followed twisted and turned in on itself as it flowed sluggishly through the impenetrable jungle.

Huge creatures were seen at a distance thrashing about in the muddied waters, but as soon as the raft neared they vanished beneath the surface.

'If one of those things comes up beneath us we'll all find ourselves in the water,' Neroli noted.

'They vanish long before we reach them,' Tandra said. 'But if they wish to attack us then I can see little we can do about it.'

'I had thought the Skulkes a serious problem,' Neroli commented, 'but they forced us only to take Raissa and her companions as our allies. Then the whispered madness struck but still we survived. To have lost two of our number to unseen dangers sseems so unfair.'

'Bram has been watching the stars of late and assures me that we are near our destination,' Tandra told her. 'In a few days the river will turn north and we will leave the raft and strike out west.'

'Not too soon for my liking,' Neroli shuddered. 'How much of this jungle will be left for us to cross on foot?'

Tandra shook her head, then raised her eyes towards the western horizon. It was time to find a campsite for the night. As the raft touched the muddied bank, the party quickly leapt ashore.

Again the attack came without warning. Xever and Yolane were still on the raft, gathering what was left of their supplies, while the remainder of the party with weapons drawn cleared the campsite. The sounds of cutting echoed in the silence of the jungle as the party slashed their way further from the river. A Skulke dropped noiselessly from the branches and struck Bram on the shoulder, burying its teeth deep into his neck.

Bram cursed loudly, then dropped his sword and grabbed the creature, tearing it from his neck and smashing it against a tree's rough bough. More Skulkes dropped silently from the trees and swarmed over the entire party.

Snatching his sword up from where it had fallen, Bram lashed out about him. 'Back to the raft!' he shouted.

Raissa and Tavira cut an opening through the Skulkes long enough for the party to turn and run for the raft. Bram reached out with his trident and cut a Skulke from Faina-lai's back. Several of the small creatures tried to block their path but the party ran them into the ground, crushing them under foot.

Tandra heard a faint cry from behind her and turned to see the struggling Kaela fall under the weight of the Skulkes' attack. She called to Bram, turned and raced to Kaela's aid. Kicking out at the swarming Skulkes, Tandra bent down and dragged the musician to his feet. Nearly a dozen Skulkes clung to him as Tandra dragged him towards the raft. Bram sheathed his sword and began to cut at their attackers with his trident. His left arm was soaked in the Skulkes' sticky yellow blood and the thick red blood of their victims.

Between them they managed to get Kaela down to the raft. Raissa and Neroli were ready with the steering poles and they pushed out from the bank as soon as Kaela was thrown on board. Tandra and Bram leapt for safety with several of the Skulkes following. Sian-vesna and Tavira soon saw to the creatures who had boarded the raft.

As Tandra looked round she realised that two of the party were missing.

'Where are Yolane and Xever?' she asked.

'There was no sign of them when we reached the raft,' Neroli said. 'The supplies they were collecting are still here, but they are gone. We called out for them but there was no answer, and with the Skulkes so close we could do little else but leave.'

'What if they had wandered off and are still back there?' Sian-vesna asked.

'There was no time for them to wander anywhere,' Tandra reasoned. 'We had not been gone for all that long, and they were supposed to gather the supplies and follow us. Whatever happened to them took place while they were still on board. I am afraid we have lost another two of our companions.'

The raft seemed much larger now as the party continued downriver. In a few days they would be free of the river and the deaths it had brought them. Sian-vesna and Faina-lai were busy with those who had been injured in the attack.

Kaela was in a bad way. He had lost a lot of blood and was severely weakened. Bram was feverish from the bites he had taken and Faina-lai watched him closely. Raissa and Tavira bore only a few bites to their lower legs, their armoured thighs having offered no hold for the Skulkes.

Tandra had received surprisingly few injuries and thanked the Life Bringer for her luck, but she was afraid it could not hold for the remainder of the journey. The sun was fast setting and they had not found another place suitable for a campsite.

'Anywhere will have to do,' Neroli observed. 'Soon it will be too dark to see.'

Tandra agreed and as they manhandled the raft into the bank their eyes flicked nervously across the thick concealing vegetation.

Tandra licked her lips. What manner of attack would the Belial surprise them with this time? She jumped to the riverbank and searched the foliage nervously. There was no sign of recent visitors and there looked to be plenty of deadfall. Waving for the others, she began to kick an area free of leaves ready for the fire, her eyes never leaving the surrounding jungle.

The sounds of the jungle were comforting. They had now learned that the jungle's silence heralded the Skulkes. But while the sounds assured them that there were none of the creatures nearby it did not stop each member of the party from jumping as any particularly loud or close cry echoed from the jungle.

Bram stood beside the fire, consumed by a fever. The sweat poured from his body—he felt weak and could barely lift his sword. Tandra could see that he could hardly stand, but he had insisted on helping. She was not sure whether he truly felt the need to protect the camp or the thought of being left on the raft worried him. Her strongest fears were for the remainder of the party. Except for Kaela, none was as ill as Bram but they all showed a nervous disposition which placed them on the edge of sanity.

Each sound or shadow had one or another of them jumping. The snapping of a stick in the fire had weapons drawn and fearful eyes searching the jungle's shadows. If they did not get a good night's rest soon, then the party would fall apart.

Bram left the camp and made his way down to the river, where he leaned against a large crooked tree. Closing his eyes, he tried to shake off the dizzy sensation which threatened to overcome him. But it was no good. His head slipped to one side and he slid into an exhausted sleep.

Bram did not know how long he had slept, but when he opened his eyes he felt somewhat refreshed. He looked up at the star-filled sky through the partial cover of the trees and estimated that there were still a few hours till dawn.

He steadied himself against a tree, closed his eyes and stretched his weary neck. When he opened his eyes he stared out towards the river once again. Its open expanse was the only area not seduced by the shadows of the jungle. As he was about to turn back to the camp, he noticed a disturbance in the water.

A dark shape lifted itself from the water and eased itself forward towards the camp. When it passed the raft Bram could hear it sniffing at the timbers, as if trying for a scent. Bram pushed himself off the tree and cautiously began to retrace his steps towards the camp. He heard the creature follow.

Exhausted and bleeding from a dozen injuries caused by the clinging thorn-covered vines, Bram staggered into the silent camp. He looked down on the still shapes as he caught his breath, then kicked the dark form closest to him.

'Awake!' he called out. 'There is something heading this way from the river. Something large.'

Tandra climbed to her feet and went to Bram's side, knuckling the sleep from her eyes. He was exhausted. Lifting one of his arms about her shoulder she led him from the camp away from the river. Raissa and Tavira waited until the last of the party had left the camp before following. Everything they owned save weapons was left behind. Bram's nervous stares over his shoulders caused them to hurry their pace. As they entered the deeper shadows of the jungle they heard the stealthy movements of the creature as it stalked them.

Neroli and Faina-lai supported Kaela while Sianvesna led the way. She had lifted her medallion from beneath her tunic and was whispering to herself as she forced her way through the tangled vines, tripping over unseen obstacles and stumbling deeper into the jungle. Every so often they would stop to catch their breath, and each time Raissa would call that the creature still followed.

'How can it follow us in this darkness?' Tandra whispered.

'It must have taken our scent from the raft,' Bram said. 'With our scent this fresh it will have no trouble following us.'

'Then we are going to have to kill it,' Tandra declared.

'Yes,' Bram agreed. 'But not here, not now. Wait until the sun has risen. Then we will be able to get a look at the thing and work out some method of attack.'

'But the sunrise is still an hour or more away,' Tandra complained. 'The further we run, the further we are from the river and the raft. And none of us are up to this—we are all exhausted.'

'We have no choice,' Bram continued. 'If it is going to follow us then we must keep going until we find a suitable place to meet it.'

Sian-vesna had been listening to Bram and Tandra. But she had also been talking with Charybdis and he had told her what he had done. If his help was to save them she was going to have to steer the party towards the north-east, even further from the river.

'This way,' she called.

Too tired to argue, the others followed her in silence. Covered in blood as they clawed at wickedly barbed vines, the party had been incessantly attacked by large biting insects. But as the sun rose the party stopped their staggering advance and turned, ready to face the creature which still followed them.

Sian-vesna knew that they would have to hold the creature at bay for only a short time before Charybdis' help arrived, but she was not sure they could even manage that. Kaela lay on the ground unmoving and Bram sat, his back to a tree, eyes closed, his body bathed in sweat. He trembled and Sian-vesna could hear his teeth chattering.

Faina-lai was asleep on her feet. What little strength the old Crafter had was now gone and she would be of little use in the coming fight.

The crashing of saplings and the snapping of vines warned of the creature's approach. Then from out of the shadows it appeared.

Tavira cursed at the sight of the monstrosity. As a child she had watched as small water beetles wrapped their abdomens in bubbles of air before diving deep into the water, but the beetle which lumbered out of the jungle was monstrously large, the black glistening shell protecting its body as tall as Tavira.

The huge beetle forced its way through the foliage and stopped, regarding the party. Beneath its small, almost hidden eyes there was a large pair of mandibles which slowly opened and closed as it turned its attention from one of the party to another.

Bram stepped forward and directed a blow at the beetle's head, but the size of the creature belied its speed. Before the sword stroke could land, the beetle had turned and raised its mandibles, catching the weapon in a vice-like hold. Cursing, Bram tried to wrest his sword from the grip of the beetle but he was far too weak.

Tavira ran to the other side of the beetle and attacked. Her sword rebounded from the black shell with the sound of ringing steel. The beetle turned away from Bram and struck out at Tavira who threw herself backward, barely escaping the attack. Bram had followed the movement of the beetle, loath to relinquish his sword still gripped firmly in its mandibles.

Raissa and Neroli rushed the beetle simultaneously, but again the creature turned sharply, this time dragging the sword from Bram's hand. Charging forward it met the attack of the pair, trampling them both beneath its clawed feet. Tandra risked a blow at the beetle as it passed, but her light blade simply skidded from the hard shell.

The beetle spun around and attacked again. Neither Raissa nor Neroli had moved after being trampled and Tavira was still winded from her attack. Bram cursed and drew his knife. Tandra dropped to the ground as the beetle rushed past and attacked its legs, hoping to cripple it, but her rapier's blade merely skittered along the shell-armoured leg.

Bram jumped to one side at the last moment and grabbed hold of the beetle's uppermost shell as it passed. He then pulled himself up on its back. He struck at the beetle repeatedly, but made no headway against the formidable shell. Tandra darted in and again struck at one of the beetle's legs. This time her narrow blade found a gap in the shell of the leg's joint but the beetle moved as she struck and her blade was trapped, then snapped off at the hilt.

Faina-lai rushed forward and retrieved Bram's sword, lifting it and throwing it to Tandra just as the beetle struck. Grasping the old Crafter in its mandibles, it lifted its head and cut the old woman in two. Her blood covered its shell with a dark gleam.

As the beetle made to turn again, another crash came from the jungle and an armoured apparition stormed into the small clearing wielding a massive broadsword. The armoured figure rushed forward and delivered such a blow that the jungle rang with the sound. The beetle's shell cracked and a thin white liquid seeped from the wound staining the shell.

The beetle grasped the armoured figure and lifted it from the ground. Dropping its sword, the figure placed a hand on each of the curved sections of the mandible and applied pressure. A sharp crack echoed throughout the clearing as one of the beetle's curved blades broke. Its whole body shaking, the beetle staggered from the clearing.

The armoured stranger knelt down, picked up the broadsword it had dropped and hurried from the clearing.

'Follow it!' Sian-vesna shouted over her shoulder.

Stunned and injured, the party followed without question. Bram took his sword from Tandra and glanced down at Faina-lai's remains. Kaela helped Neroli to her feet while Tavira and Raissa supported each other as they staggered after Sian-vesna. They had not run far before they found themselves at a broad river. Without pausing, the armoured figure rushed into the water and disappeared.

Sian-vesna skidded to a halt and drew in the air her lungs had been denied on her crazed run. Then she pointed to a large fallen log which she and Tandra shoved into the water. Signalling for the others to find a perch, Sian-vesna pushed the log from the bank. Those who gripped the log kicked out in an attempt to drive them across the river while those who had managed to find a perch paddled with their hands for all they were worth.

No-one had voiced a question since Sian-vesna had called for them to follow. They knew that the beetle they had just fought would not be the only one in the Belial and the armoured stranger was the only one who had the strength to defeat such a creature.

Their apprehension at crossing the water was outweighed by a fear of losing sight of their saviour. An armoured head appeared from the water just ahead of the log and was ploughing its way ashore. The current had taken both the stranger and the log downriver and they were well out of sight of the point where they had entered the river by the time they struck firm ground.

Abandoning the log, they dragged themselves up the bank and through the thick vegetation until they stood looking down on a beautiful wide valley. As they stared they realised that they were free of the Belial and the dangers it had presented them. But more to the point, at the base of a long gentle slope, they could see a large village and touching the edge of its northern side stood a tall green-clad tower.

20

MONKSHOOD

Izak Vy Bryn and his Oathman welcomed the return of Orren-ker.

'Have you decided?' he asked.

'We have,' Orren-ker answered. 'We have decided that five lives are a small price to pay to hear the word of your God.'

'Then you have chosen the five?' Izak asked, his joy showing through.

'We have,' Orren-ker confirmed. 'They are Mahira, Phaidra, Fallon, Jesh and myself.'

'That is good,' Izak exclaimed. 'It is rare to see a person who understands the ways of God, especially an unbeliever. We will start our journey immediately.'

Izak Vy Bryn shouted orders and the natives leapt to their feet and began to gather their few possessions. A dozen or more of the natives jogged from the camp. They carried small oval shields made of a dark overlapping shell and long-bladed spears. Soon after, the remainder of the party followed. Men followed the progress of the party to the north and south, their roles to report anything hidden from the main party below the horizon. Another group of natives hung well back, ensuring they were not followed.

Garrig had insisted that he accompany them but Orren-ker had pointed out that should the party reach the tower and succeed in their mission then they would need him and the *Windsong* safe, waiting for their return. Garrig suggested that when the *Windsong* returned he leave the bay and sail north then east in an effort to lose any natives who remained.

The party travelled swiftly and silently. Occasionally Izak would send a runner forward or to either flank to gather information of what might lie ahead, but if anything unexpected was found the Cathars saw no evidence of this.

The terrain changed slowly until the party was walking through a knee-length grass of the richest green. Long stems capped with yellow seeds bowed their heads under the weight. A gentle breeze whispering across the plain gave the impression that the party was crossing a sea of green, its tossing waves crested with yellow.

Orren-ker spent a great deal of the day travelling beside Izak, learning what he could from him.

'It seems that all they care about are the offerings they are required to make,' Orren-ker told his colleagues. 'The loss of life means nothing to them. Izak explained that the offerings must be alive when they are thrown into the Totem. They started by weeding out those in their society they deemed useless. Once this was done they then looked to their neighbours until only the Emulys remained.

'The Emulys follow a different God. Though it seems that their God also requires the blood offerings if his words are to be heard. The Emulys raid the Kolecki gathering captives.'

'Then we could be attacked at any time between here and the Kolecki encampment,' Phaidra observed.

'That is what Izak fears,' Orren-ker confirmed.

As the sun sank below the horizon it seemed to ignite the plain. The yellow seed stems of the grass captured the dying rays, causing the entire plain to burn within a golden light. Izak ordered a halt and a night camp was set. Sentries were placed well out from the camp and several fires were built.

'What in the Ten Living Hells are they burning?' Fallon coughed. 'Since leaving the beach I've seen no trees other than those of the Belial, and no-one has dared to go near them.'

'Whatever it is, its aroma is quite rich,' Phaidra offered.

'If you had watched more carefully you would see what it is they burn,' Mahira noted. 'I'm not sure what they call it, but there must be some quite large animals that travel this plain.'

Fallon sniffed and then her eyes opened wide. Mahira nodded her head and laughed. When Phaidra finally realised what the fuel was she too joined in the laughter.

Izak appeared and smiled as he watched the Cathars.

'It is as it should be,' he preached. 'Those going to meet God should be happy with the thought that their lifelong suffering will soon end.'

Mahira shook her head as she watched the Koel

stride away, 'How can anyone believe in that?'

'I have known many Cathars who have given up their lives defending their fellow Cathars and their charges,' Orren-ker said.

'But that is different,' Mahira replied.

'Is it?' Orren-ker countered.

Several of the Kolecki began to work around a large leather pot suspended over the glowing coals, pouring in a large amount of water, followed by two handfuls of dried leaves and a yellow powder. Strips of dried meat from a leather sack were diced and thrown into the thickening stew, as were several handfuls of dried vegetables.

Fallon moved closer and drew in a deep breath, but all she could smell were the smouldering pats of fuel beneath the pot. Her eyes watering, she returned to the others.

Jesh had followed the others silently as they crossed the plain. Even now he sat quietly, watching the Cathars as they laughed and joked with each other. He had left no-one behind when he had offered to go with them. His only true friend on board had been lost at the dark pool on that accursed island.

The pot of stew was poured into six smaller ones and the Kolecki squatted about the pots, each armed with a fistful of dry-looking travel bread which they used to scoop out the stew. As they ate there was a great deal of smiling and grinning.

Phaidra tore a section of bread from her piece and dipped it into the stew, lifting it quickly to her mouth. The closest Kolecki watched silently as Phaidra swallowed. Suddenly her eyes snapped wide and her face turned red. She snatched for the closest waterskin and raised it to her mouth, drinking greedily. When she lowered the bag her companions could see tears in her eyes.

'Perfect,' she croaked.

The watching Kolecki burst out laughing and slapped each other on the back. Some explained what had happened to those who had not seen it and soon the entire camp was filled with laughter.

'It seems the stew is somewhat heavily spiced,' Mahira remarked calmly as she slid forward and drew some of it from the pot. Slipping it into her mouth she chewed it several times and swallowed. Holding her expression as best she could, she waited. As the food hit her stomach it seemed to erupt, a burning sensation rose in her throat and threatened to lift off the top of her head. She felt her eyes water and her face blush. Turning to one of the Kolecki she nodded, and the laughter began again. The camp quickly settled down and when the meal was eaten and forgotten everyone sought out a comfortable place to sleep.

The camp rose early and after a quick meal was soon on its way. They had been travelling for only a short time before a call from the south drew everyone's attention. One of the outrunners waved his shield above his head and pointed towards the south with his spear. At first Orren-ker could see nothing, then he spotted a faint black dot on the horizon. Even as he watched, the black shape took form.

'Death!' shouted one of the natives, and soon the call was taken up by all. 'Death approaches.'

'What is it?' Jesh asked nervously.

'Death Crow!' Mahira called. 'And a big one by the looks of it.'

The large black bird was now plainly visible. It was high up, riding a wind that did not reach the ground. Its wings were extended unmoving as the huge bird hung in the air without effort.

The Kolecki quickly drew together, their spears raised to fend off the bird. Mahira could not help but notice how the cowering party resembled a rather large pincushion her mother had used while she was sewing.

When the Death Crow was directly overhead it banked to one side and began a lazy turn, its head tilted, its eyes examining the party. Then it dropped without warning.

A loud cry came from the bird as it plummeted towards them. Mahira thought that it must surely crash in the very heart of the cowering party. But the bird opened its wings with an audible snap as its talons flashed in and snatched up one of the Kolecki.

Kicking and screaming the Kolecki was carried off to the south, his screams quickly fading in the distance.

As the poor victim was snatched from the ground, the rest of the Kolecki rose, took up their equipment and returned to their march. Only a very few heads were turned towards the south and many of those sought only to ensure that the bird did not return.

'Callous bastards,' Mahira said. 'One of their kin dies and they show no sign of concern.'

'They are greatly different from us,' Jesh managed. The attack of the Death Crow had been terrifying. He had never seen anything like that giant bird before, and hoped that he never would again.

'We must hurry,' Izak ordered. He pointed to the
faint dot on the horizon which was the Death Crow.
'Once it has reached its nest it will return. Many
times a party has been trapped on the plain as, one
by one, they were snapped up by a Death Crow and
flown away to its nest and young ones.'

The party moved east, but most eyes turned fre-
quently towards the southern sky, straining to catch
the first glimpse of the returning bird.

'There!' rose a cry from one of the outrunners. 'It
returns.'

The party deployed itself once again. Shields
were raised and spears lifted, ready to welcome the
huge attacker.

'If this didn't work before, why are they attempting it again?' Phaidra asked.

'Savages!' Mahira said contemptuously. 'Once
they get used to doing something one way they find
it very hard to change.'

As the Kolecki cowered beneath their spears and
shields Mahira angrily gestured towards Fallon.

'Give me your bow,' she snapped.

Fallon handed it over and Mahira quickly strung
it, then tested its strength. Taking three arrows from
Fallon, she nocked one and held the others loosely
in her left hand. As the Death Crow reached the
party and began its spiral, Mahira drew back her
arm and released the shaft. She had judged her shot
well and the arrow sped upward, striking the bird
just beneath its massive right wing.

The Death Crow screamed and reached for the
arrow with its huge beak. Tearing out feathers as
well as the arrow, the bird vented its anger with
another terrifying scream.

371

Mahira tilted down a second shaft and nocked it. In one fluid motion she drew back and released. This time the arrow lodged itself in one of the wings, but if the bird felt it there was no reaction. Falling to one side, the Death Crow dived towards the party. Again, it rose from its dive at the last possible moment, another of the Kolecki struggling in its grasp. As before, the party rose and moved off without a second glance at their lost companion.

'It will return shortly,' Izak spat.

'Why not stop and fight?' Mahira asked.

Izak looked at the Cathar, his face filled with amazement. 'It is not done,' he said.

'But you do try to defend yourself?' Phaidra checked.

'It is always done,' Izak agreed. 'We defend ourselves and the Death Crow strikes and one of the Kolecki meets his ancestors.'

'But if you change your defensive pattern you could at least drive the Death Crows off.'

Izak shrugged. 'It has always been done this way. Why would we change?'

Not long after the party moved on, they heard the outrunner's call once more.

'Death!'

As the Death Crow swooped in again Mahira struck it twice, but the bird cared nothing for the slight injuries. Snapping into the party, it began to rise once more, this time with a struggling Jesh in its grasp.

Phaidra grabbed the spear of the closest Kolecki and threw it with all her strength. The spear struck the bird just below its shoulder and it staggered in flight. Mahira released another shaft and was rewarded this time by a scream as the arrow struck the bird in the neck.

The Death crow arched its neck and released Jesh. Then, as if balancing on one wing, it turned and sought out those who had caused the pain. Its small black eyes searched the ground, another cry escaping its beak as it sighted the panicking Kolecki.

Fallon and Phaidra snatched up spears and met the bird's attack with one of their own. Again Phaidra hit the bird just below the shoulder. This time the Death Crow folded its injured wing and crashed to the ground.

Kolecki and Cathars scattered as the Death Crow skidded in amongst them and a cloud of dust and torn grass was flung skyward. Mahira was the first to react, dropping the bow and drawing her longsword. Phaidra drew her shortsword and raced to her companion's side while Fallon, unable to reach her bow where it had fallen, drew two knives and leapt for the bird's back.

Mahira's first attack was deflected by a slashing beak and she was knocked from her feet as the bird tried to regain its feet, its wings thrashing the air. Orren-ker drew a stone from his pouch and readied his sling. As the bird turned its attention to the stunned Mahira he released the stone, striking it between the eyes.

The Death Crow drew its head back and climbed shakily to its feet. Fallon gripped one knife in her teeth and used the bird's coarse feathers to steady herself as she climbed its twisting back.

When she reached the bird's neck Fallon thrust with both knives, their keen blades biting deep. The Death Crow leapt several metres into the air.

Fallon's only hold on the bird was her grip on the hilts of her two knives. Knuckles white, she held on as the bird tried to rid itself of the unfamiliar weight upon its back and the new pain in its neck. As it crashed screaming to the ground Mahira rushed forward and drove her longsword deep into its side. A wing flexed and Mahira was thrown to one side.

Phaidra stepped forward and with a patience born of years of experience she waited for just the right moment. When the bird flexed its neck to shake Fallon free, Phaidra struck, the razor-edged blade of her shortsword all but severing the bird's head.

Fallon half climbed and half fell from the bird's back. Wiping her knives on her leggings, she sheathed them and went to Mahira's aid. The veteran Cathar had only just regained her feet and was looking rather unsteady.

The Kolecki gathered silently about the slain Death Crow, several of them prodding the corpse with their spears. A soft murmur rose from the awed Kolecki as, one by one, they turned their attention from the body to the Cathars.

Mahira knelt beside the injured Jesh. His shirt was sodden with blood which was flowing freely from his nose and mouth.

'He has been severely damaged inside,' Mahira diagnosed as Fallon knelt beside her.

'Is there nothing we can do for him?' Fallon asked.

Orren-ker examined Jesh and then slowly shook his head. 'He has passed on,' he whispered.

'So far from the sea,' Phaidra noted sadly. 'What will we do with his body?'

'Just cover it with rocks,' Orren-ker ordered. 'The Death Crow's mate is still alive and may seek this one out when it does not return with more food.'

As Phaidra and Fallon covered the dead seaman with rocks, Mahira and Orren-ker studied the Kolecki. They were still gathered about the fallen body of the Death Crow.

'Is there likely to be trouble over this?' Mahira asked.

'I don't know,' Orren-Ker answered. 'They seem a religious people and the Death Crow was their vision of death itself. They may be angry at our having slain it.'

Izak Vy Bryn backed slowly from his praying brethren, his back bent, his head held firmly in both hands. For a moment he rocked back and forth like the others, then he straightened and approached Orren-ker and Mahira.

'Well, we'll soon find out,' Mahira whispered, her right hand resting comfortably on the hilt of her longsword.

'A great thing has happened,' Izak sang. 'One of the minions of Death has itself been slain. This is a deed to be spoken of for years to come.'

'The deed may be great,' Mahira cried, 'but it was costly.' She tilted her head towards the growing burial cairn.

Izak shrugged. 'All things die.'

'We must hurry,' Orren-ker directed. 'This one's mate will soon investigate.'

Izak shook his head and smiled. 'During this season the male sits on its nest of twisted branches and bones, protecting the one jet-black egg. The female hunts, only returning to the nest when it has found prey. With the death of the female the male will be unable to leave the nest and seek her out until the egg has hatched.

'Only then will it hunt for food for the young one. The hunting area of the winged Death is large and there will be no others in this region for many years, perhaps longer if the male dies of starvation before the egg hatches.'

The body of the Death Crow had not been disturbed, but as Izak signalled the journey to continue he approached the body and drew five of the large black feathers from its tail. Returning to the Cathars, he presented one to each of them and slid the last into a space in the rock cairn.

'It is only right that the slayers of Death should be recognised,' he intoned.

'Has a winged Death been slain before?' Phaidra asked.

'Not in my lifetime,' Izak acknowledged. 'But it is written that there was once a great warrior of the Kolecki who slew many of the winged Death bringers as a penance to the Totem.'

'How was this done?'

'We do not know,' Izak said. 'But after what we have seen this day there will perhaps be a reckoning between the Kolecki and the Death Crows of the Belial.'

The party resumed their journey, all eyes watching to the south for more Death Crows. When one of the sentries rushed in, pointing wildly to the north, Bram thought it must have been another attack, but the Kolecki did not seem disturbed by the news. They continued their trek and before long a number of large squat figures appeared on the horizon. Like huge black beetles, the slow-moving shapes crawled steadily across the open plain.

'Now we know where they get the fuel from,' Tandra laughed.

'Are they dangerous?' Sian-vesna asked.

'No,' the Koel answered. 'They are Bautilaz. They roam harmlessly across the plain in large herds and are too large to be preyed on by the Death Crows. We hunt them occasionally for their shells.'

Bram counted almost a hundred of the giant beetles eating their way across the plain, and he could hear a faint clicking noise drifting on the wind.

Garrig scrambled to the top of the watch tree as soon as he heard the sentry's cry. He reached the uppermost branches just in time to see the *Windsong* round the point. Those beneath him raised a shout when they too saw the vessel appear.

The sails were rough-patched and there was a section of new timber just behind the bow where it was obvious she had been damaged and then hastily repaired.

The crew rushed down to the water's edge where they shouted and laughed, shaking their crewmates and waving madly. Answering calls echoed across the water from the bireme as she swung side-on to the beach. Garrig glanced over his shoulder. He had not trusted the Kolecki and realised that if they planned to betray the bargain, the danger time would be now.

'Leave everything and swim for the *Windsong*,' Garrig ordered. Joining his men Garrig swam strongly towards the *Windsong*. Eager hands stretched down, plucking the seamen from the water as they reached the vessel's hull.

'Well met, Uzziel,' Garrig said as he was dragged on board.

The helmsman reached forward and took Garrig by the elbow, helping him from the rail. 'I am sorry we took so long to return, but we took damage.'

Garrig nodded. With Uzziel in tow, he made for the stern cabin. 'Get us under way and then report to me,' he ordered.

As Garrig had made his way towards the stern cabin he saw signs of damage everywhere, but this was not the place to put ashore and carry out repairs.

When Uzziel joined him, Garrig invited the helmsman to tell of their ordeal.

'Once we worked our way from the bay we sailed up the coast seeking a place of safety. I knew that you would be hard pressed on the beach, but without the *Windsong* all would have been lost.'

Garrig nodded.

'Before we could return a storm blew up out of the west and we were forced to run before it or risk being hurled onto ragged coast. By the time the storm had blown itself out we were taking water and two of the crew had been lost overboard. Undermanned and with our sails in tatters, we limped into a small bay. There was a large rock hidden in the surf and as we beached, we struck it.

'The repairs would not have taken long if I'd had the full crew, but with half of them with you and half of those I had armed and watching for any sign of the natives we were hard pushed to complete the repairs and return for you.'

'But you succeeded,' Garrig said to Uzziel. 'Congratulations.'

'I notice that the Cathars are not with you.'

'They have started on their journey inland to the tower they seek. We will run north up the coast and then east. Once they have reached the tower they will seek us out along the northern coast in some small bay or other.'

'I hope the winds favour them,' Uzziel offered.

'They are going to need it,' Garrig noted gravely. 'They are going to need all the help they can get.'

Charybdis strode the plaza of his city angry at what was transpiring. He had offered the suggestion to Sian-vesna that the party split up in the hope of removing some of the Cathars from the hunt. The northern waters were dangerous at any time, and the natives living about the tower knew only death.

But now it seemed that Orren-ker's party would reach the tower first. If that happened and they managed to overcome the wraith guardians, then Charybdis would lose his chance of gaining control of the tower. He cursed loudly, his voice echoing through the city. So close. He had been so close.

Charybdis entered his tower and hurried to the uppermost room. As he watched the party's progress, he felt a sensation of terror rising within him. Searching further afield he found that there was a Lychgate in the lands of the Emulys just south of the tower. The Emulys worshipped at the ring of skulls surrounding the circle of standing stones.

Leaning intently over the Lychgem, he studied the Lychgate and the area surrounding it. The stone

altar rested upon four short stone pillars and the
paved area around it was edged with a wall of
bleached white skulls surrounded by six tall standing stones, two of them capped by a long block of
stone.

Near the low wall of skulls, a young girl watched
over a herd of sheep. She stubbed her toe on an
object hidden in the long rich grass. Bending down
she freed a small skull from the grass which she held
up to the light for a better look. The skull was old
and veined with cracks. As Charybdis watched he
heard a faint whisper offering the girl words of
encouragement. The girl lowered the skull and
began to examine the low walls surrounding the
altar as if she had noticed them for the first time.
No-one, not even the priests of the Emulys, could
enter the paved area. It was written that while the
stones offered great wealth, they also offered certain
death.

Raising her staff, she approached the wall of
skulls and stood at a narrow opening. She allowed
her mind to fill with the riches she knew she would
find beneath the altar. They seemed so real she
could almost touch them and the whispered
promises of the stones grew louder.

She hoped that she would not be punished for
desecrating the place of worship, but the treasure
would make her and her family rich. Stepping onto
the paving stones, she walked cautiously toward the
raised altar. When she reached the carved block of
stone she put the skull down and allowed her fingers to glide across the cold surface. As they passed
over the stone she felt slight impressions and
allowed her fingers to trace them.

Suddenly there was a blinding light and a howling wind filled her ears. Buffeted by the wind, the girl held tight to the altar, her eyes screwed closed against the painful light.

She did not see the figure step through the Lychgate, nor did she see the serrated-edged axe as it cut downward, removing her head from her shoulders. Blood ran across the dry altarstone, filling the tiny engravings. A cold cry of satisfaction echoed between the low stone walls as if the sound had not been allowed to leave the confines of the paved area.

Placing his axe down upon the altar the Iledrith, Xend the Axe, removed his great helm and set it beside the bloodied blade. His face was a travesty of human features. His eyes were red with no pupils and were separated by a wide, flat nose. His mouth was small and two incisors pushed their way from the lower jaw, forcing up the top lip. But most grotesque of all was the pink hairless head, covered by overlocking scales where skin should have sat.

21

Xend

Xend watched as the blood of the young girl filled every crevice of the runes. As the runes on the altar appeared, the matching symbols on the Lychgate glowed a deep red. Xend's body was still beyond the Lychgate, but the blood of the sacrifice allowed him to hold the gate open. It had been many decades since this Lychgate had last been opened, and that had been for a brief time only as his appearance had driven the curious from the sacred ring.

He needed much more blood if he was to bring his body through the Lychgate and exist once more in the world of light. His body was severely weakened by his overlong stay in the Lychworld, but as he cast out about him with his senses he was able to feel the throb of life from a small settlement nearby.

Of Xend's projected image, only his gloves and weapons were substantial. But the power of his mind was still far beyond anything these feeble creatures could know.

Slowly at first and then much faster, Xend the Axe sensed the folk from the settlement moving towards the sacred ring of standing stones. Xend knew nothing of these people or their beliefs, and he didn't care to. If enough blood was spilt upon the altar then he could pass through the Lychgate and seek out those who had imprisoned him.

The Emulys drew closer to the circle, and at the first sign of Xend within it they rushed forward, throwing themselves on the ground before the standing stones. With foreheads pressed hard to the dry ground, they cried out their thanks to their God for the delivery of a guardian to help them in their war with the Kolecki.

Only one person did not cry with delight. Instead, she looked amongst the scattered flock, seeking out her daughter. When she finally looked towards the altar and saw her daughter's lifeless body lying upon it, she cried out with rage and leapt forward. The Emulys jumped to their feet and grabbed the mother as she tried to pass them. Screaming and swearing, the distraught woman cursed the Iledrith and, shaking free of her captors, turned and fled. Many made to follow her but the Iledrith called them back.

'Stay!' Xend ordered. 'She is as grains of sand before the wind. Come to me. Come to me and rejoice.'

As one the remainder of the Emulys climbed to their feet, the men stood their ground and the females surged forward. Xend met them at the opening in the skull circle, his axe raised. Uncaring, the Emulys rushed forward as Xend drew the serrated blade of his axe across throat after throat. The

383

paving stones about the altar were swamped and Xend's armour shone as the red leather soaked up the blood which poured from the altarstone.

Gutters channelled the blood to the base of the altar where it gathered until another blinding flash of light erupted from the Lychgate. For the briefest of moments it looked as if another of the Iledrith had used the gate. Xend stepped forward, his real body merging with that of his image. Feeling the strength flow through his body, he raised his blood-ied axe skyward and screamed out his challenge.

The roar caused the remaining Emulys to throw themselves down and cover their ears as Xend's challenge echoed about the land. Their eyes hidden, they did not see the first of the Iledrith Loremasters step through the Lychgate and take his place at his master's side.

Charybdis heard the wail of the Iledrith through the power of the Lychgem, since the fingers of rock in the Lychworld were the shadowy forms of the tow-ers in this world. The pillars of pulsating Lychstreams which rose from their summits were linked to the gems of the towers. When the Lychgate had been opened, Charybdis felt the disturbance ripple through the liflode of the tower.

Staring deep into the Lychgem, Charybdis cursed his luck as he watched the scene unfold at the altar beside the Lychgate. Not only were the four Cathars still heading towards the tower, none of them under his compulsion, but one of the Iledrith had been released upon an unsuspecting and unde-fended world. Should the Iledrith reach the tower first and gain mastery over the Lychgem, then it could use the tower's stored power to aid its cause. Charybdis was not happy at the thought of losing a tower, but the idea of it falling into the hands of the Iledrith terrified him.

Since the confrontation with the Iledrith at the strange altar, Orren-ker had been trying hard to remember exactly what had transpired. He had felt a strong sense of danger and had rushed towards his companions, not really knowing where they were or what danger they faced.

Once he had found them he had shrunk back at the sight of the tall red-armoured creature they were battling, and for the briefest of moments he felt a panic well up inside him. Then he had heard the voice. The voice had been calm and it told Orren-ker exactly what he had to do to ward off the creature and save his companions.

Orren-ker had listened and obeyed. Ferne had died, but she was already dead when Orren-ker arrived, and he had managed to save the other two. Since leaving the island it was as if a veil had dropped over his memories. Now, the actions he had taken and the words he had heard were once more open to his mind.

A short time ago a terrifying cry had forced the Kolecki to increase their speed toward their home. Orren-ker had asked Izak what the noise was but the Koel simply shook his head, his eyes wide with fright as he ordered the pace increased.

Now, as they hurried onward, Orren-ker felt a sense of disquiet as he glanced back over his shoulder. There was a danger close by but he could not quite place where it was. All he knew was that something was wrong and the Kolecki also knew it.

Orren-ker looked up and saw the top of a tall green-clad tower. They had reached the Monkshood Tower. It sat beside a large sprawling village but Orren-ker had eyes for the tower alone. After so many hardships and deaths it was strange to be standing at the tower's base.

Izak and his party told of the fight with the Emulys on the beach and the slaying of the Death Crow. When they spoke of the strange cry they had heard the village fell silent.

'It is indeed a good omen that you four are with us,' an old Kolecki explained to the four Cathars. 'For the cry you heard was that of an unholy Iledrith, released from its imprisonment to cause havoc in the world. As our ancient tales foretold, the Iledrith have again entered our land. And as before, we are given the means of defeating it.'

'What did he say about the Iledrith?' Phaidra asked.

'It seems there is one hereabouts,' Orren-ker told her.

'But you drove off the other one,' Mahira pressed. 'You can do the same again. Can't you?' A tremor in her voice revealed her fear.

'The one we encountered was merely a shadow. The Iledrith itself was always safe beyond the Lychgate. But it seems that this time an Iledrith has actually crossed the boundary into our world.'

'What can we do?' Fallon asked.

'We can do as we planned,' Orren-ker stated. 'We must enter the tower and defeat the wraiths which guard it. Then, with the power of the tower, we can destroy the Iledrith or at least drive it back from where it came.'

'Can we succeed?' Phaidra whispered.

'No,' Orren-ker answered. 'Only I can enter the tower and fight the wraiths.'

'Alone?' Mahira cried. 'Are you insane?'

'She's right,' Fallon added. 'You can't go in there alone—it's far too dangerous.'

'While I am battling with the wraiths you will be here. As soon as I enter the tower and am attacked, the Iledrith will know. The wraiths are from the same world as the Iledrith and were once their slaves. While I do battle with them you will hold the entrance to the tower. You must ensure that none enter the tower behind me, for I will not be able to defend myself from their attack.'

'Defend the tower from whom?'

'From the Emulys,' Orren-ker warned, 'and the Iledrith.'

He slipped the medallion from round his neck and, stepping forward, he touched the pulsating gem to each of his companion's weapons. First Phaidra's shortsword, then Mahira's longsword, then finally Fallon's knives. As an afterthought he touched the remaining five arrows in Fallon's quiver before slipping the medallion back in place and striding towards the tower.

Charybdis had channelled what power he could into the weapons, but it would not be much. Mortal weapons were not made to hold the power of the Lychgems and, should he place too much of the power within the weak blades and shafts, they would be destroyed.

Orren-ker chose a spear from one of the Kolecki and touched the tip to the medallion. Weighing the spear in one hand and with his medallion gripped firmly in the other, he entered the tower. As he stepped over the threshold another terrifying scream ripped the air above the village.

Fallon was the first to see the massed Emulys as they poured over a low range of hills and swarmed towards the village. A cry went up from amongst the Kolecki, who gathered their weapons and raced forward to meet the attack. The attackers were both men and women, some carrying no weapons other than bare hands, their fingers curled like talons.

Fallon moved forward but Mahira placed a restraining hand on her arm. Mahira and Phaidra had both drawn their swords as a smaller knot of Emulys could be seen breaking away from the others. Fallon strung her bow and nocked an arrow. There were about ten in the group which approached the tower, and close behind them was a tall armoured horror.

Phaidra shuddered as she saw the familiar armour and helm. The last Iledrith she had faced had carried a war hammer. This one wielded a large double-bitted axe.

The Emulys rushed onward and the two Cathars leapt forward and met them steel on steel. Four of the Emulys died instantly and were trampled. More died as they threw themselves at the Cathars and Kolecki in a suicidal attack.

Phaidra caught the tip of a sword across her right shoulder and Mahira received a painful wound to her leg as they slowly backed towards the tower. Fallon drew a shaft back and was about to release it when she thought of the Iledrith. If Orren-ker had enhanced the strength of her shafts, then she did not want to waste them on the Emulys.

Her arrow struck the great helm of the creature and careened off. The Iledrith felt the blow and stepped back, raising the axe like a shield. Fallon drew another shaft and released it, but this time it was batted away with a flick of the axe.

Fallon nocked a third shaft but was forced to change her aim as one of the Emulys broke off his attack on the others and charged straight for her. The arrow struck the native in the chest, lifting him from his feet and throwing him back against another of the Emulys.

The Iledrith had waited, watching the struggle until the last of the Emulys had fallen. Then lifting his axe before his chest, he strode forward, filled with confidence. He cared nothing for the weak-bodied mortals who craved his blessings and fought for his cause. All he needed was their blood to soak the earth, adding more power to his already massive strength. That strength would be increased a hundredfold once he had entered the tower and crushed the Lychgem to his will.

Phaidra and Mahira met the attack of the Iledrith as one, their long and shortswords flashing back and forth. Mahira met the axe with a jarring ring while Phaidra's shortsword struck a sharp blow against the Iledrith's armoured shoulder. The blow was deflected by the armour but the Iledrith realised that something was wrong. He should not have felt the strike of the arrow or the sting of the sword but he had. Somehow the weapons of these creatures had been enhanced.

Fallon gauged her time and released her fourth shaft. It narrowly missed the visor's opening but caused the Iledrith to change from attack to defence. Phaidra and Mahira never allowed the Iledrith a moment's rest as they followed it, attacking from either side simultaneously. Yet each attack resulted in no injury to the Iledrith.

Mahira was knocked from her feet and as the Iledrith closed in, Fallon loosed her last arrow. The shaft struck the back of the Iledrith's right hand, cutting through the leather and opening up a small wound. The Iledrith snarled with rage, kicked Mahira from his path, then turned and closed on Phaidra.

Fallon drew her two knives and joined her companion. Phaidra was tiring fast but the Iledrith showed no sign of fatigue, his axe cutting an arc as he forced Phaidra and Fallon back to the tower.

Orren-ker held the spear at the ready as he climbed the stairs. He had expected to find a wraith at their base and, when he didn't find any, he whispered a prayer of thanks and continued.

The sounds of the fighting beyond the walls of the tower were muffled and it was hard for him to work out exactly what was happening outside. He knew that the others could not hold the Iledrith for long, not even with the infusion of power Charybdis had given their weapons.

Finally he reached the top of the stairs and a closed timber door. He pushed the door open with the head of the spear and a large room opened out in front of him. He stepped into the room and saw a long table and eight chairs. Short pillars surrounded the table, many holding trays of food and melted candles.

At the head of the table sat a withered man, many weeks dead, Orren-ker thought, to judge by the smell of the air. Moving to the dead man's side, Orren-ker inspected the injuries he had sustained reaching the tower. It had been these injuries which had finally killed him.

As he looked up from the body, Orren-ker saw the first of the wraiths as it darted towards him.

Dropping to the floor and rolling beneath the table Orren-ker snapped the medallion from around his neck and, with a flick of his wrist, sent the chain spinning about his hand. He placed the medallion alongside the spear and stabbed upward as the wraith leapt over him. As the spearhead entered the misty form of the wraith, it vanished in a fierce screaming wind.

Three more wraiths moved rapidly toward Orren-ker. As they neared him he brandished the spear. The wraiths had seen what had happened to the first of them and slowed their attack. In the back of his mind Orren-ker heard a familiar voice telling him how the wraiths might be destroyed. All the voice asked was to be allowed to help in some small way.

Orren-ker felt the urgency in the voice and knew that it was not telling all the truth. He pushed the words from his mind and lunged forward, impaling one of the wraiths. There was a frenzied gust of wind and the wraith vanished.

Another of the wraiths reached out and touched Orren-ker's hand as he withdrew the spear. A piercing pain lanced through his hand and arm and the medallion dropped from his fingers, its chain slipping from around his hand.

The remaining two wraiths attacked and Orren-ker had little choice but to throw the spear. As it struck one of them Orren-ker ducked beneath the table and searched for the medallion, his left arm hanging uselessly by his side. As the remaining wraith reached for him, Orren-ker's fingers closed over the curved shell of the medallion and he snatched it and threw it just as the creature's hand closed over his left ankle. The wraith vanished in a tearing gust of wind.

Orren-ker screamed in pain and fell back against the leg of the table, tears pouring from his eyes. It was all he could do to stop himself from blacking out. He grasped the lip of the table and dragged himself up until he could balance on his right leg.

With an ungainly hop he reached the transparent wall in time to see Mahira knocked from her feet by the Iledrith and then kicked aside as it attacked Phaidra. Orren-ker searched for the spear, but only a broken smoking haft remained.

He put a small amount of weight on his left ankle and cried out in pain. Even if he had a weapon with which to face the Iledrith, he would not be able to descend the stairs and aid his friends. Hobbling across the room towards the stairs he found a hidden door slightly open. He pushed on the door and pulled himself up the few stairs to a dome-roofed chamber in whose centre was set a glowing Lychgem in a shell pedestal.

Again he heard the voice in the back of his mind. This time he allowed the voice to grow and, as it grew, Orren-ker saw the faces of four companions he had thought lost. Help was close, but would it arrive in time to bar the Iledrith from the tower and the power it craved? As Orren-ker stared into the Lychgem he saw the battle below and listened to the whispered words. He was shocked. It was not the battle which had disturbed him, but for the first time he heard panic in the whispered words of Charybdis.

Fallon threw a knife and rolled to one side, the axe narrowly missing her chest. Phaidra whispered an old prayer and hurled herself at the Iledrith. Moving faster than any living creature had a right to do, the Iledrith caught her on the side of the head with the flat of its blade and threw her against the tower like a rag doll.

Fallon snatched an arrow from the chest of a dead Emulys and dived forward, driving its head into the gap behind the knee joint of the Iledrith's armour.

Xend roared in pain, then batted his attacker away with the back of his hand like some annoying insect. He pulled the arrow free, snapped it and threw it from him before returning his attention to the stunned Fallon.

Before Xend could strike, Bram threw himself across the final few metres, taking the Iledrith across its legs. Xend cried out in anger as he dropped the woman and turned to face the new threat. Tandra threw the hilt of her rapier at the Iledrith in an attempt to distract it as Bram clambered to his feet.

Tavira, Raissa and Neroli rushed past Tandra and attacked the Iledrith, their blows raining down on its head and shoulders. Forced back by the sudden assault, Xend took several heartbeats to regather his balance then lashed out, his axe opening the chest of one of his attackers. Before he could follow up his onslaught he found himself facing a tall armoured figure wielding a large broadsword.

Confident of his strength and skill, Xend aimed a blow at the attacker, only to find air as the head of his axe cut high above the ducking figure. A sharp blow to his legs forced him back another pace, but as he moved, he brought his axe downward in an arc.

The axe caught his attacker across the helmet and Xend laughed as the armoured figure was thrown from him. As Xend advanced once more on the tower, Raissa stepped over the still body of Tavira and tried to reach the visored face of the Iledrith but the axe was wielded in such a way that she could find no opening.

Neroli darted in to strike, but Xend dropped his left hand from the hilt of his axe and backhanded her up against the wall of the tower. Bram dropped his sword and leapt for the Iledrith's back and locked his arms about the being's helmet, trying to tear it from its head. But the Iledrith simply shrugged its massive shoulders and Bram was sent flying.

Before Xend could reach the tower a blow struck him across his back. Wheeling round, Xend found himself face to face with the armoured assailant, a huge dent marking his helmet where Xend had struck him. Xend was taken aback by the sight of the armoured figure. No-one had ever survived one of his blows before.

Xend and the figure traded blows, neither one able to make a killing strike. Slowly Xend worked his attacker around until his back was to the tower and he had no place to retreat. Then he summoned the last of his strength and launched a final attack. The first blow struck the stonework of the tower, cutting through the strange plant and sending sparks flying as the blade of his axe struck the liflode. Xend's second attack struck the armoured figure on the shoulder and his third opened a rent in his assailant's breastplate.

A sudden wind sprang from the gash in the armour and for the briefest of instants Xend saw the form of a wraith pour forth before it was trapped by the light of day and torn to shreds. The lifeless armour folded and fell to the ground at Xend's feet. As Xend made to step over the inanimate armour, he felt a fresh attack. He turned and found the last of the humans gathered before him. They were bruised and bloodied and he decided that he would not kill them. Reaching out, he ignored the weak blows and grasped one of the stunned women by her hair.

With his face pressed close against Fallon's, Xend allowed himself a brief smile when he thought of what he had in store for her. But his smile vanished as a searing pain stabbed deep into his left shoulder, forcing him to drop the woman. He turned and faced his new enemy.

Orren-ker stood at the base of the tower, his sling spinning slowly about his head. With a flick of his wrist he released one thong of the sling and watched as the glowing projectile sped across the distance to the Iledrith. Instead of a stone the sling released a small ball of blue crackling fire which raised the hairs on the necks of those nearby.

When he felt the pent-up force of the blow Xend knew that he had been bested. Someone had reached the tower and tapped into the power it held. But there was more. Behind the power Xend felt another force. To fight that power now would not aid his cause.

Xend turned and ran for the Lychgate, where he paused and searched for his enemy. The one who had driven him off was still by the tower, but he was not the one who mattered. In the background, like a shadow, Xend saw his true enemy and marked him well. With a curt order, his followers re-entered the Lychgate. Xend looked once more towards the tower. He might have lost the power of the Lychgem but with the mastery of the tower, another of the Lychgates would be free of its wardings, the way open for another of his brethren to taste the light of Kyrthos.

Now that the Iledrith was gone and the Kolecki had driven the last of the Emulys off, Sian-vesna knelt beside the unconscious forms of Phaidra, Fallon and Mahira lying at the tower's base.

Raissa examined the door to the tower but it was closed and made fast, and no amount of effort could open it. Bram even set a small fire against it, but though the flames licked hungrily at the wood at first, they flickered and then the fire died.

Tandra raised her eyes to the top of the tower, shading them against the glare. 'Is he dead?' she wondered out loud.

'It's possible,' Bram replied. 'In all the fighting we might have missed any noise from the tower.'

'For a brief instant I thought I saw him,' Mahira said. She was leaning against the stonework of the tower, holding her head. Her eyes were glazed and, as she tried to rise, she lost her balance and slipped back. 'He was standing at the base of the stairs, his sling in one hand. It was then that the Iledrith fled.'

Phaidra shook her head and then regretted the movement, as it released fresh waves of pain. 'I saw nothing,' she whispered.

'I thought I saw something,' Bram noted. 'It was just before that armoured nightmare turned and fled. But as I think back, I'm damned if I can remember what I saw.'

'How long do we wait?' Fallon asked.

Sian-vesna supported Fallon as she stood and made her way towards the Kolecki village.

'If he has not returned by sunset then we will leave,' Tandra said at last.

'But . . . ?' Mahira protested.

'If he has not returned by sunset then he never will,' Bram declared.

They buried Neroli and Tavira at the base of the tower and Kaela played a gentle tune as the tired and injured party stood silently around the grave. Raissa whispered her farewells to her companion's grave, rejoicing that Tavira was now one step closer to God.

As the setting sun cast long shadows across the open plain, the Cathars and their companions slowly gathered their belongings and left the tower's base, heading towards the Kolecki village. Every few paces one of them turned and stared up at the tower, as if looking for a sign of Orren-ker.

Mahira, Phaidra, Fallon, Tandra, Bram and Sian-vesna silently wished their lost companion a swift journey, while Raissa thanked God that the tower had not been breeched by the Iledrith. But again, as with the Snakeweed Tower, the tower itself was now sealed against further entry.

Only Kaela did not look back at the tower. He had whispered his goodbyes over the fresh grave and there was nothing more to be said or seen.

Orren-ker knew that they could not see him. Soon they would finish grieving and head off north, towards the *Windsong*. He had used the stored power of the gem to reach out to the coast and watch as Garrig's crew busied themselves with repairs to their bireme.

His companions would be safe. The Iledrith had returned to his realm beyond the Lychgate and the Emulys were defeated and scattered across the southern plain. It was the Kolecki's intentions to push them all the way to the Belial, and then further, until their long-time enemy was swallowed up by the shadows of the jungle.

When the last of the sun's feeble light was gone, Orren-ker turned his back on his friends and raised his hand to where his medallion had hung. Like the spear when he had thrown it at the wraith, it had been destroyed, but what did he need with trinkets when he now shared the power of the Monkshood Tower.

Shared? It was a strange word. He was alone yet he knew that the voice which had guided him during his struggles with the wraiths and the Iledrith was never far away. Perhaps it was a good thing, perhaps not. As he grew used to the power, he would need an ally.

Charybdis could not believe his luck. In such a short time he had gained four towers, each of them locked to his every whim. He now controlled all the towers east of the Berdun River. By throwing his strength behind the Cerussians and their allies he would be able to weaken the western lands enough to then gain more of the Living Towers and the power locked deep within them

Tarynn stared out over the wind-swept ocean, watching the storm as it built itself up even further. Wind lashed the Cerussian coast, throwing spray high into the air as it drove the waves against the rocky shore. Tarynn had always liked this time of year, and now he was able to enjoy it to the full.

He stood in the large chamber, a half-finished meal resting on the table behind him. By the door stood a wraith. It was not the one which had nearly killed him, but another. He did not trust the creature, even though it was a minion of Charybdis, sent here by him to help protect the tower from any who would harm it.

Tarynn had watched as the Cathars tried to destroy the tower, but they had failed. He had watched as they left, glancing nervously over their shoulders as if afraid the tower might reach out for their unprotected backs.

He had also watched as Kallem won the Snakeweed Tower, and now he rejoiced along with Charybdis and Kallem as they watched Orren-ker take up the mantle of Master of the Monkshood Tower.

Now they were united, four towers to protect all of Kyrthos. And blood would be spilled should any try to stand between them and their goal.

EPILOGUE

Tuatara felt the warding on the Lychgate drop. He had spent many generations experimenting in his study high above his stronghold, Terai, and was totally unprepared for the collapsing of the wards holding him in the Lychworld.

He moved down the spiral staircase to the lower level of his keep and passed through its massive doors into a small courtyard. Beyond the courtyard was the Lychworld. A raging storm was passing to the west as Tuatara made his way to the slight rise which held the Lychgate. As he reached out and felt the power flow once more through the runes, he cursed his lack of readiness.

Turning on his heels in a swirl of robes, he returned to his keep and descended even further into its dim recesses. Like all of his race he had Loremasters, the product of a successful breeding between Iledrith and human kind, with the Iledrith winning out, allowing the Loremasters to manipulate the Lore of the Lychworld and that of Kyrthos.

However, he had considerably more Loremasters than his brothers as he had decided that they would sway the balance of power.

Unlike the other Iledrith, his Dey were of the same breeding program but they leaned more towards the human side of their ancestry, giving them great strength and intelligence. His army was made up of the remainder but unfortunately, unlike the other Iledrith, Tuatara had allowed their numbers to dwindle.

At the lowest level of his keep Tuatara entered a large room. The floor was covered in a deep layer of rotting straw and nestled in the centre of the room were several large eggs, taller even than Tuatara. Forming small pyramids about the outer edge of the room were a number of smaller eggs.

Tuatara moved effortlessly about the room, examining each of the eggs in turn. One of them rewarded him with a slight sound. Placing his scaled hands upon its shell, Tuatara permitted some of his strength to trickle through his fingers and enter the egg. Then he allowed himself a brief smile. The smaller eggs would replace the army he had wasted. They were a product of Iledrith and human breeding, but Tuatara had added something else, something which would give them the extra strength they would need in the coming war.

But perhaps his greatest prize was the Terata. If all his plans were to come to fruition, then these eggs would hatch out into creatures which he would release on his enemies.

Happy with the progress of his work, Tuatara left the room and climbed once more into the harsh red light of day. He knew that, should he try, he would find one willing to risk all to open the Lychgate, but he was in no hurry. While the others wasted their forces in the coming clashes with the humans, he would hold his forces back. Then, at the right time, he would strike all his enemies a blow they would not be able to withstand.

THE STORY WILL CONTINUE IN BOOK TWO OF THE LIVING TOWERS TRILOGY, *WOLFSBAINE TOWER*.